OF NAKED SINS AN

sensational than

LIFE AT THE COLUMNS

This is the stunning saga of a plantation upriver from Natchez in the glorious and terrible days before the Civil War.

It is the frightening story of the Deavorses, a family torn by all the lustful sins and hidden guilts of a world half white and half black.

LAVON DEAVORS: An ambitious man who gave up his share of the ancestral plantation to live a life of luxury on the Continent. Now penniless, he has returned, determined to regain his forfeited heritage.

ATHEL DEAVORS: A good man who has welcomed home his wastrel brother and may live to regret it.

LAWTON DEAVORS: Athel's son; the rightful heir to The Columns.

JOLEEN DEAVORS: The beautiful and lustful daughter of Athel who has cast her eyes in forbidden places.

The Plantation

George McNeill

A Bernard Geis Associates Book

BANTAM BOOKS
TORONTO NEW YORK LONDON

THE PLANTATION
A Bantam Book / June 1975

Published simultaneously in the United States and Canada

Bantam Books are published by Bantam Books, Inc. Its trademark, consisting of the words "Bantam Books" and the portrayal of a bantam, is registered in the United States Patent Office and in other countries. Marca Registrada. Bantam Books, Inc., 666 Fifth Avenue, New York, New York 10019.

PRINTED IN THE UNITED STATES OF AMERICA

Contents

The Plantation

Prologue

Natchez, Spring, 1831

There was the sound of horses in the darkness. The mob strained forward. There were shouts. Several guns were fired into the air. Two white men dragged a Negro out of the darkness. They forced him to lie between two green pine logs on the ground. Green pine burns with a low flame and slowly roasts a man instead of flaring up and killing him quickly. The Negro's lips quivered. He cried softly but said nothing. The men tied loops of wire to his ankles and wrists and fastened these wires to the logs. Then they stepped back. A hush fell over the mob, a hush so total and sudden it seemed almost religious.

A man whose left forearm ended in a wooden stub dipped a cup into a vat of paraffin beside a woodpile and poured the paraffin over the logs. The paraffin flamed up; then the logs caught fire and burned with a low blue flame.

There was not a sound from the mob. On the Mississippi River, a few yards away, a paddle-wheeler blew its whistle. The logs began to crackle. Termites crawled from cracks and fled the heat. Thick smoke rose up. Crickets chirped in the hot shadows. A night bird cried from a catawba tree.

At the first inhuman scream, several men slipped away from the mob. The Negro screamed again and again. Wind blew up from the river. The smell of burning resin and flesh swept over the mob. A redheaded boy on the edge of the crowd vomited. Several more men fled the scene. But the others stood quietly. They drank from jugs of Monongahela whiskey and stared into the flames.

The fire now grew white. The smoke was white

and gray. The Negro screamed one last time. Then he was silent. The wind shifted back toward the river. A murmur passed through the crowd. The men began to talk softly and pass their jugs around as they waited for the second slave to be brought up.

It was a hot April night on the mud flats beneath the Natchez bluffs. The men drank more whiskey as they became restless. Several men debated whether the two charred logs should be used again or whether two new logs should be taken from the woodpile.

Two fresh logs were laid out on the ground as the second Negro was brought into the faint light from the fire. He struggled against the cords that bound his wrists behind his back. He was a big man and much younger than the first. Blood trickled into his left eye from a cut on his forehead. Flies buzzed indolently at the blood.

The slave's resistance aroused the mob's fury. Men shouted and cursed, and guns were fired into the air. The one-armed man stoked the fire, and another man prepared several torches. The Negro fought his cords, but he only caused his wrists to bleed. The mob surged forward several feet as the men drank and watched the struggling slave. Those nearest to him saw the hatred and defiance in his face change to fear as he looked at the charred corpse of the first Negro.

A man dressed quite differently from the rough clothes of the mob stood hidden in a vast canebrake a few yards behind the slave. This man wore the ruffles and high-fashioned clothes of a gentleman. Only minutes ago, in a mansion high on the bluffs, his foppish manners and cynical wit had amused the planters who drank sherry and port and whiskey and pretended they did not know that, down on the flats, a mob of rednecks and rivermen was lynching two slaves accused of attacking a white woman.

The man took a lace handkerchief from his sleeve and patted perspiration from his face. He wore two pistols, and there was another pistol in the saddle of the horse he had tied a hundred yards back in the cane. He carried a long cloak and wore a hat pulled down to shadow his face. Now he slipped into the cloak.

The fire was roaring. The mob backed off. A strange hush fell over the men. Blood dripped from the Negro's head and from the cord cuts in his frantically twisting wrists.

The man in the cane bent down and took out two flints. He struck them together. Sparks leaped against the dry cane. A brittle cane stalk began to smoke. The man crept forward several feet to the edge of the clearing. The cane flamed up, and the fire instantly spread. The mob was startled by the sudden fire and thick smoke. Under this cover of smoke, the man ran the few feet to the woodpile. He kicked over the paraffin vat. It soaked several logs. The man snatched up a torch and ignited the wood.

The paraffin blazed like an explosion. The one-armed man ran blindly from the flames. The mob retreated in panic. The men holding the Negro released him and stumbled from the heat and smoke. The man in the cloak ran to the Negro. He took a knife from his coat and sliced through the cords.

He motioned to the cane. The Negro followed him through the smoke. As the man had calculated—and risked—the wind had fanned the flames toward the river, enabling them to stumble through the smoke and run toward the horse that was rearing up in fright.

But the mob's panic had now passed, and the men realized what had happened. Cursing and shouting, they chased through the smoke and into the cane.

The man in the cloak steadied his horse. He mounted the horse and gave his hand to help the slave climb up behind him. A shot snapped past them. Another. They galloped through the cane, coughing from the smoke.

A dozen men stopped and fought for breath. They cursed and coughed.

"What in hell was that?" a man asked.

"Couldn't be but one thing," another man gasped. "That goddamn Underground Railroad again!"

BOOK I

The Prodigal

Chapter 1

There had never been another place in America like Natchez-under-the-Hill. In all his travels on the Continent and in Morocco, Lavon Deavors had not seen anything like it. It stretched along the Mississippi River for over a mile beneath bluffs that rose two hundred feet to the parks and mansions of Natchez. Shacks and shanties and lean-tos hugged the mud flats below the bluffs, while houseboats and barges crowded the wharves. They housed the indigent and fugitive, who had been swept up and down the river and had finally ended in Natchez, and also provided space for hundreds of whorehouses, taverns, and gambling dens.

On a hot May afternoon Lavon stood on the dock beside the paddle-wheeler *Kentucky*, which had just brought him upriver from New Orleans. He looked from the bluffs to the mud flats and wondered if anything had changed in the years he had been away. His friends in London and Paris had romantic ideas about the plantation South of Georgia, Virginia, and the Carolinas. A few of these friends had visited famous plantations and cities such as Charleston, Richmond, and Savannah. But they knew nothing of this part of the South. This was wilderness. This was frontier country. There were a few large plantations outside Natchez, and the little city thought itself sophisticated, but the real nature of this land was condensed under the bluffs to Lavon's right. Or has it been tamed? he asked himself. He walked from the dock and decided to have a look before hiring a carriage for the last leg of his long journey.

Water lapped through the cracks of the wooden sidewalks. The humidity was stifling. Heat mirages shimmered up from the brackish water, and a stench rose from the warm red mud. Pigs rooted in the mud and fought dogs for the garbage.

Lavon stepped inside a tavern that crouched over the river on wooden stilts. He ordered whiskey and paid with one of his few remaining coins. The whiskey tasted good, but the tavern depressed Lavon. It was a small room hung with cigar smoke and filled with sullen men who, from their talk and clothes, Lavon took to be minor functionaries from the port and clerks from the chandleries and warehouses.

He left and walked along another sunken sidewalk. He passed gambling dens where dandies in outlandish clothes threw dice and talked horse racing with well-dressed pimps and hustlers. In other dens polemen played cards and drank from jugs. These men were giants, and their drinking and fighting ability were legend along the river. Their arms and shoulders bulged with the muscles built up from years of poling heavy flatboats down the Mississippi.

Lavon paused to watch a cockfight in a mud pit. A rust-colored rooster sank its talons into its opponent's skull and ripped out an eye. Blood-splattered men shouted and clapped and hurried to take their winnings from the loser's owner.

While drinking whiskey at an open stand on a mud flat. Lavon heard distant music from a spinet. Claire Devonshire, his last mistress before he ran out of money, had played her spinet in her little house in London's Stewart Park. How odd to hear such music under the hill, Lavon told himself. The music's source became an idle quest.

Lavon pushed along a crowded sidewalk. Old women in tattered dresses hawked crawfish. Trappers thrust stinking, bloodstained pelts at Lavon. Negroes idled in gloomy doorways and talked with immigrants, marked by their language. Emaciated children played with fish heads and dodged drunken polemen, whose weight sank the sidewalks deeper into the water.

On a half-sunken barge a dozen Indians in ragged buckskins thumped cane drums and performed a pitiful dance. These Choctaw and Chickasaw had once ruled this land and had inflicted a humiliating defeat on the French. But first the French, then the Spanish, the English, and the Americans had subjugated and demoralized the Indians, and now this group did their dance and the leader held out his palms to Lavon and begged, "A bit, sir . . . some whiskey, sir . . . me good boy . . . you like war dance. . . ."

Black whores lounged on the deck of a long barge. They called to Lavon. A teen-age girl licked her lips and made sucking sounds. Another opened her green dress and fondled her breasts.

Lavon walked on. The spinet was being played on the next barge. It was a huge red barge. Its windows were shuttered and its door was shut. The red barge was famous, and Lavon remembered visiting it when he was in school. In its perfumed rooms of plush carpets and red draperies and crystal chandeliers were beautiful octoroon and quadroon whores brought up from New Orleans. They were skilled in music and dancing as well as sex. The barge's owner was a six-foot-eight-inch-tall mulatto named Annie Easter. Annie opened her door only to the most select of customers.

Lavon forced himself to move on. He would have liked to lie on the silken sheets and make love to a beautiful young quadroon, but he didn't have enough money to tip Annie's servants, much less pay for one of her girls.

The sidewalk was two inches below water now. A man was lying across the sidewalk, his face in the water. He'll drown, Lavon told himself. He pulled the man's face up. Empty eye sockets stared at Lavon. He dropped the head and stumbled down the sidewalk, past more barges where white and black and yellow whores displayed themselves.

Two black men were fighting at an intersection. They fell into the water. Nobody stopped to look. The water grew red. Lavon walked faster.

He stopped abruptly. He was nauseated from the stench and filth and heat. There might be a thousand taverns, whorehouses, and gambling dens ahead. He could walk under the hill for hours, and it would only get worse as he got farther from the docks. And he realized he was only procrastinating because he was hesitant to face his family at long last.

Lavon decided to return to the docks by a route that took him along the mud flats directly under the bluffs. He told himself he was glad he had taken this walk because it made him realize to what level he might have fallen if he had remained on the Continent without money.

Two slaves, haltered by a rope around their necks, were being led into a building.

"What's that building, boy?" Lavon asked a black man who was selling catfish.

"That there? That be a nigger pen there, sir."

"A nigger pen? What's that?"

"For slaves just brought down from Virginny or one of them North places."

"A slave trader?" Lavon said. "When I lived here they weren't allowed to set up permanent quarters in the city."

"The man there, he sells niggers, yassuh. Folks say he be here permanent. He just come back with a new load, from what I hear tell. Them two niggers yoked up, I 'spect they part of the new ones just arrived."

Lavon decided to have a look inside. He broadened his step to avoid a pool of mud, but looked at his wretched boots and planted his next step in the mud. Better they look soiled than out of repair, he told himself.

The building was ramshackle but had recently been whitewashed. Lavon thought he remembered the place, but he could not recall why. He passed a pen of dogs that snarled at him. A few feet away was a set of stocks.

Lavon paused at the door and studied a notice stuck to a pole:

REMSON COLLINS JUST ARRIVED FROM VIRGINIA WITH A CHOICE LOT OF NIGGERS, INCLUDING SEAMSTRESSES, IRONERS, WASHERS,

MECHANICS, CARPENTERS, COOKS, BLACKSMITHS, AND PRIME PLANTATION HANDS, AS WELL AS PRIME NIGGERS FOR BREEDING. INTENDING TO ESTABLISH MYSELF HERE PERMANENTLY, I WISH TO ANNOUNCE THAT THROUGHOUT THE SEASON MY STOCK WILL BE CONSTANTLY REPLENISHED WITH CHOICE NIGGERS.

Lavon shook his head. So slave traders had indeed descended on Natchez and begun to set up permanent quarters instead of selling on the streets. Well, he reminded himself, he had been away eight years, and anything could have happened in this godforsaken wilderness.

He walked through the open door and down a hallway that led to a courtyard, which was dominated by an oak tree draped with moss that touched the ground at the ends of sagging limbs. Along the left wall were a dozen fig trees, and the mud was purple with the pulp of fallen figs. Some thirty slaves milled around the trees or sat on pads of moss. There were a half-dozen black men stripped to the waist. Their bodies glistened with sweat. Except for two middle-aged women who fanned themselves with banana leaves, the other slaves were all young women or teen-age girls.

A white man was releasing the slaves Lavon had seen outside. They rubbed their wrists and flexed their shoulders. One man mopped his face with a cloth. The other drank from a gourd. The white man motioned the two blacks to a table. They sat down and ate from a bowl with their fingers.

Another white man came from a door in the right wall. He was followed by two girls who were no more than eighteen. One was short and black, with a body that was just shy of plump. The other was tall and slim. Her skin was yellowish. Both girls took hesitant steps and stared at the ground. The man's head bobbed as he talked. He shook his head and fussed with the shorter girl's calico dress.

Lavon told himself to be on his way. He turned to leave.

"Sir, you lookin' to buy yourself a nigger?" the man called.

Lavon stepped back into the courtyard. The man was hurrying over. He stopped abruptly as he got a good look at Lavon's clothes.

"What you want here?" he asked.

Lavon sometimes forgot how shabby his outfit was, and when forced to take note of his appearance by someone he considered inferior, he had difficulty controlling his anger.

"I was looking over your niggers," Lavon said. "Good day."

Again he started down the hall, but his exit was blocked by a white man with a wooden arm, who was dragging a sack along the floor. He and Lavon looked at each other, and, like the buildings, the man hovered in Lavon's memory. He would not have remembered him but for the wooden stub.

"I know you from somewheres," the man said. He squinted up into Lavon's face. "I know I knows you, but I ain't seen you in a coon's age. You used to come drinkin' when I had me the alehouse here."

"That's correct," Lavon said. "I have come here, though, on only a few occasions, and that was years ago." He recalled drunken nights in the alehouse. The man's name was Chunky, and he loved to demonstrate how he could punch open an ale barrel with his wooden stub.

"You're a Deavors, I swear," Chunky said. "The one that went off, went north to New York, or Paris, France, or one of them places. I'd know a Deavors anyplace. But they done said you're dead."

"It would seem they're wrong," Lavon said. "Now, if you'll get out of my way, I must leave."

"Just a minute, Mr. Deavors."

Lavon looked around. The other man was walking toward him.

"I'm new to Adams County, sir," the man said. "Just bought this place from Chunky last year. But, of course, everybody knows about the Deavors family. How can I help you, Mr. Deavors? My name is Remson Collins."

"We have no business to conduct, Mr. Collins," Lavon said.

"I noticed you lookin' at the two girls, Mr. Deavors," Collins said. "I picked 'em out special up to Richmond. I got me a fine eye. Why, I used to trade cattle 'fore I took to niggerin'. Would you like a closer look at the girls?"

"I wouldn't be interested," Lavon said.

But he was interested. He had not touched a woman for nearly a month.

"Well, sir, why not come on back to the shade and at least have somethin' to drink," Collins said. "If you headin' out to the plantation, you got a long ride."

"I am thirsty," Lavon said.

"Then you come right on back here," Collins said. "Chunky, you better look after the stock."

"Sure thing, Remson," Chunky said. He walked away.

The stock. . . . What a disgusting way to refer to the slaves, Lavon told himself as he followed Collins across the courtyard. He thought of leaving. Word might get back to his family or their friends. Someone might see him. He was back so short a time, and already he was consorting with the lowest sort of men.

His shirt was matted to his back. Sweat stung his eyes. His boots creaked in the mud. He wanted the whiskey desperately.

Chapter 2

The two girls looked up as Lavon passed. They were even younger than he had realized, no more than sixteen or seventeen. Collins escorted Lavon around the oak, past an auction platform, and seated him at a table covered with white muslin. The table was crowded with ledgers, bottles of patent medicine, spoons, links of chain, a Bible, shackles, rope, a leather whip, two vases of nasturtiums, a jug, and two cups.

Collins sat down. He poured whiskey into the cups. Lavon nodded thanks as he accepted the cup Collins offered. He took a swallow. The whiskey was terrible. It hit his disbelieving stomach like a rock, but he drank again and wiped his mouth with the back of his hand.

"Well, now, Mr. Deavors," Collins said. "From what I heard, it would appear you been away. Doin' some travelin'? . . ."

"I've been on the Continent," Lavon said. "And in Morocco." He was amused at Collins' effort to understand how any Deavors could find himself in such wretched garments.

"That a fact?" Collins said. "Me, I do a lot of travelin', but it's always here in this country. I come down from Richmond couple of days ago with a load of stock. October to May's the season, and I'm pushin' it here at the end, but business been so good, I plumb near sold out. You ever been to Richmond, Mr. Deavors?"

"My ship stopped in Richmond harbor, but I didn't go ashore," Lavon said. He sipped whiskey and looked around the courtyard. The slaves were lounging in the shadows. The two girls sat on a barrel, their heads tilted together as they talked. They held hands. The men who had just arrived stood naked while Chunky measured them for clothes.

"Did those two niggers come down from Richmond?" Lavon asked.

"No, no, I bought 'em off a fella down to Woodville. Off the sheriff, in actual fact. Fella had him a little farm and couldn't make a note after he'd put up the niggers for collateral."

"How do you get your niggers down from Richmond?" Lavon asked. "Bring them on a coastal steamer?"

"Why, no, Mr. Deavors, matter of fact, I don't. Costs too much, among other things. No, I shackle 'em together and make up a coffle and march the niggers overland. This time I come down the Natchez Trace from Nashville."

"How do you go about buying the niggers?" Lavon asked. He had never talked to a slave trader before, and despite his repulsion at the man and his trade, he was curious.

Collins bolted down the whiskey and leaned forward. His head went up and down as the words poured out. He said that on a buying trip he staked out an area. On the last trip it was a few counties around Richmond. He attended plantation and courthouse sales, sheriffs' auctions, foreclosures. He advertised in local journals. It seemed he specialized in mechanics, which were scarce in Mississippi, and especially in women who would make good breeders.

"I see," Lavon said. He drank whiskey. This bastard was not only a trader, but was actually going to breed his people as though they were cattle.

Collins seemed delighted to have found a man of quality to hear his complaints and problems. He said the local planters did not understand the hazards and expenses of his trade. They were angry because he charged seven to eight hundred dollars for a prime breeder or mechanic. Actually, he said, if these folks knew the trouble, expense, and danger of bringing the niggers down from Virginia . . .

And by God, he gave fair measure. He didn't do like some, buy old men and tint their hair dark and pull out their whiskers. He didn't buy sick niggers and give them rum so they would look sprightly for a buyer. And he didn't go to some sheriff and take his murderers and thieves for a song and sell these criminals to unsuspecting farmers.

Lavon watched the clever eyes dart about. Collins wore two ruby rings. A planter who boarded the ship in Richmond had mentioned that prime slaves there were selling for two or three hundred dollars. So Collins was making a handsome profit, obviously.

He watched Collins pour whiskey into his cup. "Thank you," he mumbled.

Collins' head began to bob again as he talked of

the dangers on the march down. They came through savage country, he said. The slaves tried to escape. There were bandits at every bend of the road, and a gang of slave rustlers up near the Tennessee border.

"Man's got a right to make a little profit after risks like that, Mr. Deavors," Collins said, but Lavon barely heard him.

He was staring at the girls again. Chunky went over to the black girl and said something to her. He poured whiskey from a jug and gave her the cup. She hesitated, then drank the whiskey. Chunky talked to her again. She drank whiskey, and it spilled over her chin and wet the front of her dress. Chunky smiled. The girl nodded and unbuttoned the dress. She discarded the calico and knelt on the moss. Chunky gave her more whiskey. Lavon stared at her black skin, glistening like wet velvet. She was so young and ripe, and perhaps even a virgin. Her breasts were large and uptilted. Beads of moisture fell from the long nipples. One of the new black men crawled over to her and took the cup and drank whiskey. The man put his hand on her leg and leaned over and kissed her. She lay down beside him. Lavon glanced around. The couple lay in a sea of black and brown flesh that seemed to undulate with a common sexual stirring. The other young girl, the high yellow, was watching the kissing couple with wide eyes. Lavon drank whiskey. He thought of the firm breasts, the lean, strong legs. He hadn't touched a Negro girl in years.

"They sure are fine-lookin', Mr. Deavors."

Lavon turned around. He had forgotten Collins for a moment. He drank more whiskey than he wanted. It rode in his throat, and he forced it down. The silence stretched. He wanted no more talk with this man. His stomach protested even the smell of the whiskey. He shifted on the wooden seat. Despite the shade, the heat was weighing him down as surely as if he had been covered with wet sheets. He sucked in his breath and smelled figs rotting in the sun.

He did not want to stay, but he could not bring himself to leave. He had to say something. "How did you get into this business?" he asked without interest. He would hear the man's answer and then be on his way for sure.

"Well, sir, I saw some years ago that tradin' niggers was goin' to be worth more'n tradin' cattle," Collins said. Once more he began to speak rapidly. "The farms up to Virginny and Maryland, why, sir, they bein' farmed out. And there's no new land left up there. Not like out here in the West, where a man can farm out his lot and move on down the road and find untouched soil rich and cheap as can be. Well, now, what you think's goin' to happen in them states up there, Mr. Deavors?"

"I wouldn't know," Lavon said. He looked through the moss. The slaves were naked, and Chunky was washing them down with buckets of water. The black girl and the man were walking into a little open cubicle directly opposite Lavon and Collins.

". . . become one big breeding pen." Collins' voice caught Lavon's attention again. "Folks already floodin' in here for this rich land. And folks up there, they findin' it lots more profitable to breed their stock and sell the surplus niggers than to work new acreage with 'em. Uh, you goin' to be stayin' for good out to the plantation? . . ."

"Yes, Mr. Collins, I'll be staying for good at the Columns," Lavon said. He shoved back his stool and stood up. "But I can forestall your next query. It has always been my family's policy neither to buy nor to sell slaves."

"That's not what I was leadin' up to, Mr. Deavors," Collins said. "Though you might change your mind in the future. Man's got to change with the times, sir." And to Lavon's annoyance, Collins rattled on again. "Why, in Alabama they outlawed slave tradin' for three years, from 1827 until last year, and it didn't work out. You know, I've never been able to follow the logic of them as owns slaves and gets rich off 'em on a plantation and yet opposes them as do the tradin' and breedin' of slaves." Collins was whining. "One feeds off the other, sure as fat dogs fart, and it's all a natural part of slavin'. . . ."

"No, Mr. Collins, it's not the same thing," Lavon snapped. "Hell, there's no need to argue it further." What had come over him, sitting in this courtyard, arguing with a slave breeder?

Lavon turned, and stopped. The girl was lying down on a bed in the cubicle. She was naked. Her lush body was silhouetted in the dim light. She opened her thighs wide. The man lay between her thighs. The girl lay still a moment while the man writhed around. Then they began to move together. The girl squeezed her legs across his back. Lavon heard the squeak of the bed and the sounds of their lovemaking.

His penis began to stiffen. He shifted his weight. He thought of the girl. She would be bred again and again for the rest of her life. But now she was so young. She would be tight. All this sex was new to her. Lavon stared at her heaving body. She was groaning now. He could almost sense the damp heat of her vagina.

"Now, Mr. Deavors, it was more a discussion than an actual argument," Collins was saying. "Why don't you sit back down and have some more whiskey. And tell you what. Maybe you'd like to mount the nigger while the buck's got her all worked up. Never been fucked before, and see, she takes to it like a pig to the sugar house. She's one fine piece of 'tang." Collins no longer whined. He spoke with the confidence of a man who knows he has finally found merchandise that is irresistible to a buyer.

"I must be going," Lavon said.

"Now, please, just a minute, Mr. Deavors," Collins said. "Chunky! Chunky, bring Moselle over here for Mr. Deavors to examine. Now, Moselle, she's the high yellow you was lookin' at. She's still a virgin. You can be first. I done picked her out special for breedin'. But like as not, 'tween times with the bucks I'll put her up as a fancy lady for white men."

"I don't have time to inspect the girl," Lavon said.

But he stood and watched Chunky lead Moselle through the moss. Her yellow skin glowed with moisture. It looked like warm honey. She walked awkwardly, with an excessive swing to her buttocks. Her eyes met Lavon's. She held his gaze, with her head high.

"Now, Moselle, she's prime stuff, too, Mr. Deavors," Collins said. "Come here, girl."

Moselle stepped in front of Collins. He unbuttoned her dress and bared her breasts.

"See how firm them breasts are," Collins said. He shoved a finger against her breasts. "And she's soft and solid in all the right places. Got a flat stomach. Pull up your dress, girl. Come on, now, be a good girl and you'll have molasses with your cornbread tonight."

Moselle looked from Lavon's eyes. She stared at the ground as she pulled up the calico. Collins patted her stomach.

"And look at them thighs," Collins said. He skated his palm over her thighs. "Not nobody touched all this. It's all yours. You be the first one. . . ."

Lavon looked from the thighs to the downturned head. Past Moselle, through moss waving in a breeze, Lavon saw the frantic motions of the couple's lovemaking. The girl was grunting and raking her nails down the man's back. Across the courtyard the other slaves moved languidly on the moss. They were naked. Some were kissing. Others passed the whiskey jug.

Lavon looked back at Moselle's lithe body. He was aroused almost beyond endurance. All he had to do was take the girl back to a cubicle.

Yet he was outraged at the whole idea of a breeding pen. And his sense of being a gentleman was offended at what Collins was doing to Moselle. This girl might be only a slave—and Lavon had taken many a slave girl when he was young—but it humiliated her to stand there and be displayed and prodded like a cow.

"I'm not interested, Mr. Collins," Lavon said. "I must be on my way."

"Well, here, Mr. Deavors," Collins said. "Take the jug with you, sir. You got a long ride out to the plantation."

Lavon took the jug, but he gave Collins the last of his coins.

"Not no need to pay. . . ."

"Mr. Collins, I always pay for my whiskey," Lavon said. He was damned if he would leave owing Collins a favor.

He turned and walked from the courtyard.

Chapter 3

The road passed through swamp and a forest so fertile that vines and bushes spilled against the road and threatened to devour it. Trees bent over the road, brushing the buggy as it passed, their leaves and gray moss forming a tunnel that blotted out the sun and seemed to liquefy the heat. Yet, at stretches, this growth was given an oddly formal air by banks of rose hedges and water oaks that arranged themselves in stately groves, and despite the fact that they had never had the touch of man, resembled the carefully furnished parks of English estates. To Lavon, these rose and oak parks were similar to the countryside of Hertfordshire.

He took little notice of the land, actually, for it had not changed in the eight years since he last saw it. Despite the occasional resemblance to England, it was desolate and godforsaken. He had not seen a house or other sign of human life for over two hours.

His eyes closed, but opened immediately as the right wheel slid out of the rut. The wheel was wobbling ominously.

The buggy forded a stream, and Lavon directed Simon, the black driver, to take the right road at a fork. The better-traveled road to the left led to Benton, a primitive log-hut hamlet.

"Faster, Simon, whip the horse on," Lavon shouted.

The whip cracked over the horse's back, and the buggy moved faster, the erratic wheel mashing a rattlesnake that crawled from a log. They drove around a curve. A horseman materialized on the shadowed road. Instinctively, Lavon pulled out his pistol and sighted the man's chest. He clamped his left hand on the driver's box and steadied his pistol hand on the arm.

The rider also had a pistol, but he had difficulty controlling his horse, and he was no match for Lavon, whose finger hovered at the trigger while he shouted for Simon to stop his horse.

"Don't shoot, don't shoot!" the rider called.

"Declare yourself," Lavon said. The man had come abreast of the buggy, and Lavon's pistol moved with him, keeping the rider always an instant from death, for Lavon handled his pistol with the assurance of a man who had used it many times, as indeed he had in his encounters with bandits on roads in Europe and Morocco.

"I'm a Benton merchant, on my way home," the rider said. "You startled me, so I pulled my weapon. I seldom see anyone on this road."

"Throw your pistol to the ground," Lavon said. "Do as I say, sir, without hesitation, if you want to live."

The man was slim and pale, and he might well be a shopkeeper. But there was a furtiveness to his dark eyes and a pose to his manner that heightened Lavon's suspicions. And he wore leather, hardly the garments of a shopkeeper. The man hesitated a moment, then dropped his pistol to the road.

"Dismount," Lavon said. "Come off your horse slowly and carefully."

The man dismounted. "I'm only a poor merchant . . ." he started.

"Be quiet," Lavon said. "Hold your palms up. Yes, those are not the hands of a storekeeper. Over here with you. And you, Simon, keep that horse still, damn you."

Lavon searched the man. He found a bag of gold pieces and a silver watch inlaid with diamonds. He laughed as he put the items in his coat.

"You must be selling a lot of flour and meal, merchant," he said. "Now, get on down the road with you. Don't mount yet. Walk your horse away. And don't let yourself be seen around here again."

The man stared at Lavon with hatred and disbelief. Lavon raised his pistol to the man's chest, and the man stepped back, grabbing the reins and leading his horse down the road. Lavon smiled as he climbed into the buggy.

"Drive on, Simon," he said. "And don't mention what just happened to anyone."

Simon nodded and drove away. Lavon looked over his shoulder. The man was moving into deep shadow, but Lavon sighted his back. A difficult shot, he told himself, but he would bet he could still drop the man. It was no more difficult a shot than the one that had felled that bandit outside Naples two springs earlier.

The man disappeared. Lavon put his pistol away and settled back in the seat, but he could not sit comfortably, for the horse had taken the wheels out of the rut again. Simon snapped his whip and finally brought the horse to a trot. Lavon hoisted the jug, and as whiskey poured into his mouth, the buggy lurched into the rut and the rim of the jug cut Lavon's lip. He tasted blood with his whiskey.

The dense growth was receding. The buggy passed through a pine forest with a rock-edged pool, where, as a boy, Lavon had once found a nest of moccasins in the rocks while swimming. Farther back in the pines he had taken his first woman, a slave girl named Dorrie, when he was sixteen.

He drank and wiped blood and whiskey from his lips. He warned himself to drink no more, for he had not eaten since a breakfast of grits and fatback, and he felt drunkenness just beyond the next swallow or two. The pine forest was giving way to meadow land. Another minute and Simon reined up in front of a wood-slat gate that led into the Deavors plantation.

He looked around dubiously.

"Go on, boy, open the gate; drive through," he said.

Simon obeyed with obvious reluctance and drove onto a wider road lined with cedar trees. Lavon straightened himself and looked at his threadbare garments. Two years ago, when they had been tailored, he had thought them the finest garments in all London, but now they showed him for what he was—a man totally impoverished but for his jug and pistol.

No, he reminded himself. He had just come into a little wealth. He pulled out the watch and examined it carefully. It was an antique watch, obviously an heirloom and quite valuable.

Wide fields appeared through the cedars, acre after acre of cotton on both sides of the road, with smaller plots of corn, a peck of which, with four pounds of pork, was each slave's weekly food ration. Or has my gullible brother increased his niggers' food allowance? Lavon asked himself.

He saw the slaves then on the horizon to his left, working a hill that sloped down to a swamp. The plow gangs trudged behind their mules, urged on by the shouts of a mounted black driver. Nearby a hoe gang of women was kept at its work by a driver who touched their backs tenderly with his lash. Not a head turned as the buggy passed. Lavon was startled to see a white woman hoeing in the nearest row, then realized it was Nettie. She had been a small thing when he last saw her, no more than nine or ten, the perfectly white child of a mulatto woman and some unknown white man.

"Faster, boy!" Lavon shouted. Simon nodded and cracked his whip.

Lavon saw a carriage ahead, and he shoved the jug to the floor, ready to meet the first of his family or some old friend. But this carriage held no member of the Deavors family, nor anyone his family would be likely to know. It was an odd carriage with a wooden cagelike contraption on its rear that contained several large dogs. A horse was tied to the side of the carriage.

In the back was a middle-aged fat man. He wore

a ruffled white shirt, and over it a gold coat with silver buttons. A black hat rested on his oversized head. His hands were wrapped together around the stock of a rifle. The man seemed to be sleeping, his face resting on his shoulder.

If this man was merely fat, his driver was obese, an ancient black man who bobbed up and down on the carriage, though the vehicle was barely moving. The man wore a narrow-brimmed hat and a purple velvet coat with gold buttons fastened to his neck, where it bulged as though about to break open. He slept with his chin on his chest. His face glistened with sweat.

The dogs barked as Lavon's buggy overtook the carriage, and he saw that they were nasty animals, lips curled back over their teeth and saliva drooling out. Neither their barking nor the rattle of the buggy brought the slightest response from either of the men. Despite the fine outfit, Lavon looked on the white man with scorn, for the dogs meant the man had come out to track a runaway slave.

Simon's buggy lurched as the rear wheel nearly slid off the axle. Lavon was slammed against the side, and the buggy came to a halt, tilting dangerously. He eased himself out and looked at the damage. His head pounded from the blow against the buggy's side. He turned on Simon, and the man shrank away from the expected blows.

"Idiot!" Lavon shouted. He cursed Simon soundly. The carriage was passing, but Lavon decided against asking help from a man with slave dogs. He retrieved his jug and took a swallow of whiskey. His lip ached.

"Can you repair the wheel?" he asked. He thought of walking on to the house, but felt bad enough about returning in these garments, and decided against arriving on foot as well.

"Yassuh, reckon I can, but it got to be lifted up and held," Simon said.

Lavon glanced at the field. "Go over and fetch a couple of strong boys and bring them back," he said.

"Yassuh, I can do that," Simon said. "But what I goin' to tell the driver, he asks? Massuh, they know you here to this place?"

"You don't have to tell the driver anything," Lavon said. "Except that a white man needs two strong niggers to help him. Now, get moving, and don't try my patience any longer."

"Yassuh," Simon said, and walked away.

Lavon brushed sweat from his face and drank from the jug.

Chapter 4

Before his arrival that May evening, Lavon existed in his family's thoughts only in the sense of another deceased relative.

The Deavors had last seen Lavon on a similar spring evening, the day of his twenty-second birthday, when he fled the Columns in a drunken rage after being rebuked by his brother Athel for abusing a slave girl who refused to sleep with him.

Before that, Lavon had drifted through part terms in half a dozen schools in Natchez, Mobile, and New Orleans. He found that so much as a week at the Columns left him with a boredom that touched desperation. The year before his departure, when he came of age, he had taken a cash settlement as his portion of the inheritance, telling himself he wanted no part of running a plantation in what he considered a wilderness.

His money was on deposit in a Natchez bank, and he had killed one horse and maimed another in getting to Natchez and to his money on that spring night eight years earlier. During the next few days he settled his affairs in town, making arrangements for letters of credit. He then filled a purse with gold pieces and set off down the Mississippi for New Orleans.

From New Orleans he took passage to New York and then London. His bitterness mellowed, and he came to feel only pity for his brother Athel, and for Athel's family, isolated in their wilderness between the Mississippi and Homochitto rivers. He wrote occasionally during the years he lived in London, Paris, Rome, Tangier—carefully censored letters—and Athel wrote him every month.

Lavon had last written five years earlier. A dozen letters from Athel went unanswered as Lavon moved about and lost all contact with the Deavors. Athel was grief-stricken as the months passed with no word of Lavon. A year went by, another, and Athel suffered not only from the fear his brother was dead but also from the guilt of having a Deavors disappear in such a manner, the first time this had happened, as far as Athel could discover. Finally, like others in his family, Athel accepted the thought that he would never see Lavon again.

Athel was forty now, and for many years the plantation, the family, and what he called his people had been his only interests. He went into Natchez only a few times each year, content with his work and with the pleasure of hunting, fishing, and riding. He particularly enjoyed plantation social life, the occasional fancy parties held in the broad gallery or just sitting in the parlor sipping whiskey and smoking with men from the other plantations.

When he had a competent overseer, he was a truly happy man, for the Columns had twelve hundred acres of cotton under cultivation by some two hundred slaves. Athel felt no need for expansion or increased profit. He was willing to let an overseer run the place efficiently enough to equal the previous year's earnings, but in such an isolated location it was not easy to find such a competent man. When, as this spring, Athel found himself in charge of the plantation, without assistance, he would plunge into the work with energy and enthusiasm for a few weeks, but would soon grow weary of the routine and turn much of the day-to-day supervision over to his drivers, foremen, and mechanics.

Athel was a tall man, taller than Lavon by half an inch, and although he liked his food and whiskey, the plantation work, daily riding, and strenuous activity that hunting required combined to keep him in good physical condition and spare him the fat that was replacing muscle on his younger brother's body.

Athel's hair was light brown, like Lavon's, though in the past year strands of gray had appeared. His eyes were the same deep blue as his brother's; his face was also rather round, but it bore no trace of the dimples that crinkled Lavon's cheeks when he smiled.

Estelle, Athel's wife, could be called a handsome but not a beautiful woman. She was tall and quite thin, with dark eyes and black hair. Estelle was marked by an almost desperate nervous energy. She was much sterner with the children and the slaves than Athel, though totally dedicated to the well-being of both. She tolerated Athel's propensity for entertaining and drinking but did not enjoy being a hostess and seldom touched so much as a glass of port or Madeira.

Estelle agreed with her husband that their people should never be sold and that they should never purchase new slaves. She did believe, however, that the slaves should be disciplined more stringently and should work harder, and she was forever fretting at Athel's leniency with their people. She did not mind the little gifts or the tobacco or molasses he gave them at Christmas, nor the free days he let them enjoy at the end of the harvest, but she objected to his practice of giving them whiskey and letting them have dances on several occasions each year.

Athel and Estelle had three children. Tillman was twelve, a sickly boy with pale blue eyes. Joleen was a tall, voluptuous girl of seventeen. She had wheat-colored hair, deep blue eyes, and a savage scar high on her right thigh that she had suffered two years earlier when thrown from a horse in the woods. Lawton was two years older than Joleen. He had first seen this scar when he came home from the institute in Natchez for spring vacation. Whenever his obsession with Joleen consumed him, he first thought of the scar.

Chapter 5

Joleen raised herself in the stirrups, and from the cover of the thorn vine, she watched Lawton and Ambrose, the black stable boy, walk from the swamp, rifles barrel-down. Each slow step indicated their exhaustion from an afternoon of hunting in the heat. Joleen herself was exhausted, for she had tied her horse at the swamp's edge and followed the boys for hours.

She sat down and walked the horse a few yards through a shallow bayou green with slime. Gnats and mosquitoes swarmed at her face, and she brushed at them with her free hand.

The boys had stopped, and Lawton rested his leg on a stump. Ambrose said something, and Lawton laughed. Joleen dismounted and led her horse through a plum thicket. She had hoped when Lawton came home from school last weekend that he would spend more time with her, but it was starting out like every vacation. All he wanted was to hunt, fish, or ride with Ambrose, continually taking the boy from his stable work.

Joleen felt rather strange, not only weary, her body prickling from the heat, but also excited in a way she only vaguely realized was sexual. She smiled as she remembered actually beating Lawton on horseback the day before, and people said he was the best rider in Adams County. He had given her a five-furlong start, but he always had done the same in the past, and he always won. The race yesterday had been about the only occasion Lawton had acknowledged her existence, she told herself again. He seemed to have time only for Ambrose.

Except Sunday, after church, when he went for a

walk with that giggling, empty-headed Lily Crawford. Lily might be all of seventeen, but she acted about as grown-up as Tillman, and Joleen could not see what her brother found interesting or attractive about the girl, when he clearly had his pick of any young lady in Benton, if not the whole county. Oh, Lily Crawford had a pretty enough face, and long blond curls, but for a girl her age, she was skinny as a rail. It looked as if they seldom fed her at home. The girl had no bosom at all, Joleen reminded herself as she looked down at her own well-formed breasts. And Lily was scared to death of horses, guns, and snakes.

The boys were disappearing over the crest of the hill. Joleen walked up the hill to the last cover, a stunted magnolia tree. There was a carriage on the road, heading for the house. She could not make it out clearly in the fading light, but supposed it was that man with his dogs to track down Essie; he had been gone four days now. And farther back on the road was an old buggy tilting to one side. A white man stood beside the buggy, drinking from a jug.

Ambrose was walking on, but Lawton had stopped to watch the hoe gang. The women had begun to drift toward the quarters, except for Nettie, who paused to take a drink of water from a pickaninny with a clay jug. Joleen realized that Lawton was staring at Nettie.

As always, Joleen felt sick when she thought of this field hand who seemed white in every respect except for the gestures and manner of speaking that marked her a slave. A few years earlier, Joleen's father had given Nettie housework, but the girl was sullen and at times impolite and made everyone, white and black, quite uncomfortable.

Could Lawton be interested in the girl? Joleen asked herself suddenly.

Some months ago Joleen had learned that white boys on plantations sometimes had relations with slave girls. At first, when Louella Flowers told her, she had been shocked and angered and refused to believe it. Then her friend Nadine Sumrall, who was seventeen, had told her that, yes, it did happen sometimes, terrible as it was, and that only a few weeks earlier she herself had overheard her parents discussing the sale of a slave girl who had had relations with her brother, Theron.

Joleen and her girl friends never talked in detail about sex. They hardly ever discussed any part of the body, and they used terms like "he was intimate with her" and "they had intimate relations" and "she had a passionate friendship with him." Joleen was vague on some of the details of sex with a man, but she had learned from her older girl friends a smattering of general information and misinformation.

Joleen's physical precocity had attracted older boys since she was twelve, and on dark porches at dances she had been daring enough many times to let some sixteen-year-old kiss her. Several times during the last few months she had allowed boys to fondle her breasts during a kiss. She found this pleasant and natural, exciting as much because it was daring as because of the physical reaction on her part.

Talks with older friends, and her own experiences, had let her know ways in which boys revealed they were interested in or excited by a girl. And on several occasions she was certain Lawton had shown some of those indications of physical interest in her. At this point Joleen's thoughts diffused quickly, as they always did, for she was unconsciously apprehensive of following any thought relating to sex to a firm conclusion.

Lawton had disappeared. Joleen mounted the horse and dug her heels into his flanks, moving him to a trot. She rode from the fields, past the log washhouse, where Mulverne stood with a basket of laundry resting on her hip. Rows of sheets hung heavy on the lines behind the house. Joleen nodded as she passed, and Mulverne said, "Evenin', Miss Joleen." Mulverne was lighter-skinned than most mulattoes and was Nettie's mother.

Four long rows of gray wooden shacks stood to Joleen's left, and she rode between them and the big house. Naked children played in the dusty streets formed by the shacks, and smoke curled from the chimney of the nursery, where a dozen suckers were tended by old Aunt Froney, who was also the midwife.

Joleen caught Lawton and Ambrose as they walked along the fence that enclosed the plantation's vegetable garden. They both looked up, and Ambrose said, "Evenin', Miss Joleen," but Lawton only nodded. Joleen glanced into his blue eyes, then rode on angrily. She dismounted and led her horse into the barn.

Ed, the blacksmith and hostler, took the reins. "Have a good ride, Miss Joleen?" he asked. He was a stocky, very dark man with enormous shoulders and arms. His left ear was partly missing, and Joleen had heard that someone had bitten it off in a fight.

"A nice ride, Ed," she said. "Hope I didn't wear him out. We're both tired."

Ed patted the horse's damp flanks. "He's a strong one. Needed a good workout. Don't you worry none. I'll rub him down good and see he gets some extra oats."

Joleen walked toward the door, adjusting her steps so she wouldn't leave the barn before the boys arrived. Her timing was perfect.

Ambrose nodded and spoke again as he hurried past. A moment later Ed was shouting, "Boy, where you been all afternoon? Don't you know you got work to do? Don't matter none Mist' Lawton's done come home. You not goin' to 'mount to a hill of beans you don't settle down, and already Miss 'Stelle she done complainin' the place got too many skilled niggers as it is. . . ."

Lawton didn't come in; Joleen hurried out as she realized he might be halfway to the house by now. But he was dragging himself along so slowly that he seemed to be lagging with each step.

"You got Ambrose in trouble," she said as they walked toward the house, interrupting the ground pecking of six chickens, who squawked, flapped their wings, and scurried away in a haze of dust.

"Didn't realize how late it was," Lawton said. He was looking down, and held his rifle as though it weighed a ton. Joleen knew instinctively it wasn't only exhaustion and heat, but that something was troubling him.

"Where's your kill?" she asked, though she was

aware precisely how meager their kill had been, despite the fact that Lawton was the best shot she knew, better even than her father. "Long as you spent, you must have bagged yourself an armful of game, Lawton." He would not look at her, and this annoyed her.

He shook his head. "Just a couple of old squirrels, not worth bringin' home."

"Daddy took me huntin' last week, and I shot a possum," Joleen said.

Now he looked at her and grinned in the mocking way she hated. "You? Shoot a possum? Last time I saw you fire a gun, it knocked you down, Joleen. And Daddy wouldn't let you shoot, not a girl." Their eyes locked. They stared at each other, brother and sister, with identical blue eyes, the same blond hair, the same round face, full lips, and dimples.

"He did, Lawton. I promise you he did. Well, he did help me hold the gun and aim it."

Lawton laughed. "Stick to girl things, Joleen. And leave huntin' to the men. Why, I heard Mama say you hardly learned to cook. That's what a girl should be interested in, things like cookin' and sewin'. Don't you want to grow up to be a proper lady, Joleen?"

"Like that skinny old Lily Crawford?" Joleen asked. "Is that your idea of growin' up to be a real lady, Lawton?"

They stopped, staring at each other. His cheeks were red. Hers must be too, she realized, because they felt so warm. Her resentment, exhaustion, and the smothering heat brought her to a dangerous point, the first time Joleen might have been goaded into taunting Lawton in some physical way. Her body was tense and glowing with that odd feeling she could not quite identify here in the last moments of her innocence.

The sound of footsteps turned them from their confrontation. Their father was coming up the path from the back swamp.

"Any luck with your huntin'?" he asked Lawton. "Did you take Joleen with you?"

Lawton glanced at Joleen. "No, not much luck,"

he said. "I went with Ambrose. We only shot a couple of squirrels."

"I went ridin'," Joleen said. "If I'm goin' to be taught to use a gun, I'd rather go with somebody who can come back from an afternoon of huntin' and have somethin' to show for it."

Athel smiled, and she returned the smile, glancing at Lawton with satisfaction.

"Perhaps your brother is takin' on too many city ways in Natchez," Athel said. "Maybe he's forgotten how to use a gun."

"It's not my idea to attend the institute," Lawton said. "I'd gladly come back here for good."

"No, son, I was only jestin'," Athel said. "You must have some education, get yourself ready for the college in New Orleans."

Athel kissed Joleen's cheek, hugged Lawton, and with an arm on the shoulder of each child, steered them toward the house. Joleen felt good, the best of feelings, the way she always felt when she was alone with her father and brother.

"Daddy, you keep on teachin' me to shoot," she said, "and sometime later, when Lawton comes back all citified, I'll instruct him how to shoot more than some grandfather of a squirrel."

"I can shoot better than you with my eyes closed," Lawton said.

"I guess you might have been shootin' with your eyes closed this afternoon, Lawton," she said. "And yesterday, Daddy, I beat him on horseback."

"Yes, after I gave her a five-furlong start," Lawton said.

"That's enough, you two," Athel said, squeezing them both on the shoulder. "Are you hungry? I could eat a bear myself."

Joleen and Lawton agreed they were hungry.

"What were you doin' in the back swamp?" Joleen asked. "Lookin' for Essie again? I saw a carriage on the road and took it to be the man with the dogs. But he was movin' so slow, he could be midnight gettin' here. And there was a buggy, too, Daddy. Leanin' to one side. And some white man drinkin' from a jug."

"Purvis Swan and his dogs should have been here by now," Athel said. "But I can't imagine who the other fella could be, Joleen. No, I wasn't lookin' for Essie. I was seein' about the hogs out in the swamp. Two of the sows had piglets. A dozen in all, it would seem. I don't intend to be caught short again this autumn and have to buy either corn or pork from some Yankee merchant."

"Will Swan be able to track Essie down?" Lawton asked. "I've seen Swan in Natchez. He seems a foul man, despite his airs, and he keeps the lowest sort of company."

"They say he has the finest dogs around," Athel said. "I hate to resort to such a man, but I have no other recourse, I'm afraid. I don't understand what possessed Essie to run away again. I swear, I'll never understand the boy, Lawton."

"Maybe he left the county," Joleen said.

"No, no, I doubt that," Athel said. "Not with his family here."

"Lately I've noticed more men like Swan in Natchez," Lawton said. "Low men with trackin' dogs, men tradin' slaves. Why, they even set up a sort of slave pen on the river. And talk is, a man named Collins from up to Virginia is plannin' to breed slaves there."

"Men like that are the dregs of our peculiar institution," Athel said. "I suppose we have to endure some of these wretched men . . . oh, I mean men with dogs, Lawton, certainly not traffickers and breeders. I suppose trackers are like hangmen, son. Society must have them to do some foul work, but they can only be despised, perhaps pitied. Well, enough of this talk. Come on, we must wash up for supper. And I'm lookin' forward to some tobacco."

Smoke drifted from the kitchen and brought the smell of frying birds. The smell reminded Joleen how hungry she was.

They started up the back steps to the gallery, but Athel turned. "Wait up," he said, "somebody's coming."

Chapter 6

Filch, the plow-gang driver, ran toward them. He was a round man with a big stomach, and his running made Joleen smile.

"Hate to bother you right at suppertime, Mist' Athel," Filch said. "But white man up on the house road, his buggy broke down, and he sent for a couple of boys to help fix it, and 'course I sent 'em, but that man, he don't look like he belong on the place, look like trash, got a big jug of whiskey. Thought maybe you ought to know."

"Yes, Joleen saw him, too, Filch," Athel said. "I don't like to have somebody of that appearance around, especially with the sun settin'. You better go down and find out what he wants. Get a horse from Ed. As a matter of fact, take him with you. Let Ed talk to the man. He'll know what to say."

"Yassuh, Mist' Athel," Filch said. He nodded and walked away.

"I think I hear a carriage out front," Lawton said. "It could be that stranger. I'll go see."

"No, most likely it's Swan," Athel said. "I'll deal with him. Son, would you go to the storeroom and bring me in some tobacco? I just remembered I'm out of it in the parlor. And if I'm late, tell your mother not to wait supper on me."

Joleen watched her father walk down the gallery. Lawton turned and trotted away without a word to her. She ran after Lawton, upset that her father had asked him and not her to fetch the tobacco. In the past, he'd always asked her. It was her special task.

"Wait up, I'll go with you," she called.

Lawton did not turn around. He moved faster,

again scattering the chickens. "You might need help, Lawton," she called. "A boy who can only shoot two squirrels after a day of huntin' might have trouble sightin' the right tobacco." Joleen bit her lip. This was too much. What was getting into her?

Lawton glanced over his shoulder but did not speak. He was nearly running now, as though he might reach the storehouse and lock her out. Joleen could not match Lawton's long stride. Her efforts to catch him revived the dormant heat that had made her miserable. She again felt exhausted, angry, and excited as she chased Lawton into the rectangular log building. As always, her nostrils were assaulted by the strong smells of tobacco, coffee, and spices.

The only light came through the cracked door and the one thin window high in the back wall. Lawton moved from the patch of light at the door. Joleen stepped forward and bumped into him before realizing he had stopped.

He turned on her. "Damnit, Joleen, stop pesterin' me, you hear? Go away! Get on out of here."

"Daddy would skin you alive if he knew you were usin' language like that in front of a girl," Joleen said.

Lawton lit a lamp. "Are you a girl, Joleen?" he asked. "Well, nobody thinks of you as one, not the way you run around tryin' to do boy things. And look at that dress. It's a proper mess. Why, in Natchez they'd laugh you off the streets for wearin' that old thing, Joleen."

"I am too a girl," Joleen snapped. Lawton's words had angered her. Her eyes were adjusting to the flickering light. She stared at Lawton's eyes. Her lower lip quivered slightly. She did not understand the ways her body felt strange. These were new sensations.

She breathed in the spices, the tobacco, the coffee. The smell was pungent. It burned her nostrils and heightened her awareness of her senses, her body.

"Then act like one," Lawton said. "Go play with Tillman. And leave me alone. And stop tryin' to learn to shoot. Learn to cook and dress proper."

"I thought you liked the way I dress, Lawton,"

she blurted. She almost added: You must, the way you stare at me when you think I don't notice.

Lawton did not speak. His eyes moved from hers.

Joleen realized they were alone in a dark place, the kind of place where she had twice let a boy kiss her and touch her breasts. And Lawton was nervous and unsure in exactly the same way other boys were when alone with her. Her own brother, who had just told her she wasn't really a girl. Brothers and sisters were not supposed to kiss and touch, she knew. But the realization that she was nearing forbidden ground only made her even more excited.

Lawton was still silent, his eyes moving from the wavering flame to a chicken that had wandered into the door, anywhere but back to Joleen's eyes.

"Do you like the way Lily Crawford dresses?" Joleen asked.

"Lily knows how to look like a lady," Lawton said. "And she wears a bonnet in public, like a lady should. You never wear a bonnet, even to church."

Joleen stood there, savoring the tantalizing new feelings that aroused her. She smiled slightly at the corners of her lips. It was difficult to tell in the dim light, but Lawton's face seemed much redder.

Seconds passed, and Lawton did not speak or move. Joleen was surprised that he didn't scoop up the tobacco and leave the storeroom. He shifted his feet slightly, and Joleen began to suspect the reason he did not leave. The suspicion thrilled her in a physical way she had never known. She had seen it happen before when she pressed against a boy for a kiss. The boy would be embarrassed and mutter excuses for not being able to go back in and dance with her.

Could this have happened to Lawton? To her own brother? And only from being alone with her, without even touching her? Could she have aroused him that much?

"Well, we better fetch the tobacco and get in and get washed up," she said. "Come on, Lawton."

"You go in, Joleen," he mumbled. "I'll get the tobacco."

"No, I'll stay and help you," Joleen said. "I've been gettin' the tobacco for Daddy, and he's usin' a different blend, so I better make sure you get the right kind, Lawton."

"I know the right kind. I do know, Joleen, really I do. Now, go on. Leave. Please."

"Oh, come on, Lawton, what's wrong?" she asked with all the innocence she could put into her voice. "Go and fetch it, if you insist. I'll just watch and make sure you get the right blend."

Joleen was beginning to feel a little uneasy, but this only added to the thrill of the game. She wondered suddenly how she would react if he actually kissed her or touched her. She didn't know, but she did feel a tinge of apprehension at the idea that her game with Lawton might soon move to something physical, something sexual that might be difficult to control.

Lawton backed away slowly. He turned and nearly tripped over a pile of gunnysacks. His movements were so awkward that he might have been an invalid taking his first steps after a spell in bed.

"That's the wrong kind," Joleen said. "That vat, to the left. Oh. see, you don't have any idea. Here, let me get it, Lawton."

"No, stay away," he said. "Damn you, stay away from me, Joleen."

"I only want to help, Lawton," she said sweetly. "Here, help me over the gunnysacks."

She grabbed his arm, and as she stepped over the sacks, he twisted his arm violently. Her hands flailed out and caught his retreating arm as she stumbled.

"Let me go," he shouted. But she held on, first from fright, but a second later because she didn't want to let go.

Lawton fell back. Joleen fell against him. They crashed onto the gunnysacks. Lawton cushioned Joleen's fall, but her weight pinned him to the floor.

Joleen knew she was hurting him, but she did not move. Her mind was not functioning. She was driven by instinct and intuition, as she usually was at pivotal moments. She lay there waiting for Lawton's move, well aware beyond any doubt that she had sexually aroused her brother.

For a moment Joleen feared he was really hurt. He groaned, but he was not groaning in pain, she realized. He was making the kind of sounds a boy made when she opened her lips for his tongue and let him squeeze her breasts.

Lawton jerked as though touched with fire. He pushed at Joleen and feebly tried to shove her off. She resisted, and they wrestled for a moment. The wrestling became a mutual writhing as she lay between his thighs. The feel of his stiff penis thrilled her, then scared her more than she would have thought. Never had her body responded in such delicious ways.

The whole thing lasted less than a minute. It could easily be construed as merely Lawton's effort to get free of a troublesome little sister. Joleen quickly rolled from between his thighs. Her skirt was caught up high on her legs. She paused an instant before smoothing the skirt down and climbing to her feet.

The bewildering sensual feelings again made Joleen uneasy, for she did not know how to respond to the new demands and pleasures of her body. Her nipples felt quite odd—sore and hard and tender.

She took a small bowl and scooped up tobacco. "I've got it," she said. "Are you hurt, Lawton? Are you all right?"

He had climbed to his knees. He nodded and grunted. She hesitated but did not prolong the moment. Instinctively, without a decision of the mind, she knew she had carried the incident as far as she dared.

She hurried outside and paused on the steps. She gulped in hot, fresh air that brought the scent of honeysuckle. Her nostrils tingled with the storeroom smells. And these pungent smells would always be linked to what had happened in the storeroom with Lawton.

She walked quickly to the house. Her skin was beaded with moisture. The smells lingered in her nostrils. She entered the gallery. A smile crossed her lips, and her fever deepened in a most pleasant way. She wanted to run up the stairs, wanted to reach her room so that she could tear off her clothes and be alone with the body she had discovered in a new way in the storeroom.

Chapter 7

Athel watched the carriage creep into sight between the oleander and azalea bushes that grew profusely throughout the huge plantation. The driver's chin rested on his chest, but he pulled it up abruptly and sat straight as he popped the whip over the unconcerned horse's back, a gesture Athel considered absurd, since the next moment the man reined up the horse at the hitching post.

The dogs in the rear compartment had heard plantation dogs in the distance, and they began to whimper. Purvis Swan climbed down from the carriage, and his efforts took a full minute. He drew himself up to his height of nearly six feet, so that his bulk did not seem so excessive, and walked with a parody of authority. The driver's chin fell to his chest again.

"My 'pologies for arrivin' at suppertime, Mr. Deavors," Swan said. "But I was delayed at the Sumrall place."

"That is all right, Mr. Swan," Athel said.

"If you give me a little information 'bout the nigger, sir," Swan said. "Then I'll get on with my work and leave you to your supper."

"Can you track at night?" Athel asked.

"Why, Mr. Deavors, I got the best nigger dogs in Adams County," Swan said. "Yessiree, I do believe they could track down the smartest nigger on the darkest night. Once my dogs onto a nigger's trail, that nigger's got 'bout as much chance as a one-legged man in a ass-kickin' contest. No, I don't normally run my dogs at night. But this is the very time of the day many a nigger'll come sneakin' up, at suppertime, to get a bit of fatback or try for a little poontang 'fore curfew."

"I doubt if he went far," Athel said. "He has family in the quarters and seems devoted to them. I'll never understand why he runs away. This is the third time. Came back of his own accord once, and last year we caught him the second day. This time he's been out for four days."

"Could you tell me somethin' 'bout the boy?" Swan asked.

"His name is Essie," Athel said. "He's about . . . oh, Essie must be in his early thirties. He never married, got his mother and a sister here on the place. He's our wheelwright. A good mechanic. He's a burly man, usually seems in good spirits. I've never known him to take a drink. Despite his size, from all I know he's a gentle man. Once you track him down, I doubt you'll have any resistance."

"Well, hope not," Swan said. "But you never can tell 'bout niggers, Mr. Deavors. Let me get my things, and then, if you'll show me the place where his family lives, the place he was last seen, where you think he went into the swamp, then I'll leave you to your supper. I know for folks like you here on the Columns suppertime is a big part of the day. Yessiree, now take a fellow what got a few acres, couple of niggers. Why, he mostly new to the county, mostly trash, Mr. Deavors. Come dark, he most likely to sop up some sorghum with cornbread and fatback, same as his niggers. But I don't like to deal with folks like that. I deal mostly with the quality. Try to dress proper, keep my boy lookin' like he belongs to a man 'preciates he's invited to the finest plantations. I try to bring a little dignity to niggerin', Mr. Deavors."

Athel walked down the steps while Swan was talking. "My supper is waitin', Mr. Swan," he said sharply.

"You be finished with me in two shakes of a sheep's tail, Mr. Deavors," Swan said. "By the way, fella was up to your road, dangerous-lookin' man, to my way of thinkin', come past in a run-down buggy. He might of thought I was sound asleep, but I always keep one eye open. His buggy threw a wheel, and he's up on the road still, I reckon, and I thought . . ."

"Yes, one of my drivers told me about him, Mr. Swan," Athel said. "I've sent a couple of men to deal with him."

"That a fact?" Swan said. He turned to his carriage. "DuPre, get off your black tail and get to work."

DuPre's head rose quickly from his chest, his eyes opening and his body shaking as though he was shocked at such treatment. He took out a red handkerchief and patted moisture from his face before lowering himself to the ground.

Athel stood impatiently while DuPre helped Swan remove his gold coat and slip into a brown coat of rough cloth. Swan stuck a pistol in the fob of his trousers and took up a long, vicious whip and a rifle in his right hand. DuPre untied the horse, and Swan took the reins in his left hand.

DuPre released the dogs and hauled himself back up onto his soft seat without a word. The carriage tilted dangerously with his bulk. He sank into the carriage box, and an instant later his chin rested on his chest.

Athel's irritation increased as he smelled smoke from the kitchen. "Come, Mr. Swan, I'll take you back to the quarters," he said.

"Yes, Mr. Deavors, I don't want to make you late for your supper."

Athel walked off, and Swan lumbered after him, losing his air of authority as his weight seemed too much for his spine to cope with. They walked in silence for a couple of minutes, past azalea and oleander bushes. The wind had come up, bringing the smell of honeysuckle from the trellis on the other side of the drive. Smoke curled gray from the washhouse chimney and from the chimneys of the shacks they approached.

"I was thinkin' when I catch the boy, Mr. Deavors," Swan said, walking faster and huffing out his breath as he tried to keep up with Athel's long stride. "Do you do your own whippin' here to the place, or do you normally send your niggers to the jail to be whipped? Folks say there's no better man at whippin' niggers than Purvis Swan, and I might add, once I whip a runaway nigger, he ain't likely to run away again."

"I don't whip my people, Mr. Swan," Athel said.

"But a boy what's run away three times . . ."

"Mr. Swan, I'm perfectly capable of disciplinin' my people in my own manner."

"Sure you are, Mr. Deavors," Swan said. "Didn't mean to imply nothin' else."

"Don't hurt the boy once you catch him," Athel said. "He isn't armed, and he isn't likely to offer resistance."

"Sure, I understand, Mr. Deavors."

Athel led Swan down the road between two rows of shacks. He realized how quiet the quarters were, when usually at this time his people were chopping firewood, eating supper at their doorsteps, tending to their little plots of vegetables, or visiting and talking before curfew. He saw a few solemn faces at the windows and sensed that, as Swan's dogs had a reputation among the plantation owners, so the man himself was well known among the slaves of Adams County.

Lavon settled back in the buggy as Simon, the wheel now repaired, drove off slowly. The road began to rise slightly, and they passed the last of the cotton fields and cedars and entered a grove of magnolias, their broad white flowers perfuming the air in a way Lavon had forgotten. Among the magnolias were wooden benches, and to the right, a leaning pine-wood gazebo.

Two horsemen hurtled from the magnolias, and the buggy horse shied and reared. Lavon jerked out his pistol but saw it was a pair of slaves. He put the pistol away.

"Mist' Athel, he sent down to see what business you have here," one of the slaves said.

Lavon saw it was Ed, the blacksmith. The other man he didn't recognize, and assumed he was a field hand.

"You ought to say 'sir' to a white man, Ed," Lavon said.

"Do I know you . . . sir?" Ed asked, straining down for a better look.

"You know me, Ed," Lavon said. "Well, don't you know me?" His anger rose. He was hot and thirsty. The whiskey backed up in his throat. His lip ached. He He dared this black man to give him the smallest kind was sick of dealing with slaves and poor white trash. of trouble.

"You Mist' Athel's brother, the one what left all them years ago?" Ed asked.

"Yes, that's right. Don't you remember my name?"

Ed shook his head.

"Good," Lavon said. "Then you won't run back and say anything to my family. Do you understand that? I don't want them to know I'm coming."

"Yes, sir," Ed said. "I won't say nothin'. Come on, Filch."

Lavon watched the men disappear through the magnolias. "Get moving, Simon," he said.

Beyond the magnolias, the road curved through a formal flower garden, the bright colors of sweet peas, nasturtiums, and roses vivid even in the fading light. There was another curve, and the road paralleled the long, leaning trellis overgrown with scuppernong vines, honeysuckle, and the brilliant purple bougainvillea leaves that Lavon had been pleased to find also in Tangier.

As they drove around the end of the trellis, Lavon sat up straight. The house came into view beneath the massive oaks and pines that filtered sunlight even on the brightest days. The house had not changed, so far as Lavon could tell. It was a large, rambling two-story house of weathered white clapboard with a wide gallery down the center to the back and a wide porch across the front and right side. The dining room jutted out from the back, connected to the detached log kitchen by a covered but open-sided passage.

Twelve massive white columns dominated the front of the house, alternating Corinthian and Doric columns that had been brought downriver by Lavon's grandfather. The columns were a legend around

Natchez, and from time to time local scholars made the four-hour trek to study them.

In the thick grass of the front lawn was a profusion of oleander and azalea bushes. The azalea blossoms had withered in late March, but the oleanders were dripping with pink and purple flowers.

Simon stopped the buggy behind the carriage with the dog cage. Dogs, horse, and white man were gone, but the black man still slept in the driving box. Simon glanced around at Lavon, then at the house, as if to show he was not accustomed to driving his buggy to such plantations. Despite having been passed through by the two slaves, he still obviously doubted his passenger would be well received.

A tall, gray-haired Negro came bustling across the porch.

"Here, boy, what you doin' stoppin' at the front door this way?" he called. "You, sir, what is your business here?"

Lavon climbed from the buggy. "Cellus, don't you recognize me? Have I changed that much?"

Cellus stared at Lavon. "Mistuh Lavon? That is you? No, can't say I would recognize you right off."

"Well, it's been eight years, Cellus," Lavon said. "I've grown heavier over the years."

"Yes, you do seem to have changed," Cellus said in the patronizing tone Lavon recalled only too well. Lavon's parents had drowned in a steamboat accident in the Mississippi when he was fifteen, and though Athel had always been lenient and indulgent and overlooked most of Lavon's transgressions, Cellus had always been stern and condemning. The man seemed not to have aged a day. He had no wrinkles. His hair had been gray as long as Lavon could remember. He had no idea how old Cellus was. He might be forty, or he might be sixty. There was no hint of age or stoop to his awesome shoulders, and his back was ramrod straight, as always.

"Where's the family?" Lavon asked. "Where's my brother?"

"They be to the dinin' room, havin' supper," Cellus said.

"Pay the nigger, Cellus," Lavon said. "I'm short of cash at the moment."

Cellus looked slowly at the man in the buggy and back to Lavon, who grew uneasy beneath the dark eyes and huge brows, the rigid and unforgiving face.

Cellus mumbled to himself and moved toward the buggy. "You got no luggage?" he called as Lavon walked up the steps.

"No, I have no luggage," Lavon said.

"You want your jug of whiskey?"

"Give it to the nigger," Lavon said, and stalked across the porch.

The family was seated at the table waiting for Athel. No one had started eating except Tillman, who had taken a sip of milk and broken off a piece of cornbread.

The dining room was oblong and paneled with pine. An enormous brick fireplace lay dormant in one outside wall. A mahogany buffet dominated the opposite wall, while a mahogany China cabinet stood beside the door that led into the house. All eight windows were raised, and a breeze fluttered the white curtains. The outside door was open, and occasionally a hound dog wandered in and settled himself on the floor, eyeing the table and letting it be known he was ready for anything that fell from the table or was thrown to him.

Athel followed a gray dog through the door and mumbled apologies to Estelle as he sat down. He poured a glass of whiskey and took a drink. Whiskey and milk were the only beverages on the long oak table.

Estelle nodded to Norvina, a twenty-year-old mulatto whose mother, Beatrice, was the cook. Norvina, in turn, motioned to two very dark twelve-year-old girls outside the door. The girls, whose names were Bonita and Flora, were often taken for twins, though they were no relation at all. The only way a stranger could tell them apart was that Bonita always wore a red ribbon in her hair. The girls scurried down the passage to the kitchen and returned in a minute carrying steaming platters of food. They shuttled back and forth with platters as the Deavors began to eat.

Supper consisted of sweet potatoes roasted in ashes, black-eyed peas and crowder peas with chunks of fatback, fried ham, fried pork chops, fried birds, fried eggs, cold baked turkey, possum, and cornbread.

"Best cornbread I've ever tasted, Norvina," Athel said as he took another piece and spread on thick, creamy butter. "How does your mother get it to come out like this?"

"She uses just the meal, water, and salt, nothin' more," Norvina said. "Ruins a good cornbread to add eggs or butter or milk, Mist' Athel."

"Do you think Swan will find Essie this evenin'?" Estelle asked.

"I reckon he might," Athel said. He sipped his whiskey. "The man seems to know his work." He looked down the table at Lawton. Something seemed to be troubling him. His face was flushed, and he barely picked at his food.

"I wonder if Essie ran away because we let that other boy learn to be a wheelwright too?" Estelle asked. "That might could be the reason. Essie seems a proud boy. We should hire out some of our people. We're gettin' too many mechanics on the place."

Athel took a long time to chew a bite of possum. This had become a running argument, the idea of hiring out mechanics during slack periods. The children sensed the coming argument, and as though they had planned it, each began to pay excessive attention to his food.

"I know what Haskell Sumrall said after church Sunday," Athel said. "I know it's gettin' to be the practice in the county to let a slack mechanic work on the river or in some mill or home, Estelle, but I've heard bad reports about these ventures. You never know how a man is goin' to treat a slave, especially one not his own. Why, don't forget what Aunt Delma told us on her last visit from Natchez, that the captain of a paddle-wheeler was treatin' his hired slaves so bad the sheriff had to take them back and return them to their owners. Found one boy's back all cut up from the lash, another had lost two fingers, and then we ought to consider—"

A shot interrupted Athel. He bolted up.

"Damn fool Swan!" he said. "I told him not to hurt Essie, but I should have known better."

Lawton shoved his chair back and stood up. "I'll come with you," he said.

"No, son, stay here," Athel said. "There could be trouble." He turned for the hall. "Cellus," he shouted. "Bring me my gun."

He stopped after two steps. A tall, shabby man stood in the hall, his face bathed in shadows.

Chapter 8

Athel walked to the hall. "What do you want, sir?" he asked brusquely.

He had barely spoken the last word when the man took a step forward. Athel looked into his brother's face.

"Lavon?" he gasped. "You . . . How . . . ?"

"Yes, Athel, I've returned," Lavon said.

Lavon extended his hand, and Athel grasped the hand. He drew Lavon forward and embraced him. Tears rose in Athel's eyes.

"What has happened to you?" he asked. "Where have you . . . ?"

There was another shot. He pulled back.

"What's wrong?" Lavon asked.

"Essie ran away," Athel said. "I hired a man with nigger dogs and warned him not to hurt the boy. . . . Cellus, damn you, where's my gun?"

Cellus ran down the hall and handed Athel his rifle.

"I must see about Essie," Athel said, staring at his

brother's face as though still trying to convince himself Lavon had really returned.

"I'll come with you," Lavon said.

"Yes, yes, I am so . . . Ah, Lavon, I never thought I would see you again in this life. I . . . Come, we must hurry."

Lavon followed Athel into the yard. The quarters were quiet. Not a light burned in the shacks. A wind was up. The air was still humid, and both men began to sweat as they ran down the trail to the swamp.

The baying of dogs in the darkness made Athel forget Lavon's return, for the sound meant the dogs had cornered Essie and tasted blood. Lavon fell in behind Athel on the dark trail. A thorn vine ripped his jacket. He lost the path for a step, and mud oozed over the top of his boots. The howling grew nearer. Lavon had forgotten the terrifying sound of dogs on the kill. An animal splashed in nearby water. The water smelled fetid.

"Swan!" Athel called. "Where are you? Hold your dogs, damn you! Don't fire again!"

"Mr. Deavors?" Swan answered from the darkness. "Stand still, sir. I'm gettin' toward the dogs now. They holdin' the nigger at bay, but they might attack you if you come up on 'em."

"Call off your dogs if they have the boy," Athel shouted. "I don't want him hurt."

"He attacked me with a limb," Swan whined.

"Essie!" Athel called. "Essie, can you hear me? Where are you?"

Only the dogs answered. They were quite close now. There was a confusion of sounds, with the snarling of the dogs, the footsteps in the undergrowth, the thrashing of water. Lavon remembered Essie now. He was a huge man. Lavon pulled out his pistol as something crashed through the bushes. What if Essie attacked him instead of Swan?

But it was a dog that emerged from the dark, not the slave, a brutal animal with blood dripping from lips that curled back over its teeth. The dog seemed confused by the presence of the men. Lavon brought his pistol over his left arm and sighted the dog as it crouched to spring.

A scream turned the animal back into the bushes. Another scream brought Athel past Lavon.

"Damnit, Swan, call off the dogs!" Athel shouted.

Lavon went through the undergrowth and came on a moonlit clearing, where Essie writhed on the ground, flailing at the dogs, who darted forward to bite his arms and legs. Swan and Athel stood at opposite sides of the clearing. Each man had his gun raised.

Essie, in his terror, thought they meant to kill him. "Don't shoot me, don't kill me!" he cried up at Athel.

Lavon realized he could turn the moment to his advantage and win Essie's gratitude. He shoved Athel's rifle away and reached Swan in two strides and wrenched the gun from his hands.

"Don't kill the boy!" Lavon shouted.

For a moment, Lavon thought he had made a fatal error, for the dogs turned on him, snarling as they went after the man who had attacked their master. Lavon stumbled back. His foot caught in a cypress root, and he fell to the ground. He lost his pistol and jerked up his hands to fend off the dogs.

Swan's whip cut the air. "Nester! Blue! Jackson!" he shouted. The dogs stopped. They turned toward Swan in bewilderment.

Lavon retrieved his pistol and stood up. Essie crawled to a birch and clawed the bark to get himself off the ground. His shirt and trousers were in shreds, and he bled from a dozen wounds along his legs and arms.

Athel looked searchingly at Lavon, then turned to Essie's aid. Swan quieted his dogs.

"We have to get Essie out of the swamp," Athel said. "His wounds need tendin' quickly. Can you walk, Essie? Good. Now, you walk on ahead, and don't you try to run off, you hear me?"

Essie stumbled from the clearing. After a few steps, Athel and Lavon had to take his arms and help him up the path. Swan kept his dogs well back, occasionally cursing and cracking his whip.

Cellus and Ed waited at the top of the path. Athel charged Ed with the task of locking Essie in the slave jail adjacent to the storeroom. Aunt Froney was summoned to treat Essie's wounds. Filch was sent to get the doctor.

Swan came up to Athel. His face was red, and he had difficulty breathing. "Nigger came out of nowhere with a limb," he said. "Fired at him to save my life. Didn't hit him. Then he plumb got away for a few minutes, Mr. Deavors. Got out there in the dark, got into some of them little creeks and bogs, and he was quiet, quiet as a rat pissin' on cotton, almost outsmarted my dogs a couple of times. Not like a nigger to be so smart. And the dogs, they was so worked up with the chasin', and him havin' attacked me . . . well, it was all the boy's fault."

"He could have been killed," Athel said. "He's my wheelwright, Mr. Swan. Do you know how valuable he is? Now he's all chewed up and no use as far as work is concerned for a long while."

"Of more use than if he'd got away," Swan said. "Dogs didn't bite him deep. Just nipped him. Niggers ain't like white people, Mr. Deavors. Blood's not the same. Don't hurt him to bleed a little. Bleed some of that meanness out. He'll mend up quick. I guarantee it."

Athel dismissed Swan with a shake of his head. He instructed Cellus to escort Swan to the house and give him his fee.

Athel made sure Essie was being treated; then he and Lavon walked to the house. They did not speak. The impact of Lavon's return again swept over Athel. He did not know what to say. For his part, Lavon remained silent to organize his story.

Athel stopped at the back steps. "Welcome home, Lavon," he said quietly. Again he embraced Lavon, and tears fell down his cheeks.

The brothers started toward the gallery. Athel put his arm around Lavon's shoulder. Lavon spun the tale of his predicament: A business venture in Tangier had left him impoverished, he had been cheated by partners he considered men of honor, and being in a savage country, he was left without recourse to law. The truth was that he had simply squandered his entire inheritance on high living.

Athel stopped. "Why didn't you write me?"

"I did, Athel. I wrote on several desperate occasions," Lavon said. "In all honesty, I feared you had abandoned me. And one can't depend on the postal service in such a place."

"And I wrote to you," Athel said. "But when time passed and I received no reply, I finally stopped writing. I should have persisted, I see now. I should have employed agents to trace you."

"No, it's all my fault," Lavon said. "I should never have been so reckless as to leave here, Athel. All that followed came from that rash act. That, and compounding the folly with a stubborn pride that would not let me come home immediately from Morocco when I failed to hear from you."

"I'll make amends for my failure to keep in touch with you," Athel said. "But for now, do you want a drink? A bath? Do you want to rest? And you must be famished."

"I need both a bath and a rest," Lavon said. "But first, some food and whiskey, Athel." Lavon's voice broke with genuine emotion. "You can't know what it's been like. It seems I've been traveling for an eternity . . . always by some unlikely conveyance or other."

Lawton had crept down the gallery a few minutes earlier and seen his father embrace Lavon, seen the tears in his father's eyes. He had never seen his father cry or show so much emotion. Lawton was so touched that for the first time since he had left the storeroom, he forgot his guilt and obsession.

The brothers noticed Lawton, and Athel motioned for him to come forward. Lavon shook the boy's hand as Athel told Lawton that, by an act of providence, his uncle had been returned to them.

Joleen appeared in the doorway, and Lavon was

struck by her eyes, which looked straight at him. He embraced her quickly and stepped back, aroused by the feel of her body. But it was more the bold eyes and knowing smile at the corners of her lips that told him of her imminent sexual awakening. Though so young, she was the most provocative woman he had seen for a long time.

Lavon exchanged pleasantries with them. They were both unusually quiet in the presence of this uncle they had not thought about in years. They had only fragmentary memories of him. The homecoming continued as they entered the dining room. Tillman came forward shyly at his father's beckoning.

All Lavon knew about Tillman was that Estelle had nearly died at his birth. Tillman talked so quietly that Lavon had difficulty understanding him. He was a tall boy for his age, but very thin. There was a brooding quality to his dark eyes that disturbed Lavon.

Estelle had stepped outside to order fresh cornbread from Norvina. She came from the passageway, followed by Ed. Lavon assumed that Ed had told her about his arrival and Essie's capture. Ed glanced sharply at Lavon and walked back down the passageway.

Lavon walked over to Estelle. He smiled. In every gesture he showed only deference and repentant looks. He searched her eyes, hoping for an indication that she no longer disliked and distrusted him.

Suddenly, and awkwardly for Lavon, he embraced her. She stiffened. "Thank the Lord you're alive and well, Lavon," she said as she pulled away.

She could bring herself to say no more, and even this she said merely in deference to Athel. She still despised Lavon, and while she would not wish him dead, she had often prayed that he be alive and well so long as he stayed on other continents.

"Lavon is famished," Athel said. "Sit here, Lavon. I see a place has been laid for you. Estelle, this is a night for celebration. I'm overcome. I don't know what to say."

"There will be hot cornbread in a minute, Lavon," Estelle said.

They all sat down. Athel poured whiskey for Lavon and for himself. They began to talk. Lavon asked about other family members. Athel told him of the death of a cousin and the drowning of a great-uncle in the Gulf of Mexico.

"Cousin Buford died of the cholera last spring in Natchez," Athel said. "Aunt Delma still lives there. She was out visitin' a few weeks back."

"And everyone here, the immediate family, you've all been well?" Lavon asked. He sipped the whiskey. Estelle motioned to Bonita and Flora, and they started serving him.

"We've all been well lately," Athel said. "Lawton and Joleen are never ill. Tillman had the grippe two winters runnin', and last year the scarlet fever. But he's healthy this year, so far."

"The place seems to be prospering," Lavon said. "I can't wait to get out and walk around tomorrow. Have you planted any new acreage?"

"Oh, some three hundred new acres since you left," Athel said. "But only to replace farmed-out land. Still the same acreage in cotton. I did purchase a thousand acres last year, but it's only been used for grazing. Yes, we've been fortunate, Lavon. The place has prospered. My main disappointment has been my inability to find a decent overseer. But I keep talkin' about us. Tell me, what of your news? Did you ever marry? Tell us what has happened with you."

"No, I never married," Lavon said. "Really, there's not that much to tell, Athel. Later, if you like, I can discuss my business failure in Tangier. But I'm sure the others do not wish to hear of my business affairs."

"Then tell us of your adventures," Athel said. He felt he had made a mistake to inquire of personal matters that must be both painful and embarrassing to his brother.

The cornbread arrived. Lavon helped himself to a large slice. He patted on butter and ate ravenously. The food was better than anything he had eaten for months. He thought wryly of his dining companions on the Continent and the constant jests he had made to them about the bland fried food his family ate on the plantation.

Lavon drank whiskey. "My adventures?" he asked. He shook his head. He leaned forward and began to weave his stories, looking from one child to another as he spoke of a snake charmer in Tangier, a camel race in Fez, a bullfight in Spain, a bear-and-dog fight in London, a grand ball in Paris.

He talked easily, charming the children as he mentioned what to them were storybook cities, as naturally as they might speak of Benton or Natchez. And he was careful not to seem condescending, for he sometimes turned the stories back on himself in such a way as to show humility and make them laugh at his plight.

Yes, he told himself, he could win the children. And Athel did not seem to have changed. But Estelle sat with her back straight, as always. Her eyes were narrowed. She still felt the same way about him, but he told himself he would somehow overcome her opposition.

There was a sound. Lavon glanced around. Cellus stood in the door, watching him. Lavon looked from the eyes that seemed to accuse him of crimes he had not yet thought of. Cellus walked over to Athel. He bent down and whispered something. Athel's head turned toward Lavon but looked away quickly. He nodded and sighed. Cellus looked at Lavon again, then left.

Lavon told the children another story. His heart pounded, and he caught himself glancing around to see if Cellus was still there. He was gone. Lavon forced a smile at Joleen and asked himself what in the world Cellus had said to Athel, because it obviously had to do with him. He waited for Athel to say something, but he remained silent. Lavon rambled on with his tale. He promised himself that when his plans came to fruition, his first act would be to sell Cellus as a field hand to a sugarcane plantation.

He glanced at Athel again. What in hell had that goddamn nigger said about him?

BOOK II

Brother and Sister

Chapter 9

Lavon sipped wine and watched people talk and flirt and drink. The wine was good French white, a Sancerre. Mildly dry, the way he liked wine. It was the first decent drink he had tasted since leaving the Continent. He was sick of the whiskey he had consumed since his arrival two weeks earlier, though he had been thankful for every drop.

He stood in the midst of the county's finest families. It was a dressed-up group that had come to his Aunt Delma's mansion in Natchez. They considered themselves sophisticated, this cluster of people who, as a doctor had told Lavon, "make Natchez a new Athens in this barbaric sea of mud and swamp."

Lavon recalled evenings in Paris and London salons. He smiled as he listened to the talk, and his eyes examined the ladies' garments. He posed well in the middle of the group, a handsome man in his newly tailored suit. Athel had taken him to the finest tailor in the city. Lavon told himself that this rag would do well enough in Natchez, but when he returned to London, he would have a good laugh with his tailor there over the local man's work.

The parlor was a large room, but with his aunt's propensity for filling up rooms with furniture and guests, it was crowded. The furniture was Georgian, the walls were red plush, and there was a jungle of growing things, particularly potted palms. Above the crowd, two pukhas—oblong ceiling fans—stirred the air, pulled by slaves tugging ropes.

The air was growing heavy. Lavon took out his handkerchief and wiped moisture from his face. Damn lazy niggers are falling asleep in the heat, he told himself.

He finished the wine. Without command a slave extended a tray, and Lavon took another glass. He looked around the room, past his sister-in-law, Estelle, who was talking to a group of women. His gaze settled on a painting of passenger pigeons on the wall above Estelle's head. He tried to remember the man who had painted it. The man had been one of Aunt Delma's favorites when Lavon was young. He was always in her salon. He gave French and dancing lessons to the daughters of the town's wealthy and tried to earn a living selling his paintings. But he hadn't fared too well in Natchez. There were not that many young ladies for his French and dancing lessons, and except for Aunt Delma, not many people were interested in his pictures of birds. Audubon—that was the fellow's name, he recalled.

Lavon suddenly realized that Estelle was staring at him. He nodded, smiled, and looked away. She had thought he was staring at her. Lavon smiled to himself and drank wine. He had sooner look at a pigeon than at his sister-in-law.

Damn the woman. She was always watching him. She was polite but cold. He could not reach her. This was unusual; there were few people he could not reach if he wanted, particularly women.

When he thought of Estelle, it disturbed him. She was the major obstacle to his plans, and she could influence Athel against him. Athel himself seemed pleased with his conduct in the two weeks since his return. He had been polite, deferential, sober, repentant, and hard-working. Hard-working? Goddamnit, he had been up at dawn for ten days running and dragged his outraged body out to help supervise the niggers' work, though he knew nothing of growing cotton.

Lavon knew he could do what he wished, could stay drunk and whore around, and Athel would let him live at the Columns and give him occasional cash. But if he wished to get back the half-ownership he had relinquished, he had to seem dedicated to the goddamn plantation and willing to work it for the rest of his life.

Lavon was not certain now how easy this would be. Athel had changed somewhat. Oh, he was still generous. He was willing to accept responsibility for things not his fault. But he was not so quick to give in to Lavon's whims and demands as he had been years ago. And now he had children growing up, and he wanted the plantation for them.

Lavon had abandoned any idea of settling down at the Columns. All he wanted was to secure half-ownership of the plantation and turn his financial affairs over to Natchez attorneys and get out of the godforsaken place and return to Europe. He sipped wine and asked himself how he had ever thought he could endure more than a few months living out in those swamps.

"Thank you . . . evening, ma'am." Lavon smiled as old Mrs. Delsano welcomed him back. She also smiled and appraised him with the eye of a woman with an unmarried daughter.

She walked away. Laughter turned his attention to a corner of the room where Aunt Delma and several women were talking to the German lawyer Lavon had met earlier. Lavon studied the man. He spoke easily, smiling from one lady to another as though he had absolute confidence in his charm. The man's name was Aaron Clauson. He had come down from the German community in Ohio a few weeks earlier. He was foppish at times. He dressed as a dandy, with too many ruffles and flourishes for Lavon's taste.

The man's dark eyes disturbed Lavon. They were too shrewd, too knowing, as though they were the one part of a mask that couldn't be molded to his disguise. Lavon felt himself a master of the pose, and was beginning to wonder if he might be in the presence of another.

Joleen joined the women. She, too, laughed at the man's talk. Lavon had not seen her look on anyone in such a manner. Certainly she had not looked at him in such a way, though she seemed to like him well enough.

Aunt Delma looked around and spotted Lavon.

"Come over and join us," she called. "Mr. Clauson is telling us anecdotes about President Jackson."

Lavon joined the group. "You've met everyone here, haven't you, Lavon?" Aunt Delma asked. "Yes, of course you have, dear." She drank from her glass of Madeira.

"When we met, sir, I didn't realize you had recently returned from a tour of the Continent," Aaron said. He spoke with an accent. "Which cities did you like best?"

"I wasn't touring, Mr. Clauson," Lavon said. "I lived in Europe for several years. As for my favorites, it would be difficult to choose between Paris and London. Except, of course, for the disagreeable weather in London."

"I quite agree," Aaron said. "You know, ladies, an Englishman was asked when summer occurred in England. And the man replied, 'Why, it's usually one weekend in July.' "

Lavon forced himself to laugh with the ladies. He then told a story about losing his way in the London fog and climbing into what he thought was a cab, only to discover it was a police wagon. The ladies laughed. Lavon and Aaron eyed each other.

"Are you really leaving Natchez this evenin', Mr. Clauson?" Joleen asked.

"Yes, Miss Deavors, I fear I must," Aaron said. "A planter south of Woodville needs my assistance. I must reach him tomorrow. And of course, I could not leave earlier and miss an evening here."

"But there's no coach," Lavon said.

"No, I must go on horseback," Aaron said.

"You plan to ride that road at night?" Aunt Delma said.

"I'll ride fast, I assure you," Aaron said. "And I'll be armed with a brace of pistols. Though if forced to use one of the guns, I'm not sure I'll know what part is the trigger."

The ladies laughed. Lavon excused himself and walked away. He took another glass of wine. He had been mistaken to think the man was so shrewd. He was a fool and a fop, and that was that.

The pukhas waved faster. A warm breeze swept the room. Lavon stood alone and sipped his wine. He saw that Lawton was talking to the little Sumrall girl. Rather, the girl was talking, and Lawton was listening and nodding. Lavon could never gauge the boy's moods, but he suspected Lawton was having problems with sex. He was at that age. Earlier Lavon had seen Lawton kissing Lily Crawford on the back porch. Now he was red-faced and seemed flustered.

Well, Lavon told himself, Lawton was a good-looking boy, and if the Crawford girl wouldn't provide sex, there was enough 'tang on the plantation to keep him busy for the summer.

Lawton watched Lavon walk over to a group of older women. He wished he had his uncle's easy way of getting along with people, particularly women. Nadine Sumrall's talk bored him, and though he knew how desperate she was not to be left alone, he would have bribed someone to take his place. Lawton drank punch, and his eyes wandered the room. Lily Crawford was talking to three boys. Joleen was still talking to that lawyer from upriver. That was all right, better than when she walked out onto the porch with Rayford Caldwell.

Lawton scolded himself for watching Joleen. But he could not help himself. It was as compulsive as the fantasies and the accompanying masturbation every day since the incident in the storehouse. He had endured contrasting feelings of excitement, guilt, anxiety, and ecstasy. Guiltily, he had avoided Joleen as much as possible. But his mind betrayed him with constant thoughts of her lips, her thigh with the scar, her breasts, her smile.

Lawton shifted his weight to his left leg. His penis had hardened with his thoughts. Nadine was talking about her new dress, and Lawton nodded and drank punch.

Across the room, Joleen smiled at him. He resented that smile on the corners of her lips. He looked away. His cheeks were warm. What was happening to him? He had to do something. He was desperate. What if she suspected how he felt about her, and after the way he had been treating her?

He had to do something, anything. He thought of the white slave. He could have the girl. He knew he could. Nettie excited him. Not as much as Joleen, but a little bit. He had to have a woman. But Nettie was a slave. It was wrong to take advantage of slave girls. His father had told him that. She looked totally white. But she was still a slave.

Theron Sumrall joined them. He started talking to his sister. Lawton excused himself and walked across the room. He stopped by his father and a group of men. Though he wanted to join the grown-up talk, he stayed on the periphery of the group.

". . . rain doesn't slack up soon, the cotton's goin' to be in trouble," Haskell Sumrall was saying. He was Nadine and Theron's father and owned a large plantation near Benton.

"It's not the rain that worries me so much as my lazy niggers," another man said. "Hot weather like this comes, and they just won't do their damn work. Don't want to get out till the sun's up, and think they ought to quit 'fore nine in the evenin'. I sometimes think somebody's goin' among the people, stirrin' up trouble."

"I hear James Murrell's bunch took off a score of niggers last week up near Port Gibson," Haskell Sumrall said. "That kind of thing is bound to cause unrest. Word gets 'round. I'll swear, even when my people haven't seen a strange nigger for weeks, they seem to know about every act of disobedience by every nigger in the state. I hear they increasin' the slave patrols up near Rodney and Port Gibson, and I think we ought to be doin' the same thing down here."

Lawton drifted away. He took more punch and wished he could drink whiskey like the men. He had tasted whiskey and did not much like it, but it would make him feel grown-up.

Joleen was smiling at that lawyer. The man held his glass with two fingers. His handkerchief stuck out from his coat sleeve. He was elegantly dressed, Lawton told himself. A little too elegant.

Why would Joleen want to talk to the man so long? And why was she smiling, first at the lawyer and then at Lawton across the room? And in that tantalizing way of hers? Lawton turned away in frustration. Lily was standing by the punchbowl. He hurried over to her. He hoped he would be able to walk her out to the back porch and kiss her again, but he knew that if he did, he would close his eyes and it would be Joleen's lips he pressed against, and Joleen's body he touched.

When he reached Lily, his cheeks were burning.

Chapter 10

Aaron Clauson rode north along the trace. He wore a leather outfit and carried two pistols.

He met no riders during the first half-hour, and he relaxed. But he was still anxious, not only because of his mission, but because he had heard the talk about James Murrell. Aaron knew Murrell was as likely to kill a white rider for his money as to steal a slave. Each week in Natchez there was some new tale of Murrell or other thieves along the trace. A mile back, Aaron had passed the skull of a decapitated murderer on a pole, marking the site of his crime. There was now less of the lynch law that had once prevailed on the trace, but Aaron knew it was still common for angry men to kill a bandit or murderer and cut off his head.

Aaron's horse shied as a possum ran across the road. Aaron tensed with his horse's movement, then settled back in the saddle and wiped sweat from his face. A ground fog was rising. This was a hazard on the road, but a blessing if the fog held until he reached his destination.

How odd, he thought, to be riding through the Mississippi night on this errand. When Levi Coffin first suggested in the spring that he move to Natchez and pose as a lawyer, he had thought that suggestion preposterous. Yet here he was, coming from a planters' party and heading for a rendezvous with five black men.

He shifted in the saddle and thought of the gathering at Mrs. Deavors' house. He had been in Natchez only a few weeks, and already he was weary of the social life and the talk of the planters. Some of those men, such as Athel Deavors, actually considered themselves humanitarians because they did not sell or whip slaves.

This is no time for moral speculation, Aaron told himself. He must concentrate on his mission tonight, for he was not pleased with the plan he had devised and put into effect. But his thoughts would not hold to his plan, and he thought of Joleen Deavors' smile and her blue eyes. He knew he should be wary of that smile, for it was truly enigmatic. One could read into it anything he wanted, from sexual invitation to scorn.

And she was young. She could be no more than seventeen or eighteen. Merely another lovely daughter of a planter. He had met dozens of them. Yet, there was some quality to Joleen that set her apart. . . .

Aaron heard a horse moving up fast behind him. He pulled a pistol and looked around, debating whether to seek cover at the side of the road. But the rider was close enough to have seen him. Aaron's palms were sweating. He gripped the pistol tighter and held it across his chest. For a moment Aaron thought the rider would go past him without a word. The man might have been blind, for he paid no heed to Aaron, and this was unlikely on the trace at night.

The man looked around suddenly. His face in the moonlight startled Aaron. His face was long, and the eyes were too large and white. His beard fell below his chin, and his white hair flew behind him as he hunched forward in the saddle.

The rider slowed his horse to match Aaron's pace.

"Good evening, sir!" he shouted. "Where are you bound?"

"I'm going up near Jackson," Aaron said.

"Are you going to do the Lord's work?" the man asked.

"What, sir?" Aaron asked. He did not understand what the man meant. The eyes held him, and the voice, too, was hypnotic.

"The Lord's work!" the man shouted.

Then Aaron knew where he had heard that voice and seen that face. A week earlier he had wandered out to a camp meeting where this man preached to a crowd of hundreds and worked them to a frenzy. He was Lorenzo Dow, the most famous of the preachers who rode the trace, to rail against the sins common to frontier life.

Aaron put up his pistol. "The Lord's work?" he said. "Yes, I suppose you could say I am doing the Lord's work." He was amused to be discussing religion with this preacher on the Natchez Trace.

"And so be I," Dow said. "I must save souls tonight. I must save souls. They await me in Port Gibson. I must save them from damnation. Are you saved from damnation, sir?"

"I believe I am," Aaron said.

"Then I must ride on," Dow said. "Remember this: Tigapa! It stands for Trust in God and Push Ahead. Tigapa. Repeat it when you doubt your faith, and save your soul from hell fire. Good night, sir."

Dow leaned forward and gave his horse rein. He disappeared into the darkness, his hair flowing behind, as though unable to keep pace with the horse.

Aaron rode faster. Twice he heard approaching horsemen and hid in cover at the side of the road. He encountered no slave patrols, and he took this as a good sign. An hour later he rode into Rodney, a boom town that was a center for cotton shipping. It also had more than its share of the kind of sin Dow detested. Aaron moved slowly along a street lined with shacks and lean-tos and turned onto a trail that led toward the river but that passed no buildings.

The fog was heavy among creeks that twisted down to the river. Aaron reached the weeping willow and waited for the signal. He rode another hundred yards, but there was no light ahead. He touched the hilt of his pistol. He listened for signs of warning. All he heard were frogs and insects.

The flashing light startled him. He trotted toward the light, his hand still hovering at his gun. A few seconds later he saw a Negro man holding a lantern at the edge of a plum thicket. Aaron dismounted and shook hands with the man.

"How are you, Clarence?" Aaron asked. He had met the man several times the previous week, and they had planned tonight's mission. Clarence was a free Negro who had come to Mississippi four months earlier as Levi Coffin's agent.

"I was anxious about you, Aaron," Clarence said. "Did you run into any patrols?"

"No, only lone riders," Aaron said. "Are the slaves here? Are there any problems?"

"No, I spoke to the man on the boat this evening," Clarence said. "The only problem will be if we don't get the slaves aboard before the man's master returns from Port Gibson. Come on, we ought to get started."

Clarence led the way into the thicket. Four black men sat on the ground eating plums. They stood up and stared at Aaron. He shook hands with them to reassure them, but still he saw the fear and suspicion in their faces. They trusted Clarence because he was a Negro, but now they had to trust a white man.

The planters had their talk of James Murrell and his rustling, but Aaron had heard slave talk of other Murrell tactics. He wondered if these men knew of Murrell's trick of luring a slave away with promises of freedom, then forcing the slave to allow himself to be "sold" in another state, only to run off the next day. Murrell would force the man to be sold and to run away again and again, and the slave had no choice. When the slave became a liability, he was murdered.

They left the thicket, found a trail that paralleled the Mississippi, and passed through oak and cypress groves. Aaron rode at the head of the column, and Clarence brought up the rear. After a quarter-mile they turned onto a road. This road twisted around until it, too, paralleled the river, which was a half-mile away.

Bayous and bogs lined the sides of the road, but the water was clear of growth. It was "famous" water, for it was filled with moccasins. Besides being deadly, the water offered no cover, so if a slave patrol confronted the men, they had no place to flee. There was no justification for slaves to be out at night without a white man. So Aaron's role was essential.

Aaron found himself glancing around to see if anyone was coming up behind. This is no good, he told himself. He felt naïve. Even if he successfully passed a slave patrol, he would be recognized. He had not considered that. In the future he would have to plan better.

They had gone a half-mile when Aaron heard sounds ahead. He halted the column. The slaves gathered together and began to whisper. Aaron feared the men would panic if they were challenged.

There was nothing to do but go on. The column was formed again. Aaron rode off slowly. The fog was thinning out. Four horsemen took form. Aaron's hands were damp on the reins. He held up a hand, and the column halted. He rode forward a few yards to meet the patrol.

"Evenin'," the leader said. He and the other men were armed with rifles. "Where you bound with your niggers, sir?"

"I've hired them out to the lumberyard up the river," Aaron said. "The owner wants them tonight so they can start off at first light tomorrow."

The other men had gone past Aaron. They were looking at the slaves and talking. One of the men came back and whispered to the leader. Aaron eased his hand to the hilt of a pistol. He knew they were suspicious, yet he did not know how far they would go with a man of property. One never knew with these patrols. They might be reluctant to challenge him. Yet the patrols were often composed of poor men who resented the planters and enjoyed being in a position of authority over a wealthy man.

"My name's Seth Parsons," the leader said. "What is your name, sir?" He moved closer and studied

Aaron's face. "I find it odd that you be out this time of night with your boys. And we got to be careful, what with all the slave stealin' and rustlin' goin' on, and the talk of an uprisin'. Murrell's men are about these parts. . . ."

"Sir, do I look like one of Murrell's men?" Aaron asked indignantly. "I know you have your duty, but I will not be insulted on the public roads by men who, in all truth, are dressed as if they themselves might be brigands. My name is Calvin Thigpen, and I've journeyed all the way up from Woodville. If you hinder me any longer or insult me again, you will pay, sir. I promise you that."

Parsons was clearly stunned by Aaron's outburst. He was wavering. Aaron knew he might not get another opportunity. "Come on, boys," he called. "Get moving."

Aaron rode off. He gripped his pistol. He waited for a challenge. He rode ten paces. Twenty paces. How foolhardy this plan was. Even if they escaped, Parsons would know what he looked like. After fifty paces he glanced around. The patrol was riding off, but Parsons lingered behind the others.

The fog was rising. Aaron rode faster. The slaves broke into a trot. When Aaron looked around again, he could no longer see the patrol. He relaxed and wiped his palms.

They turned onto a trail to the river and reached the cover of moss-draped oaks. Aaron and the slaves waited while Clarence crept to a small paddle-wheeler two hundred yards up the river. He returned five minutes later. Aaron and Clarence shook hands, and Aaron watched until the men were safely on board.

Aaron rode out of the oaks at a trot. He galloped through the fog and reached the trail to the plum grove. He paused and debated whether to try to find a fresh horse. It's better to get out of the area immediately, he told himself.

A horseman came slowly from the fog. It was Parsons. He reined up beside Aaron.

"No, sir, don't try to ride off," he said. "Where's your niggers, Mr. Thigpen?"

"At the lumberyard," Aaron said. "I warned you before not to insult me. . . ."

"No, sir, you couldn't have made the yard this fast. And then I remembered somethin'. Tomorrow's Sunday. That there place don't do no work on a Sunday. I thought somethin' was funny. Others thought I was bein' too suspicious, but I was right."

Slowly he brought up his rifle. He was an old man, and the gun was heavy in his hands. Aaron shot him through the chest and raced onto the trail.

Chapter 11

Rainfall was heavier than usual the first two weeks in July. The slaves were sent to the fields half an hour earlier. They began work a few minutes before daybreak after a cold breakfast in their cabins. Filch drove his hoe gangs hard, because the rain made the grass grow faster than the cotton. Two girls walked the rows with water jugs so the slaves wouldn't have to pause but a moment for a drink.

At noon the women were given a half-hour to sit in the fields and eat the snacks they had brought in the morning. The men led their mules to open-sided stalls, where they ate lunch and rested for two hours while the mules drank water and ate as much oats as they wanted. Work continued until half-past eight. The slaves trudged back home to cook dinner, chop firewood, work their vegetable plots, tend their chickens, and visit. At nine-thirty a driver walked the rows of shacks, blowing the curfew horn and checking to see that all the fires were out. When he made the rounds ten minutes later, all the slaves were expected to be in bed.

Despite heavy rain, the talk among the planters was that the crop would be the best in years. When men gathered over whiskey and cigars, conversation never drifted far from the price per bale or what the market might be like in New Orleans or Europe.

Sometimes the talk would turn to the latest story about President Jackson and his wife, but more likely, nonplanting talk would be concerned with some new rumor of a slave insurrection or the theft of more slaves by James Murrell and his men. Murrell would have needed an army to take away the number of slaves he was accused of stealing, but he was blamed for each missing Negro. And there were hundreds of missing blacks at any given time, though most of them were runaways who were caught or who wandered back after a few days of hiding in the swamps and stealing food at night.

For the past few weeks, this talk had centered around Seth Parsons' murder and the theft of five slaves. On a Sunday afternoon a dozen planters sat on the Deavors' front porch drinking whiskey and lamenting the fact that a white man had been involved in the theft and murder but that no one in the patrol but Parsons had seen his face clearly.

Lavon sat in the background. He nursed his whiskey and endured talk he had first found boring and now despised. Each morning Lavon dragged himself up at dawn. Twice he had been badly sunburned. Mosquitoes ate him alive each evening in the fields, and chiggers, ticks, and mites bypassed every slave to reach his legs and ankles. He had killed copperheads and moccasins, heard the warnings of rattlers, and had nearly stepped on a coral snake, the deadliest of all because its venom went to the nerves instead of the blood. He had lost twenty pounds in the heat, and every night he ached in all his bones.

Lavon had never learned anything about cotton, so he knew less than any of the slaves. They were critical of his supervision, particularly the drivers and mechanics, except for Essie, the runaway, who treated him with respect and would do anything he wanted. Essie had not been punished for running away, and since he thought Lavon had saved his life in the swamp, he also assumed Lavon was responsible for his lenient treatment.

Lavon had tempered his drinking and fought down his sexual excitement, for he knew he was on parole at the Columns. If he showed any indication of his true intentions, he would have no chance of owning half the plantation again. Even with his pose as a reformed wastrel and his hard work, his hopes were decreasing with each day. Estelle made little attempt to hide her contempt for Lavon, and he knew she talked against him at every opportunity. Cellus scorned him openly, and Lavon suspected that Cellus had sent word to the hands not to kowtow to him. He knew Cellus had warned them: God help any girl who let Lavon get near her.

Athel was still generous and forgiving. Lavon knew he could drink and whore forever and his brother would let him stay and even give him money. But Lavon could spend a month's allowance in a day. He had to have wealth, and he had to have independence. Therefore he needed the income from half the plantation, and he had to get out of the swamps and spend that income in some civilized place.

So he held to his hopes and sought his brother's approval. He stayed sober, worked hard in the sun, killed snakes, talked crops. He was polite and deferential. He waited out his parole, hour by hour and day by day.

On this afternoon Lavon talked market conditions and boll weevils. He smiled at Haskell Sumrall and agreed that a new cotton gin was just what Benton needed. He looked at his watch for the third time, but the hands seemed unable to move in the heat.

Finally the men drifted out to their carriages and headed home. Lavon lay down in his room for five minutes. He walked out and sat on the porch for ten minutes. He went out back, and then to the front again.

It was so early. Hours must pass before he could sleep.

Athel found him half an hour later in the magnolia grove.

"Did you enjoy the afternoon, Lavon?" he asked.

"Of course," Lavon said. "It's always a pleasure to discuss cotton, and I'm eager to learn all I can."

"I'm glad," Athel said.

He and Lavon walked toward the gazebo. Athel sought the softest words for what he had to say. He knew how restless and bored his brother was. It had taken him all these weeks, but he was coming to accept what both Estelle and Cellus maintained—that Lavon had not changed and was only posing for some purpose. Athel wanted to give Lavon more time to prove himself. Most of all, he wanted to avoid any confrontation with Lavon. But now he had no choice.

They stopped in the shadow of the gazebo. "Lavon, may I see your watch, please?" Athel asked.

Lavon handed Athel the watch.

"Yes, this is Haskell Sumrall's watch," Athel said. "This afternoon he saw you take it out and thought he recognized it. Haskell lost it to a bandit in the spring. Yet you told me you purchased the watch on the Continent, Lavon."

"I . . . He must be mistaken," Lavon said. He had checked the watch for an inscription but had not realized it might be recognized.

"No, there aren't two watches like this in the world," Athel said. "It's been in the family for generations. See, the diamonds form a scrolled 'S.' "

Lavon looked into Athel's eyes. Athel's eyes were not accusing. They were hurt. They wanted to believe. Lavon resented the necessity of building one more clever lie. A mosquito buzzed at his head. He slapped at the sound and popped himself on the ear.

"Actually, I bought the watch in Natchez," Lavon said. "I bought it off a man when I arrived, and . . ." He lacked any enthusiasm for the lie. He slapped at the mosquito again. Joleen was riding through the grove. She waved, but he ignored her. In his state of enforced celibacy, her budding sexuality was driving him to the breaking point.

"But you said you were destitute. . . . Lavon, Cellus talked to your driver the night you arrived. The nigger said you confronted a bandit on the road and took . . . some items from the man. Why didn't you tell me? Why did you . . . ?" Athel, too, lacked the desire to continue. "All right, Lavon. I don't care. But the watch belongs to Haskell, and I must return it to him. If you like, I'll compensate you for its value."

"No, no, give it to Haskell," Lavon said.

Athel put the watch in his pocket.

They walked on through the trees. "I was in the swamp earlier, and the piglets are growing faster than I expected," Athel said.

Lavon thought it a weak ploy to change the conversation, but he gratefully discussed hog slaughtering and the price of Yankee pork. When they parted at the front porch, Lavon walked around the house. He told himself time was running out. He had to come up with a plan or he would be lost. And he had to do something about that goddamn Cellus. He swore to himself that he would have Cellus' black balls before he was finished. He walked around the house again and then began pacing the vegetable garden.

Lavon emerged from the garden plot ten minutes later, hot and thirsty. He cursed gnats and mosquitoes and barely grunted at Lawton, who was coming out of the barn. Finally Lavon went to bed and lay awake for hours.

Chapter 12

The next day, Lawton walked through the slave quarters. He nodded at slaves who lounged in the doorways or hoed in their gardens. Normally Lawton would linger and talk on a hot afternoon, but he didn't say a word. He went down the path to a grove of fig trees and watched a spider making a web that reflected the sunlight. The smell of rotting figs was sweet.

He watched birds hop drunkenly about the ground as they ate fallen figs. He didn't know what to do. He could go riding. He could go hunting. He had to do something so he would stop thinking about sex. When he could stop having fantasies about Joleen, he only found that Nettie took her place. No one had ever smiled at him the way Nettie smiled. And last Friday, as they talked, she ran her tongue around her lips. She had just come from the fields, and her dress was pasted to her body.

"Sure she wants your ass, but stay away from her," Ambrose said the next day. "She's crazy, Lawton. She's not a nigger, really, you know, and she knows she can't ever be a white. Believe me, that girl don't do nothin' without havin' some gain in mind. If she swings that ass at you, it's 'cause she thinks she'll get somethin' from you. Nobody's been able to touch her. She's too highfalutin. Don't want to be a nigger. Lord God, Filch, he's been after her since his wife died. And Essie, why, Essie'd marry her in a minute. . . ."

Ambrose had trailed off the sentence as Noelle passed them. Her smile was equally inviting to them both. She was a dark slim girl with big buttocks.

"Now, you can have that one," Ambrose said. "No doubt 'bout it. I can tell the way she looks at you. She looked at me that way . . . 'fore I fucked her. But you stay away from Nettie 'less you want to find yourself 'tween a rock and a hard place."

Lawton asked questions about Noelle and was fascinated and excited by Ambrose's talk of sex. But the girl didn't interest him at all. Not like Nettie, with her insolent, inviting smile. And for every thought about Nettie, there were ten about Joleen.

Lawton walked deeper into the grove. He pulled a fig and ate it. He ate another fig. There was a sound. He turned. Joleen was walking toward him.

Sun lit the golden hairs along her arms. She wore an old yellow dress. As always, it angered Lawton when she dressed this way.

"What you doin', Lawton?" she asked. She smiled. Lawton hated that smile. He never knew what it meant. And the fact that it resembled Nettie's smile confused him all the more.

"Just walkin' some," he said. "Maybe I'll go huntin'."

"Here, what's that?" she asked. She touched his chin.

He stepped back. "Don't touch me."

"Why, Lawton, what on earth's wrong with you? I was just gettin' a piece of fig off your chin. Are you all right? Your face is red all of a sudden."

"There's nothin' wrong," he said. "I just don't want you touchin' me, that's all." His cheeks were warm.

"Why don't you want me to touch you, Lawton?" she asked. "You don't want to walk around with fig stickin' to your chin, do you?"

"I don't know. I just don't . . ." He looked from her eyes. There was a line of perspiration above her lips.

"I swear, Lawton, sometime you don't make any sense at all," she said, and shook her head. "You goin' huntin' with Ambrose?"

"No. Maybe I'll go with Daddy."

"I think he's busy with Uncle Lavon again, Lawton. He sure spends a lot of time with him. I saw 'em yesterday, havin' a real serious talk out by the gazebo, and then a few minutes ago there they were again, walkin' all serious like through the flower garden. I guess they might still be out there."

"No, not anymore," Lawton said. "I just saw Uncle Lavon comin' from the vegetable garden. Come to think of it, I saw him walkin' sort of in a daze through the garden yesterday."

"The vegetable garden?" she asked. "Two days in a row? It's not like him to take an interest in beans and things. What was he doin' there?"

"Like I said, just walkin'," Lawton replied. "He hardly gave me the time of day yesterday or today. I swear, I don't know about him sometimes, Joleen. At times it seems as if he doesn't belong here. Even when he's in the fields, you can tell he doesn't like it. I liked him at first, but now there's somethin' rubs me the wrong way."

"I know what you mean, Lawton," Joleen said. "I just don't feel comfortable around him. And Mama doesn't like him at all, not one bit. And neither does Cellus. Well, you get on with your huntin', Lawton. I'm goin' down here to the creek and take me a swim."

"You goin' down to the back creek?" he asked. "You know Daddy told you not to swim there. Current's too swift."

"You wouldn't tell on me, would you, Lawton?"

"I don't care," he said. "But you shouldn't be doin' it, Joleen. It's so far away. What if somethin' happened?"

"You want to come with me and make sure nothin' happens?" she said.

His cheeks were burning. His penis was hard, and he was afraid she would see it against his pants.

"Damnit, I can't go swimmin' with you," he said. "You know that."

"Oh, Lawton, don't be silly," she said. "I meant come with me and wait nearby while I swim. I didn't mean to swim with me. And you shouldn't be usin' curse words in front of me, Lawton."

"I'll curse whenever I want to, Joleen."

"Well, I guess you do it because it makes you feel grown-up, Lawton. Anyways, I'm all hot, and I want to swim. I'll see you later. And . . . Lawton?"

"What, Joleen?"

"Please, don't tell Daddy I'm goin' swimmin' in the back creek. Promise?"

"Why shouldn't I tell?"

"I wouldn't tell on you if you were doin' somethin' naughty, Lawton. You know that, don't you?"

"I guess so, Joleen." He stared at the sweat above her lips. How could he have chills up his spine when he felt so hot?

"I wouldn't ever tell on you, Lawton, no matter what you did," she said. "No matter how naughty. And if you like, I'll do somethin' nice for you . . . for not tellin'."

"I don't want you to do anything, Joleen, except to stop pesterin' me."

"I haven't been pesterin' you. When was the last time I asked you to teach me to shoot? . . . So you just go on and hunt some old squirrels, and I'll take me a swim."

"I . . . well, have a good swim, Joleen. And you be careful, you hear me? Damnit." He felt he had to add the "damnit." "And I won't tell Daddy."

"I know you won't, Lawton," she said. "Here, I didn't get all the fig off your chin."

He tensed. She touched his face. Her fingers were warm. He stared into her eyes, then looked away. Suddenly she was gone. He couldn't move. His legs were weak. His stomach felt hollow. He closed his eyes, and inside his jumbled head he saw her naked in the water. He clearly saw the scar on her thigh.

He began to walk aimlessly around the edge of the swamp.

Lawton walked the swamp trail beside the creek. At times, sunlight streamed down and lit a clearing, but he avoided the bright light and walked in the hot shadows. He nearly slipped on a log while crossing the creek, although he had crossed the log a hundred times without trouble.

Nothing but physical force could stop him now. No power of guilt or fear of discovery would be strong enough. He saw the blackberry bushes that marked the creek's pool. He listened, but all he heard were swamp noises and a blue jay's cry. He crouched and moved through the bushes.

Joleen lay on her back in the sand. She still wore her dress, but it was pulled high over her thighs. She had been wading, and water dripped from her thighs. Lawton sank into the bushes. He stared at the white scar. He was nauseated from heat and excitement. Joleen opened her thighs. Her dress was pulled higher. Lawton stared at the golden hairs. His hand rubbed over his penis, but he pulled it away.

Joleen stood up. He thought she meant to leave, and crouched lower, but she walked to the water and removed all her clothes. She tensed on her toes. Her breasts were wonderfully exciting. The nipples were bright red. She ran her palms over her hips and thighs. Lawton began to rub his penis through his pants. He couldn't stop, much as he tried.

Joleen went into the creek and swam for a couple of minutes. She came out dripping water and stood on her toes again, turning slowly. Then she lay down in the sand on her back, her thighs apart. Lawton looked at the curly hairs that glistened with moisture. He realized he was taking down his pants. He paused only a moment. Then he slid his hand over his stiff penis and started masturbating.

Joleen's breasts heaved with her breathing. Her stomach was flat. Her navel was large. The scar was ugly and white on her smooth, tanned skin. How could a scar be there on her perfect thighs? And how could it be the most beautiful part of her? He masturbated faster. He realized he was grunting. He tried to quiet himself. There seemed no flesh to his penis, only tender nerve endings.

Several times Joleen seemed to be glancing in his direction. Surely she didn't see him? Or had she heard him? He was only a few yards away. And for an instant he thought she smiled and posed her body.

But he couldn't believe she saw him. It was impossible. This was Joleen, his little sister.

Joleen rubbed her thighs together, then opened them wide. Lawton was so close he could faintly see the lips of her vagina through the hairs. Fantasy came in a rush—touching the scar, kissing the scar, his lips against the wet flesh, his tongue sliding over the flesh to lick through the moist hairs.

He climaxed with a force he had never known. The sensation nearly doubled him over. His stomach churned. Sweat poured from his face.

He wiped himself and closed his pants and crept away.

Chapter 13

The rain soaked Lavon as he walked to the house. He brushed past Cellus in the gallery and went into the parlor and poured a glass of whiskey. Water dripped onto the carpet. He looked at the puddle. Estelle would be angry. "Brought it all the way upriver from New Orleans," she often said. He drank more whiskey and looked around at the heavy oak furniture, the curtains and beaded lamps swaying in the wind. The room was oppressive. It seemed to hug in on Lavon. He was sweating. His ankles ached from chigger bites.

Only ten in the morning, he told himself. He felt he had been in the field for ten straight days. Two and a half months since his return, and he just could not endure this life any longer. Damn Athel for not finding an overseer. Damn the rain. Damn the grass and damn the cotton and damn the niggers. Damn everybody! Since the discovery of the watch, everyone's attitude toward him had changed.

His anger and frustration grew as he poured more whiskey. He was desperate, and he had no recourse. There was nowhere else to go and nothing else to do. He worked his butt off in those fields, worked like an overseer. Hell, he worked like a nigger, with only some hunting and planter talk for "pleasure." He had his room and board and whiskey and nothing else. Athel would never give him back the ownership he had relinquished.

He drained his glass and filled it. All he owned was the purse of coins he had taken from the bandit. Damnit, he had to live in style. He had to have excitement and fine wine and luxury and women. And goddamnit, he had to be independent. He wanted to answer to no man, least of all his brother, who watched and judged and was compassionate and forgave.

"You ruinin' the rug."

Lavon turned. Cellus stood in the door.

"Damn the rug!" Lavon said. "Get out of here and leave me alone, Cellus."

"Miss 'Stelle, she goin' to be displeased if you don't stop drippin' on the rug. And she got company. Miss Pearl Sumrall visitin'. You better go get dry."

"Cellus, get your ass out of here!"

Cellus did not move. He looked at Lavon without expression. Lavon's knuckles were white as he squeezed the glass. All his life this slave had stared at him this way. He wondered if Cellus had not taken one look at him coming from the womb and decided he was unfit to be a Deavors. Every time he did something wrong through the years, Cellus was the one who caught him. Every time he had touched a slave girl or had too much whiskey or struck a black man, Cellus knew. Cellus had told Athel about the incident with the bandit. Cellus had talked against him continually since his return. And Athel heeded this slave with the unmoving face and the rigid back.

Cellus would not look away. Lavon knew he would never look away. They could stare all day, and Lavon would be the one to finally move his eyes. The bastard was only a slave, and he had never shown the least respect for Lavon.

"You drippin' in 'nother spot," Cellus said.

"You turn around and you get your ass out of here, damnit," Lavon said. "Better yet, if you're so goddamn worried about the carpet, get a cloth and wipe it up. You hear me? Move, damnit!"

Cellus did not move as Lavon set down his glass and stepped toward him.

"What's wrong with you?" Lavon shouted. "Have you forgotten you're a slave? You're my nigger, and by God, you'll do what I tell you or I'll have your black ass."

"I'm Mist' Athel's slave, not yours. And I don't do housework."

"You'll do what I tell you!" Lavon shouted. "Clean up that goddamn water."

Cellus did not speak. He did not move. Lavon had to follow through now, for house slaves had gathered in the hall, eavesdropping in fascination, and if Cellus got away with this, the slaves would never respect Lavon again.

"Nigger . . ." he started. He had never been angrier.

"Mist' Athel, he be hurt you actin' this way," Cellus said. "Seems like you make a practice of hurtin' your family."

"Clean up that goddamn water," Lavon said. "I won't tell you again." Cellus did not move.

Lavon grabbed Cellus' arm and pulled him forward. "Get down on the floor and clean up that puddle!" he shouted.

Cellus pulled free and brushed at the sleeve as though Lavon's touch had contaminated him. Lavon struck him hard across the face with the back of his hand. Cellus stepped back into a table, knocking it over. Porcelain figurines crashed to the floor. Cellus brought himself to his full height. His hands doubled into huge fists. Lavon read the anger in Cellus' face, and he knew Cellus could easily break him in half. The realization of Cellus' strength added impotence to Lavon's anger.

"Lavon, what are you doin'?" Estelle called. She ran in from the gallery. Mrs. Sumrall stood in the door.

"This nigger insulted me for the last time," Lavon said. "I'll teach him to remember he's a slave and to respect his master."

"You're not his master," Estelle said. "Lavon, don't you dare touch him again. Look at you! Not yet noon, and you're reekin' of whiskey."

"I want him whipped," Lavon said.

"Whip Cellus? No one is whipped at the Columns. You know that. Oh, look, you've hurt him. His nose is bleedin'. How dare you strike him!"

"I'll be all right, Miss 'Stelle," Cellus said. "He was too drunk to do me no harm."

"Damnit, I want him whipped," Lavon said. His

voice was guttural. He looked past Estelle, past Mrs. Sumrall's pinched face, past the house slaves clustered in the doorway. Ed and Ambrose were pushing their way into the room.

"What's wrong, Miss 'Stelle?" Ed asked. "I heard all the shoutin' out to the back."

"Ed, take Cellus out and whip him," Lavon said.

"No, I won't do that," Ed said. He looked at Estelle.

"Lavon, control yourself," she said. "Now, I don't want anymore trouble with you. Athel will be in at noon, and he can deal with you. Though, Lord knows, I don't know what we're goin' to do with you."

"He gets whipped," Lavon said. "I'll do it myself."

"Have you lost your reason?" Estelle said. "Norvina, come in here. Go back to the kitchen with Cellus and stop the bleedin' in his nose."

"I'm all right, Miss 'Stelle," Cellus said. "I can take care of it."

Cellus walked away. Lavon went after him. Estelle stepped between them. Lavon turned on her. Cellus glanced over his shoulder and shook his head. Lavon trembled with his helplessness.

For half a minute he stood trembling. His anger frightened him. He picked up the decanter of whiskey and shoved his way through the slaves at the door.

Lavon woke up the next evening in the Parker House, one of Natchez' finest hotels. He had a terrible hangover. His suit was muddy. He called a slave to help him dress and stumbled down to the dining room for supper and whiskey. He was sitting at the long table, picking at his ham, when memory began to structure itself. He began to recall fragments of what had happened.

He could remember the scene at the Columns well enough. And the wild ride to Natchez. He even recalled the first few taverns he visited and the woman he took into the back room at one of them. Beyond that, he could remember nothing. He nibbled at the dinner and drank whiskey. In the misery of his hangover he felt the other men were staring at him and whispering about him. No one talked to him.

Slowly his predicament came to him. He was finished at the Columns. He had only the purse of coins. The door of every decent home in the county would be closed to him. He shoved back his chair and left the dining room.

The manager confronted him in the sitting room.

"Sir, I must ask you to vacate the premises," he said. He was a bald man who wore spectacles.

"I don't intend to leave," Lavon said. "And I will not be insulted this way."

"You were very intoxicated last night, sir," the manager said. "Perhaps you don't recall your behavior. Had I been here, I would have refused you a room, but my clerk was intimidated by your threatening manner and your mention that you lived at the Columns."

"I do live at the Columns."

The man drew up his sharp chin. "I rather doubt it after your behavior to your brother, sir."

"My brother? Here?" The faintest memory came to Lavon. Athel had been in the hotel, hadn't he? But Lavon could remember nothing definite.

"Of course, there's no need for you to return to your room, since you have no luggage," the man said. "Parker House never rents to men of your appearance and behavior, no matter what their family connections."

"Prepare my bill, and you may be certain I'll leave," Lavon said.

"There is no bill," the man said. "I spoke to your brother. He settled your bill."

"You what? You bastard! I have money, damnit. I'm a Deavors, and I have money!" Lavon shoved the purse in the man's face and shook the coins.

The manager backed into a corner. Lavon advanced on him. "Cyrus, Frank!" the man shouted. "Get him off me. He's drunk and crazy again."

Two tall men came toward Lavon. He pivoted and brought up his fists. But he quickly dropped his hands and walked out of the hotel.

It was early dusk, and the heat was still awesome.

His head throbbed. People moved out of his way. A horse shied as he lurched across the street. A dog barked from behind a picket fence. Lavon walked without thought along a boulevard and through a park where oleanders bloomed pink and purple beneath sycamore trees. He passed a street of fine houses behind deep lawns. He walked faster and faster, because he feared his anger and knew if he did not walk it off, he would start drinking again.

Half an hour later he stood in a park on a bluff overlooking the Mississippi. Louisiana was hazy on the horizon across the river. Water oaks shaded the park. There were formal beds of red and yellow roses, and their smell was sweet in the soft wind. He stepped to the edge of the bluff. Far below lay the mud flats, wooden sidewalks, shanties, and houseboats of Natchez-under-the-Hill. People looked small, and they moved slowly in the stifling heat.

Lavon's head was swimming. His legs were unsteady. He had a moment of vertigo and stepped back from the precipice. He tried to swallow down the whiskey taste and gagged.

A paddle-wheeler was loading cargo at the pier for New Orleans boats. There might be time to buy passage. If not, there would soon be another boat leaving. He had to leave Natchez before he lost all his sense of honor and self-respect.

He walked from the park and hired a carriage.

Chapter 14

The second whiskey went down easier, and Lavon orderd a third from the one-eyed man behind the waterfront bar. He heard the paddle-wheeler's whistle. He could be in New Orleans tomorrow. But he thought again of his coins. He had spent a great deal of money since leaving the Columns. He could pay for the trip downriver and even buy cheap passage to the Continent. But he would arrive penniless, and that would be no good.

Staying here was no good either, he told himself. His money would soon run out, and no one would help him. The whiskey burned his throat and angered his stomach. Could he seek employment? Work as a clerk in a ribbon store? As a law clerk? He laughed bitterly and drank more whiskey.

Lavon left the tavern and wandered the wooden sidewalks. Water lapped through the cracks. Fish heads and scum floated between the sidewalks. The heat was stifling. Lavon went into a tavern and gambling den crowded with trappers and polemen playing dice and cards.

He found he could now recall much of the scene in the hotel with Athel. Athel used words like "disappointed" and "hurt," and he talked about "another chance if you change" and "apologize to Cellus and Estelle. . . ." Lavon had not only told Athel to go to hell but told him what he thought of him, what he thought of Estelle.

He saw Athel's face, Cellus' face, Estelle's face. Scene after scene played in his mind, and he saw himself posing, lying, begging, and all for nothing.

"For nothing!" he said aloud.

Lavon poured down whiskey, and for a moment he surveyed his predicament as though a detached spectator. There seemed nothing he could do. He had money enough for only a short time, and then he would be destitute. Every door in Natchez would be closed to him. His detachment dissipated, and hatred took its place as he thought of his family.

A man in deerskins stumbled along the bar and fell against Lavon's arm as he raised his cup. Whiskey poured over Lavon's coat. He grabbed the man.

"You spilled my whiskey," he said.

The man tore from Lavon's hand. "To hell with you!" he shouted.

He swung, but he was drunk, and Lavon stepped

aside and smashed his fist into the man's face. The man staggered against the bar. When he straightened up, he held a knife. Lavon pulled his pistol. The bartender came between them. He, too, had a pistol. A man by the door raised a rifle. Lavon sobered quickly and left the place.

He told himself to get out from under the hill. Get out and go where? he asked himself.

He drank whiskey at a stand on a mud flat. His boots sank into the mud. Mulatto women posed in the doorways of hovels and opened their dresses to tempt Lavon. Children played in the water. Half a dozen ragged men shouted abuse at each other in Italian. Lavon walked on. The sidewalk was three inches below water. There was music and laughter and screaming, and everywhere the smell of sweat and urine and decaying food in the heat.

Lavon walked faster. The sky was dark purple. Lanterns were lit. He passed whorehouses, gambling dens, taverns, drinking stands, and cockfights, and finally he looked on as a whiskey-crazed crowd of polemen passed jugs and screamed while two huge hounds savaged each other in a mud pit. Lavon could stand no more. He headed back toward the mud flats under the bluffs and told himself he must stop drinking and do something.

A gambling den on stilts above the water attracted Lavon. The dice went against him, and he lost two coins. Smoke was so thick his eyes watered. He left and stumbled along the sidewalks and the mud. His feet were soaked. A group of men was squatting in the mud and drinking. They looked up and began to whisper. Two of them stood up as Lavon passed. He put his hand to his pistol. The men did not follow him. He told himself again to get up the bluffs while he was still able. But he had no place to go, and no desire except for more whiskey.

He drank in the first halfway decent tavern he had found under the hill. A second cup was placed before him, though he did not remember ordering it. When he finished that, another whiskey was served.

"I didn't . . ."

"Man there at the end of the bar sent these down," the bartender said.

Lavon looked around. He didn't recognize the fat man, who smiled and nodded, though there was something familiar about him. Courtesy dictated he buy the man a drink in return. The man picked up his cup and came down the bar.

"Thank you for the whiskey, sir," he said.

"And thank you," Lavon said. Where had he met the man?

"I haven't seen you here to this place before, Mr. Deavors," the man said. "I don't like to run with the sort comes here, but sometimes I get me a hankerin' to come down off the bluffs."

"No, I don't normally come down here either," Lavon said. "Pardon me, but where do I know you from? Your face is familiar, but . . ."

"Why, actually, we never met proper, Mr. Deavors. But I saw you out to the Columns. Name's Purvis Swan, sir."

Swan extended his hand. Lavon shook the hand. Now he remembered. The man with the nigger dogs.

"Give us some drinkin' whiskey," Swan said to the bartender. "Somethin' good. Not that Monongahela whiskey you been servin'."

"I don't think . . ."

"Come on, just one. Night's still early, Mr. Deavors. Lots of whiskey and pussy under the hill." His laugh was obscene.

"Just one drink, Mr. Swan," Lavon said. He told himself he was not yet reduced to drinking with a man who ran nigger dogs. He would have the one drink and leave.

An hour later Lavon stared at an untouched cup of whiskey and listened to Swan talk about his plans. His scorn for the man had not diminished, but Swan had flattered him, courted him, and now Lavon knew Swan was trying to interest him in some kind of scheme. It was obvious that Swan had heard of his trouble at the Columns.

"I've done just fine with the dogs," Swan was

saying. "Put aside a little money, and been lookin' 'round how to invest it, and, you know, ain't nothin' goin' to make a man more money than bringin' down niggers and sellin' 'em. Yessiree, been thinkin' I might go into that business soon's I raise a little more money, and take in a partner. If I could find the right sort of man . . ."

"That's good, Mr. Swan," Lavon said. He picked up the cup but took only a small swallow. He recalled Remson Collins' talk in the slave pen. Collins was making a fortune with his slave trading. It was a despicable trade, but a man could bring down just one coffle of niggers, just one, and sell them for a small fortune. Lavon told himself that staying in Natchez was out of the question. But he had to return to Europe with enough money to set himself up in something. He recalled the brutal jests about men he knew in London who became impoverished.

"Course, findin' the right partner's not no easy job," Swan said. "Oh, I could find a dozen men, but I want the right sort, man with some character, kind of man can deal with the quality, can bring some dignity to niggerin'. . . ."

Lavon drank whiskey. He considered what he had been hearing. This pompous fool was offering to take him into the nigger-dog and slave-trading business! He wasn't yet low enough to dream of such a wretched trade.

He ordered another round of drinks. He put a coin on the bar and wondered how long his money would last. He could not be penniless again. He had to have wealth and the life it provided. But more urgently he had to have cash, and in the very near future. He drank whiskey. He had sunk into a pit, into the world of Purvis Swan. His desperation was spurred by the realization that he was not as deep in the pit as he would be when he ran out of money.

"Here, Mr. Deavors," Swan said. "I'll get us some more whiskey."

"I've had my fill of whiskey," Lavon said.

"Yessir, I've about grown weary of it myself, Mr. Deavors." Swan's eyes were bloodshot. He smiled, and fat rolled up around his mouth. "My boy's waitin' with the carriage. Can I drop you off somewhere?"

"I . . . No, thank you, Mr. Swan." Where could he go? Where would he sleep tonight? Any decent hotel might refuse to give him a room.

"Tell you what," Swan said. "How 'bout you come on 'long to my house, Mr. Deavors. I get my nigger to fix us a little late supper, and I got me some genuine brandy there. Come all the way up from New Orleans. Pure French brandy, says so right on the bottle."

"Thank you, but I don't . . ." Lavon stood up. He nodded wearily. "Well, yes, I appreciate the invitation."

Lavon stumbled along the wooden walk, avoiding fish heads and debris. He was overwhelmed with hatred for Athel and his family. He had grown up at the Columns. It was his plantation, too. Now he was walking under the hill with Purvis Swan.

He slipped on a fish head and nearly fell into the water. Swan grabbed his arm and helped him along. Lavon pulled away and straightened his body. Each breath brought the smell of garbage from the mud.

Lavon vowed he would do anything to get out of the pit.

Chapter 15

The prospect of a record cotton crop could not overcome Athel's depression as the stories filtered out that Lavon was working with Purvis Swan. Athel took long walks in the woods or rode for hours and brooded about what he should do. Even if a Deavors had taken employment as a clerk or become a merchant it would have hurt the family pride, because no Deavors had ever had any profession but planter, doctor, or attorney. Lavon's work with the nigger dogs was so startling that Athel could think of no way to deal with the situation.

Athel's brooding always led him back to the scene in the Natchez hotel, when Lavon denounced him and the family and said all his actions since his return had been only a pose. For once Athel felt no guilt about the situation. No, he told himself as he rode slowly through a meadow, whose shadows hummed with crickets, there was some flaw in Lavon's character. He would never change. No one could have done anything differently with Lavon. There had been no possibility of letting him own part of the plantation. Lavon's abuse of Cellus and his behavior toward Estelle were inexcusable. The fault was entirely his. But Athel did feel compassion for his brother, as well as a strong responsibility to the family. He would have to take some action to extricate Lavon from his present situation.

Athel dismounted and led his horse along a brook shaded by loblolly pines. His boots crunched the brittle needles. The air smelled of the pines. Athel walked for half an hour before mounting and galloping toward the house.

There was nothing else to do, he told himself. He would ride into Natchez this afternoon and make arrangements for Lavon to be given a sum of money, with the understanding that he leave Natchez at once.

The August heat was truly awesome, with temperatures reaching one hundred each day and the humidity creeping higher and higher. The slaves tended the tall cotton plants and fought the weeds, but they worked with a lethargy and paced themselves with a stubbornness that no threat or promise of reward from the drivers could change.

The slaves had been glad two weeks earlier when word came down from the house that Lavon was gone. They had considered his attempts to supervise them as a nuisance, at times laughable, but many knew Lavon's temper and what it meant to cross him. All of them read the threat in his narrowed eyes when he stood over them, trembling in the heat, and cursed them in several languages. Essie was the exception. Essie felt that in some way Lavon had been forced to leave because he had helped him.

Had Cellus' nature allowed him to dance, he would have done a jig the morning Lavon left. He wore his bruises like decorations from a battle he had won. The house slaves remarked that he looked younger than he had in years. Estelle had permitted herself a smile at Cellus that day and had even poured herself a rare glass of claret, which she sipped alone in the study off the parlor.

When Athel came in and told her he was going into town to arrange for money so that Lavon could leave Natchez, Estelle would gladly have tripled the amount. When Athel left, she enjoyed a second glass of claret.

Tillman was glad his uncle had left, because he knew how much he upset the family. Yet he had mixed feelings. On this afternoon Tillman sat beneath the house and thought of Lavon's tales of Morocco, Spain, France, Italy, and England. He had woven these tales into his fantasy life, and without realizing it, the leader of the toy soldiers that personified the fantasies was always his uncle. He moved his soldiers through the mounds of dust that were sand dunes in the Moroccan desert.

Tillman's hand curled around a soldier as he heard his mother shouting at a slave above him. His breathing became labored when his mother used that tone of voice with anyone, because it was the tone with which she scolded him. An hour earlier she had spoken to him in that voice because he knocked over a vase in the parlor. He could not help such things at times, because he would suddenly forget everything. He would forget where he was, and for a full minute his mind would be blank. Then his mind would function, and he would realize that a vase had been broken, or he would find himself in the road and suddenly have to jump from the path of a racing carriage.

When he was scolded, he ran under the house and played in the cool dust for hours. His mind roamed where it wished in its lazy jumble of images and colors and fairy lands, where all the beautiful princesses looked like his mother.

He heard Joleen and Lawton talking at the back of the house. He crawled toward their voices, careful not to raise a cloud of dust that would give him away. But he could not understand what they were saying, so he returned to his soldiers. They never wanted to play with him anymore, and he never knew what to say to them. They seemed so tall and so grown-up and so sure of themselves. And it was too hot and too bright out in the yard. And Lawton might ask him to go hunting. Tillman hated the sound of a gun. The shot would cause his heart to pound, and he would clap his hands to his ears and run away. A dead or bleeding animal would make him cry. No, he liked to sit here in his cool dust and pretend he was one of the soldiers marching over the sand dunes to an ivory and cedar city where the princess waited to be rescued.

At the Columns, no two people had thought less about Lavon than Lawton and Joleen. They had been disturbed by his abuse of Cellus, and Lawton had been angered when told of Lavon's conduct toward his mother. But his anger quickly faded. He was far too concerned with his sexual problems to give his uncle any further thought. Whenever possible he followed Joleen and watched as she swam in the creek.

Now he stood in the shade of the house and stared at the beads of moisture on her lip. Their talk was idle summer talk that would have seemed innocent to anyone overhearing it. They spoke of a party in Benton, of a new colt, a possible trip into Natchez.

Lawton stiffened as Joleen brushed a piece of lint from his shirt. The past couple of weeks she had touched him often, casually picking lint from his shirt or a leaf from his hair. It seemed innocent, yet at times Lawton doubted Joleen's true naïveté. The look in her eyes and the smile on the edge of her lips were just the ways that Nettie taunted him. The last time he had watched Joleen at the creek he even wondered whether she was deliberately posing her naked body for him. He could not throw off these suspicions, yet he could not accept them. This was Joleen, little Joleen, his own sister.

Nor could he let his fantasies lead him to visions of making love to his sister. More and more, then, the fantasies involved kissing Joleen's lips, kissing her breasts, kissing along the thigh with the scar to the golden hairs and the pink lips.

Yet he could go no further, no matter how the fantasy excited him, for older boys at the institute had spoken with scorn about men who used their mouths on women.

"What did you say, Joleen?" he asked. He had not been listening carefully. "Oh, yes, if you like, when we go into Natchez I'll take you to buy one of the Italian creams." He spoke impatiently. Impatience and anger were the only defenses against his feelings for Joleen.

"If you can find the time," she said. "I also thought you might like to help me look at material for a dress for the Sumralls' party."

"That's girl doin'," he said. "I'm not interested in lookin' at any old material, damnit."

"It's not really important, Lawton," she said. "It's just that you're constantly complainin' about the way I dress."

They talked about the new colt again. She smiled. His cheeks were red. He wouldn't look into her eyes. And he couldn't stand still. She was at ease with him and with their sensual game.

She had come to know her body this summer and to enjoy and accept as natural the delicious feelings in her breasts and nipples, or between her thighs, when she touched herself or rubbed a cloth over her body while bathing, or when she galloped on her horse. She delighted in her ability to make Lawton's face go red. She knew that he followed her when she swam, and she posed for him and waited for him to make a move. So far he hadn't, but she knew beyond a doubt that he would. Something physical would happen between them. She did not fantasize what this would be. There were no clear visions in her mind when she rubbed herself with the washcloth while sitting in a steaming bath.

But she thought of Lawton at such times, and thought of him wanting her, thought of him telling her how pretty she was, thought of him confessing his obsession and apologizing for all the mean things he had said to her and for the ways he had criticized her for being a girl or being younger. Each time he scolded her or was impatient with her he goaded her sense of power over him. She was not a cruel girl, and she would play this game only with someone as strong as or stronger than she. Lawton was older, stronger physically, expert in skills she admired, chased after by other girls. She loved him dearly without ever clearly thinking of this love. Again, without thinking clearly, she considered him almost an extension of herself. She knew that many people commented that they looked alike. Lawton was the perfect adversary for her inchoate and impatient sexuality.

"What you goin' to do now, Lawton?" she asked, and picked another piece of lint from his shirt. He stepped back.

"I told you, don't do that, Joleen," he said. She caught his worried eyes. He looked away when she smiled.

"Oh, silly, you can't walk around with lint on your shirt," she said. "Why don't we go for a walk, Lawton? Down to the creek, where it's cooler."

"No, I don't want to go for a walk, Joleen. Stop pesterin' me."

"I'm not pesterin' you, Lawton," she said. "But I thought you'd like to go down to the creek with me. I'm so hot, Lawton."

"Then damnit, go by yourself," he blurted. "How much time you think I can spend with you, Joleen?"

"Why, Lawton, I thought lately you liked spending time with me," she said. "And why are you talkin' mean to me?"

"I'm not," he said. "You're just . . . I like bein' with you sometimes, Joleen. But damnit, you're my little sister . . ."

"I swear, Lawton," she said. "You're just tryin' to make me mad. I'm not little anymore. Am I, Lawton?

And you're not that much older. Am I still little, Lawton?"

They looked at each other. Suddenly her cheeks were warm, and she knew they were red.

He shrugged. "Oh, you're growin' up, all right," he said. "But you're still . . . well, I don't know, Joleen. You act more childish sometimes than you think."

"So you think I'm still childish . . ." She broke off the sentence. No, she would not lose her temper. Soon enough she would have Lawton where she wanted him. She took a step backward as though physically acknowledging that she stepped back from the confrontation.

"I'm goin' out to the barn," Lawton said.

"I'm goin' down to the creek," she said. "I'll see you later."

"What?" he asked. "What do you mean?"

"I mean at supper, Lawton," she said. "What did you think I meant?"

"Nothin'," he mumbled, and walked toward the barn.

Joleen headed for the creek, walking slowly in the heat. She wondered what would happen if she posed naked for him and then confronted him there where he was hiding. What would he do? The idea excited her, but as she passed through the quarters, her thoughts turned from Lawton to the German lawyer Aaron Clauson she had met earlier in the summer at Aunt Delma's. She thought of him often, though not with the sexual feeling she had when she thought of Lawton. The man intrigued her. She had never met anyone like him. He had a way of looking right at her that differed from the glance of any other man she had ever met. And he seemed to be interested in her. But she had no way of knowing. Joleen was confident of her desirability, and the fact that Aaron Clauson was an enigma made him all the more interesting.

She told herself that the next time she saw him in Natchez, she would make sure he was interested in her.

Lawton rode off with no destination in mind, and an hour later found himself on the Benton road. He was proud of himself because he had resisted the temptation to follow Joleen to the creek. He had even been able to stop thinking about sex. This had been especially difficult, since he had passed Nettie in the field and she had given him one of her looks.

Now he rode slowly, inhaling the pine smells and considering the talk he'd had with his father earlier in the week. His father had asked if Lawton wanted to go on to school in New Orleans this coming September instead of returning to the institute in Natchez. Lawton did not want to go off to New Orleans, and he was thinking of some way to tell his father without seeming ungrateful.

At the crossroads near the creek he heard dogs baying and saw the dust from a fast-moving horse. He reined up and watched an odd-looking carriage pass. The carriage had a dog cage on the rear that contained five hounds. An obese black man bobbed up and down in the driving box. His chin rested on his chest. In the back seat sat a fat white man. The man held a whip and a rifle. He nodded at Lawton.

Another man was sitting beside the fat man. He turned. Lawton was stunned. The man was his Uncle Lavon. He had heard that Lavon was running nigger dogs—but actually to see him with the dogs was a shock. Lavon looked directly at Lawton but did not speak. Lawton had never seen such a look of hatred on anyone's face.

Lawton sat still long after the carriage had disappeared. He could not forget that look, as though Lavon blamed *him* for his predicament of being in the carriage with the fat man and the dogs.

Chapter 16

The carriage stopped in front of the Delsano plantation, and Lavon turned to see the family sitting on the front porch. Two slaves passed around tall glasses. Juan Delsano glanced at the carriage and leaned down to his wife. She stood up and led their three children inside.

"You wait here," Swan said. "I'll handle the particulars."

He lumbered toward the house, and Lavon looked past him to Juan Delsano's stern face. Lavon looked away quickly. He had last seen the man when he visited the Columns earlier in the summer. Delsano had spoken about "the riffraff that's driftin' in to make their money off any foul occupation that concerns our niggers." He added the usual pious declaration that it was "a shame we have no choice but to deal with them." Natchez had been owned by Spain in the previous century, and the old Spanish families like the Delsanos were particularly proud and snobbish.

The dogs growled in Lavon's ear. Flies buzzed around the dogs, and one fly touched Lavon's ear. He shook his head. Mosquitoes joined the buzzing. The horse swished his tail at some flies, and the carriage started rocking.

"Damn you, DuPre, hold that goddamn horse steady!" Lavon shouted.

DuPre nodded. He quieted the horse. Lavon wiped sweat from his forehead. He slapped at a mosquito, then scratched a bump on the back of his hand. Would Swan talk all day? The man might have palsy of the mouth, the way he ran out of control. All he needed was to find out which nigger was missing and which cabin he lived in; but no, Swan would talk on and on about his dogs and how he appreciated being hired by the quality.

Lavon thought of seeing Lawton a few minutes ago. He had dreaded coming this near the Columns, yet had known it was unavoidable. That little bastard would inherit the plantation someday. All Lavon's hard work, and yet Lawton would be master of the Columns. And he, Lavon—what would he be doing? Still running nigger dogs and sharing a little house with Purvis Swan? He loathed Swan, and loathed him all the more because of Swan's generosity and flattery.

"Not just an employee, I mean a full partner," Swan had told Lavon. "We split fifty-fifty. We goin' to make us a heap of money." And Swan had a contract of partnership drawn up.

The worst moment had come when Swan was showing Lavon how to whip a runaway. After Lavon had forced himself to hit the man five times, Swan had smiled and said, "Mr. Deavors, you takin' to niggerin' like you was born to it. Yessiree, you goin' to work out real fine in this line of work."

Lavon had stalked off and gotten drunk. He nearly took his few coins and bought passage on the first vessel leaving Natchez. But he stayed. He forced his hatred and self-loathing deeper inside, and placated them with whiskey and two high-yellow whores on a houseboat in the river.

The only way he could pull himself out of this trap was to have money. A great deal of money. Swan's talk of the profits from slave trading fed his hopes. Despite his dislike of trading, he told himself if he could whip niggers and run the goddamn dogs, surely he could bring down one coffle of slaves and sell them. But it could be months before they earned enough money for that.

Swan returned, and DuPre climbed down and helped him into his work outfit. "This here is more serious than I'd imagined," Swan said as they led their horses back to the quarters. The dogs trailed after them.

"What do you mean?" Lavon asked.

"Mr. Delsano says he got five boys missin', and a

strange white man was seen out back couple of nights ago," Swan said. "Seems maybe the boys didn't just run away, but got some rustler takin' 'em off. Thought we might ought to tell the sheriff, but reckon we'll give it a shot first, 'count it could mean a nice little bit of money. You don't mind, do you?"

"No, I don't mind," Lavon said. The danger was the only part of the work he enjoyed.

They examined the cabins where the runaways lived and talked to several women, who cowered from the dogs. Swan led the way down a trail that divided at the edge of the swamp.

"Reckon we ought to split up here," Swan said. "You take Nester and Blue, Mr. Deavors, and go down that there trail to the left. I'll take the others and circle toward you, down that little path through the oaks. The trails meet back in the swamp. From what Mr. Delsano told me, this is where the white man was seen and is the most likely way for the niggers to have gone. See there—look at old Nester rarin' to get down the trail. He's on to somethin', sure as a pig's ass is pork, Mr. Deavors."

They tied their horses and went into the swamp. Lavon held the two dogs on long leashes. He carried a rifle in his right hand. There were two pistols in his pockets. Lavon walked cautiously, though he knew the dogs would warn him if the slaves were near. Nester and Blue strained against the leash, and Lavon had difficulty controlling them. They were huge spotted hounds, scarred on the back and belly, and a piece of Nester's left ear was missing.

Lavon was miserable in the damp heat. He swallowed and thought of the chilled wine at Swan's house. Lavon looked forward to the wine after all the whiskey he had consumed during the summer. Swan had rushed out at Lavon's first mention of wine and bought two cases from the captain of a New Orleans paddle-wheeler.

Now each evening Swan drank white wine and praised its virtues as though he had never let whiskey pass his lips. Swan would sit on the porch beside a trellis filled with morning glory, a fragile glass in his monstrous hand. He smiled into the setting sun as though he could not believe the fortune that had let him snare a Deavors as a partner.

The dogs were growling low in their throats. Lavon strained to see ahead, but there were only deep shadows beneath the trees and clusters of moss and vines. A putrid smell rose from the damp ground. A movement to the left snapped Lavon's head around, but it was only a snake arching its body in a bayou.

The dogs yelped. They fought the leash. Lavon freed them, and they bounded down the trail. Lavon advanced slowly, his finger on the trigger of his rifle. He stopped and listened, but all he heard was the howling of the dogs. Lavon found them pointing a bush where a piece of cloth was caught on a thorn.

He followed the dogs down the trail once more, and soon the dogs were whining and growling. They ran into the darkness ahead, and he ran after them. The thrill of the chase drove him on. For the first time in days he pulled himself out of his apathy, self-loathing, and hatred. He welcomed the adrenaline that pushed him faster and faster. The dogs howled ahead. He ignored the limbs and vines that slapped at his head and shoulders.

The dogs were baying now. Lavon slowed his pace and brought up his rifle. He heard human sounds. Someone was running. There was a shout. A shot rang out. He crouched behind a magnolia and moved forward. Dogs snarled. Someone screamed.

"Mr. Deavors!" Swan cried from Lavon's right. "I see 'em! The niggers! And a white man!"

Lavon came on a clearing where a campfire smoldered. Five catfish were roasting on sticks over the coals. He skirted the edge of the clearing and ran toward the screams and snarling. A hundred yards up the trail, the dogs were attacking two black men, who writhed on the ground. Three more slaves clung to the low-lying branches of a water oak.

The other dogs joined Nester and Blue. Both slaves were bleeding and screaming. Lavon advanced on the dogs, but he knew better than to try to run them from their kill. He would leave that to Swan.

In a moment Swan crashed through the growth. His whip cut the air, and the dogs crept back.

"They was two white men," Swan gasped. "They plumb got away. Took a shot at me. I might of wounded one of 'em."

"Can the dogs catch them?" Lavon asked. He did not want the chase to end so easily.

"Well, reckon they could, Mr. Deavors," Swan said. "They the finest dogs in the county. But I don't hold to the idea of chasin' two armed white men what know this swamp. We get paid for takin' back niggers. Let the sheriff hunt them rustlers."

Swan leashed his dogs. Lavon shackled the slaves. The men were terror-stricken and begged not to be whipped.

"Them white men, they done come and took us off to this place one by one and told us they'd shoot us if we tried to get back," one of the men pleaded. "They was goin' to fetch two more and take us off tonight."

"Hush up, nigger," Swan said. "That's 'tween you and your master. I'm goin' to tell him 'bout the rustlers."

They started down the trail, and Swan had difficulty keeping his dogs from attacking the slaves. Lavon's intensity drained with each step as the humidity smothered him. He began to brood as they reached the plantation and Swan made his boastful report to Juan Delsano.

"Imagine that, Mr. Deavors," Swan said for the third time since leaving the plantation. "They done give us a twenty-five-dollar bonus for gettin' back the niggers and chasin' off them white men. Course, I done laid it on kind of thick 'bout having to fight off them rustlers. Now, of course, half of it's yours, sure 'nough, but I think we ought not to spend it but put it aside as money toward the time we got 'nough to go up to Richmond and buy us some slaves for sellin'. Few more months like this and we'll sure 'nough have us the money."

"Sure, let's save the money," Lavon said. A few

more months, he said to himself. A few more days of this, and he might strangle Swan.

The carriage finally reached Swan's house. His cook met them on the front porch. She handed Lavon an envelope.

"Man left it here a short time ago," she said. "Told me it was mighty 'portant."

Lavon recognized Athel's handwriting. He ripped open the envelope and read the message: ". . . instructed my bank to give you five thousand dollars on presentation of this letter . . . better for all concerned if you return to Continent immediately . . . bank will send you money quarterly . . . would like to see you before you leave . . . understanding . . . still love . . . brothers . . . family . . ."

Lavon squeezed the paper so tight his hand ached. He dropped the letter to the ground. His brother was sending him off to Europe as a remittance man. Athel would dole out a pittance of money to soothe his conscience and make sure no Deavors was involved in a low trade.

"Are you all right, Mr. Deavors?" Swan asked. "You want some of that wine?"

Lavon stared through the wilted morning glories a moment, then turned to Swan.

"How soon can you be ready to leave for Richmond?" he asked.

Chapter 17

Lawton scraped his hand against the wall as he crept along the dark side porch of the Sumrall house. The only light came from a moon hazed by erratic clouds. Whiskey churned in his stomach. He felt strange, both good and bad and certainly a bit giddy. He wondered if he was drunk. Earlier, when he had gone up to Theron Sumrall's room to drink from the jug Theron had stolen from his father, it had been exciting. Lawton had felt very grown-up, drinking like adults. Now he felt guilty, and he was afraid his father or mother would smell the whiskey on his breath.

There was a sound around on the back porch. Lawton stopped. He heard nothing more from the back, only the music, talk, and laughter from the parlor and the front lawn. The loudest sound to him was his own breathing.

Lawton inched forward again, though he told himself to go back to the party. If Joleen was back there with some boy, it was none of his business. But he thought of the way she flirted with Rayford Caldwell. Boys at the institute said that Rayford had experience with whores and knew all kinds of ways to kiss and arouse women.

"No, Rayford, don't do that!" Joleen's voice startled Lawton. "Well, all right, just one more kiss, Rayford. But not like the last one. . . ."

Lawton stood at the corner. He heard their heavy breathing. In spite of himself, he found himself stepping around the corner. Rayford had his arm around Joleen while they kissed. Lawton ran across the porch. Rayford pulled away from Joleen's body, but he was off balance as he turned, and Lawton shoved him to the floor and stood over him with his hands doubled into fists.

"Lawton, what's wrong with you?" Joleen asked. "You go away and leave me alone."

Her top button was unfastened. Her breathing was heavy. Rayford climbed to his feet. Lawton advanced on him and hit him a glancing blow to the cheek. Rayford stumbled back but found his balance. His fists came up. He was two years older than Lawton and outweighed him by thirty pounds. He sidestepped a punch and cut Lawton's nose with a sharp blow.

Lawton fell back against the wall. He tasted blood and snorted out his breath as he moved forward.

"Stop it, both of you!" Joleen shouted. She stepped

between them. "Rayford, go on, leave us alone. Go on, now, or I won't see you again."

"He hit me first," Rayford said.

"Please, Rayford," Joleen said.

Rayford shrugged and walked away. Lawton touched his nose. A flash of pain met his touch. He wiped at the nose and swallowed blood.

"Here, let me see," Joleen said.

"No, stay away, Joleen," He backed against the wall.

"You're bleedin', Lawton. He must have really hurt you. Here, let me get the blood off."

"No, I'm all right."

He let her dab at his nose with her handkerchief. Their eyes met, and he looked away. He smelled her perfume. He had never known her to wear perfume before.

"What got into you, Lawton?" she asked.

There might have been the faintest smile on her lips, but he couldn't be sure in the moonlight. His nostrils were flooded with the sweet perfume. His penis began to grow hard.

"You were kissin' him," Lawton said.

"There's nothin' wrong with kissin' a boy," she said.

"There is, too, like this," he said. "Just kissin' any old boy. Standin' on a dark porch with a boy like Rayford. Lord, what would people think if they saw you?"

"Had you rather I kiss Rayford out front where everybody could watch us, Lawton?" He hadn't seen her move, but she seemed closer. Her breasts nearly touched his chest. He pressed harder against the wall.

"You shouldn't be kissin' him at all."

"You kiss Lily, Lawton."

"Damnit, that's not the same, Joleen." She caught him staring down at her breasts, and he looked away. She dabbed at his nose and hurt him. He flinched.

"I didn't mean to hurt you, Lawton," she said. "It's stopped bleedin' now, I think. And why isn't it the same?"

"I don't want . . . How do you know I kiss Lily, Joleen?"

"I saw you, Lawton. More than once."

"Damnit, you shouldn't be sneakin' around spyin' on me, Joleen."

"Well, you were spyin' on me, Lawton. And it's not the first time. Is it?"

"What do you mean?" His heart pounded. His penis was harder. Her perfume smothered him. He hated the perfume.

"Oh, you know," she said.

His penis ached against his tight pants. He was feverish. His stomach heaved with the whiskey. Its taste was sweet in his throat. He was desperate. What did she know? Did she really know he had watched while she swam naked? And surely she couldn't know he had taken down his pants. Anger was his only defense.

"I don't know anything, Joleen," he said. "Damnit, why are you standin' so close? And where did you get that perfume? And why'd you put on so much? Look at you. Why, your dress is unfastened. You're actin' cheap, the way you behaved with Rayford. Like some woman on the river, doin' all kinds of bad things. . . ."

She did not speak for a minute. She did not move. Her face was glazed with moisture. A rivulet of sweat ran down her neck and under her dress. Her whole body must be damp with perspiration. Moisture would be dripping off her stomach. Moisture would be trickling over the ugly white scar on her thigh. The hairs would be beaded with moisture the way he had seen them when he watched her from the bushes.

"Am I all that bad, Lawton?" she asked. There was an edge to her voice. "So you think I'm just like some cheap woman in one of those places on the river? Why do you try to hurt me, Lawton, talkin' like that? I don't say bad things to you. But you've done something really bad, and we both know it. Just look at you. Aren't you ashamed?"

He tried to shift his weight so that his penis wouldn't be obvious against his pants. Had she seen the bulge? But how would she know? She was his little sister. How could she stand there and ask him questions? His suspicions about her innocence were stronger than ever now. Without quite realizing it, he began to look at her in a different way. But he did not know what to say. The perfume seemed stronger. He shifted his weight again.

"I'm not ashamed," he finally muttered, and avoided her eyes.

"Well, you ought to be," she said. "Drinkin' whiskey like that, Lawton. Why, what would Daddy say?"

"Whiskey? Is that what you . . . ? I can drink if I want to, Joleen. Men drink whiskey. It's not the first time, either. I had whiskey on my last birthday. And last Christmas I had some."

"But you're actin' so strange, Lawton," she said. "You've had a lot of whiskey, haven't you? And it wouldn't be the same, you sneakin' it. Daddy would really be upset if he knew. You better be careful. You better sober up. And you better get that whiskey off your breath. Course, I won't tell on you. And you wouldn't tell on me. Would you? About Rayford tonight? Or about swimmin' in the back creek? We shouldn't tell on each other for bein' naughty, Lawton."

"I haven't been naughty," he said. "Just had me a little whiskey. I wouldn't tell on you, Joleen. But I . . . Damnit, Joleen . . . I . . ."

"Haven't you been naughty?" she asked. She touched his nose. He stiffened at the pain. Her finger brushed his lips. "It would be better if you told me everything, Lawton. And you ought to apologize. For what you said to me. Comparin' me to some woman under the hill. Just because I was kissin' Rayford."

"I mean it, Joleen. I'm not goin' to apologize."

"You might be sorry if you don't, Lawton. I bet I could make you sorry for talkin' to me that way."

"I don't know what you mean, Joleen. Leave me alone, damnit. That old perfume's makin' me sick. And you . . . What's that?"

They both turned. There was a sound around the corner. They waited, but there was no further sound, only the noises from the party.

"We better go back up front, Joleen," Lawton said. "Before somebody finds us back here."

"What difference would that make, Lawton?"

"Hell, Joleen, I mean, we've been back here alone in the dark a long time."

"Well, silly, all we're doin' is talkin'. What's wrong with that? And what if we'd been doin' somethin' else? We can do anything we want, Lawton. As long as it's between us. It would be easier if you were honest with me."

"I am honest, Joleen. What's there to be honest about? I just . . . Damnit, Joleen, keep your hands off my face."

"I saw Lily touch your face like that once, Lawton."

"You ought to know the difference, Joleen. Lily's . . . she's . . . well, she's older than you. And damnit, she's not my little sister."

"Do you like the way Lily kisses, Lawton?"

"That's none of your business. Stop talkin' that way, Joleen. What's gotten into you? I'm not goin' to talk about kissin' and stuff like that with you. You got me so upset I can't think straight. We better go back inside."

"I don't think you can, Lawton. People will know . . ."

"Know what?" Without thinking, he glanced down at his pants.

"Why, that you've been drinkin' whiskey. And honestly, Lawton, I think you're a little drunk."

"I'm not drunk, either. You don't know. You wouldn't know about whiskey and boy things, Joleen."

"I know a lot more than you think, Lawton. No, you shouldn't go back inside yet. Daddy's goin' to skin you alive if he smells that whiskey. I was just thinkin'. You know, there's that patch of mint out back, by the willows. I think we ought to get some, and you could chew it and take away the whiskey smell. And you could apologize to me on the way."

"I'm not goin' out there with you, Joleen. And I'm not goin' to apologize, neither. Just look at you. Your dress is unfastened."

"Do you like the dress, Lawton? I got a blue one because I know you like blue. I had it made special.

You're always fussin' at me for not lookin' like a proper lady, and here I go and get a dress made special, and you haven't said a word about it."

"It's a pretty dress, Joleen," he mumbled.

He could not clear his thoughts, though if he had, it would have done him little good. His mind would have told him not to walk out back with Joleen. But it would have been pitiful advice against a sexual excitement so intense that his loins ached and his stomach was drawn tight.

"Come on, Lawton," Joleen said softly. She took his hand. He pulled away.

"Joleen . . . I . . . I guess I better chew some mint," he said. "But we better hurry and get back."

They walked off the porch and took a path through the vegetable garden and away from the kitchen, where the slaves were laughing and talking.

Chapter 18

"Slow down, Lawton," Joleen said. "You don't have to run. Here, how's your nose?" They stopped. She leaned up and touched his nose. Her lips were close. He thought of kissing Lily and pretending he was kissing Joleen.

He stepped back. "It's stopped hurtin', Joleen," he said. They walked on.

He smelled the mint before they reached it. The smell was sharp in the heat. He recalled the pungent odors in the storeroom the day he and Joleen got the tobacco. With the mint came the smell of her perfume. He was truly intoxicated, but the whiskey was the smallest part of the intoxication. Walking was difficult. Joleen's hand brushed his, and he flinched. Yet, just as nothing could have stopped him as he went along the path to watch Joleen in the water, so nothing could stop him now.

"Here we are," Joleen said.

"Yes," he said.

He looked at her. Her eyes held him. Weeping willows screened them from the house. As on the porch, she seemed to materialize very close to him, but he wasn't conscious that she had actually moved.

"Well, I'm waitin', Lawton," she said.

"Waitin' for what?"

"Why, for you to apologize for what you compared me to. Some woman on the river. And sayin' I'm cheap. Why do you want to hurt me, Lawton?"

"I don't," he said. "But it's true sometimes, Joleen. I don't mean you're cheap. But you do things a girl like you shouldn't do. . . ." There was no conviction in his scolding. Yet he held to it. The realization of his vulnerability only made him hold on stronger. It was all that remained of his will, and the perfume and the lips and the eyes were making short work of that small remnant.

"Then maybe we're the pot and the kettle, Lawton," Joleen said. "Here, let's get the mint."

She bent down. He knelt beside her. Again they stared at each other. She picked a sprig of mint and handed it to him. Her hand lingered on his hand. He pulled away. He was surprised that his hand was unsteady. He chewed mint. The taste was sharp. He turned and spat out the mint.

"You better chew some more," she said. "Here."

This time she put the mint to his mouth. Her fingers touched his lips. He had never realized how sensitive his lips were. She dropped the mint. He sucked his breath and stared into her eyes. The grass was damp, and he felt the moisture soaking his knees. Joleen's lips were closer. Suddenly he was kissing her.

Joleen's lips were soft and warm and damp. He groaned at the sensation. With the sensation came the shock of what he was doing. This was Joleen. . . .

She opened her mouth and twisted the kiss. Her tongue flicked the roof of his mouth. Her tongue was a far greater shock than anything his poor mind could have imagined. All summer he had been driven to sensual frenzy by what his eyes could see and what his mind could fantasize, and the only tactile fulfillment of his urge had been Joleen's fingers picking lint or leaves from his clothes or fragments of fig from his chin. The touch of her lips and tongue was the most erotic thing that had ever happened to Lawton. He knelt there with his arms drawn in against his body while she licked and sucked his lips and tongue until he moaned and his balls ached. She nibbled at his tongue. His mind lurched forward desperately: This was Joleen, he was kissing Joleen....

He pulled his lips away. "I'm sorry ... I don't ..." He couldn't find the words. Sweat poured from his face. "Joleen, I don't ..."

Her face was moist and pink. A strand of golden hair was plastered to her forehead. Her dimples showed as she smiled. And it was a smile of sheer provocation.

Joleen had only to open her mouth and he moved his head awkwardly forward. She smiled and inched her face back. His lips sought her mouth as she smiled and teased. The taste of her mouth had obsessed him, and he would do anything to touch any part of her with his lips and tongue. She leaned forward and kissed him again. She put her hands on his shoulders. His kiss was desperate, awkward. She sucked his frantic tongue, and her fingers caressed his neck and ears and hair. Lawton groaned and put his arms around her. Her breasts moved against his chest. His balls ached.

Lawton's mind did not function now. His body was permeated with an excitement that seemed to bring all nerve ends to the surface of his skin. Joleen lay back on the damp grass. He lay on top of her. They kissed again. His fingers trembled as he unbuttoned her dress. His breathing was ragged. He heard himself moaning.

Lawton moved his hand beneath her dress. He touched her breast. The sensation was overwhelming. He hunched against her thigh. His fingers stroked her nipples. It was a desperate, delicate stroking of the forbidden bud of flesh, the most forbidden act Lawton had ever performed, to squeeze those nipples that he had often seen at the creek, that he had fantasized beneath Joleen's dress as they talked casually. His face lay beside hers. There was no expression on her face. He kissed her cheek, then began to lick the perspiration from her face.

Joleen pulled his hand from her nipples.

"Please, Joleen," he gasped. "Please let me. You're so beautiful. Don't make me stop. . . . I want to . . . to touch and kiss you all over. . . ."

"Don't tear my dress, Lawton," she gasped. "Don't tear my dress. . . ."

"I won't. . . ."

He tried to kiss her lips, but she moved her head to avoid the kiss. Her nails scratched at his scalp. His hands dug beneath her body, fought through grass and soft earth. He grasped her buttocks. She writhed against his hands and kissed his ear.

"Careful, Lawton," she whispered. Her tongue was hot and wet in his ear. "Be careful. Don't hurry. Take off my dress. . . . You'll ruin it. . . ."

He began to undress Joleen. His hands shook. He nearly tore the dress, and she snapped at him. He fumbled out an apology, and then she spoke softly and soothingly and instructed him. Dumbly he obeyed her instructions as he forced gentleness into his movements. He removed her dress, then her undergarments.

He knelt above her. She lay naked on the wet grass, her legs spread apart and arched up at the knees. Her smile was twisted on the corners of her lips. It was an enigmatic smile. Her face was rosy now. Her breasts heaved with her ragged breathing. Lawton devoured her body with his eyes, as he had done while watching her at the creek. Even in the moonlight the scar was alien and white on her deeply tanned thighs. He touched the scar. He jerked his finger away as though stung. Joleen smiled and breathed deeply. She pressed her thighs together, then opened them wide. He saw the pink lips beneath the curly mat of hair, covered with beads of moisture.

"It's all right, Lawton," she whispered. He leaned down but hesitated. She touched his head. "Don't worry. It's all right. But you have to talk to me first.

You have to be . . . honest. . . . No, no, don't take off your pants, Lawton. . . . Talk to me. . . ."

He put his head between her thighs. "I want you, Joleen," he gasped. "More than anyone. You're so beautiful. You're not little. I want to . . . kiss you all over." He stroked her dripping thighs and trembled. "I'm sorry I fussed at you all summer and said bad things about you. . . . I'll do anything for you, Joleen. . . ."

"Promise you won't take your pants off, no matter what," she said.

"I promise. . . ." He touched the jagged scar. He stared into the mat of hair inches away and became obsessed with the pink lips.

"All right, Lawton. Do what you want. . . ."

Joleen curled her leg against Lawton's head. The pressure was very gentle. He skated his lips over her thigh. The skin was slick with moisture and very warm. The hairs tickled his nose. He jerked his face back. Joleen's leg curled against his head again. Her fingers twisted in his hair. She arched her legs. He lowered his head and slipped his tongue into her navel and relished the drop of sweat he found there.

Fantasy lit his mind. He was staring at her naked and dripping body coming from the creek. His penis throbbed in its confinement. His nipples were tight. He pressed his face against her stomach. He began to suck and lick at the heaving stomach, to become intoxicated with the moisture he found there. He was truly obsessed with Joleen's body now, with the warm flesh, with the sweat. He cupped her breasts. Her nipples were very hard. He kissed down to her thighs. His tongue sought the scar. He slid his hands under her writhing buttocks. They were so slippery he had difficulty holding them.

Lawton reared up on his knees with his face pressed against the scar. Joleen's thighs squeezed his head as he licked past the scar. The pressure hurt his ears. He breathed through his mouth. He was now thoroughly maddened and obsessed. He wanted to worship Joleen's body, to consume the body, to be ruled by the flesh that had taunted him for months. He endured the vise of her thighs and surrendered to the totality of her flesh and her sweat and the faint smell he approached.

Joleen relaxed her thighs. The hairs touched his nose. He smelled mint. And grass. And sweat. They mingled with the mild and maddening smell of her wet vagina. Again her thighs locked his head. For an instant he could not breathe, and he nearly choked.

Her thighs relaxed. His tongue slid past the hairs and probed the tight opening. The texture of the pulpy, burning flesh sent shivers over his body. He kissed and sucked the vagina while he squirmed against the ground. Joleen's thighs were strong and demanding. He sucked and whimpered and drove his tongue deeper.

Lawton could not breathe. He twisted away. In his frenzy he licked the sweat from Joleen's thighs. He looked up the length of her body. She was on her elbows. Her mouth was open. Her breasts heaved with her frantic breathing. Her face was scarlet. Her eyes were half-closed.

Joleen's fingers shoved at his head. She spread her thighs while he kissed and tongued her vagina. She stiffened spasmodically, again and again, and thrust her body against his face. Then she collapsed on the ground.

He still sucked, but she pushed his face away. His face dripped with moisture from her body and his own sweat. He rolled over onto his back.

Joleen climbed to her knees, then stood up. She breathed with her mouth open while she fumbled into her clothes. Guilt and shame rose within him, but neither could abate his continuing excitement.

"I'm goin' on back," Joleen mumbled.

He crawled to his knees. "Joleen, I don't . . . I didn't mean . . ." He put a hand on the ground and shoved himself up. "Oh, God. . . ."

Joleen brushed his lips with her mouth. "It's all right, Lawton. It's all right. It's just between us, Lawton."

She walked away. Lawton sank to his knees. He ached desperately. He glanced around. Fireflies mocked him. Mosquitoes buzzed at his ear. He saw a drooping willow and crawled through the leaves.

He snapped off a button getting his pants down. He formed a fist. He masturbated quickly. His climax poured out and hurt him, and he collapsed on the ground.

Chapter 19

The fading sunlight glistened on the chains of the slaves who marched along the trace in front of Lavon. There were thirty-eight slaves in the coffle now. A wheelwright had died of a heart attack outside Nashville and a laundress had died of exhaustion as they crossed the Mississippi-Alabama line. Lavon had cursed their luck in losing slaves for whom they had paid cash, but Swan insisted their luck had been good so far.

"I've known men to lose half a dozen on this sort of trek," Swan had said at breakfast as they squatted around the fire and ate fatback and stale bread. "And it's not usual to bring the niggers down in early-September heat. We rushin' the season tryin' to be first, so we can expect to lose a couple."

Lavon twisted in the saddle. He was sore from riding and exhausted from the pace of their journey and the constant tension of tending to the slaves. His only satisfaction was to think of the money these blacks would bring in Natchez. He had run the sums through his mind a thousand times, and so it angered him to watch a slave being buried and have to subtract six or seven hundred dollars from the profits.

But the deaths had a deeper impact than loss of money, for Lavon couldn't repress a feeling of guilt that the slaves had died while in his possession. He knew they died because of the rigors of a forced march in the heat. Anger could drive Lavon to punish a slave severely, and he had brutalized many slaves in his life. On this trip, however, he had seen enough of the underbelly of the peculiar institution to make him sick.

Lavon had visited dozens of auctions and sheriff and plantation sales. He had lived with the fear, panic, and hatred of slaves who did not want to be sold away from their homes. He had seen six-year-old children dragged screaming from their mothers and taken off for sale. He had seen couples married for thirty years become hysterical when sold separately. At one such separation outside Richmond, an old man had fought to join his wife, who had to be whipped away from him. The man had gone berserk and attacked a trader with a length of chain, then thrown himself into a fire and burned to death.

On the first day of the march, Lavon and Swan had been able to move the slaves only a few miles from Richmond. The whips had to be used again and again, and Lavon had to learn how to sting a slave into obedience without injuring him severely. Later, as they marched through strange country, apathy had set in among the slaves, and several refused to eat. Yet, the first time they were unshackled for a rest, four men ran away and had to be hunted down with nigger dogs. Now they were yoked around the neck with iron rings, and the yokes were linked with chains. One wrist of each slave was also manacled to the slave in front and behind with five feet of chain each way.

Lavon discovered that promises and bribes, as well as whippings and threats, could move the coffle, so he doled out molasses and promised grand new lives in Natchez, new clothes, whiskey, gentle masters. He knew that lash marks would lower a slave's value. And he was sick of whippings. To whip an insolent black man was one thing, but how could he whip a woman who refused to walk and who cried for her children?

The sun was setting behind tall pines. The pine forests had stretched for miles, covering gullies and gentle hills overgrown with vines. Lavon took a swallow from his water bag, then splashed water on his face. Two more nights on the trace and they would be in Natchez. They would rest and bathe the slaves, dress them up, calm them down, give them a little whiskey, and sell them. Of course, he knew the planters who bought his slaves would look on him with the same scorn as the planters who had sold him slaves in Virginia. They considered traders necessary but hated dealing with them.

"Damn them all to hell!" he muttered.

He thought of the money, of taking the paddle-wheeler to New Orleans and a ship to the Continent. He would have cash with which to start over in Europe. That was all that mattered now, his profit from the slaves that would allow him to leave Natchez.

"Mr. Deavors!" Swan called from the front of the coffle. The slaves shuffled to a stop. Lavon rode forward. A man was lying on the ground. He was vomiting. His body shook.

"Another one sick from the heat, I guess," Lavon said. "What is that, six today?"

"Would be," Swan said. " 'Cept he seems different. I think maybe he's pukin' up his guts 'cause he ate somethin' bad."

"What can we do with him? It does seem to be more than exhaustion."

"Reckon we ought to get him in the shade and let him rest," Swan said. "You know, I was a little worried 'bout that fatback we bought off that farmer last night."

"But he would have been sick before now if it was something he ate," Lavon said. "And no one else got sick from the fatback."

"Guess so," Swan said. "Let's get him away from the others 'fore he spooks 'em."

They unshackled the man, and Swan helped him to the shade of the pines. Lavon herded the other slaves into the shade two hundred yards up the road. He led the mule with the water barrel to the coffle and gave each slave a half-gourd of water. They huddled together and whispered as they watched the sick slave up the road. The man was doubled over on his knees, vomiting violently. His body jerked, and he screamed and clutched his stomach.

Lavon couldn't watch the sick man any longer.

He told himself he couldn't take even one more day of this. He hadn't bathed in days. The slaves smelled of sweat and filth. They looked at him with dead eyes and expressionless faces. A fat woman suddenly bent over and vomited. The woman beside her began to chant and rock back and forth.

The slave with Swan was screaming again. Was this man going to die on them too? Thoughts of the money from the remaining slaves couldn't overcome Lavon's misery. He stood limp with exhaustion and heat. He did not want to deal with the man's agony. Finally the screaming stopped, and Swan walked over.

"Worst seems to be over," Swan said. "Lord God, he was vomitin' blood, shittin' like crazy. He's one sick nigger, Mr. Deavors. What we goin' to do with him? He ought to see a doctor, and in any case, he can't start walkin' again."

"Well, we can put him on the spare horse," Lavon said. "We ought to stop for the night soon. I'd like to get set up before dark."

"We ought to do that for certain," Swan said. "We don't want somethin' like last night."

They had marched past sunset the previous night, and while passing through a canebrake, had encountered three armed men. Lavon and Swan had pulled their own guns. There had been some dangerous moments, because the slaves nearly panicked, and Lavon and Swan had had to worry about the possible panic as well as the threat of the men, who would not yield the narrow road to let them pass. The three finally wavered and rode off, but Swan and Lavon were convinced the men were bandits or rustlers.

"Is there any lodging near here?" Lavon asked. "Some kind of inn or stand? I don't fancy another night in the open."

"I recollect there's a stand down the road a short spell," Swan said. "I was just thinkin' 'bout it. We gettin' low on nigger food, and they might know the whereabouts of a doctor."

Lavon formed the line again while Swan put the slave on the spare horse. Swan shackled the man's wrists around the horse's stomach.

"Looks too sick to be fakin', but don't hurt none to make sure," Swan said. He took the horse's reins and rode to the front of the coffle.

Lavon brought up the rear of the line. The slaves moved slower than before, despite all his combined threats and promises. Two more slaves vomited, but Swan rode back and prodded the men on with the butt of his whip.

"See, now, bet you they fakin' it," he said. "Ate some grass or somethin' to make 'em look sick so they can get a ride. You got to be on 'em tooth and toenail, Mr. Deavors."

Swan rode back to the front of the line. The coffle shuffled off. The slave on the horse was screaming again. Lavon wiped sweat from his face with the back of his hand. Would he never end this journey with the fat fool and these blacks? He hated to see the slaves suffer, and even more he hated to be near them when they were sick. He hoped there was a doctor in the vicinity. He twisted in the saddle and asked himself how men could buy and sell blacks and not be affected by it, not become twisted and inhuman in every aspect of their lives. He felt more depressed than at any other time of his life, and despite his thought of the money, he told himself again and again that this was the last time he would lower himself to this barely human state.

Swan was shouting and cracking his whip. Lavon asked himself at which times he had despised Swan most in Virginia. Had it been when Swan led him into some tavern where traders and trackers and whippers drank, or when he grew sick of such men and led Swan into a decent establishment, only to have gentlemen snicker and shake their heads as Swan talked about "bringin' dignity to niggerin' "?

Thunder rolled in the distance. Clouds were forming on the horizon. The slaves moved closer together and whispered as they glanced at the tangled undergrowth of a hill that sloped down to a creek. This night, Lavon told himself. And tomorrow. And one more night. Then he would be selling the slaves in Natchez.

He had to think of the money, all that money,

enough to set himself up in Europe. To hell with the scorn of the planters or the judgment of Athel and his family. Lavon told himself that the Columns was as much his as his brother's, despite any rash youthful settlement he might have made. It was certainly more his home than Estelle's. The money he had taken from Athel and used to buy these slaves was a small price for Athel to pay. After all, Athel had the whole goddamn plantation.

It was unthinkable that he would return to Europe and live at the whim of Athel and the bank, hoping each quarter that the next payment arrived on time. Yet a nagging thought forced itself forward. He had been counting his profits and telling himself he could be set up in Europe. Set up how? he now asked himself. All he had ever done was live a life of wealth, leisure, and pleasure. He had no skills and no profession, and if he undertook any trade, he would be laughed out of the social circles he knew in London and Paris.

He laughed bitterly and told himself he did have a profession. He ran nigger dogs and sold slaves.

"Move on along there, goddamnit!" Lavon shouted. He cracked his whip at the slaves, who were barely shuffling toward the brackish creek. Dark gray clouds were crouching on the horizon. The short gaps between lightning and thunder meant rain was near.

"How much farther to this stand?" Lavon called.

"Way I recollect, it should be quarter-mile past the bridge," Swan said. "Creek twists back, and the stand sets out over the water. Now, this here stand, Mr. Deavors, it ain't what you'd call no first-class establishment."

"It would have to be better than sleeping in the open, with the rain coming up," Lavon said.

The bridge consisted of a dozen logs on low pilings, crossed with planks. Water lapped at the rotting wood. The lead slaves refused to walk onto the bridge, and Swan had to put the whip to two of them. The slaves' weight made the pilings sway. The thunder and lightning were steady for a full minute. A cool wind came up. Lavon was afraid the bridge would give way before he got off, but the pilings held, and he rode onto the bank.

The land was low on this side of the creek. They passed marshes filled with cane and green slime. The stubs of dead trees jutted up from the marsh like huge ruined teeth. Half a dozen slaves vomited, but Lavon and Swan forced the coffle on with whips and the promise that in a few minutes they would stop for the night.

Hulking cypress trees grew along the road, and through their leaves sheet lightning lit the gray sky. These trees frightened the slaves. Lavon had gone back to speed up the rear of the coffle, when a shout turned him around. The coffle had stopped, and the lead slaves were screaming and backing up. A woman's chant was picked up by the other slaves.

"What in hell's the matter with the goddamn niggers now?" Lavon asked as he galloped up.

Then he saw the ten poles stuck in the mud. Rotting skulls were fastened to two of the poles. Skeletal hands and feet hung from the other eight.

"Them belonged to the Hankses, father and son," Swan said. "You heard 'bout them Hankses?"

"No, I haven't," Lavon said. "We better get . . ."

"Oh, they wasn't no garden-variety robbers and murderers," Swan said. "Made Murrell's bunch look like Sunday-school boys. Them Hankses not only robbed and killed. They tortured men, women, and children, beat 'em up, loved to rape women 'fore slittin' their throats. Story is they'd take a horseman and tie him to his horse and whip the horse off a high bluff into the river. And they—"

"Yes, yes, but we have to do something with the slaves."

"I ain't told you all," Swan said. "Favorite way they'd get rid of somebody was to rip open his stomach and fill him with stones and sink him in the water. When they was finally caught, some men who'd lost family to 'em held 'em on the ground and sawed off their hands and feet and heads while they was still livin'."

The slaves' chanting was loud and eerie. Lavon

looked around. They had formed a half-circle. Lightning came in sheets again, mingled with deafening thunder. Fat raindrops hit Lavon's face.

"Let's get moving," he said. "It's going to rain like hell."

It took Lavon and Swan ten minutes of cursing, whipping, and finally, a shot fired in the air, to get the slaves moving. A dozen slaves claimed they were too sick to walk, but they were forced forward. The rain fell in torrents. Beneath the dark clouds and cypress limbs it seemed midnight on the muddy road. Lavon was soaked to the skin by the time he saw the lights of the stand. These stands were common along the trace. They were simply farmhouses that rented beds to travelers and provided food and whiskey. Lavon had heard that some stands were little more than havens for robbers who waited for travelers to bed down. Meriwether Lewis, Thomas Jefferson's secretary and friend, who explored the West with William Clark, had been murdered in such a stand on the trace.

This stand consisted of an unplastered log house attached to a large lean-to barn. The house stuck out over the creek, supported on long wooden poles. Swan herded the slaves into the barn, while Lavon went inside the house. A toothless woman and two sullen, emaciated boys of seventeen or eighteen sat at a table cluttered with dishes and scraps of food. A dog rose from the woman's feet and growled and bared its teeth at Lavon.

"They spare beds in the other room," the woman said. "Supper's cookin'. You can put your niggers in the barn. Whole thing'll cost you eight dollars, countin' meal for your niggers and oats for your horses."

Lavon looked at the woman's pig eyes and saw the furtive glances of her sons.

"My partner and I will sleep in the barn with our niggers," Lavon said. "We'll eat out there. We'll want two jugs of whiskey. And fresh water. Something to sleep on. Have your boys bring the stuff out. We're tired and hungry. . . ."

"Money in advance, mister," the woman said,

working her sunken gums together. "Be nine dollars with the whiskey."

"Half in advance, half in the morning," Lavon said.

"Hell, Ma, it's rainin'," one of the boys whined. "I don't want to go sloppin' up a bunch of niggers in the rain."

"Get off your butt, Billy Frank," the woman said. "There's cash money to be made. You, too, Provine."

Lavon gave the woman four and a half dollars and watched her eyes devour the contents of his purse.

"You have much trouble with bandits around here?" he asked.

"No more'n any other place hereabouts," the woman said. "If you hear anybody goin' 'bout in the night, it'll just be my boys."

"If I see anybody near the barn tonight, I'll blow his goddamn head off," Lavon said, touching his pistol. "My partner and I will sleep in turns. We have some sick niggers. Is there a doctor in the vicinity?"

"No, not no doctor 'round here," the woman said. "I hear tell they's one down to Natchez."

Lavon joined Swan, who agreed they should stay in the barn and sleep in turns. Lavon slept little, despite his exhaustion and the whiskey he drank. No one came lurking in the dark, but a dozen slaves spent the night suffering from vomiting and diarrhea. Just before dawn the slave who had been put over the horse died. Swan suggested they throw him in the water, but Lavon insisted on having two slaves dig a shallow grave for the man.

At sunup they formed the coffle and started off. Lavon and Swan took turns on Lavon's horse. Eight sick slaves were slumped over Swan's horse, the extra horse, and the mule. And thus the weary caravan continued on its grim journey.

Chapter 20

It was a day of dark skies, steady rain, and stifling heat and humidity. By noon fifteen slaves were sick with diarrhea and vomiting. A second slave died as Lavon ate a lunch of bread and fatback. They buried the man and brutalized the coffle into line again. They slung sick blacks over all three horses and the mule, and set off with Lavon and Swan walking, whip in one hand, whiskey jug in the other.

Lavon felt little sympathy for the dead and dying slaves, and much more compassion for himself. He was nauseated from treating the filthy, vomiting slaves in the heat and feared he was coming down with their ailment. He was near total exhaustion. He worried that the time would come when the slaves would refuse to move despite any threats, promises, whippings, or shots in the air.

At dusk they drove the coffle into a clearing beneath water oaks at the edge of a swamp. They collapsed against the trunk of a tree and drank whiskey while the slaves moaned and screamed a few yards away.

"We might as well face it, Mr. Deavors," Swan said. "We got big trouble. Them niggers is sick, gettin' sicker, they dyin', goin' to lots more die. They got the bloody flux. I didn't want to admit it, but that's what they got, and it'll wipe 'em out sure as fat dogs fart. We be lucky we don't come down with it. Lord God, I skimped and saved to buy me a coffle, now I'm goin' to be wiped out." He turned up the jug and drank until whiskey spilled over his chin.

Lavon did not reply. He had feared for hours that the slaves had some dread disease, but he had been incapable of admitting it to himself. He had been too exhausted and too disgusted to think or act clearly. His mind refused to accept the obvious.

The bloody flux, as Swan called it, was simply cholera. He had seen enough of it in Europe and Morocco to be acquainted with it, but in his desperation he had refused to recognize the obvious symptoms. He knew there was danger that he might come down with the disease, but, strangely, compared to the ruin he faced, the fear had little effect on him. He had sold his honor to become a trader, and it was all for nothing!

"Yes, they'll spread it before morning, and they'll probably all die," Lavon said. "This has all been for nothing. Christ, with luck we'll struggle into Natchez with two skinny niggers that nobody will buy."

He drank whiskey. He would be back there in the pit again. Back to running "nigger dogs" and whipping runaways. There would be no more money from Athel. It might take them years to save enough to bring down another coffle, years of living with Purvis Swan.

"God help me," Lavon mumbled.

"What's that you sayin', Mr. Deavors?" Swan asked.

"No, goddamnit," Lavon said. He jumped up. "No, I'm not going to sit here drinking and wallowing in pity. . . ."

"Whatever can we do?" Swan asked. He heaved himself up. "Even if we could find ourselves a doctor, it'd be too late. And 'sides, he might spread the word."

"To begin with, we can do what we should've done hours ago," Lavon said. "We can separate those that don't show any symptoms of the disease. Damnit, how stupid of me not to do something before! We can take the healthy ones into Natchez tonight and sell them first light. If a slave gets sick, we'll hide him quickly. Don't you see, damnit? We might at least get most of our investment back."

"We could do that, Mr. Deavors," Swan said. "You right, we ought to cut the sick ones. Your idea's better'n nothin'. When they die off, we'll keep buryin' 'em."

They started over to the slaves, but Swan stopped.

"What's wrong?" Lavon asked. "We can't lose another minute."

"We forgettin' one thing, Mr. Deavors," he said. "What 'bout all them as is sick when we leave for Natchez? Sick but not dead? What we goin' to do with them? We can't leave 'em to be found and have word get 'round. And we can't take 'em into Natchez." His body sagged. "So it looks like we beat, after all."

"No, goddamnit," Lavon said. "I'm not losing everything and going back to Natchez without money, back to grubbing for a living. We'll dump them all, every goddamn slave with cholera. We'll find some deep bayou and dump every one of them."

"But they still livin'. . . ."

"Living and dead, to hell with them," Lavon said. "They're going to die anyway."

"I don't know, Mr. Deavors," Swan said. "Dumpin' the ones still livin' . . . Well, maybe you're right. They only niggers. But I don't know. . . ."

"Don't think about it," Lavon said. "Think about the goddamn money. Think about being dead broke in Natchez."

"I don't have to think no more," Swan said.

The slaves were docile as they were unfettered, though two young men tried to crawl into the bushes, and Swan had to drag them back. There were murmurs and groans as the sick and dying were separated from those who showed no symptoms. Lavon and Swan talked soothingly of a doctor's arrival, of treatment, of whiskey, of being a few miles from Natchez, of no more forced marching.

The two men worked with a fury, covered with blood and vomit, as they pushed themselves with whiskey. Fear of catching the disease was a minor part of Lavon's worries. He was driven by a monomania as he forced back a woman who had crawled into the swamp, and he fettered her once more to a man whose body was jerking with agony. Most of the slaves remained docile as they were formed into two groups, but occasionally the agony of the pain and dehydration sent a spasm of strength through a slave, and he had to be clubbed unconscious. Lightning and thunder terrified the healthy slaves, and they began to chant as a heavy rain fell.

Swan and Lavon walked away from the two groups. "How we goin' to work this, now?" Swan asked.

"We'll have to get the sick and dead ones down to a bayou or creek in the swamp," Lavon said. "But, Christ, that will take both of us, and we can't leave the others alone."

"The horses could drag 'em down. . . ."

"No, the slaves would fight that," Lavon said. "Even sick and dying, they'd fight and scream, and the horses would become unmanageable. There's nothing else to do. We'll have to . . . kill them here and have the horses drag them to the water. The other group, well, we can chain them to a tree. . . ."

"Lord God, Mr. Deavors," Swan said. "I never done nothin' like that in all my born days. And I done plenty." He drank whiskey.

Lavon also drank whiskey. "They're just niggers, Swan," he said. "Don't think about it. Think of the goddamn money. Come on."

Lavon's body was poised between collapse and a desperate strength. He was so tensed that he could feel the bulge of muscles in his arms. Sweat poured from his body. His eyes hurt. His stomach was one solid unit. He could easily have cried, and he felt the salt of tears in his eyes. Swan had not moved. Lavon stared at the man and hated him as though he personified all that Lavon had become.

"Well, I guess . . ." Swan started.

Lavon shoved Swan. "Get moving, goddamnit!" he shouted. "We're going to lose everything! What if someone finds us here? Shots might be heard. We better use our rifle butts."

They drank more whiskey and worked quickly in the rain. They forced the healthy slaves deeper into the oak grove and secured them to two trees with chains and padlocks. They picked up their rifles and returned to the dead and infected slaves. The slaves had been trying to crawl away but had merely hindered each other with their confused movements. Several of the slaves looked up in terror. They seemed to sense what was going to happen.

A man lunged at Swan's legs and screamed as he knocked Swan off his feet. The man clawed at Swan's throat. Lavon tore off half the man's skull with a blow from his rifle butt. The slaves were moving, struggling in all directions, but halting each other because of the chains that linked them. A woman threw a stone that grazed Lavon's head, and it infuriated him. He caught the woman on the forehead with his rifle butt and snapped her neck.

Swan clubbed down two pleading women and kicked a man who bit his leg. Lavon began to shiver, though he was not feverish. His hands shook as he clubbed down another slave. He and Swan staggered about the slaves, swinging their rifles, until all the slaves lay still, some two dozen of them. Perspiration dripped into Lavon's eyes. His throat contracted. Breathing was difficult because of the stench. But he did not pause. He and Swan hitched the three horses to the chain, though the horses were difficult to manage.

Finally Lavon managed to control the horses. He lit a torch, and with this light, he and Swan forced the horses to drag the dead and dying slaves to a bayou, where the eyes and snout of an alligator were lit by lightning. Lavon threw stones, and the alligator disappeared.

Several slaves regained consciousness and began to moan and grab feebly at bushes and clumps of grass. Lavon ignored them as he and Swan filled a gunnysack with rocks and fastened it to the chain. Lavon waded into the water with a long stick. Something bumped his leg, and he panicked, thinking it was the alligator. It was only a turtle. The water was shallow for a few feet, then dropped off sharply. Swan had to whip the horses into the water, and then he mounted one horse and rode them in deeper. Finally the slaves were unfastened from the horses, and they sank into the water. Two living eyes stared up at Lavon. And groans became bubbles in the water.

Lavon staggered back, shaking and dry-heaving. He collapsed in the mud, with his head between his knees, and began to weep.

BOOK III

The Abolitionist

Chapter 21

The Deavorses sat in the first-class lounge of the paddle-wheeler *Andrew Jackson* on a cloudy September morning. A black waiter poured tea for everyone except Athel, who drank whiskey, and Aunt Delma, who sipped Madeira from a teacup.

The family had come to see Lawton off. He was going to New Orleans to school. There was little talk. Joleen and Tillman said nothing at all. Everyone was waiting for Haskell Sumrall's return and the news he would bring about Lavon.

"Now, you be careful of the company you keep in that city, Lawton," Estelle said. "Professor LeBeau will meet the boat, and I expect you to follow his guidance in the choice of your friends."

"Yes'm," Lawton said, and avoided his mother's eyes.

She had been opposed to Athel's suggestion that Lawton go to New Orleans a year early. She would have fought the idea, but she sensed that Lawton was unhappy and that going away was important to him. His change of attitude surprised everyone. In the past he had never been happier than when he was at home, and he was an indifferent student at best.

Joleen was the only one not surprised by Lawton's decision to go away. She felt rather guilty about what had happened with her brother, and this was one of the few times in her life she had felt guilt about anything. This guilt came not so much from the sexual encounter itself as from its obviously disastrous effect on him. The day after the incident, Lawton had accepted an invitation to spend a week on the Woodville plantation of a classmate from the institute. When Lawton returned, he was subdued and spent most of his time alone. He would not look at Joleen, and he seldom spoke to her. He missed half his meals, and his parents were clearly worried about him. So was Joleen. She had an impulse to talk to him but decided it was better to leave him alone.

When Lawton had put his mouth between her thighs, she experienced a series of climaxes unlike any physical experience she had ever had. She had loved it, loved every delicious movement of his lips and tongue, which drove her to writhe and gasp. She loved it all the more because it was the climax of the summer-long game between them, and she had clearly won.

But she sobered quickly when she realized his terrible reaction. She knew they could not continue the game. She did not need any further triumph over Lawton. She loved him and respected him, and she could no longer maintain this respect if he groveled at her feet and she had to watch his self-respect crumbling. She did not sit down and think this all out. As always at crucial times, she acted more through a sure instinct than any conscious thought process.

Her instinct was weakened by guilt only a short time. Her main worry, aside from Lawton's suffering, was the fear that her relationship with Lawton would never again be the same. But she felt the incident would fade and that she and Lawton would continue to love each other. She hated to see him go, but knew it was best that he get away and be alone for a time.

There was a residue of sexual tension between them, but she did not concern herself with it. Joleen's main problem was that Lawton's lips and tongue had taken her to such sexual intensity that she found the usual kissing and petting on dark porches to be first boring and then trival, even when she grew bolder and let a boy slide his hands over her thighs one night. Nor did she want some boy who did not excite her to give her pleasure with his mouth. She would not consider real sex with any man she did not truly love and desire. So she began to use her hands on her body more frequently and to have increasingly graphic fantasies about sex with an older man who would excite her and know how to make love in such a way that she would again experience those delicious spasms.

Her mind wandered as she sat musing in the hot lounge of the *Andrew Jackson* this September morning, and as usual she thought of the German lawyer Aaron Clauson. She was determined to see him again very soon, even if she had to contrive the rendezvous in some bold and unladylike manner.

Haskell Sumrall joined the family. He was Theron's father, and it was in his backyard that Joleen and Lawton had had their sexual adventure. He ordered a whiskey and paused before speaking. This confirmed Athel's worst fears.

"It's true, Athel," he said finally as he sat down. "Lavon is sellin' slaves on Seville Street, with that man Swan, who runs nigger dogs. He was auctionin' the last of the lot when I arrived. I didn't speak to him. There seemed nothin' to say."

"No, there's nothin' to say to my brother," Athel said.

"It's a scandal," Aunt Delma said. "A Deavors sellin' flesh on the public streets! We should do somethin', Athel. The family can't let this continue. My own nephew, indeed! If he ever comes to my house again, I'll set the dogs on him. He's become common as bug dust."

"There's little we can do," Athel said. "I could talk to him, but it would do no good. Lavon's beyond help, beyond redemption."

"I'm afraid there's more to report," Haskell said. "There was some curiosity and suspicion because he sold his niggers so soon after arrivin' and at less than market prices. Oh, he found enough buyers. But while I was there, a man returned with a slave he had purchased and claimed the man had become violently ill. Lavon refused to give back the man's money."

Athel shook his head. He could think of nothing to say. When the bank had sent word that Lavon had picked up the money, Athel was hurt that Lavon did not get in touch with him, but relieved that Lavon had returned to Europe. The hurt had been replaced with disbelief when he was informed, only that morning, that Lavon had been up to Richmond and returned with a coffle of slaves for sale. He had not wanted to believe the news, so Haskell Sumrall had offered to visit the slave auction and find out the truth.

Now that Athel had the truth, he was possessed by a rare anger. He sat silently and drank his whiskey while Estelle fussed about Lawton's behavior in New Orleans.

Each time his mother admonished him about New Orleans, Lawton feared she knew what he had done. He had lived with the fear of discovery since the night with Joleen. He mumbled and nodded as his mother spoke, but he would not look at her. He had never been more miserable.

He had felt so wretched after masturbating that night that he was physically sick and had vomited beneath the willow. Early the next morning he went to Woodville. When he returned to the plantation, he lived only for this day, when he could flee to New Orleans. At times he told himself he could never return to the Columns.

His shame did not end with Joleen.

Two weeks later he was swimming in a pool in the back pasture when he heard someone in the nearby woods. He was scrambling from the water when Nettie walked from the trees. He froze, embarrassed that he was naked.

"Go away, Nettie," he yelled. "Damn it, you shouldn't be here, girl! You should be in the fields."

"I done told Filch I'm sick," she said. "I was just goin' to take myself a swim, Mist' Lawton. We could swim together."

Lawton protested and cursed her. But it was impossible to maintain any sense of dignity or authority when he stood in front of her with a red face and a stiff penis. Nettie was an attractive girl with large breasts, and a slim body. Her smile promised everything, yet it was a haughty smile for a slave. A slave, yet she was white—this made her irresistible to Lawton, despite Ambrose's warning and his own conscience, which told him it was wrong to have sex with a slave. His mind might have been his appendix for all the effect it had on him.

She slipped from her dress. She wore nothing underneath. He stared at her breasts and the flat red nipples. Her legs were muscled from field work. Her vagina was covered by a tangle of dark curly hair.

"Sure is hot today, water feel good," Nettie said as she walked toward Lawton.

Lawton retreated toward the water. He thought of some threat, but the thought died the same instant.

"Sure is," he mumbled.

Lawton drew back, but Nettie ran past him into the water. She turned suddenly and splashed water into his face.

"Hey, stop that!" he shouted.

Nettie's answer was to splash him again. She laughed and ran deeper into the pool. Lawton ran after her and caught up with her as the water lapped against her nipples. He scooped water in both hands and threw it over her head. They both laughed, and when she tried to splash him, he lunged forward and caught her wrist.

She tried to jerk away, and her body tightened. The next instant she moved against Lawton. He gasped at the sensation. Her breasts pressed against him. Her vagina rubbed against his rigid penis. And her lips sucked at his mouth. They kissed. Her tongue tantalized the roof of his mouth. He fondled her buttocks, slick in the water.

Lawton began to move through a hot, sensual daydream that left him mindless and driven only by his senses. The water was warm, the day was scalding, Nettie's body burned as though her flesh was molten. They were in the water . . . and then they were lying down on the bank and Lawton was groaning softly as she bit his nipples, licked his stomach, took his penis in her hot mouth and sucked him. When he was ready to explode in her mouth, she pulled away, and he rolled over and fell between her thighs. He writhed against her body, and his hands rubbed her buttocks and thighs while they kissed.

He felt fever and chills up his back as Nettie helped him guide his penis into her vagina. She was wet. And the vagina was hot and tight. So tight and so hot. His first few thrusts hurt them both. She squeezed him with her strong legs and pressed the muscles of her vagina in rhythm with his thrusts. His climax came very quickly.

They said nothing as they dressed. Nettie smiled and walked away. For a week he made love to Nettie every evening when she came from the fields. He lived in the sensual haze that overrode any thoughts of conscience, though after each time with Nettie his guilt grew deeper. Finally he rebuffed her one evening, and after that he stayed away.

He brooded even more and spent hours alone on his horse and waited for the day when he could leave the plantation. He considered himself a sinful, terrible young man who could not control his desires. He had had sex first with his sister and then with a slave girl.

The boat's whistle interrupted his thoughts.

"Time for guests to go ashore," the waiter said. "We be gettin' underway shortly, ladies and gentlemen."

Everyone stood up. Lawton felt sad and lonely, and he steeled himself for the hugs and kisses and tears.

"Why, where's Tillman?" Estelle asked.

"The young massuh?" the waiter asked. "He done gone off the boat some minutes ago."

Chapter 22

Lavon ordered another cup of rum and leaned against the bar of the outdoor stand. He looked down Seville Street at the deserted auction block where he and Swan had managed to sell nine slaves. Lavon was on the point of emotional and physical collapse as he took the rum from a Spanish mulatto with a gold tooth. He told himself to drink the rum and move on before some other buyer returned with a sick slave and insisted on getting back his money. Three men had already returned with vomiting, dehydrated slaves, and there had been some ugly scenes. Once Lavon had even pulled his pistol.

Lavon drank the rum and wiped his face with the back of his hand. His legs were giving way. He had to lean against the bar. He had reached some lethal point beyond mere drunkenness. All night and all this morning he had been driven by an intensity that overcame physical weakness and kept him on his feet. He was dirty and unshaven, and his clothes reeked of sweat. He might have cried again. He might have vomited. He might have sunk to the mud. He was nauseated and feared he had cholera. He drained his cup and ordered another but told himself that after this he had to leave. He had to rest. He had to get clean. He had to sober up. He had to see a doctor.

Rum rode in his throat, and he forced it down. He saw himself killing the slaves and dumping them in the bayou. He saw the eyes sinking into the water.

What had he done? What had he become? And all for next to nothing!

"For nothing," he whispered.

In their panic he and Swan had sold the slaves at ridiculously low prices. They had made back only a small part of their investment. Three slaves had become sick during the bidding, and they had pulled them from the block and hidden them in a canebrake. Swan was out now dumping them in the river.

Lavon looked down the street and was startled to see his nephew standing by the auction block. Tillman was staring at him. Lavon glanced around. He expected to see Athel or some other member of his family. All he saw were the shoddily dressed shoppers who were bargaining in the outdoor stalls and markets that glutted Seville Street.

Lavon turned away and drank more rum. What in hell did the boy want? And where was Athel? Or had

Tillman wandered off alone? He was a strange boy; no doubt about that. But why would he come to Seville Street alone? Surely Athel was around somewhere.

"Damn you!" he said aloud. "Damn you all!"

He forced himself to stand up straight, though it took all his strength to give up the support of the bar. If Athel wanted a confrontation, he would have one. He only hoped his brother was angry and insulting. He could endure that far better than forgiveness or compassion.

Tillman still stared at Lavon. He had not moved. There was no sign of Athel. Lavon remembered the moment earlier in the morning when he had looked into the crowd and seen Haskell Sumrall. He hated the look on Sumrall's face. When he looked back a few minutes later, Sumrall was gone. Of course, if Athel was in town, Sumrall would have told him. And if Tillman was here, surely Athel was nearby. Lavon tried to muster his anger, but it was futile.

He had murdered and sold slaves, and he had given up so much in honor and self-respect for so little money. He could not return to Europe. He was back down in the pit. He drank rum and choked from the fetid market smells, while his goddamn nephew stood there staring at him like the judgment of God.

Who was this boy to judge him, no matter what he had done! Who was Athel to judge him, damnit! Somehow he would gain back his honor. He would wipe out all this. He would be wealthy and respected. He swallowed back tears and repeated the vow.

Lavon looked down the street. Athel was standing beside Tillman. Lavon straightened up. He had to steady himself with a hand on the bar.

Athel did not look at Lavon. He took Tillman's hand, and they walked away.

Lavon collapsed against the bar. He ordered rum. He rested on his elbows and sniffled as he cursed the memory of the dying slaves. What he had done was wrong, but what else could he have done? By all rights, he owned half of a plantation, goddamnit! When he had been forced off the Columns, his family might as well have taken his honor as well. They had forced him down into this life. Lavon picked up his cup with both hands, and the cup brought him the fantasy he wanted: he owned the Columns, and Athel and his family came crawling to him like mendicants.

Chapter 23

Much of summer remains late into a Mississippi autumn. In late November the Deavorses' slaves picked cotton in weather that daily reached the seventies and at times touched eighty. Only the earlier sunsets limited their work, and on two straight Sundays they were ordered into the fields. The cotton yield was unusually high, and the rule was that the cotton should be picked by Thanksgiving.

Half an hour before daylight, one of Athel's drivers blew a horn and the slaves got up and prepared their food for the day. At first daylight a second horn was blown, and the slaves trudged to the fields. A driver visited each slave house to make certain every able-bodied slave was headed for the fields. The drivers kept the slaves at their work with a mild severity, but as always, Athel depended more on promises than threats. The slaves knew that if the harvest was good they could expect rewards of molasses, tobacco, chickens, and whiskey. They also worked hard because they knew that in a short time the grueling work would end. On the night of the annual harvest ball they would have their own party in the barn, with dancing and whiskey, and then they would be given a few days off.

The normal force of field hands was increased during the final weeks of harvest in an effort to win the race against the weather. A prolonged period of rain could ruin a good crop and wipe out a year's work. Many slaves who normally performed specialized tasks found themselves in the fields in November. In addition, there was a system of rating slaves as "partial-hands" during harvest. Young children would be considered "quarter-hands," which meant they were expected to pick one-fourth as much as a prime field hand. An older child might be considered a "half-hand" or a "three-quarter-hand." Conversely, the older slaves were considered "three-quarter-hands," "half-hands," or "quarter-hands." They were all expected to march out into the fields for at least a few hours of work during November. Thus Athel's work force was increased by the equivalent of over a dozen "full hands" by the use of this rating system.

After two days of rain during the first week of the month, the weather held good. In previous years Athel had employed the "task system" of harvesting. Under this system each slave was given a fixed quota of cotton to be picked, and he could not leave the field until he finished his work. But the drivers reported that the system did not work well, because a slave, in his eagerness to finish early, often did sloppy work, and a strong slave became resentful if given a larger goal than a weaker slave.

Athel had read in an agricultural journal that more and more planters were using a "gang system," in which a group of slaves under a driver was assigned to a certain number of acres, and none of the slaves could leave the field until those acres were picked. Athel decided, with some reservations, to try the gang system, and by November he was relieved to observe that the picking was going faster and smoother than in previous years.

The cotton picking was not the only frenzy of activity on the plantation. The cotton had to be loaded on wagons and transported to the Benton gin, where it was pressed and prepared for shipping, first to Natchez and then by boat to New Orleans. There were still vegetables to be gathered and preserved. Corn had to be shucked and winter fodder prepared. And the pigs had to be collected from the swamps and slaughtered and cured.

In addition, the house slaves were kept busy with

the autumn cleaning. They replaced the curtains with winter draperies. All the winter covers were aired and the rugs beaten. Estelle took stock of the slaves' winter clothing needs and made a trip into Natchez to buy the items that could not be made on the plantation. Each male slave was given a pair of wool pants, two cotton shirts, and a wool jacket, as well as a pair of "nigger brogans," which were heavy, bootlike shoes. Each woman received two cotton dresses, a woolen coat, and a pair of heavy shoes. Estelle also purchased trinkets, small gifts, and tobacco for the slaves' Christmas gifts.

The harvest was the best in years, and the slaves seemed more than usually content. Normally, this harvest time would be especially festive for the Deavorses, since November 21 was Joleen's eighteenth birthday and her party was held in conjunction with the harvest ball. But this year's festivities were marred by Lawton's absence and the shame that Lavon had brought to the family.

Only one letter had come up from New Orleans, and in it Lawton discussed the most general kind of activities. He said he was doing well in history but having difficulty with geometry and Latin. He made no mention of missing the plantation. Estelle wrote him every two weeks and filled the letters with news of the family as well as pleas that he behave himself. Athel wrote twice and told of the record harvest. He offered no advice to Lawton. Athel wanted to give his son a free rein, for he knew Lawton would almost certainly be taking advantage of the city's whorehouses. Athel was no Puritan, and he thought such experience would not hurt Lawton; in any case, it was inevitable, as it had been for him when he went downriver to school. He only hoped the boy heeded his advice that he frequent only the best houses and take certain hygienic precautions.

Athel suspected that Lawton had had sexual experiences with some slave girl during the summer. He assumed this was why Lawton abruptly changed his mind and decided to go away to school. Athel had dreaded the time when his son was old enough to be tempted by the slave girls. In this Athel was rigid. He believed it wrong for a white man to take advantage of a slave's position to satisfy his sexual whims.

Athel went about his work and missed Lawton terribly, for if Lawton were in Natchez he would have come out several weekends during the fall. Athel thought Lawton's education was important, but he hoped he disliked the city and kept his love of the plantation.

From time to time the family had word of Lavon's activities. Once, in Natchez, Athel saw his brother riding in the carriage with the dog cage. Athel's anger had changed back to compassion and then to anger again. No matter what his feelings of the moment, he told himself constantly that he should do something to change the situation. He simply could not have his brother continue in his despicable line of work. But he could think of nothing he could do about it. And he had not discussed Lavon since the day on the paddle-wheeler.

Lavon became only a memory to Joleen, who was caught up in the housekeeping activities of harvest time as well as preparation for her birthday party and the harvest ball. And her Aunt Delma was also giving her a party in Natchez.

"It's time she was properly introduced to Natchez society," Aunt Delma said. "She's such a lovely and active girl. Lord, I'm surprised she doesn't die of boredom out there on the plantation."

The Deavorses and the Sumralls had employed a tutor, and five days a week Joleen and Tillman went over to the Sumrall plantation for lessons. Joleen had been a good pupil with other tutors, but this fall she was restless and inattentive during the lessons. She devoted far more effort than usual to selecting her clothes, and she constantly fussed with her hair and preened and examined her body as she stood naked in front of her full-length mirror.

She missed Lawton, but she had few sexual thoughts of her brother. She hoped he was not suffering anymore because of what had happened between them. She felt no real guilt about the incident. She simply missed Lawton. The plantation seemed empty without him.

Joleen had not kissed a boy for more than three months. She did not want their clumsy kissing and petting. She savored the delicious feelings between her thighs as she rode her horse, and she courted her body with her fingers during hot baths. This courting became a frequent ritual as she lay in the steaming water with her head back and breathed through her mouth. She stroked her tight nipples and slid her fingers against her vagina for exquisite minutes while she thought of Aaron Clauson's lips pressed against her mouth, thought of his hands squeezing her nipples, thought of his naked body pressed against her opening thighs. Joleen's stomach would quiver, then tighten. Her nipples would ache with a tender pain. She would press her fingers hard against her vagina. Her thighs would go rigid as her release brought murmurs from her lips. Sometimes at the instant of her climax she would gasp, "Aaron, Aaron . . ."

Joleen thought back with some self-scorn about the summer. She was impatient to be a sexually mature and fulfilled woman—impatient and apprehensive and a little frightened, in an exciting way. She had not seen Aaron in several months, but this only heightened his appeal. She remembered his interest in her at their June meeting and convinced herself she had only to see him again to win him. After all, she was so much more mature and desirable now!

"Mr. Clauson will be there for your party, dear," Aunt Delma had replied to her hesitant question. "His invitation will be delivered by hand."

Chapter 24

The Deavorses' ball was an annual event, and an invitation was considered a mark of a family's social standing in the county. Guests who came from Natchez or other places several hours away stayed overnight at the Columns or at neighboring plantations. Aunt Delma spent several days visiting, as she did each year. She found plantation life deadly boring except when there was a party, and her arrival with two cases of Madeira was the official signal that the festivities had begun, even if it was two days before the ball.

The gallery was cleared out, and a platform was built at the back end. Athel hired an orchestra from the finest hotel in Natchez. The walls were decorated with rust, red, and brown leaves. Candles whose earth colors matched the leaves were set in floor-stand candelabra along the walls.

The women tried to outdo each other with their finery, and men who seldom dressed up chose this occasion to wear outfits they had purchased in New Orleans. Cellus orchestrated the work of the slaves who parked the carriages of the guests and the slaves who circulated with punch and whiskey to fill guests' glasses. It was considered a breach of hospitality to let a guest's glass stand empty. Two slaves stood behind a table ladling out more punch and whiskey, as well as sherry, port, brandy, and Madeira. In the dining room was a buffet of cured ham, green ham, turkey, crawfish, roast beef, sweet potato, crowder peas, salad, aspics, cheese, sherbet, and mincemeat and pumpkin pies.

Joleen was stunning in a low-cut blue dress. She danced and flirted, and for the first time she was allowed a glass of punch with whiskey. She was also allowed to stay up past the midnight curfew that usually sent her to bed. When her mother wasn't present, she took another cup of punch, and later a third. Athel saw her and indulged her without comment. He had never seen her happier. Joleen found she liked the strong punch. She became intoxicated, but the punch had little to do with her euphoria. She told herself her life was truly beginning on this November evening. She had been only a child, but now she felt suddenly that she was a woman.

Every unmarried man fought for her attention and her approval. She would soon be at an age to marry. Had she been penniless, wealthy and socially prominent men would have courted her for her beauty, charm, and self-confidence. But she would bring a large dowry and a family name that had been prominent back to the days when the Deavorses were lairds in Scotland.

The orchestra was resting, and Joleen heard a fiddler out in the barn. She remembered that the slaves were having a party there. She loved everyone tonight. She loved the plantation. She loved all the people. She wanted to share her happiness with the slaves. She decided to go out to the barn.

The fiddling and dancing stopped abruptly as she entered. For a moment she felt self-conscious. Then the slaves clustered around her. There were cries of "Happy birthday, Miss Joleen," and "Happy birthday, young miss." The women went on and on about her dress and touched it as though they couldn't believe anything that beautiful could be real.

The slaves were drinking whiskey and rum, and Joleen realized her punch glass was empty.

"Could I please have some whiskey?" she asked Filch, who held a jug.

Filch glanced at Ed. Ed knew that her mother would disapprove and that her father would not approve but would give in. He hesitated, then took the jug. He poured her one swallow of whiskey.

"Don't you tell your folks, Miss Joleen," he whispered.

She raised her glass in toast, and the slaves toasted

her back with their cups and jugs. She choked on the whiskey but forced it down, though it brought tears to her eyes. Everyone laughed. Finally she returned to the house.

At midnight a table of gifts was brought into the gallery. Joleen opened all the gifts and thanked everyone. But there was nothing from her family.

"Come on out front," her father said. She walked out with him and stopped on the porch. On the lawn stood the most beautiful horse she had ever seen. It was a chestnut mare that Athel had bought in Natchez in October and kept in a paddock there. Ed had brought it out from town in the afternoon.

Joleen ran to the horse and rubbed its coat. The horse was proud and shy and doubtful of its strange surroundings and its new mistress.

"I want to ride him," Joleen said.

Despite her father's protests, she would not be denied. A compromise was reached. Ed held the reins and led the horse around the front yard while she sat on its back and talked soothingly into its ear.

Joleen did not go to bed until two. At six she was up and became so intent on getting to her new horse that she barely noticed that she had her first hangover. By half-past six she was riding her horse in the paddock under Ed's careful supervision.

During the next few days Joleen was preoccupied with the horse and with the thought that she would see Aaron Clauson in Natchez. Saturday morning the family went into Natchez. Joleen spent the afternoon helping her aunt prepare for the party.

Saturday evening the house blazed with candles, and slaves holding more candles lined the driveway. Aunt Delma was a wealthy woman who owned two plantations and considerable property. She was a widow with no children, and she spent lavishly to present her niece to Natchez society.

There were two orchestras, one in the parlor and one on the front lawn. The food was memorable, the whiskey and wine and punch plentiful, and people dressed as though visiting royalty. Joleen wore a pale green dress, cut lower than her mother approved. Eligible men courted her and danced with her. Women were sweet and flattering but envious. She drank punch and made no effort to hide it from her mother. And she drank more than her mother knew, for Aunt Delma loved Joleen's high spirits. She led her niece into the study from time to time and filled her glass.

It was a magnificent evening for Joleen. She was the center of every man's attention and every woman's comment. At midnight her aunt announced a grand waltz. The floor was cleared. The candles were put out. Thirty slaves stood on chairs with paraffin lanterns, and she and her father led the waltz in the dazzling light.

But Aaron Clauson had not come. Finally Joleen spoke to Aunt Delma.

"He was invited," Aunt Delma said. "He was expected, dear. His invitation was delivered by hand. I don't understand his absence."

Joleen's euphoria collapsed. She moped around and found that the punch tasted terrible. The flattering men bored her, and she began to answer their compliments tartly. She was tired and wished everyone would go home so she could go to bed.

A half-hour later she looked past a portly young doctor, who was paying her court, and saw Aaron at the door. She checked the impulse to go over to him. He paid his respects to her aunt, to her mother, to half a dozen women. Finally he walked over to Joleen.

"Happy birthday, Miss Deavors," he said, and bowed slightly. He gave her a single red rose. "I returned from a business trip this evening to find your aunt's invitation. The shops were closed, so I can offer you only this rose as a gift."

"It's lovely," she said. "I love roses." Then she saw the other side of his face. It was bruised, and there was a bandage over his left ear. "Sir, what has happened to you?"

"I tried to ride a reluctant horse," he said. "The beast threw me. Stupid animal. But not quite so stupid as I was. I should have known better than to mount a stubborn horse with spirit. May I have the honor of this dance?"

"Thank you," Joleen said.

He danced better than anyone she had ever known. His talk was witty and charming. He was so handsome, with his dark eyes and dark hair. There was a strength and purpose as he led her about the floor that did not go with his foppish style and self-deprecating manner. She felt he was concealing something, and this upset her. But what disturbed her far more was that, as he danced with her and charmed her, his thoughts seemed elsewhere. His eyes were furtive at times. He made a caustic comment about slavery and planters that shocked her. The next minute he dismissed the comment and told a humorous story.

Joleen was as charming, witty, and flirtatious as she could be. She was even bold enough to mention that she was warm and that there seemed to be a breeze on the lawn. Any other man would have broken his leg to walk her outside.

"I must say good night," Aaron told her. "Best wishes for your birthday."

He left. Joleen was stunned. Her cheeks were hot.

"Would you honor me with this dance?" the stout doctor asked.

"No, leave me alone, I don't want to dance," she snapped.

Joleen snatched a cup of punch from a slave's tray. She took a sip, then turned and purposely let the cup slip from her fingers and smash against the floor.

Chapter 25

A dozen squealing children drove Lavon into the darkness of Swan's garden, where he drank unforgivable wine and watched the candles being lit on the Christmas tree in the parlor. Swan's friend on the paddle-wheeler no longer brought up the white wine Lavon had found pleasant in September. Now he sold a sweet rosé that Lavon felt rotted his teeth with each sip. He told himself it should come in iron containers, since it could surely eat through glass. Swan could not tell the difference.

The talk and laughter floated out to Lavon's refuge behind a stunted banana tree. Every new-rich, social-climbing family in Adams County must have accepted Swan's invitation for a "swell Christmas affair." They all came, with their unfortunate manners, unfashionable clothes, and unmanageable children, because one of their hosts was a Deavors.

A real live Deavors, Lavon told himself. Swan might as well have exhibited him in a cage and charged admission. These people cursed the members of the planter aristocracy, but they would sell their wretched children for the chance to meet one as a social equal.

It's goin' to be a party like nothing' ever seen in this neck of the woods," Swan had said. "Goin' to be two fiddlers from the finest whorehouse on the river. Goin' to be possum and pork and ham hocks and rabbit and chitlins and chicken, goin' to be whiskey and rum and that there wine. . . ."

If white people like these visited a plantation, the slaves would send them around to the back door, Lavon told himself. And these guests were lowering themselves to visit Swan's house. They would never ask the man to their own homes. They came now because a Deavors was present. Even in their bourgeois world a man who ran nigger dogs was beneath them.

The guests were the successful slave traders, the men who doctored sick slaves, the small merchants of Seville Street, the captains of small paddle-wheelers, the tavern owners, and the farmers who were struggling to reach the exalted status that would allow them to be called planters. That lofty rank was accorded a man when he owned no fewer than twenty slaves.

For weeks Lavon had run the dogs alone because Swan had come down with cholera. Swan nearly died. Lavon was nauseated for a few days, but he was spared the disease. Now Swan had recovered with a vengeance.

It had taken Lavon a month to overcome the guilty nightmares in which he relived the slave-killing horror. He was now able to swallow his guilt and accept the stark reality of his situation. His rationalization was a daily ritual. He had done things he disliked. He had acted in a drunken panic. He would never do such things again. Given his present situation, he had no choice but to survive any way he could. He had lost his self-respect and his honor. All he could do was earn enough money to buy them back.

And all this had happened because he was forced to leave the Columns. Anyone else in a similar situation might have done the same thing.

His rationalization worked well. He cut down on his drinking and schemed and fantasized. He would own a large plantation of his own. He would once more be a man of wealth and honor. And if he had to bring down another coffle of slaves, he would do it right this time. He would take damn good care of the slaves on the journey. And he would be shrewd in buying and selling.

But where would he get the money? He had to have cash to carry out his plans. It would take an eternity of running the dogs to save enough money.

"Mr. Deavors, you out there?" Swan called from the porch. "They got the candles lit."

Lavon returned to the parlor. He talked to women who confronted him with blushing unmarried daughters. The girls would give anything to catch a Deavors.

Mrs. Runnels worked her way through the women and stood beside Lavon. She was a skinny, fast-talking woman whose husband, Slidell, treated sick slaves, though he had no medical degree.

"And you remember my daughter Frannie, don't you?" Mrs. Runnels asked. "Frannie's takin' dancin' lessons. Tell Mr. Deavors all 'bout your dancin' lessons, honey. Come on up here. Don't be shy. He likes dancin' and all that cultured stuff, just like you. Frannie's crazy 'bout culture, Mr. Deavors."

"Yes, Frannie, tell me about your dancing," Lavon said.

Frannie mumbled about an upcoming recital. She looked into his eyes only once. She seemed afraid of him. He tried to imagine her dancing and nearly smiled. She was an attractive green-eyed girl with large breasts and a provocative pout to her lips. Her brown hair was long and silky. But she was so awkward. She seemed to lack every social grace.

Slidell Runnels joined them. He smiled at his daughter, then told Lavon how good his business was. He said he had tripled his income in the past year and taken on two apprentices.

"That's 'cause I know the insides of a nigger is different than the insides of a white man," Runnels said. His dark little eyes sparkled as he talked. "The blood's different, liver's different, everythin'. You can't treat a nigger same way as a white man."

Lavon was amused at first. He knew about these charlatans who contended slaves had to be doctored differently. They left a wake of suffering and death behind as they preyed on poor farmers who could not afford a real doctor.

But as Runnels talked about his success and the cash he had in a bank, and praised his daughter, Lavon was no longer amused. That cash was Frannie's dowry. Only the day before, Swan had mentioned Runnel's growing wealth. "Times I think I should have gone into treatin' niggers 'stead of chasin' 'em," Swan had said.

With a large cash dowry, Lavon could bring down another coffle from Virginia. Frannie was looking at him again. She was really quite an attractive girl.

Lavon smiled. "When did you say your dance recital was being held?" he asked.

As usual, Christmas was a festive occasion at the Columns. But it was the gloomiest Christmas of Athel's life. First Lawton wrote and asked permission to spend the holidays in New Orleans with school friends. Athel reluctantly sent his approval. Then, as Athel sat in the study on Christmas Eve, Cellus came in and told Athel that Nettie was pregnant and that the word in the quarters was that Lawton was the father. Athel had feared something like this. Of course, this was why the boy was anxious to attend school in New Orleans and why he didn't want to come home for Christmas.

"Are you certain Lawton is the father?" he asked. "Could it possibly be anyone else?"

"No, sir, I'm 'fraid not," Cellus said. "That girl would never let anyone near her. She been talkin' 'bout Mist' Lawton, playin' up to him. Ambrose says he knows for sure it was Mist' Lawton, says he warned the boy 'bout Nettie. No, sir, I'm dead certain myself. I know this is bad news, but I know you'll want to deal with it 'fore it gets too far 'long. Tell you the truth, that girl don't fit here, bein' neither black nor white. I 'spect she planned the whole thing to get herself sent away."

"But you, Cellus, are you certain?"

Cellus looked at Athel a long moment before answering. "Yes, Mist' Athel. I'm dead certain."

"And Lawton ran off to New Orleans rather than face the consequences of takin' advantage of the girl. . . ."

"No, sir, you bein' too harsh on Mist' Lawton, to my way of thinkin'. Don't nobody take advantage of that girl, and I'm sure she set the whole thing up. And there's just too many young girls around. Course, it would have been better if he had stayed and faced up to it. But he ain't the first to run off when he done something wrong."

"Perhaps you're right," Athel said. He realized what Cellus was taking about; there had been a time when Athel himself was young and on a drunken night had literally ridden a horse to death; that night he had run away into Natchez to stay with Aunt Delma. He found out later that Cellus had defended him to his father, just as Cellus now defended Lawton. He looked up at the man, who towered over him. Could Cellus actually be fifty? His hair had grayed when he was young, but neither his face nor any visible part of his body had aged a day in the last twenty years. Athel remembered that without Cellus' help it would have been almost impossible for him to take over the plantation when his parents were drowned. He scolded himself for taking Cellus' loyalty and intelligence for granted.

"Why don't you sit down, Cellus?" Athel asked. "And join me in a drink."

"I'd be pleased to," Cellus said, and he lowered himself into a chair beside Athel's desk.

Athel poured two drinks. He tilted his glass to Cellus, and they drank silently for a minute.

"I was just goin' over the books, Cellus," Athel said. "You've done a fine job of keepin' the books, by the way. I don't know how I could get along without you. . . ." He trailed off the sentence. He knew how much Cellus disliked flattery. "We've had a good year with the crop. A damn good year. The people have worked hard. I want to do a little somethin' more then the usual. I think in the spring I want to build new quarters for them."

"They'll be pleased, Mist' Athel," Cellus said. "Some of them shacks gettin' pretty windy as it is." He finished his whiskey.

"More whiskey?" Athel asked.

"Thank you, but I reckon not,'" Cellus said. "There's lots to do, what with Christmas tomorrow. Everybody tends to get lazy, so I better see to things." Cellus stood up. He stepped toward the door, then turned. "And, Mist' Athel, 'bout Nettie and Mist' Lawton. He's a fine boy. He'll turn out all right, don't you worry none."

"Thank you, Cellus," Athel said. "I'm sure he will. As soon as I decide what to do about Nettie, I'll let you know."

"Yessir," Cellus said, and walked out.

Athel poured more whiskey. He told himself he had to make a decision about Nettie. It would be problem enough if Lawton had had sex with a dark slave. But Nettie looked completely white, and the baby might well be a duplicate of Lawton. Athel could not endure the thought of such a child growing up on the plantation, and of course it would be unthinkable for Lawton to live with such a thing.

So there was no choice. He would have to send the girl away. He had never sold a slave, and he would not do so now. He would free her, with the understanding that she go far away and never return. She would be better off. She had always been a misfit at the Columns. He would see that she had money so that she and the child did not suffer.

He leaned back in his chair and drank more whiskey. If the girl had seduced Lawton, it was not truly his fault. But despite what Cellus had said, Athel wished Lawton had had the character to resist the girl.

"Damnit," he said aloud.

If only Lawton had told him the truth. It was weak of Lawton to run off and hide in New Orleans.

Athel closed his eyes and tried to stop thinking about Lawton. He succeeded, but only to find himself brooding about Lavon.

"What's happenin' to the Deavorses?" he said aloud.

Chapter 26

Lawton glanced anxiously at the girl who sat beside him, and then at her aunt on the opposite seat of the buggy. Neither had spoken for a quarter of an hour. They merely smiled and nodded at his comments about the wild azaleas in full flower, the budding camellias, and the white dogwood blossoms.

The girl's name was Lucinda Claiborne. Two months earlier, in January, she had accepted Lawton's marriage proposal. Normally, the marriage would have taken place in New Orleans, but Lucinda's parents were dead, and she lived with her Aunt Carrie, who was traveling with her now. The Claibornes were a prominent but impoverished family, and Aunt Carrie could not afford a proper wedding. So the wedding was being held at the Columns.

Lawton had met Lucinda in October after a month in which he saw little of his classrooms but a great deal of the inside of many whorehouses and taverns. He could not resist the sex that was so readily available, though he felt depraved each time he left a whorehouse.

On an October Sunday, Lawton attended a tea dance at a girls' academy and was introduced to Lucinda. He thought her pretty enough in a bland way. But each time he saw her—and he saw her as often as he could—her face took on new subtleties of beauty, her blue eyes grew deeper and bolder, and her auburn hair became more lustrous.

The first few times they were together, she was shy and hesitant. She deferred to Lawton and encouraged him to talk. He was gratified to watch her lose her shyness and pull out of herself as they spent more time together. Lucinda was so fresh, her smile so pure. He felt that meeting her had changed his life, indeed had saved him from a life of depravity.

Lawton was desperately in love with her.

"We'll soon be on Deavors land," he said. "See, we're crossin' the creek now. That road goes down to Benton. And this is our road. Are you tired, Lucinda? And you, Aunt Carrie? It's been a long ride out here."

"Lawton, please stop fretting about me," Lucinda said. "I'm not nearly as fragile as you think, and I've enjoyed every minute of the trip."

"I'll survive," Aunt Carrie said. "But I have to admit I'll be glad when we get there."

Lawton looked at Lucinda. Their eyes met. She smiled, and Lawton looked away.

He glanced out at a pine grove. Just a mile now, he told himself. The horses moved faster. Ed gave them more rein. Cellus sat beside Ed, and behind them Essie drove a wagon that held their luggage.

Aunt Delma had been the only member of the family to meet the boat. She had taken Lawton aside and told him that Tillman had run away again. It was nothing serious, she added. But Estelle had gone to bed with a splitting headache. Joleen had stayed with her mother, and Athel had gone out with a group of slaves to find Tillman.

Aunt Delma had taken them to her house for tea. Well, he remembered with a smile, Aunt Carrie and Lucinda had tea. Aunt Delma had sipped Madeira from a teacup, and she had served whiskey to Lawton.

While Lucinda and her aunt napped, Aunt Delma had given Lawton the news. Most of it was routine and had filled up his mother's letters. And he had seen his mother and father in February when they visited New Orleans to meet Lucinda and make plans for the wedding.

Finally Aunt Delma leaned closer. She shook her head. "Your father won't admit it, Lawton, but I think you ought to know," she said. "He's worried sick about his brother. Lavon has become too sorry to kill. He's workin' with a wretched man with slave dogs. Named Purvis Swan. He's even whippin' slaves. Your father gave him money to return to Europe, and instead he brought down slaves and sold them at public auction. A Deavors, Lawton, sellin' flesh in the Natchez streets! I wish Athel would do something. Run him out of town, if need be. But you know your father. He simply worries about it."

Lawton knew of his uncle's activities, and he was upset by them. Aunt Delma's concern for his father made him worry. His father had seemed exhausted and preoccupied when he visited New Orleans, but Lawton thought that had been because of Nettie. Lawton and his father had discussed Nettie, and Lawton had apologized for not telling his father about the affair. Lawton had felt bad, and his dormant guilt had flared up. Now he realized that Lavon's activities must also have contributed to his father's mood.

Lawton brushed beads of perspiration from his forehead. He thought of Nettie, pregnant with his child. He thought of seeing Joleen again. He worried about Tillman. His good mood had evaporated. He twisted in the seat.

Ed drove past the slat gate. "This is it!" Lawton said. "We're home. This is the Columns."

He strained forward in the seat. The fields were

plowed for planting, and he smelled the freshly turned earth. He saw a line of slaves on the horizon. He heard a shout. Filch was standing up in the stirrups of his horse, waving at Lawton. Lawton called back. Filch galloped for the house. The carriage moved faster. They passed the magnolia grove, the flowerbeds, the wall. The house came into sight. The carriage pulled up. Cellus opened the door.

Lawton looked at the house. No one appeared. His anxiety deepened. Something was wrong. Something had happened to Tillman. . . .

His mother and father appeared from around the back of the house. Tillman followed. There was kissing and hugging, and Lawton introduced his brother to Lucinda and Aunt Carrie. He wondered about Joleen. Perhaps she didn't want to see him. The next moment, she was at his side. She hugged him, and they looked at each other. There was a tinge of sexual memory, but it was swept away in her sweet smile and obvious happiness at his return. Joleen hugged Lucinda. Slowly the house slaves came out, and they were introduced.

Lawton looked at his family, at the slaves. He smelled the earth. He glanced at Lucinda. Suddenly he was very happy.

There was a week of parties, bridal showers, and frenzied activity. The wedding rehearsal was held Friday evening, and afterward Lawton went into Natchez with several friends for a bachelor party that ended up on Annie Easter's barge at three in the morning. His friends satisfied their drunken lust with the mulatto whores, but Lawton refused to touch a woman. He bought the time of a quadroon named Eugenie and listened to her play the spinet. It was nine in the morning when he returned to the Columns. He went straight to bed but slept only two hours.

The wedding was held at two o'clock in the gallery. The hall was decorated with boughs of dogwood and ropes of purple bougainvillea. A hundred guests attended. The Reverend Claude Dawson of the Benton Presbyterian Church performed the ceremony. Before the service, Miss Bernadine Claudette of Natchez played the spinet and an Italian tenor sang.

Lucinda drew gasps and whispers of approval as she walked down the aisle in a white silk dress that had been in her family for generations. Since she had no close living male relative, she was given away by the Deavorses' neighbor Haskell Sumrall. Joleen was maid of honor. Lawton's father was his best man.

Lawton and Athel stared at each other a moment as Lawton took the ring. The look that passed between them was silent acknowledgment that Lawton was a man now, that his transgression with Nettie was something of the past. Lawton was not yet twenty, but everyone knew this wedding marked him as a grown man and heir to the Columns.

Following the ceremony, the guests took three hours to rest and refresh themselves, some at the Columns and others at nearby plantations that had offered their hospitality. Forty slaves spent those three hours working furiously to prepare the grounds and the house for the reception.

Guests began arriving at six o'clock. They came from all over Mississippi and Louisiana. Their carriages stretched for a mile down the driveway. By eight there were nearly four hundred guests at the Columns. They were elegantly dressed, and their gifts filled table after table beneath a tent on the front lawn.

Two orchestras provided music. One group sat on a platform at the back of the gallery. The other was on a flower-decked platform in the front yard. Among the oleander bushes were eight tables filled with green ham, cured ham, roast beef, roast chicken, roast turkey, grilled trout and catfish, pheasant, quail, shrimp, crawfish, and oysters. Four calves and four suckling pigs were grilled in pits in the side yard. Six other tables were spread about the house and lawn. Behind each stood two slaves serving punch, whiskey, rum, wine, port, sherry, Madeira, and brandy. A dozen slaves moved among the guests, continually refilling their glasses with champagne.

As Lawton and Lucinda turned from a group of

guests, Athel called them onto the porch and introduced them to Governor Brandon. The governor asked of Lawton's plans and seemed pleased that he planned to stay on the plantation instead of returning to New Orleans.

"Ah, there's Lieutenant Davis," Athel said. "I was hoping he would be on leave and able to attend."

Lawton turned to see a tall man in uniform coming up the steps. For a man of his size, he moved with unexpected grace. The lieutenant's features were sharp and his nose aquiline. He was a handsome and imposing figure in his uniform, and his gray-blue eyes looked directly at Lawton in a way that was disturbing. But he smiled as he joined them, and the smile was gentle and gracious.

He shook hands with Athel and the governor.

"Lieutenant Davis, may I present my son Lawton and my daughter-in-law, Lucinda," Athel said. "Lawton, Lucinda, this is Lieutenant Jefferson Davis, from down in Wilkinson County."

Davis shook hands with Lawton and offered his congratulations on the marriage. Lawton was curious about the man, and more curious still when he noticed a facial tic that made Davis blink from time to time. When these tics grew particularly bad, Davis even had trouble keeping his hands from shaking.

"I understand you're thinking of resigning your commission and growing cotton in Mississippi," Governor Brandon said.

"Yes, that's a strong possibility, though I would miss the army," Davis said. "If it becomes a necessity, leaving the army, I shall surely live in Mississippi."

There was talk of the current harvest and of European cotton markets. Finally Davis excused himself.

"Poor fellow," Athel said. "He suffered a severe attack of pneumonia up in the Northwest. As a result, he has attacks of neuralgia and that tic of the eyes."

"Yes, I'm afraid the army is no career for a man in his condition," the governor said.

Lawton and Lucinda left their father and the governor and began to circulate among the guests. Lawton was weary, exhilarated, and slightly drunk. He enjoyed being host and showing off his bride. Lucinda was quiet at first, but he insisted she drink some champagne, and she began to blossom, as he knew she would. Dusk grew deep, and candelabra were lit, along with lanterns strung among the trees.

People would talk about the reception for weeks, but by the time it reached its peak of dancing and drunkenness, Lawton and Lucinda were nearing Aunt Delma's Natchez home in a carriage.

Lawton was nervous and hesitant when Lucinda came from the dressing room and joined him in bed. Candlelight bathed her face in new beauty. Lawton kissed her lips gently. She was so lovely and fragile and pure. He did not want to hurt her or frighten her. He was hesitant to put his hands on her body. She touched him first, stroking his cheek.

Lawton undressed Lucinda very slowly. He had fantasized her untouched body. And now she lay naked beside him, slim and pale. Tenderly he kissed her freckled breasts and small red nipples.

"You're so beautiful tonight," he whispered. "I love you."

"I love you, too," she said.

Lucinda's fingers played with his hair as he kissed her lips. He slid down and sucked the nipples. His fingers caressed her stomach. He felt the stiffness of her body. He touched her cool thighs. He hesitated. His hand barely touched the red hairs. He moved up again and kissed her lips. Her body was rigid now.

"Lucinda, we can wait, if you . . ."

"No, Lawton. Please . . . I want you to. . . ."

He kissed her eyes and found it difficult to think of sex with her now, to think of possessing and invading her body. Yet he wanted her beyond all reason. She had lived in his fantasies. He was obsessed with her slim, pale body.

His penis was not stiff, though he was very aroused. He kissed her breasts. He licked her stomach. His fingers stroked the soft nipples. His mouth brushed the curly hairs. Lucinda tensed.

He jerked his head away. He couldn't. He thought of Joleen.

"What's wrong, Lawton?" Lucinda asked.

"Nothin', Lucinda. I . . . I love you. I want you very much. . . ."

She kissed his cheek. He lay beside her. He stared into her eyes. Her cheeks were flushed. He wanted her so much. Yet his penis wasn't hard. He wanted to kiss her all over. But he couldn't. What would she think of him? And he wanted to slide his penis beneath those red hairs. But her body was so stiff. He would hurt her. She would be dry. She would hate it. She wasn't some nigger or some whore.

"I . . . Lucinda . . . I love you. I want to explain that . . ."

She put a finger to his lips. She kissed his cheek again. "Lawton, we're both exhausted and all. Let's not talk now. Why don't we just rest a few minutes? I love you, too."

"All right, Lucinda." He kissed her shoulder. They lay curled together. He kissed her hair. They did not speak again. Soon the day's excitement and drinking overcame them, and they slept.

Chapter 27

The next day, Lavon married Frannie in the Blood of the Lamb Baptist Church. Lorenzo Dow, the circuit-riding preacher, performed the ceremony and followed it with a half-hour sermon on sin and degradation. The fattest girl Lavon had ever seen was maid of honor. Purvis Swan was best man. Frannie's family held a reception in their home, a six-room glorified dog-trot house on the edge of Natchez. Two fiddlers provided music for the fifty guests. They drank whiskey, rum, and red wine that Lavon found decent enough.

Lavon drank many glasses of the wine. He endured the guests by calculating again and again the profits he and Swan could expect with the money Frannie's father had provided as dowry. Lavon had wanted to marry Frannie in January, but her family had insisted they have "a proper courtship and engagement." Soon, soon, he told himself, he would start amassing money. Already he was looking over available land and planning his plantation. And the fantasy of his plantation always led to the one in which he owned the Columns and Athel and his family came begging to him.

When he took Frannie back to the small house he had rented, he was drunk. Frannie had allowed him nothing more than a few kisses during their engagement. At first he had been content with his frequent trips to the better whorehouses, as well as an occasional friend of Frannie's who thought the offering of a ripe young body might persuade Lavon to change his choice of a wife.

But Frannie was an attractive girl, and she had a sexiness that gradually made her more and more desirable to Lavon. He was angry at her refusal to sleep with him before the marriage. When he staggered into the bedroom on his wedding day, he turned on Frannie and ripped off her dress. She resisted, and he threw her onto the bed.

Her resistance goaded him. He was rough with her. He bit her nipples and made her gasp with pain when he shoved his fingers into her vagina. The abuse aroused Frannie. She began to respond. Her nipples tightened and grew hard. She sucked at his lips and nibbled at his fingers.

Frannie was wet when he shoved his penis into her vagina. He took her with all his strength and fury, as though to make her pay for his plight. He climaxed quickly and collapsed. In five minutes he was snoring.

Lavon and Swan left at dawn the next day for Richmond. They spent three weeks at the Virginia market, plantation, and sheriff sales. They were tougher and shrewder in bargaining. They insisted on a written guarantee of a slave's good health and character. Finally they formed a coffle of seventy-six slaves, mostly mechanics and prime field hands. The heat was less oppressive than on the trek the previous September. They maintained a far slower pace. They made sure the slaves had enough rest and good food. Halfway down, they hired a doctor to examine the slaves and treat four who were ill with minor ailments. One slave died on the trace, but Lavon was elated to reach Natchez with seventy-five slaves.

After the debacle of their last sale, they had a bad reputation, and the first day they sold only one slave. Lavon made a show of giving a healthy slave to a farmer who had purchased a dying slave from them in September. He displayed the warrants attesting to the slaves' good health and character. He had a Natchez doctor examine the slaves and pronounce them healthy. It was planting time, and skilled slaves were in demand. Sales picked up. Within two weeks they had sold all their slaves. The possession of nearly twenty-five thousand dollars did much to ease what guilt Lavon felt. He still detested being a slave dealer, but he told himself it was only temporary and that he had taken damn good care of the niggers on this trip. He purchased fifty acres of rich cotton soil and dreamed of his plantation and of someday adding this acreage to the Columns.

He bought an expensive suit from a tailor, and on a hot April afternoon he sat in the parlor of the Stanton Hotel and drank brandy. He told himself that someday he would own half the land in the county. He would treat his niggers well. He would be a man of honor and self-respect, and his brother and his family would become dependent on him for everything. Oh, once they became abject, he would be generous with them, of course.

"Lavon, I've been insulted!"

Frannie's whining voice cut into his thoughts. He turned as she perched on the chair beside him. Her eyes were red from crying.

"Christ, what happened?" he asked.

"The Blue Bird Tea Room," she said. "On High Street. They didn't even want to serve me. I had to cause a scene to get served."

"Why did you go there, Frannie?"

"I'm as good as anybody," she said, and sniffled. "And the ladies there, Lavon. They snickered, and I know they were talkin' about my dress. Lavon, do somethin'. You're a Deavors. . . ."

He finished his brandy and stood up. "I'm going to do something, Frannie. In the meantime, you do as I've told you, and forget your social pretensions. Hell, a few months ago you wouldn't have thought of having tea there. Now, come on. I'm tired, and I want to go home."

He marched her to the house he had come to despise. They did not speak. He glanced at her dress. It was ill-fitting and out of fashion, though it was not cheap. He could easily imagine the ladies snickering at her. His Aunt Delma might well have been there. Or even Estelle. He hated them all for insulting his wife. And goddamnit, they would pay. But he hated Frannie as much. He would make her into a proper lady if it killed her.

In early May, Lavon and Swan brought down one hundred and twelve slaves from Virginia. Two died during the march. They made a handsome profit. They hired two men to run the dogs and whip the slaves and paid them a wage from the money they took in. Lavon bought more land, including sixty acres adjacent to the Columns. He turned a great deal of business to Frannie's father in return for a fee.

Lavon often served on the slave patrols. He was always chosen as leader. Any patrol he headed was far more efficient and more active than the usual group. Therefore he returned more runaways, and many farmers became indebted to him. He enjoyed this petty prestige and realized that someday he could turn the favors to his advantage.

On a July night one of his patrols captured four runaways belonging to a former Ohio farmer who had moved to Mississippi the previous year. The next day the man insisted on buying Lavon drinks. The day was in the high nineties, and they drank in a tavern with an open front. Lavon glanced across the street and stiffened as he saw his Aunt Delma and Joleen talking to a man Lavon vaguely recognized. He was a lawyer, the German lawyer he had met the previous summer at Aunt Delma's. He paid no attention to the man, whom he remembered as a fop and a fool. But he stared at Joleen's beautiful face and the thrust of her breasts against her dress. He had forgotten how beautiful and provocative she was.

"I know that fella there," the farmer said. "Took me a minute, but I know him now. Used to live up to Ohio. Town called Cincinnati, I think. He's done some lawyerin' for my brother. Good man in court, my brother said. Good man all around."

"I met him," Lavon said. "I took him to be a fool."

"Well, he may be, sir. But I wouldn't want to tell him that to his face. Word is he killed a man in a duel 'count of bein' insulted. That was a few years back. Clauson, that there's his name. He's a hot-tempered one, that fella. But he sure knowed the law. My brother hated to give up his services."

Lavon turned to the farmer. Surely he wasn't talking about the man Lavon had met at Aunt Delma's, the one who stood across the street. "You're sure this is the same man? And your brother gave up his services because he fought a duel, because of his temper?"

"Hell, no, Mr. Deavors," the farmer said. "That didn't have nothin' to do with it. My brother found out Clauson's one of them bloody Christ-killers. He didn't want no truck with no Jew. . . ."

Chapter 28

Aaron Clauson forced his horse through the storm. The road was deep in mud. He hunched against the rain that lashed his face. The rain's sound, as well as the thunder and lightning, blunted any noises that might have warned him of a slave patrol's approach. He shook his head and wiped water from his eyes with the back of his hand. For over an hour a raincoat had protected him from the storm, but with the temperature hovering at ninety-five and the humidity high, he had to discard it.

He was hesitant to ride fast, yet he was desperate. Clarence, the free Negro, and eleven runaways were hiding in a grove of catawba trees three hours south of Natchez. Aaron had arranged for their passage on a ship to Mexico. At midnight they were to meet a longboat that would take them to the ship. But if they left their cover and tried to reach the river, they would almost surely be intercepted by one of the many patrols that was out tonight. Aaron feared that Clarence would follow through with their plan, because he did not know of the news that had reached Adams County earlier in the day. Two weeks ago, up in Virginia, a Negro named Nat Turner had led a slave rebellion. Sixty whites had been killed by the slaves, and in putting down the rebellion, whites had killed scores of Negroes. Turner was still at large.

For hours rumors had spread fear and hatred through Adams County. By coincidence, two runaway slaves in Natchez had tried to steal some pork and fatback from an elderly white woman, and when she resisted, they struck the woman before fleeing. Aaron had heard the true version from the woman's brother at the courthouse in the early afternoon, but by the time he heard the incident discussed in a tavern at early dusk, it had been blown out of proportion. Drunken and hate-filled farmers and laborers tried to outdo one another with tales of how the woman had been raped and butchered. Every man in the tavern had some additional tale of how slaves were running away to the swamps and arming themselves. The slaves had known of the Turner uprising in advance, an old man said. The man claimed he heard it from a government official.

"They's multitudes of niggers armed all over," he said. "And word is the Turner nigger hisself, he ain't sittin' up there to Virginny. He's headed this way."

"They'll swarm out of the swamps, armed tooth and toenail, and kill and rape and loot," someone else said. "Why we sittin' 'round? Shit, I don't own no niggers, and I say to hell with them as do. We got to act first."

"I say kill ever' nigger in the county," a gap-toothed man said. "We can't take no chances."

"I go 'long with Cyrus," another man said. "Lord God, they over two thousand nigger men 'round Natchez. Arm them niggers, and we ain't got no chance. And word is, they's abolitionists and Yankee agents brimmin' with money and guns been seen travelin' all over Mississippi the past week, stirrin' up the niggers."

As he left the tavern, Aaron saw a group of whites chase down a lone black man. The man claimed he was on an errand for his master, but he had no pass. The law requiring passes for slaves away from their masters was never enforced. When Aaron saw the whites turn into a mob that beat the Negro to the ground, he realized how nasty the mood was. Fortunately, the slave's owner was nearby and rescued him.

Another slave, caught on the open road a few minutes before Aaron rode by, was less fortunate. It was night by then, and the slave tried to escape from a group of loggers. They ran him down. In his fear, he struck a white man. He was knocked to the ground and kicked to death.

Aaron's tensed horse shied and reared up. He gripped the reins tightly as the horse lurched to the left. In a flash of lightning Aaron saw the coiled snake. He steadied his horse and slowed its pace. He had seen many snakes on the road tonight, panicked and driven from cover by the storm.

A quarter of an hour later the rain let up. The thunder became a murmur. The lightning was feeble through the leaves and moss. Aaron rode faster. He went around a sharp curve and came on a dismounted slave patrol. They were passing around a jug. Two men jerked up their rifles and followed Aaron's approach through their sights.

"Whoa, sir, stop and declare yourself," an elderly man said.

Aaron reined up. The rifles were lowered, but the men gathered around him. A lantern was thrust up, and the men examined his face. Aaron thought he had seen one of the men. He dared not lie about his name.

"My name is Aaron Clauson, sir," he said. "What is the meaning of this? Why are you stopping me?"

"What are you doin' out this time of night, Mr. Clauson?" the old man asked. He was obviously the patrol's leader.

"Why, sir, I don't believe that's any of your affair," Aaron said, but immediately he regretted his choice of a haughty and defiant manner. These men were drunk and exhausted by the heat.

"We don't need no smart aleck tonight," a fat man called from the back of the group. "Why, he talks like a Yankee."

"Mr. Clauson, it's been a long day for us," the leader said. "Now, you know 'bout the news from up to Virginny. 'Bout the niggers risin' up and killin' all them whites. Word is, the head nigger himself is headin' this way. We a duly sworn patrol, and we intend to do our duty. Not only is the woods crawling with armed niggers, but we got the word they teemin' with Yankee agents, too."

"I see, of course," Aaron said. "I heard of the Virginia uprising. It's just that . . . I was frightened when I rode up on your group and you had rifles pointed at me. Every time I hear a sound in the bushes, I'm afraid it's some slave or abolitionist. Thank God there are patrols on all the roads."

"But what you doin' out on a back road in a rainstorm this time of night?" the fat man asked. " 'Specially if you so all-fired scared of the niggers?"

"I'm a lawyer," Aaron said. "I have a client down here who needs to see me tonight."

The man with the lantern stepped forward. "Wouldn't no lawyer go out on a night like this. Say, lawyer, ain't I seen you to Natchez? Just a few days ago. I done took a wagon load of Madeira from the boat up to Miz Delma Deavors' place. You was havin' tea with her, sittin' out in the yard."

"That's right," Aaron said. "Now I remember you. I couldn't see your face in the dark."

"Well, then, you not no abolitionist," the leader said. "Not if Miz Delma knows you good 'nough to take tea with you. You headin' down to the Columns to do business with the Deavorses?"

"I . . . yes . . . yes, I'm going to the Deavorses' plantation," Aaron said. "Athel Deavors sent an urgent message asking me to ride down at once. Something to do with his slaves. I think he must be worried about the . . . insurrection. He wants my advice about his slaves. Hell, as far as I'm concerned, he can kill the lot of them." The lie came easily, and Aaron knew it would please these angry men.

"Damn right, sir," the fat man shouted.

"We had that in mind, just talkin' 'bout it," someone else said.

"You be careful," the leader said. "Area's swarmin' with dangerous niggers. That Turner nigger killed near to a thousand up in Hampton County, Virginny, and we aim to see that don't happen here, if we have to kill ten thousand niggers 'fore sunup."

"I'll be careful," Aaron said.

"They 'nother patrol few miles down the road," the leader said. "So you not goin' to be far from help. Matter of fact, that there patrol's headed by a Deavors. Lavon Deavors. He's the brother, I think. The one what sells niggers. Guess he don't have much truck with his family."

"No, not from what I hear," Aaron said.

He nodded to the men and eased his horse from the group. He rode slowly until he was out of sight, then moved the horse into a gallop. The patrol that the leader mentioned might well be near the catawba grove. Aaron remembered the Deavors brother from the June party of the previous year. Now it seemed he had been disowned by his family and reduced to hunting runaways and selling slaves. The Deavorses would hate that, Aaron knew. They prided themselves on being humane masters. They neither bought nor sold slaves.

But they owned human beings! Owned them as though they were animals. It was only a rationalization for such planters to think of themselves as humane. . . . But Aaron was too tense and too exhausted for moral speculation. The horse galloped through a deep mudhole. Mud was thrown up into Aaron's face. He wiped the mud away and took a deep breath that brought the smell of festering lilies.

He thought of the patrol he had encountered and the one ahead. Normally men tried to avoid the legal duty that demanded they give up a week of nights every three months to ride with a patrol. But with word of the Turner insurrection and the fear of an uprising in Adams County, men were flooding the patrols. From what Aaron had heard, many patrols included men who were not legally sworn to the oath. There was always a residue of hatred of Negroes among poorer farmers and laborers. Now they were worried about their families, goaded by the damp heat, and ready to believe any rumor they heard. The slave patrols gave them some sense of legality for their fear and hatred.

A finger of lightning lit a cypress tree. Snakes crawled about the roots that grew twisted above the ground. Aaron felt terribly alone. His redeeming sense of humor failed him. At times he could become self-amused at his situation here among these primitive, slave-owning Christians. But not tonight. These vaguely legal patrols reminded him of vaguely legal pogroms in

Germany and Poland. He had come to America twenty-four years ago, when he was nine. But his memory of pogroms was vivid.

"I know you're lonely down there in Mississippi," Levi Coffin had told Aaron earlier in the summer when Aaron returned to Cincinnati for a visit. "You should think of taking a wife, Aaron. Marry some Natchez girl. It will help you seem a more normal part of the community."

Take a wife? Aaron said to himself. Yes, he would like to get married. But who could he live with? Who could he trust? Who could he burden with the secret of his work? And actually he had two secrets. He considered himself an agnostic, but he felt a strong sense of being Jewish. And at times the religious beliefs surfaced, to surprise him with their tenacity.

He thought he had learned to control his anger. On many occasions he had listened to anti-Jewish talk and held his wrath in check. For the greater good of his work, he would continue to submerge what he was. His pose had worked. It would have been more difficult, probably impossible, if it were known he was Jewish. Sooner or later his background would probably be discovered, but until then his pose served him well.

What would he tell his bride if he got married? Would he tell her the truth? Would he . . . convert? "No," he muttered. He would pose. And lie. But he would not make that public gesture of repudiation.

And which of the pretty slave-owning girls would he consider as a wife?

As always, he thought of Joleen Deavors. And as always, he told himself that the largest part of her attraction was physical. Yet he couldn't deny that he was drawn to the girl for more reasons than her beautiful face and body. Each time he saw Joleen, she seemed more mature and more intelligent. She had changed a great deal since the night of her birthday party in Natchez last fall. She was much more poised with him. She had gained confidence, and her wit could be deadly. At times he feared she saw through his pose. But she was young and spoiled, and in a crisis she would probably revert to type and be helpless or even give him away.

He shook his head and shifted in the saddle. Would this ride never end? And would he never . . . ?

Aaron almost rode into the dangling legs before he saw the body. The horse reared and nearly threw Aaron. He reined the horse in and looked around at the black man hanging from an oak tree. Blood ran from the man's eye sockets, his nose, his mouth, and the slashed neck. The blood fell over his chest and past the intestines that dripped from his stomach.

Aaron's mouth opened. His stomach heaved. His nostrils drew in the smell of blood. He dry-heaved twice, three times. He could barely control the horse, but finally reined him down. Nausea swelled at the back of his throat. He tasted bile. He drooped forward in the saddle and rode on a mile while he sucked in gulps of humid air.

He realized he was passing through the grove of tall ferns. At the end of the grove was the barely visible trail that led to the catawba trees. He rode down the trail and reached the catawbas. Coals glowed in a shallow pit. The coals lit the body of a black man.

Aaron reined in his horse. With his other hand he fumbled the covers from his pistols. A shot jerked his head up. Someone shouted. There was a scream. He glanced around at the darkness. He was too late. And what could one man do against a patrol?

He rode on slowly. There were gunshots and screams in the darkness. He saw the distant light of torches. This was madness, he told himself. He could do nothing now. He should leave, ride back to the other patrol and confess his fear and provide an alibi for himself. It was foolish to risk the entire operation with his capture. . . .

"Hey, nigger, whooee, we goin' to have your balls!"

Aaron saw a torch moving nearer. He heard horses. There was a scream.

"Massuh, don't do it . . . I'm sorry . . . Clarence, help me!"

"He's gettin' away," someone shouted.

"No, there he goes! Mr. Deavors, we done flushed 'nother nigger."

"Don't kill him. Take him alive."

A blur of movement turned Aaron's head to the left. He saw the torches moving, and in front of him he saw a black man stumbling through a bed of ferns. Two white men were riding leisurely. Aaron moved his horse toward the men, keeping behind the cover of the ferns and trees.

"Mr. Deavors don't want us to kill the nigger," the lead rider called.

"I say have his black balls," the second rider said. "Don't pay no mind to Deavors."

Aaron pulled a pistol. The sound of his horse startled the lead rider, who reached for his own pistol. But he was too slow. Aaron killed him with a shot through the chest.

"Yankees!" the second man shouted. He dropped his torch and fired. The shot creased Aaron's left shoulder. Pain scalded the arm. Aaron rode toward the man and brought up his other pistol. The shot blew away half the man's face.

The slave had disappeared. Aaron reined in his horse. His left arm hung useless in its pain. The pain made his stomach churn. He pulled the rifle from his saddle. He heard horses moving closer. More torches were visible now. Aaron swallowed and tasted blood; he felt weak. There was nothing he could do. He had to escape. He galloped away from the approaching horses.

"Over here, Mr. Deavors!" someone shouted. "I think I see him. And Lord Jesus, there's Rancy dead on the ground. Done been murdered!"

A shot cracked past Aaron's head. He lowered his body over the horse and rode for the cover of a willow tree. Now he had to move slowly, because it was difficult to see. A limb creased his ear. Vines and moss slapped his face. He breathed through his mouth. He tasted bile and blood.

A form blurred into his sight—a man on horseback with a pistol raised. Aaron tried to bring up his rifle, but his left arm was useless and the movement of his right arm was slow. The rider closed on him.

A shot . . . pain ripped his side. Through a haze he saw the man bring up another pistol. Aaron rode straight for the man. His boldness made the man hesitate a moment. In that moment Aaron swung his rifle and shot the man in the face. The man dropped from the saddle.

The rifle fell from Aaron's hand. He slumped forward and lost the reins. He dug his fingers into the horse's mane. His strength was gone. Chills raked his body.

There were shouts and the sound of horses from all around, yet they seemed far away. Aaron's horse galloped on. Suddenly the horse reared up. Aaron was thrown to the ground. The shock of pain made him vomit. Spasms jerked his body. He swallowed so much blood he nearly choked.

"I hear his horse over this way," someone shouted.

Aaron clawed at the grass and pulled himself beneath the limbs of a weeping willow. He lay on his back and gave in to his agony.

There were sounds approaching the willow, but he heard them through a haze. Then he was unconscious.

BOOK IV

Girl into Woman

Chapter 29

A shot brought Joleen out of bed. She stood at the window and looked past the dark lawn to the first light of morning. It had been a nightmare of a night, unlike anything she had ever experienced. Even before word arrived about the Virginia insurrection, there had been an odd, frightened feeling at the Columns. She felt it while walking through the quarters in the late afternoon.

Her mother was worried about the effect of the news on their people. Her father was more concerned with the reaction of the county's white people. He called in Ed and the drivers and told them to keep the slaves in their houses. They were not to go out under any circumstances.

A slave patrol rode up at dusk, during a rainstorm, and Joleen hid inside the door while her father and Lawton talked to the men. She recognized only one, a man named Hickerson, who owned a small farm that bordered the Columns. The men were red-faced. They passed a jug around. They were very excited and angry.

The men insisted they be allowed to search the plantation for runaways and Yankee agents and to make certain all the Deavorses' slaves were locked up. Her father refused. There were angry words and more profanity than Joleen had ever heard. Finally the men left.

A few minutes later her father and Lawton took their rifles and rode off to make sure no strangers were on the plantation. Before he left, her father called Cellus into the study. He gave Cellus a rifle and told him to look after the family. Joleen had never seen a Deavors slave with a gun. She knew it was against the law to arm a slave under any circumstances.

Supper was late. Everyone was quiet. No one ate much. Haskell Sumrall and five other men rode over. They talked on the porch. Joleen heard part of their conversation. They had all taken precautions against marauding slaves, but their main fear was the patrols that seemed to be running wild. There were tales of killings and brutality not seen in the county for years.

Against her will, Joleen was sent up to bed early. She resented the fact that Lawton talked with the men and took part in guarding the plantation. He seemed very grown-up and confident. Joleen felt she was being treated like a child. Then she realized that Lucinda was worried about Lawton's safety and that Tillman was terrified, so she sat with them until they could fall asleep.

Sleep did not come for Joleen, except for a few fitful naps. Twice she heard distant gunfire. Once while she stood at the window she saw torches on the horizon. A minute later someone rode off from the house in the direction of the light. In the hours she lay awake, during the thunderstorms and smothering heat, her mind conjured up frightful pictures from the talk she had heard. She saw the drunken, hate-filled men hunting down slaves and killing them.

She did not understand this. She knew a few men were bad masters. She knew that sometimes a slave did something bad or ran away and he had to be punished. But all the slaves here at the Columns were happy. Except for Essie. Weren't they? And the slaves on the other plantations were happy. How could these white men kill slaves who were content and obedient and belonged to other white men?

Now she watched the sky blaze from pink to red behind black clouds on the horizon. She wondered about the shots she had heard. When would all this end? What had happened during the night? Was everyone all right? She felt she had been isolated in her room for an eternity. Surely she could go down now. It was daybreak.

She dressed and went down the stairs. Her mother was asleep in the parlor. The house was quiet. Joleen heard birds outside. A rooster crowed. The stillness in the house was ominous. Then she heard horsemen up on the road. Someone shouted from the yard. Joleen ran toward the gallery. Cellus stood in the door. She stopped. Cellus was holding a rifle.

He glanced past Joleen to her mother, then backed into the gallery. Joleen followed him.

"Better get back upstairs, Miss Joleen," he said. "Men ridin' up."

"Who are they, Cellus? Another patrol? What all happened durin' the night? Is everybody all right?"

"Everybody's fine," he said. "But these men in the patrols, they mighty riled up. Your daddy'd want you upstairs. . . ."

There were shouts from the front. Cellus ran into the study, across the gallery from the parlor. He stood hidden behind a curtain, his gun raised. Joleen crept to the door. Her father and Lawton stood on the front porch. They each held a rifle.

Filch rode up to the porch. "It's a patrol, Mist' Athel," he said. "Might be couple dozen men. They got somebody in a wagon. Couldn't make out clear, but seems to be a white man."

"All right, Filch," Athel said. "Go on back to the quarters. Keep all the people inside."

Filch rode around the house a moment before the horsemen appeared at the end of the wall.

Estelle came from the parlor. "Go upstairs, Joleen," she said.

"Just a minute, Mother," Joleen said. "I'm goin'."

But she did not move. The horsemen were reining up. They looked fierce and menacing. A wagon pulled up among the men. The leader dismounted and walked up the steps.

"Mornin', Mister Deavors," the man said.

"Mornin'," Athel said. "What brings you here, sir? All my niggers are locked up and guarded in the quarters, and there've been no strangers on my property."

"No, sir, well, that wasn't what we come for," the man said. He glanced back at the wagon.

"Joleen, go upstairs," Estelle said.

"Yes'm, I'm goin'," Joleen said. But she strained for a look at the man in the wagon. She couldn't see him, and her mother was tugging at her arm.

Then two men moved aside. Joleen gasped. The man in the wagon looked like Aaron! She took a step. Her heart was pounding. The man's eyes were closed. His face was cut and bruised and caked with mud. There were rags wrapped around his body, and they were the color of dried blood. He didn't even seem to be breathing!

"See, they was this awful shootin' up the road a piece, Mr. Deavors," the leader said. "Patrol shot it out with these vicious niggers. And then this here white man come ridin' along, and, well, best as we can make out, he done killed three of our men."

"And we're goin' to make the bastard pay!" someone shouted. The other men nodded and cursed.

"Joleen, I won't tell you again . . ."

Joleen pulled from her mother's hand. "No, Mother, do somethin'. That's Aaron . . . Aaron Clauson."

"Yes, but I don't see how the Columns is involved," Athel said. "Who is this man? He needs a doctor right away. I can see that from here."

"You don't recognize him?" the leader asked. "See, that there's just it. He claims to know you. Says he was on his way down here to do business. We done found him after the shootin', and he claimed he was just ridin' 'long and got caught up in the shootin'. And you don't even know the fella. . . ."

Athel walked down the steps. "Now, just a minute. He does look familiar. Lawton, isn't that the lawyer who visits your Aunt Delma? Clauson? Aaron Clauson? Sir, I must insist you get a doctor for the man immediately."

"Yessir, I think it is," Lawton said.

"So you do know him, Mr. Deavors?" the leader asked.

"I know him socially. But I've never done business with him."

"Then he's not your lawyer. He wasn't comin' down here to see you."

"Come on, let's get on with 'em!" someone shouted.

"Just a minute," Athel said. "I don't know the man well, but he's a friend of my aunt's. I certainly don't think he's the kind of man to get involved in any shootin'."

"But he's not your lawyer? He wasn't ridin' here last night to see you on urgent business?"

"Well, no . . ."

"Then he was lyin' through his teeth, Mr. Deavors," the leader said. " 'Cause that there's the excuse he give us. Wouldn't be no other reason on earth for him to be ridin' in a rainstorm in the middle of nowhere at midnight, what with Yankees and dangerous niggers all 'round. So he did kill them three men."

"All right, that may be so," Athel said. "But that's for a court to decide. And damnit, he needs a doctor. Sir, I insist you take him to the doctor in Benton right away. And then see that he's turned over to the sheriff."

"Yessir, you got my word," the leader said. "I'll do my best. But Lord God, three men murdered, and my bunch mighty riled up. Well, we better get a move on."

Joleen took a hesitant step. They were going to take Aaron away. He would die. Or they would kill him. She knew from the way the men looked at Aaron that they would kill him.

"No!" she cried. She ran onto the porch.

Everyone turned to look at her.

"Joleen, get back into the house," Athel said.

"Daddy, don't let them take him away. He's goin' to die. They're goin' to kill him."

"The leader promised me they'll take care of him."

"He needs help right now. He's hurt so bad. Oh, look at his face! Please take him inside and send for the doctor."

"We couldn't give him up, miss," the leader said. "Not with the evidence we got 'gainst him."

"Lawton, take your sister into the house," Athel said.

"Come on, Joleen," Lawton said.

He put his hand on her arm. She pulled free. She swallowed back her tears.

"No," she said. The lie came without thought. "Daddy, he . . . he was comin' down to the plantation last night . . ."

"What do you mean, Joleen? I don't . . ."

"He . . . he was comin' to see me," she said.

"Comin' to see you?" Athel asked. "In the middle of the night? Why would he do that, Joleen? I don't understand."

"Aaron's come down here to see me before . . . at night," she said. "And he was comin' last night, late. And so he certainly wasn't involved in any shootin'."

Athel stepped closer to Joleen. "Do you realize what you're sayin'?" he whispered. "Why would you do such a thing? Meet a man at night."

"Oh, Daddy, I . . . I didn't do anything bad with Aaron," she said. "He's so hurt. Please help him. Please . . ."

Athel stared at Joleen. She dared not look from his questioning eyes, but she could not bear the hurt she saw. Finally Athel walked back to the men.

"You heard what my daughter said. Mr. Clauson was indeed on his way down to the plantation. You've gravely wounded an innocent man. I'll take him now and send for the doctor."

"Now, just a minute," one of the men said. "We not goin' to give him up just 'cause of what she said."

"Sir, do you doubt my daughter's word?" Athel asked. "Do you wish this man's death on your hands? If he dies, I promise you there'll be hell to pay."

"Now, nobody's doubtin' Miss Joleen, sir," the leader said. "Her word's good 'nough for us. Come on, boys, we got things to get done."

There was some grumbling, but the patrol rode away. Athel called Lawton over.

"I can't send any of the niggers, what with patrols

runnin' crazy, son," he said. "You'll have to ride into Benton for Dr. Stacey."

Lawton nodded. He looked at Joleen. She had never seen him look at her that way, as though he did not like what he saw. As he walked off the porch, Joleen realized her mother was staring at her. Suddenly she felt terrible. Her father was also staring at her.

Cellus ran out the door. He and Athel went down the steps. Cellus lifted Aaron in his arms. Joleen shrank back as Aaron was carried past her. Blood was seeping through the rags.

Estelle followed Cellus into the house. Athel ran past them, down the gallery. "I'll get Aunt Froney," he shouted. "Take him upstairs, Cellus."

Joleen stood on the porch. Tears fell down her cheeks. She took a step toward the door, but stopped. She hesitated to enter the house, as though her lie had stripped away her honor and she had deprived herself of the right to be called a Deavors.

She thought of Aaron. He might not even be alive. But he had to be. And she had to help him, no matter what. She ran inside.

Chapter 30

Dr. Stacey credited Aunt Froney with saving Aaron's life. The midwife used her herbs and the knowledge gained from forty years' experience healing sick slaves to stop the bleeding and keep Aaron alive until the doctor arrived. It was two days before Dr. Stacey pronounced Aaron out of danger. And another three days before he was fully conscious. During this time he was nursed constantly by Aunt Froney or one of the house slaves, as well as Joleen. No one asked Joleen questions about Aaron's mysterious visits, but there was an unmistakable tension in the house and unusually long silences in the dining room.

Joleen sat many hours in front of Aaron's bed, staring at his handsome face so badly bruised and cut, and thought of the times she had met him on Natchez streets and taken tea with him and Aunt Delma. Her parents had no idea how often she had been seeing Aaron or how she felt about him. When the dressings were changed on his arm and chest, she felt vicarious pain and forced herself not to run from the room and be sick.

Always before, her fantasies about Aaron had been romantic or physical. But during those days, while Aaron slept, Joleen realized she loved him. She loved him in a way she had never loved anyone! And she wanted to marry him! Her thoughts slipped into new fantasies.

Yet a recurring thought came to Joleen: Where *was* Aaron going in that rainstorm, in the middle of the night, with most of the county frightened and locked up?

On the fourth day the tension became so bad that Joleen could no longer endure it. She would have spoken to her parents had they not asked her to join them in the parlor after supper. Supper was the longest meal Joleen had ever endured. She ate very little. Lawton wouldn't look her in the eye. Lucinda looked everywhere in the room except at Joleen. Tillman, on the contrary, stared at her constantly, as though she had grown into something quite odd in the past few days.

Finally Joleen was seated in the parlor with her parents. The doors were closed. All the windows were open, but it was a humid night, and the heavy air added to Joleen's discomfort.

"We must discuss this situation," Athel said. "This is a very serious matter, Joleen. Your mother and I feel . . . We don't understand why Mr. Clauson found it necessary to sneak down here at night or why on earth you agreed to meet him under such circumstances."

"And what did you do?" Estelle asked. "Where did you go? What did you . . . do, Joleen?"

"Oh, Mother, we didn't *do* anything," Joleen said. "I was goin' to tell you."

She paused. She hated this situation. She was caught up in a lie that dominated her life in a way she had never been dominated. She had to bend with every turn of the lie and not make any mistakes.

"Then what did you do . . . if you didn't do anything?" her mother asked.

"*Why*, Joleen?" Athel asked. "Why did Mr. Clauson find it necessary to sneak down here? He's a friend of your aunt's, a perfectly acceptable man, a lawyer of breeding and good manners. We would certainly have received him had he come callin' on you in the proper manner."

"Joleen, what will people think?" Estelle asked. "We Deavorses have a respected name in this county. You told your secret in front of all those men. And about a man you hardly know, dear. The word will spread all over Adams County."

"But the word about what?" Joleen asked. "He just came down at night a couple of times. I went outside. We just walked around and talked. And I know him lots better than you think. Ask Aunt Delma. I was seein' him very often with her in Natchez. And . . . Mother, please don't look at me that way. We didn't do . . . There was absolutely nothing . . . physical. He's never so much as kissed me, if that's what you're worried about. As far as what other people think, well, I don't care what other people think."

This is hopeless, Joleen told herself. She was tempted to blurt out the truth, to tell them she had lied to save Aaron's life. But she sensed that if she did, they would believe this was the lie and the rendezvous the truth. She couldn't think straight. A mosquito was buzzing at her ear. She brushed at the mosquito and wiped perspiration from her face. She hated all this. She truly did not care what other people thought but hated being mistress to an insatiable lie. And she knew how much she had hurt and disappointed her family.

"Joleen, what does Mr. Clauson intend to do?" Athel asked. "Before this incident, I might have considered him a suitable candidate for your hand in marriage. But I most certainly do not approve of his conduct. Yet, he has an obligation to you, if he has any sense of honor or decency at all."

"Daddy, Aaron's been so sick," Joleen said. "He certainly hasn't been thinkin' about what he's goin' to do concernin' me. He's been so sick. He's not . . . Don't blame him."

What could she say? How could she defend Aaron's character and continue her lie? Again, she worried about his real destination that night. What if he was going to see some other woman? Perhaps he didn't care anything at all about her. How could she know? And in any case, she wouldn't consider marrying him if he proposed only out of a sense of obligation.

"Joleen, dear, don't lose control of yourself," Estelle said. "Please don't cry."

"I'm not going to cry," Joleen said. But there were tears in her eyes. She sniffled and dared herself to cry.

"You still haven't answered my question," Athel said. "All right, Joleen, I believe you when you say nothin' happened. Then why was it necessary for the man to sneak down here at night, and why on earth did you sneak out to meet him?"

"Daddy . . ." she started, but she had no idea what to say. Yet she had to say something. "I . . . I don't want to talk about this anymore. Please, Daddy. Mother. It's just that, well, Aaron and I felt that, well, since he's not a planter and he's a Yankee, you might not want him to see me. That's all. It was just a sort of little game we played, meetin' secretly like that."

"Rather a dishonorable and foolish game for a grown man to be playin' with a girl," Athel said. "Though I can see that foppish side to Mr. Clauson's nature."

"I'm not a girl," Joleen said. "I'm more grown-up than you think. And I knew what I was doin'. Oh, it's hopeless. I'll never be able to explain everything to you so you'll believe me. What's the use?"

"Don't raise your voice to us, young lady," Estelle said.

"Oh, Mother . . ." Joleen started. Again she did not know what to say.

"All right, Joleen," Athel said. "We take your word that nothin' serious happened between you and Mr. Clauson. When he gains some strength, I'll have a talk with him and let him know my opinion of his conduct and see what he has to say for himself."

The gathering broke up in that mood.

Joleen had become acquainted with confusion, anxiety, and a sense of helplessness in the past few days. These were new feelings for her. She disliked all of them. When she was not sitting with Aaron—and he slept most of the time—she was alone. She had never been so alone. She spent hours wandering aimlessly about the plantation, and more hours riding. Her dealings with her family were strained and rather formal. She wondered what Lawton thought. He seldom spoke to her, and spent most of his time in the fields.

Aaron's sleep had been due partially to the severity of his wounds and partially to the drugs Dr. Stacey had given him each day. But on the fifth day, the doctor cut the drug dosage in half. In his brief periods of being awake on previous days Aaron's eyes had been hazed. But on this day his eyes were clear for the first time.

Joleen asked Aaron how he felt. He said he felt much better, though he had never been weaker. He thanked her for her family's generosity in taking care of him.

"You remember nothin' of comin' here that night?" Joleen asked.

"I fear not," he said. "I had succumbed to my wounds. What a stupid thing for me to have done, to plunge right into the midst of that shooting. I knew I was in danger from those men. They were capable of anything, Miss Deavors. Therefore, I'm deeply in your father's debt for saving me."

"My father did not save you, sir," Joleen said. She glanced toward the door. She thought she heard someone in the hall. But no one came in. She leaned closer to Aaron. "I must tell you this quickly, because my father will soon talk to you. When the patrol brought you up, they thought you were part of the insurrection. They said you claimed to be comin' down here because you were Daddy's lawyer. But Daddy said, no, you weren't. They were goin' to take you away. And I . . . I said you were comin' down here to visit me . . . secretly and all, it bein' the middle of the night. . . . I said we just . . . walked around and talked some. And I said we'd done it several times before. . . ."

"I see," Aaron said. "Then I am deeply in *your* debt." He paused. He seemed to be choosing his words carefully. She sensed something calculated in his speech, as from time to time she had sensed something false in his manner. But his dark eyes looked straight at her with assurance. "I am truly overwhelmed at your kindness. And your courage. I know this was done at some great sacrifice on your part, some great sacrifice to your . . . reputation. And you may be certain that when I speak with your father I shall let him know the truth and—"

"No, no," Joleen interrupted. "Please, sir. You must continue the lie. My father would only think you were lying now to protect both yourself and me. And my father accepted my word and backed it up with his own honor, to get you away from the patrol. So we must . . . continue the lie. Don't you understand?"

He nodded. Suddenly he looked very tired and pale.

"I understand," he said. "Of course. When I speak with your father, I shall . . . reinforce your lie. And assure him we merely talked. I shall apologize for my . . . poor judgment in coming down in such a way. And I shall tell him I hold you in the highest esteem, that I have been courting you in Natchez. And I shall . . . I shall ask his permission to marry you, if you will have me as your husband."

This was not at all as Joleen had fantasized. Her romantic illusions faded. The whole dialogue was formal and without feeling. She resented her situation. Aaron would ask for her hand from a sense of honor and duty. Her cheeks blazed. She felt herself a romantic fool.

"Simply defend my own lie, sir," she said. "You

do not have to tell my father anymore lies. As for my reputation, I am quite capable of defending it myself, you may be sure. What I did, I did out of . . . respect for the friendship that had developed between us in Natchez. I acted . . . on an impulse to save your life. Do not feel you are in any way obligated to marry me. And what makes you think I wish to marry you, sir, on any account?"

"I didn't mean to presume," he started. His head fell back to the pillows. His face was so pale that Joleen became frightened.

"Oh, don't try to talk anymore now," she said. "I forgot how weak you are. You should rest. We can talk later, if you wish."

"No, no, please stay," he said. "Miss Deavors, I have become quite fond of you the past few months. I hoped that in our increasingly frequent meetings in Natchez you . . . you had come to . . . to realize something of my feelings for you. Only the demands of my profession have kept me from courting you more frequently and more formally. May I confess that, in any case, our . . . deepening friendship would have certainly led me to ask your father for your hand. . . ."

Joleen stood up. "Fondness and friendship are not the basis for a marriage," she said. "Now, you should rest."

"Please, wait." He reached for her arm. The motion made him gasp. He had hurt himself. His face was contorted. A line of saliva dribbled from his lips. She sat down again.

"Don't hurt yourself," she said. "Lie still, please. Are you all right? Should I get Aunt Froney?"

"Not just fondness, Joleen," he gasped. He touched her hand. She stiffened. He had never touched her before. His hand was warm. And she realized he had called her Joleen. Always before he had called her Miss Deavors. His breathing was erratic. His face was even whiter. She was afraid he had hurt himself badly. She should send for Aunt Froney. But she stayed there in their first intimacy and held his hand and looked into his eyes.

"It's more than fondness," he said. He squeezed

her hand. "I love you, Joleen. I do love you. Very much. Will you marry me? For I shall certainly ask your father's consent."

Joleen stood up again. If only he would tell her where he had been going that night. Why didn't he tell her? She couldn't bring herself to ask him.

"I . . . I can't answer now," she said. "I must think. We'll talk again later. And you . . . you must be honest with me about everything. Now, you should rest. I'll send Aunt Froney up here."

"There's little pain," he said. "I'll be all right. But only if you say yes, that you'll marry me. In time . . . perhaps you will come to return my love."

"I . . . I am fond of you," she said slowly. "Perhaps more than . . . fond. There, now, I've told you my feelings, sir. I don't know about marriage. I have some doubts, considerin' the circumstances of your proposal. Please, defend my lie when my father speaks to you. That is the only urgent matter between us. As for our personal situation, we will have plenty of time to discuss that. Now, I must go, and you should rest."

Joleen hesitated, then touched his hand before leaving the room.

In the hall she paused to catch her breath. She thought of Aaron's hand, so warm and pale, thought of their first touch, first intimacy. His eyes were so dark.

He wanted to marry her. Damnit, she said to herself, why did his proposal have to come in this way!

She loved Aaron. He said he loved her. And yes, she definitely wanted to marry him. And damn the circumstances!

She walked downstairs and told herself she would accept his proposal. She wouldn't tell him right away, though. She wanted him to court her a little while. And tell her where he had been going that night.

She did not doubt that he would. When she reached the bottom step, she was thinking of her wedding. Her cheeks went warm when she realized that in the near future she and Aaron would have their wedding night.

Chapter 31

The wedding was set for the second week in February. Athel and Estelle had misgivings about Aaron. They could not forgive him for sneaking down at night to visit Joleen, even though they accepted Joleen and Aaron's word that "nothing had happened" between them.

Aaron's foppish manners disturbed Athel. However, when they rode together, Athel was impressed with Aaron's horsemanship. And Aaron was a man of good breeding. Perhaps in time he will lose some of his annoying manners, Athel told himself. And he felt strongly that the marriage was necessary to protect Joleen's reputation. Aaron swore he loved Joleen and would make her happy. And Joleen was obviously in love with Aaron. Athel could never deny Joleen anything, and she had hinted that she would marry Aaron without her family's blessing, if necessary.

Aunt Delma finally convinced Athel and Estelle that the marriage was for the best. She had been out of town on the night of the shooting. When she returned and heard the news, she had a trunk and a case of Madeira loaded into her carriage and set out for the Columns.

She was disturbed by the secret meetings, but only for a moment. When she discovered that Joleen and Aaron wished to marry, she was delighted. She liked Aaron and had watched with pleasure as he courted Joleen. Aunt Delma believed in the social conventions, but she also loved intrigue and a good time, and in her youth she had committed a few indiscretions of her own.

The wedding was what mattered, she told Athel

and Estelle. The wedding would make everything all right. As for the stories that had spread over the county, well, let the fools gossip. The Deavorses did not need anyone's approval for their conduct.

Aaron stayed at the plantation three weeks before returning to his Natchez home. Joleen nursed him constantly. She delighted in watching him grow healthier. They held hands often, and there were many secret kisses that left her warm and anxious for their wedding night.

Her happiness became complete when Aaron told her where he had been going the night she saved him.

"I never pay attention to the news, which is always dreadful on any account," he said. "So when I set off that evening to visit a client, I had no idea what was happening in Adams County or what had happened in Virginia. In any case, this client had summoned me urgently. There was . . . an affair of the heart. Or more nearly of the flesh. The man stood to be ruined if his little indiscretion was discovered. As his attorney, he asked me to handle the matter and protect his name. When stopped on the road by those dreadful men, I could not divulge the name of my client or the reason for my mission. Even now, I can't reveal his name, because he's married. Surely you understand."

Joleen nodded.

Aaron took her hand. He went on to tell her that one of the men in the first patrol had seen him with Aunt Delma and assumed his urgent business was at the Columns. So it seemed harmless enough to tell a gentle lie. Then, when he was caught up in the shooting and captured a few minutes later, he was trapped by the lie.

Joleen accepted his explanation. She wanted to believe Aaron. And she strongly criticized the actions of the drunken slave patrols. She was too involved in marriage thoughts and too much in love even to think of doubting his story.

Lawton had been stunned as he stood on the porch that turbulent morning and heard Joleen confess to secret meetings with Aaron Clauson. For a whole week Lawton could not look her in the eye, and he seldom talked to her. It was difficult to believe that "nothing happened" when she was with Aaron. He remembered only too well what had happened between himself and Joleen.

He was disappointed with Joleen. He was angry with her. But she was still Joleen, his sister. He loved her and felt protective toward her. Ultimately he would forgive her anything.

His anger toward Joleen soon dissipated, and the brunt of the anger fell on Aaron. Lawton had never liked the man and his alien manners. At times during the first few days, Lawton's anger was so strong that he wished Aaron's wounds would prove fatal. He even thought of confronting the man, accusing him, challenging him. But to what? A duel? No, it was not his place. His father would handle the matter.

Lawton finally accepted the explanation that indeed nothing physical had happened between them. And he was relieved that Joleen's honor would be protected by the marriage. Yet Lawton did not want the man to be Joleen's husband. He did not want him, with his sneaking ways and foolish Yankee manners, to become a member of the Deavors family. But Lawton's resentment faded slowly as he realized how much Joleen loved Aaron and wanted to marry him.

And Lawton's own marriage was going well. Lucinda liked the plantation more with each passing month. She felt at home now and enjoyed sewing and helping out in the kitchen. She was also fond of riding, and she and Lawton spent hours together on horseback.

Sex with Lucinda had become wholly satisfying for Lawton. She was no longer tense, and he was no longer hesitant. He gave full rein to his obsession with her slim, pale body. He enjoyed kissing and licking down from her breasts to her vagina, and Lucinda encouraged him with words and gestures. When he moved into her body, her motions of lovemaking became urgent and liquid. They made love almost every night.

With the approaching harvest, Lawton spent longer hours in the fields. He worked hard and learned more and more about managing the plantation. Under his father's prodding he took on additional authority.

He enjoyed the work, and he shared the sense of excitement that the harvest would soon be in. But he was never satisfied with his work. He would brood about a job he had supervised and wonder if he had really done it well or if his father would have done it better. He wondered if his father was really pleased with the way a certain section was picked or the way a dozen wagons were loaded for the gin. As the crucial harvest time progressed, his self-confidence eroded badly, the quality of his work suffered, and he hesitated to take on more responsibility.

One warm day early in November, as he rode from the fields, he told himself he had to do something to restore his self-confidence and impress his father. He had heard planter talk and read in agricultural journals that cotton prices would be depressed this harvest, but would probably be high the coming year. He galloped back to the house, hoping he could convince his father to hold out part of their harvest and store it on the plantation so they could get the higher price a few months later.

Chapter 32

Lavon had sent his patrol to the Columns that night with the wounded Aaron while he rode into Benton and waited. He was not yet ready to face his family at the plantation, even at the head of a patrol. He thought the German lawyer was involved in an abolitionist scheme and even let himself imagine that the patrol would uncover something at the Columns that implicated his family. But he really knew such a thing was impossible. As for Clauson, he didn't give a damn about the lawyer, but if he had not been on his way to the Columns, then he was responsible for the deaths of three men. He would surely be hanged.

An hour later the sullen patrol rode into Benton. They told Lavon that Athel had discounted the man's story but that Joleen had confessed that Clauson was on his way to visit her and that he had been down before for secret meetings. Lavon remembered seeing Joleen with Aaron. Of course, he told himself. They're having an affair. The dandyish lawyer was hardly the kind of man to be caught up in abolitionist plots and killings.

The wedding announcement did not surprise Lavon. He smiled when he thought how shocked Athel must have been to discover Joleen's indiscretions. Lavon wondered what Athel thought of the Yankee lawyer as a son-in-law. He also wondered if Athel knew the man was Jewish.

That autumn of 1831 and the early winter of 1832 brought increasing prosperity to Lavon. In October he brought down a coffle of two hundred slaves; with the profit he bought four hundred rich acres, as well as a house in Natchez. In November he built a brick slave pen with large cells for the slaves. It was built around a courtyard, where the slaves were exhibited and sold and where they could cook and exercise.

In December Lavon brought down another hundred Negroes from Virginia, while two of his agents purchased ninety slaves in South Carolina. Lavon had developed a shrewdness in selling slaves and an instinct for anticipating what kind of slaves the Mississippi farmers and planters would need in the coming months. Mechanics might be selling well in October, for example, and other traders would bring down more mechanics in December, but Lavon would decide that prime field hands would be in demand in December, and he would have more field hands than any other dealer.

Out of the many slaves he brought down, he had

kept only a man and two women for his own use. In December Frannie complained that it didn't look right to have only three slaves, so he gave her two women, though there was hardly enough work for them. He also kept out a dozen prime field hands from the December coffles and set them to work clearing his land. He planned to plant cotton in the spring.

On mild winter evenings Lavon sat on the porch of his new home and sipped wine and thought of his growing wealth. On these evenings his somewhat nebulous plans to take the Columns away from his family became firmer. He began to add tactics to his strategy.

The Columns was an oblong-shaped plantation. It was surrounded by a dozen parcels of land, some of them owned by small farmers and some by absentee landlords. Lavon planned to buy up all the land surrounding the Columns so that Athel could not secure fresh acreage in the coming years or even gain access to the Columns without passing over Lavon's land. By February Lavon owned three of these parcels. He always used a Natchez lawyer, Jason Colfax, to make these purchases so Athel wouldn't realize what was happening.

Lavon also began concentrating cash in Natchez' two banks, as well as buying stock in the banks. In the next few years he planned to see that men he could control were elected to the banks' boards of directors. Each spring Athel went confidently to one of the banks and signed a note that provided cash for the planting and for expenses until the cotton was sold the next winter. Some year, Lavon told himself, when Athel was in financial trouble, he would discover that neither bank would finance him. Or better still, Lavon would see that Athel got the loan, but under terms that would make it impossible for him to repay in time to save the Columns. Because the plantation was always the collateral for a planting loan.

Lavon had Jason Colfax purchase for him thirty percent of the Benton gin—in the lawyer's name—and looked forward to the day when he would control the gin and it would handle no cotton from the Columns. And he began to investigate ways to stop the Deavorses' cotton from getting to New Orleans markets on barges, as it usually did. Who knows, he told himself as he drank wine and listened to the crickets, one year the barges might mysteriously sink. . . .

And now Lavon had Essie working as his agent at the Columns. One Saturday in Natchez, Essie had come up to Lavon on the street. He had taken off his hat and bowed and said he had driven the family into town and had been given a couple of hours of freedom while they shopped.

"I never forgot how you saved my life and kept me from bein' whipped, Mist' Lavon," Essie said. "And what all it cost you. Sure wish you could come back as the master. You want me to do anythin' for you, no matter what, you just let me know."

Lavon thanked Essie. He said, yes, he would certainly need to call on him in the future. He hinted that he would return as the plantation's master and that Essie would make a perfect overseer, after being given his freedom. Before parting, Lavon gave Essie a five-dollar gold piece. Essie would have gone back and burned down the whole plantation if Lavon had asked him.

Lavon would relax and drink his wine and think of owning the Columns, of having his family penniless and at his mercy. But his satisfaction at his plans and the pleasure of his fantasies would buoy him for only a short time.

Two serious problems always crept into his thoughts.

The first was the new state constitution that was being prepared. There was a possibility that the constitution would contain a provision outlawing slave trading in the state. There had always been a residue of dislike, on humanitarian grounds, of slave trading. Now, in the aftermath of the Nat Turner insurrection, there was a strong practical impetus to prohibit the trading. Many Mississippians feared that Virginia and the Carolinas and Maryland were selling their malcontents, their troublemakers, their rebels and murderers and rapists, and that these slaves were pouring into the state in such numbers that the white people would soon be greatly outnumbered by dangerous and alien blacks.

Lavon had recently been told by one state senator that it looked as though the provision would be blocked. But there was no certainty.

Lavon's second problem was Purvis Swan. Now that the profits were pouring in, Swan hardly lifted a finger to do any work. He had grown fatter and more pompous than ever, and he doted on his dogs as though they were his children. Lavon had two law firms examine the contract he and Swan had signed. Both firms said it was ironbound. There was no way to break the contract. If Swan never did another day's work, he would still be entitled to half of everything Lavon earned.

On Groundhog Day Lavon returned home early from the slave pen. He had just sold four field hands from a new coffle, and he was in a good mood. But Frannie was depressed because she could not go to Joleen's wedding.

Lavon poured a glass of brandy and sank into the new winged chair that had arrived from New Orleans the day before. "You're never going to be invited out there, damnit, and you ought to know that by now. Soon enough, Frannie, you'll be mistress of the Columns, and you'll be at the top of Adams County's social world. But you have to be patient, damnit."

"That could take years," she whined. "What's the use of all those old lessons if I never get to show off what a lady I'm becomin' in front of proper society?"

"You'll get the chance soon enough," he said. "Come here. That's right."

She knelt down beside him and looked up. He smiled and kissed her cheek. She looked good in the blue dress. He had helped her pick out the material and the pattern for the dressmaker. He supervised the purchase of everything she wore. And he sent her to dancing lessons, to elocution lessons, to etiquette lessons, to language lessons, and to piano lessons. He would make a lady out of her, he had sworn to himself. She would be a proper mistress for the Columns. She was improving, he admitted, but too often she committed social errors or proved awkward in ways that embarrassed and angered him.

"I'll tell you what, Frannie," he said. "To make up for not being able to attend Joleen's wedding, I'll take you to New Orleans for a few days, and we'll go shopping."

"Oh, Lavon!" she squealed. "Oh, I've never been to New Orleans. Can we take first-class passage?"

"Of course," he said.

She kissed his forehead, then his lips.

"There's a while until supper," she said. "Why don't we lie down? And just rest and all. But I don't want you to, you know, touch me or anything."

They went upstairs to the bedroom. Frannie changed into an old yellow dress. When she lay beside him on the bed, she teased and taunted and told him she wasn't at all interested in having sex with him. He tried to kiss her. She twisted her head away. He touched her breasts. She slapped him and cursed him.

"Damn you!" he shouted. He ripped off her dress. She wore nothing underneath.

Frannie struggled furiously. She cursed and bit his hand. But he overpowered her and made violent love to her. He took a long time to climax, and then collapsed on the bed. Frannie kissed his cheek and snuggled against him. They slept until supper.

Lavon enjoyed these mock-rape sessions with Frannie. They seldom made love any other way. But there were times when he grew bored with her physically, as he grew bored with her in every other way. Then he went down the hill and along the sunken sidewalks to Annie Easter's barge, where he lay in a red-plush room and drank champagne and made love to a beautiful mulatto.

One stormy evening he drank wine with Annie in the parlor as the wind rocked the barge and howled through the portholes. Annie told him she was thinking of selling the barge and its girls.

"I've got a son in this proper Eastern school," she said. "He doesn't know a thing about this place. He's never been here. Thinks my money comes from a Louisiana plantation. I visit him up East every year. He graduates soon. He's become quite the fancy gentleman, and if he found out about this place, he'd never forgive me."

Lavon glanced around the parlor at the planters, judges, bankers, and lawyers who were talking to the girls. Some of these men had favorites with whom they were quite obsessed. If a man owned a whore barge like Annie's, he would be providing a service to the county's most powerful men. He would know all about their sexual weaknesses and whims. And for many men of some importance but limited means, these girls were quite expensive. What might such men do for the privilege of visiting these girls without paying?

"Of course, I'd want somebody who'd look after the girls," Annie was saying. "If you hear of anybody who's interested, let me know, Lavon."

"Yes, I'll keep my ears open, Annie," he said. "Well, the storm seems to have let up, so I'll be on my way."

Lavon enjoyed the light mist that still fell. He found a carriage at the docks and settled back for the ride up the hill. The more he thought of owning Annie's barge and girls, the more the idea appealed to him.

Chapter 33

Aaron sat in the back seat of a carriage driven by Ed and asked himself if this was really his life. The carriage was nearing the Columns. In a few hours he would marry Joleen. He would be wed not only to Joleen but also to the planter aristocracy he despised. He had finally confessed to the Deavorses that he was

Jewish. Their response was surprising. There had been little reaction at all, which confused him. Worst of all, as a consequence of a dowry he could not refuse, he was on the verge of becoming a slave owner.

The carriage jolted Aaron to his teeth. His humor failed him. It was February, and yet the morning was warm and humid. Nights were cool, and often there was frost, but many days were more like summer than winter. There was no snow or ice. He missed the true, cold winter of Ohio. This heat was just one more reason to curse his existence in Mississippi.

Several times in the past few weeks he had thought of leaving Natchez. But he could not. He had spent all this time and effort in establishing himself in this area, and many people depended on him. Marrying into the Deavors family made him an accepted member of the Adams County aristocracy and therefore beyond suspicion.

Yes, he told himself, this is really my life.

He thought of Joleen. Lying half-conscious in that hot, damp bedroom in September, he had been overcome with admiration and gratitude for her sacrifice and courage in telling a lie to save him from the slave patrol. He had become more and more fond of her as they met in Natchez. And he was overwhelmed by her physical presence in that dim room, with his mind floating in a haze of sedation and dull pain.

He stared up into her beautiful, sensual face, shadowed in the wavering flame of the lamp, and decided he loved her. The blue eyes captivated him. He had never seen such a lovely face. Even through the pain and weakness, his body wanted her desperately. And he told himself that in all decency he must ask for her hand, to protect her honor.

Before he was fully free of pain and back to his senses, he found himself engaged. For one whole day he felt trapped. But a few hours alone with Joleen removed this feeling. Over the weeks he had come to like her even more and to realize that he, indeed, not only loved her but also needed her. And she confessed that she loved him. He knew that she had led a sheltered and pampered life. She had little education and little knowledge of the world beyond the plantation. And her unquestioning acceptance of slavery he found abhorrent.

But she was an intelligent and inquisitive girl, he argued with himself. She was open to new ideas. She seemed ready to burst from her plantation shell, to throw off the husk of her background and heritage. And each time he saw her, she was more beautiful. She radiated an open sexuality. Her most innocent kiss on the cheek was sensuous and suggestive.

Aaron shifted in the seat. He pulled out his lace handkerchief and wiped moisture from his forehead. He let his thoughts wander to fantasies of making love to Joleen tonight. These pleasant thoughts held his mind only a minute. For despite his weeks of self-assurance that eventually Joleen, exposed to the real world beyond the Columns and under his guidance, would grow out of her background and change her views on slavery, the time of reality had now arrived.

What if she did not change her beliefs? What if she remained adamant about slavery? What would he do? Once they lived together, how long could he continue to deceive her? This very night, their wedding night, there was the possibility that a messenger from Levi Coffin would arrive at his doorstep. All this was unfair to Joleen. She loved him. She trusted him. Whatever she might be because of her background, she was at least honest with him and gave him her total being. He had never met anyone more open and outspoken, anyone with less guile or guilt.

In deceiving her and hiding from her a basic part of his nature, he was being cruel. And he was placing her in danger. He loved Joleen, yet he hardly acted like a man full of love for a woman. He rationalized the necessity for what he was doing again and again. He told himself he had dedicated his life to fighting slavery and that any sacrifice had to be made for the greater good of his work. But the rationalization was no longer effective. He had come to realize that Joleen was as important as his work.

Aaron eased away from the seat and pried his damp shirt from his back. He would simply have to wait and take his chances, and in the meantime continue his work. He would have to deceive her. But he would be a good husband. He would make his love and need evident to Joleen every hour of every day.

Aaron's frustration made him angry. It was a nebulous and undirected anger, but he had come to fear this anger, especially since the September incident. He may have saved one slave that night. He never knew for sure. But he had killed three men. And he had nearly been killed himself.

He came to regret his decision on that September night. And when he went to Ohio in December, Levi Coffin told Aaron he was quite upset and disappointed by his actions. Coffin, like many others in the abolitionist movement, was a Quaker. These men did not believe in violence under any circumstances. Coffin dismissed Aaron's contention that his first thought in pulling his pistols in September was to help save the life of a slave.

"And what if you had not seen that slave, Aaron?" Coffin asked. "Wouldn't you have shot those white men in any case, because of your anger and the hatred you felt for them? No, listen to me a moment, Aaron. I don't believe in violence, yet anyone might have responded instinctively to save that man. What worries me is that what you did is consistent with your nature, with the violent anger and the hatred of slavery that brought you to us. This wasn't the first time you killed in Mississippi. I sometimes think that, given the chance, you'd murder slave owners without mercy. . . . Forgive me my harshness in speaking so bluntly, but I see this in you, and there's no place in our movement for so much hatred, anger, and killing."

Aaron was stunned by Coffin's comments. He remained silent and listened to Coffin and the other men gathered in the secret room of Coffin's store. They told him that it was one thing to help those slaves who wished to escape, and quite another thing to literally invade the South and shoot down white men. They said that if he did not learn to curb his anger and hatred and propensity for violence in a very short time, he would become a liability in Natchez. Such shootings made many people, in the North and South, both black and white, hesitant to join their cause.

On the boat back down to Natchez, Aaron forced himself to look at his anger and hatred and his tendency to pull out his pistols and ride into any situation that he felt violated his personal sense of honor or decency or justice. Yes, he could argue that there was justification for his Mississippi shootings and that he could not simply ride away from the slaughter that September night. But he admitted to himself that he was so full of a kind of hatred and anger that Coffin was not far from the truth. Given the chance, he might well kill many slave owners without mercy.

He was sincere in his hatred of the institution of slavery, and his dedication to driving it from the earth was deep and abiding. Of this he had no doubt. He hated slavery, and it was that simple. He hated prejudice. He hated brutality. He hated injustice. He had suffered himself because he was Jewish. In Europe he had seen other Jews suffer terribly for their beliefs.

He also knew he had the courage to do what his commitment demanded. He would take any risks to free black men he might never know or have feeling for as individuals. Yes, he would help unknown black men and kill unknown white men. He had a deep commitment to a cause, but no commitment to individuals. He hated an evil institution, and this hatred fed his anger. Just as a few years earlier he had stalked the streets in Cincinnati proclaiming he was Jewish and daring anyone to insult him because of it. Yet he had no formal belief in the Jewish religion and was no part of the Jewish community.

For many years he had been alone in every emotional sense. His parents had died when he was young. He had no other family in America. He had acquaintances for drinking and riding and shooting, and mistresses for sex. He was constantly invited to parties and balls. But he had no real friends. He loved no one, and no one loved him. Except Joleen.

On the boat that December day, three months after his engagement to Joleen, he stared across the river and asked himself if he was capable of true love for a person, capable of being truly loved, capable of needing another person and being able to accept this need. How far he'd come since then! Joleen's love for him and his love and need for her were every bit as important to him as his work in freeing slaves.

"How much further to the Columns?" he asked.

"Less than half an hour now, Mist' Aaron," Ed said. "Sorry if you been joggled around back there, but Miss Joleen, she done made me promise to get you back out here quick as a wink."

"That's all right, Ed," Aaron said, though his body was aching from the journey.

He stared at a bayou, green with slime, where a moccasin arched its body from the water as it rippled along. Aaron did not want to think of Joleen or his love for her, nor of the coming wedding and reception that would initiate him into the planter world. He settled back in the seat and thought of all that was happening within the movement.

Prospects had never been so exciting or encouraging, and for the first time, what some people called the Underground Railroad was beginning to get itself organized in Ohio. All over Ohio there was a network of safe houses and churches where fugitive slaves could hide. Food and disguises and maps were stocked in these places. Aaron had brought back charts of this growing web of safe houses, as well as directions telling the best routes to travel from one house to another, and particularly which towns or roads to avoid.

There were many pro-slavery communities in Ohio that would betray any fugitive slave and see that he was returned to his master. And many slave owners went to Ohio themselves with hired agents and tracked down their fugitives and returned them to slavery. So when a slave reached Ohio, he was not necessarily safe from his master.

Some people kept a remote bedroom ready for the fugitive slaves. One farmer had a secret cellar in his barn that could hide a large family. A merchant in Mechanicsburg used an old smokehouse. A Cairo doctor hid slaves in what appeared to be a woodpile at the side of his house but was really hollowed out. Aaron had seen fugitive slaves hidden in church belfries, in hollow haystacks, and in hollowed-out bridge abutments.

Men like Aaron and Clarence helped these fugitives to flee up the Mississippi from the deep South. Slaves from border slave states arrived on foot. They were all hidden and given disguises to help them work their way north to Lake Erie. From ports like Toledo, Ashtabula Harbor, Cleveland, Sandusky, and Huron, the fugitives were put aboard boats run by friendly captains and taken to Port Burwell or Port Stanley in Canada, where their masters could not follow.

Aaron's friends had devised many tricks to help the fugitives reach Canada. In Sandusky, a lawyer corked the face and arms of a light-skinned slave and took the man right past his owner in the middle of town. A Presbyterian minister in Mechanicsburg had a simple device for getting a black man through town without suspicion. The minister kept a variety of tools on hand. A fugitive merely put a rake or a scythe over his shoulder and walked down the street as though on his way to work.

Fugitives were often disguised as members of the opposite sex. In Cleveland, a tall mulatto woman was dressed up as a wealthy white man. And a white boy went along posing as "his" servant, right past the slave's master, who was searching for the woman and threatening violence to anyone who aided her escape.

Aaron put away his pistols on his return to Natchez. There would be no more shootings, he told himself. And he still had to avoid the slightest suspicion after the September incident. He set himself to organizing willing blacks and occasional whites who were sent to him by the people in Ohio. He also recruited sympathetic paddle-wheeler captains or their black first mates.

Aaron kept his maps of Ohio safe houses and routes carefully hidden. He provided only one route to a fleeing slave. Usually he worked through agents, so that the fugitives never met him.

And he began spreading the news about Canada to the slaves so they would realize that if they ran away there was a place in which they would be safe from their masters.

Clarence, who had escaped in September, was particularly effective in visiting inland towns and plantations. He owned his own wagon and team and pretended to be a porter and teamster. He posed as a hopeless drunk and buffoon, which was the image white Mississippians had of any free Negro.

Aaron's carriage was at last approaching the stream that lay near the Deavorses' plantation. "Pull up so I can bathe my face," Aaron shouted to Ed.

The carriage stopped. Aaron got out and splashed cold water on his face.

Chapter 34

They drove down the cedar-lined drive. Aaron saw two slaves walking across a field of bedraggled cotton plants. He thought again of the albatrosslike dowry and what this marriage ceremony would mean.

It had been an evening in late September when Athel had sprung the trap on him. Aaron had just returned from a walk with Joleen. Athel asked him to step into the study. He poured whiskey and made the kind of small talk that indicated he was about to discuss something important. "We must talk about Joleen's dowry," Athel said finally. "I've given this matter much thought, and I hope the dowry I propose will be satisfactory."

"A dowry?" Aaron replied. He had not thought about a dowry. "I'm . . . I'm sure we'll have no difficulty, sir. And in any case, I'm of sufficient means to see that Joleen lives in comfort." Aaron had inherited money from his family, he had saved and invested money from the lucrative law practice he had abandoned in Ohio, and he had a good income from his Natchez law practice.

"Well, yes, I'm sure you're of sufficient means, Mr. Clauson," Athel said. "Otherwise I would have been hesitant to have you marry Joleen. But her dowry is her rightful inheritance. I've purchased a thousand acres of good land in the county, which I wish to give you."

"That's most generous, sir," Aaron said.

"I hope you'll want to build on the land," Athel said. "Though I'm sure Joleen will adjust to Natchez, she's grown up in the country and enjoys country livin'. And she's an avid rider and will want to keep horses and ride regularly. I'll confess, sir, that I hope in time you'll consider puttin' the land into cotton, even if you continue to practice law and live in Natchez."

Aaron chose his words carefully. "I'm sure we will both enjoy a country home sometime in the future. And as you know, I also love to ride. I am most gratified for your generosity." Of course, he told himself, the land would never see a single seed of cotton, but he wouldn't let Athel know that.

"And I want to give you and Joleen twenty of our people."

"Your . . . people, sir? You mean slaves? You wish to give me slaves, Mr. Deavors?"

"Of course, sir," Athel said. "You've been hiring two free niggers in Natchez, if I understand correctly. Particularly, Joleen will be pleased to have Filch and Norvina in town with her. Filch is my best driver, but recently a rattler got him on the foot, and he never fully recovered its use. He's dedicated to Joleen. I've talked to him, and he's willin' to live in Natchez. So is Norvina. She can run the house, and she's an excellent cook. But I do attach one condition, sir. You must pledge me your word that these slaves will never be sold out of the family, even under the most extreme economic circumstances."

Aaron stood up. "Sir, I must protest," he said. "I can't accept—"

Athel stood up too. He interrupted Aaron. "This is not a negotiable issue, sir," he said with more emotion than Aaron had ever seen in the man. "I am adamant on this point and will not argue. Under no circumstances are our people to be sold out of the Deavors family. We have an obligation to our people!"

"Mr. Deavors, I'm not arguing with you on that point, sir," Aaron said. This was an impossible situation! He was on the verge of becoming a slave owner and was in the position of seeming to want to sell slaves, while this planter was condemning the practice. For an instant the grotesque irony nearly caused Aaron to smile. But his situation was too serious, and he had to take the greatest care not to reveal his true feelings about slavery.

"Then you agree that these niggers will never be sold out of the family?"

"You have my word, sir, that I will never sell a slave. Yes, you most certainly have my word, Mr. Deavors."

"Thank you for your word, sir," Athel said. "I feel particularly strong about this, Mr. Clauson. Since my brother, to the shame of the Deavorses and the eternal damnation of his soul, has become a trafficker in flesh!"

Aaron was startled by Athel's outburst. The man truly hated slave trading. And he thought he was taking care of his own Negroes and providing them with the best possible lives, even though he had them enslaved. What an incredible rationalization, Aaron told himself.

Athel was waiting for him to speak. "Sir, I appreciate this further generosity, in giving us these people. But living in town, with the free blacks available, well, it hardly seems necessary for us to have these slaves . . ."

He broke off the sentence. Athel was obviously puzzled by his attitude. In one desperate and contradictory instant Aaron told himself that he would never own slaves . . . and that he must accept the slaves or be found out and have his effectiveness destroyed.

"Please clarify your position, Mr. Clauson," Athel said. "For I don't understand it. I can see no reason why you would decline these slaves and deny Joleen the company and help of people she has spent her life with and who are dedicated to her."

Aaron pulled out his handkerchief and patted his face. "It's simply that your continuing generosity overwhelms me, sir, and I was doubly touched because I know how highly you value your people. You may be assured, sir, that I will be a benevolent and protective master."

Aaron nearly choked on the word "master," but he forced himself to follow through with his pose, while telling himself that he would find a way out of the dilemma and free the slaves. In any case, he reminded himself as he stuck his handkerchief into his sleeve, it was only September. The marriage wasn't until February, and he had months to come up with some stratagem that would solve this ironic problem.

The carriage was by now passing through the magnolia grove. Only a few hours, Aaron told himself. He would be married to Joleen. He would be a Deavors. He would be a member of the planter aristocracy. And he would be a slave owner. For he had not come up with any plan to extricate himself from his dilemma. There didn't seem to be any alternative but to accept it on the surface. By day he would be served by slaves he owned, and by night he would help other slaves find their freedom. . . .

Stop it, he told himself. He *would* think of something, damnit. And it would be far easier, once he got to know these slaves. Out here they were isolated and helpless. Given a bit of freedom in Natchez, given the chance to associate with free blacks, they might run away of their own accord. If not, he could arrange for Clarence to help them, without their knowing that he himself was involved. Only six of the twenty were actually moving into Natchez with them. The others would remain on the plantation until a country house was built.

There was a blur of movement beneath a tree.

Aaron glanced over, to see Tillman staring at him through the leaves. His eyes were wide, and his mouth was open. The moment Aaron's eyes caught Tillman's, the boy vanished behind the leaves.

Chapter 35

Aaron stood among the azalea and oleander bushes on the front lawn. He sipped champagne and shook hands and made small talk while he watched Joleen flit from his side to a group of people, then return to smile up at him and join in the talk that seemed as natural to her as to the hundreds of guests at the Columns.

She was supremely beautiful in her blue dress. Earlier, as she had walked along the gallery in a white silk dress that cost over a thousand dollars in New Orleans, she seemed too beautiful to be real. Now she smiled at him again, her face still deeply tanned, her blue eyes luminous in the first purple of dusk. Her face was full of love and happiness and a sensuousness that made Aaron eager to leave the reception and return to Natchez.

He was proud of Joleen. He loved her beauty and her sexuality and her gaiety. And he felt her love for him. But she seemed so young today! She seemed truly a teen-age girl who had grown up in the country. She flirted and gushed and smiled and talked inanely to the multitudes of people who clustered around her. Aaron drank his champagne and despaired that she would ever throw off this shell of being a plantation daughter, that she would ever be able to see the evil in the institution that made this lavish wedding and reception possible.

He glanced around. Lavish was the only way to describe the reception. There were two orchestras, one from Natchez, the other from New Orleans. Whole calves and pigs roasted in pits in the back, and there were two dozen tables covered with elegant displays of food from Natchez, New Orleans, and even Europe. One table contained a dozen varieties of caviar alone. On another table were silver platters of lobster that Athel had ordered to be shipped specially from New England. Other tables contained every conceivable kind of beverage; slaves circulated among the guests, keeping their glasses filled with champagne.

Not only Joleen but also Estelle, Lucinda, and Aunt Delma wore expensive dresses made in New Orleans. The ladies had all gone down there in November for a week, and Aaron had heard that the trip cost nearly five thousand dollars.

For weeks this wedding had been the talk of Adams County society. There had been one party after another for him and Joleen, one endless, dull party after another, and during the day one shower after another for Joleen. A whole room in the house had been set aside just for the gifts. Among them were an antique diamond clasp and an antique diamond stickpin from Aunt Delma.

"Just a little while longer," Joleen whispered in his ear. He flinched in surprise as he felt the tip of her tongue. She smiled at the corners of her mouth when she pulled away.

He and Joleen moved to another group of guests. There were more handshakes. More champagne. More boring talk. Athel and Estelle joined them. A moment later, Lawton and Lucinda came up. Here we are, the happy Deavors family, Aaron said to himself. Actually, he rather liked his in-laws, particularly Athel, if only he could forget that they owned slaves.

And they had accepted him into the family with a vengeance. He had been snubbed a few times and heard a couple of caustic remarks in Natchez since revealing that he was Jewish. Two clients had dismissed him. But his being Jewish made little difference to the Deavorses. He had married Joleen, and now he belonged to the family. And that seemed to be the county's attitude. Being Jewish mattered little if one was a Deavors.

Aaron discussed horses with Lawton, but he looked past his brother-in-law, and his mind wandered. He suppressed a smile at the thought of standing here among all these Christian slave owners, here on a plantation in the back end of nowhere, in Mississippi. It was not only far from his childhood days in Munich but also another world even from Cincinnati.

Four hours earlier he had been married by a Presbyterian minister, though he had not renounced his own religion or become a Protestant. He remembered telling Joleen and her father his secret—and their unexpected reactions.

It had been an evening in early October. Aaron had come out to a small party at the Columns, and he and Joleen were walking in the flower garden. He told her he had to reveal something about himself that might well alter her feelings for him.

"Mind you," he added quickly, "I'm making no apologies for what I am."

She stopped beside a bush of yellow roses and looked up at him with her great blue eyes. "I . . . I've thought you might have somethin' to tell me," she said. "I've sensed that you've been holdin' somethin' back."

"Joleen, it's this—I'm Jewish."

"I don't think I understand," she said. "What does that mean, that you're Jewish? Is that a religious thing? Or some kind of different nationality? I honestly don't know, Aaron. Does that mean you were born in Palestine? I remember in the Bible they talked about Jews and all. Is that what you mean? Oh, please forgive me. In many ways I'm such an uneducated girl. And I've spent my life out here on the plantation. I . . . think there's a Jewish family livin' in Natchez, though I'm not certain. Tell me what bein' a Jew means, please."

"It means . . . It's not easy to explain, Joleen," he said. "In a sense, it's both religious and . . . and cultural. No, I wasn't born in Palestine, but back . . . back in biblical times the Jews were driven out of Palestine, and since then, for many hundreds of years, we've had to live all over the world, in alien lands, and try to preserve our heritage and our beliefs and our religion.

But I'm not at all a religious man, Joleen. It's not a religion to me. It's a sense of a common heritage and certain . . . beliefs. I can explain all of this in detail later, of course. What you must understand now is that throughout history we Jews have been persecuted for our culture and our religion. If you marry me, you may find yourself caught up in this persecution. Friends may turn against you. It might not be an easy life for you. Your family may disapprove. Don't you even begin to understand what I'm trying to tell you?"

"Are you tryin' to get out of our marriage?" she asked.

"No, of course not," he said. "I'm only trying to be honest with you."

"And I appreciate that, sir," she said. "I would like to hear of your religion and your customs. Though I must warn you, I might not want to adopt them. I probably wouldn't, Aaron. You see, I've simply never been one for any sort of routine or customs. Why, I have to confess I can hardly boil water, though it's the custom for girls around here to learn to cook and sew. Last time I took up a needle, I stuck myself in the finger. As for religion, well, we Deavorses, oh, we go to church and all, from time to time, but we're not too religious. And the minister will—"

"Damnit, Joleen, you don't understand," he said. "I'm different. I'm Jewish, and you . . ."

She smiled and kissed his cheek. "Of course you're different," she said. "You're a Yankee. And you're German. You're the most different man I've ever met. And you know what else makes you different? You make people think you're cynical and don't care about anything, and you're witty and all, but I know how serious you get sometimes. And now you tell me you're Jewish. Well, that just makes you a little more different. That's all. As I was sayin', the minister will marry us, of course. But I'd have to think a long time about changin' to this Jewish religion."

"No, no, that's not it at all," he said. "I'm not asking you to convert. I'm not religious myself. And I don't intend to convert to your religion, either."

"Well, I don't think you've ever been invited," she

said, and laughed. "Though I'm sure they'd be glad to have you."

"No, listen. Your minister may not even want to marry us when he learns I'm Jewish."

"Oh, he will. He'll do whatever Daddy tells him to."

"But your father. He may not want you to marry me. When he finds out I'm Jewish . . ."

"Really, Aaron, I don't understand all this," she said. "Daddy knows perfectly good and well I intend to marry you, as long as you're willin'. I mean, you are still Aaron Clauson. You're the man I love and want to marry. I don't care a fig about any old religion or custom or whatever. Now, come on, the music's startin', and I feel like dancin'."

They went back inside and danced. Aaron drank more than usual. He was relieved at Joleen's reaction. Yet he resented that she could so casually ignore something that was so important to him. She's truly an unsophisticated girl, he told himself. She has no idea what the real world is like.

That same evening, Aaron told Athel he wished to speak to him alone. They went into the study, and Athel closed the door. Aaron declined the offer of a drink.

There was no small talk. Aaron said simply, "I think I should tell you that I'm Jewish, Mr. Deavors. I've already spoken to Joleen on the matter."

Athel's face showed no emotion. He walked to the window and looked out, then turned.

"I see, Mr. Clauson," he said. "And you say you told Joleen. May I ask her reaction?"

"She had very little reaction," Aaron said. "Frankly, I was surprised at her lack of response." He described Joleen's reaction. "And I informed her I'm not a religious man. I'm not a practitioner of my religion. But I retain a strong sense of my cultural and religious heritage. I will be married in your church, sir, but I won't convert, nor will I renounce my faith."

"I see," Athel said again. He turned to the window, turned back to Aaron. "I appreciate your honesty in tellin' me this before the weddin'. I'm not surprised at Joleen's reaction. She's led a rather sheltered life on the plantation. And she's been brought up in an atmosphere devoid of religious or racial hatred. We Deavorses pride ourselves on bein' tolerant people. That's not true of everyone in Adams County, and of course Joleen may be subjected to some difficulty in the future. Though I frankly doubt it. I will be honest with you, sir. To my knowledge, there has never been a Jewish member of our family, though on at least two occasions a Deavors has married a Catholic. You say you're willin' to be married by our minister but that you're not willin' to convert to the Presbyterian Church?"

"That is correct, sir."

"And you won't ask Joleen to convert to your religion?"

"No, sir."

"Very well," Athel said. "I . . . This will make no difference, then, Mr. Clauson. In acceptin' you as my son-in-law. When I was in school in New Orleans, I had Jewish friends. As I said, we are . . . I'm sure . . . it will all work out. What I want is Joleen's happiness. She loves you and is determined to marry you. My charge to you, sir, is to make her a good husband. Your religion, your background, are . . . secondary to that."

Aaron left the room confused and disturbed. Athel's attitude seemed a little patronizing at first, though Aaron didn't doubt the man's sincerity. He wasn't certain what upset him most. Perhaps it was the fact that Athel really didn't seem too concerned, that being Jewish or not was of little importance to this planter family. Or if it was, they certainly weren't going to let him know it.

And Aaron was particularly upset when he recalled Athel's remark that the Deavorses prided themselves on their racial and religious tolerance. And yet they owned slaves!

Aaron drank a great deal of whiskey that night.

Now, at the reception, Aaron found he was drinking more than he intended. He asked himself if marrying into the Deavorses meant he would drink as much as these planters seemed to drink.

"Let's go into town," he said to Joleen.

"Yes, let's go right now," she said.

He took her hand, and they excused themselves and walked toward the house.

Chapter 36

Joleen's fantasies about sex with Aaron had been bold and vivid—though diffused—and her body had matched her mind's boldness with its intense feelings of excitement. She would lie in a hot bath while her fingers caressed her breasts and the long scar on her thigh, and she would glow with hazy images of Aaron's hands and Aaron's lips, and she would remember the strength she had felt when she touched his arms.

But now, on her wedding night, as she changed into a blue silk nightgown, her boldness and her sensual confidence deserted her. The body she had explored and pampered and aroused seemed alien. Now she wondered if Aaron would find her nearly as desirable as she hoped. She told herself he must have had many women. And she had had almost no experience with men, just with boys who did not know what they were doing.

Joleen tied the last ribbon in place and walked slowly from the dressing room.

Aaron rose from the bed to meet her. He offered her champagne, but she shook her head and stared shyly at the floor. He put a finger to her chin and lifted her head. The look in his dark eyes as he glanced from her face to her breasts pressing against the thin gown both excited her and restored some of her confidence.

"You're so very beautiful, Joleen," he said. "Almost too beautiful to . . . touch. But far too beautiful . . . not to ravish."

Her eyes had followed his gaze down, and now she looked up sharply and tilted her head.

"I'm sorry, I didn't mean to frighten you," he said. "I spoke too boldly."

Joleen smiled at the corners of her lips. "No, Aaron, your words didn't frighten me at all," she said. "They were lovely words. They . . . reassured me."

Aaron cupped her face with his hands. Within those strong hands Joleen felt the heat in her cheeks grow warmer. Aaron brushed her lips with his. New warmth rose up from her toes to her breasts, and her nipples grew tender.

She put her hands over his. They kissed with their mouths open. She startled him as she licked his tongue, and she told herself to be less bold and let him pace their lovemaking.

Aaron led her to the huge canopied bed. He lifted her up gently and kissed her eyes, then laid her down on the bed. He bent down, but pulled back and hovered above her, as though hesitant to touch her.

"I love you, Joleen," he whispered. He stroked her lips with two fingers.

"And I love you, Aaron," she said.

She took the fingers between her lips and began to suck the fingers, first softly, then deeper into her mouth, with an urgency that made her nipples tingle.

His lips replaced his fingers. They sucked the kiss, sucked each other's lips and tongue. He lowered himself to her body, and she felt his hardness, and it delighted her.

They kissed and caressed for a long time. Aaron carefully unfastened each ribbon and slid off the gown. She lay naked beneath his gaze, her legs bent at the knees and her thighs spread wide. He continued to stare down at her open body while he undressed.

Joleen stiffened as he stroked her thighs.

"You've been hurt . . . that's a bad scar," he mumbled. His finger was maddening on the soft ridge of flesh.

"I fell from a horse. . . . Do that more, please. Yes, rub it there, Aaron. . . ."

He fondled the scar and squeezed her breasts. She scratched his own taut nipples and then rose up to tantalize his ear with her tongue.

"Am I too . . . bold?" she asked as they kissed again.

"No . . . no . . . you're perfect, Joleen . . . so beautiful . . . so . . . so very sensuous . . . like a kitten."

She realized she was indeed purring with her excitement. Aaron brushed his penis across her scar. A stab of uncertainty came back to her. But only for a moment. He licked the scar, and her mind was lost in the flood of her senses. She squirmed and groaned and realized she was growing moist.

She arched her knees up sharply and opened her thighs.

Aaron was gentle and hesitant as he moved deeply inside her. She flinched and whimpered with the pain, but she begged him to continue.

The pain joined the other sensations in a sum of pleasure that caused Joleen to rake her nails across her breasts and up her sides and then dig the nails into her scalp. Aaron began to move gently inside her, and she enclosed him with her long legs and bit her arm.

". . . see your face . . . want to see . . . face . . ." she gasped. She arched up to squeeze his penis and try to suck it deeper into her tight flesh, and all the time she stared into his eyes.

While her climax built, she licked his face. Then her head fell back, and the climax seared her body. She did not relax for an instant. Already, as she savored his own climax, she felt herself growing ready once more.

They mumbled "I love you . . . love you . . ." between kisses as they continued to make love, and Joleen felt she could lie locked and undulating with Aaron inside her body forever and ever.

Chapter 37

Joleen squirmed on the chair as Signore Carlini began another piece on his violin. Joleen rather liked the music. But she did not like having to sit still for so long. She looked over at Aunt Delma, who was staring at the violinist.

Joleen realized that someone else was fidgeting in her seat. There was a movement of bright green silk. Joleen turned and caught the eye of a pretty, auburn-haired lady of about her own age. The lady smiled and nodded. Joleen smiled in return. Was she supposed to know the lady? She did not remember having met her. But she had met so many people in the three months she had been in Natchez.

There were all these new people and strange things in her life now. In her brief visits to Natchez over the years she had gained no idea of what the city was really like. Now each day she discovered something new. Some of these aspects of city living delighted her, some amazed her, and some repelled her. And everybody was always rushing around. It wasn't at all like the pace of life at the Columns. The first few weeks, she found it different and exciting, but now she wasn't so certain.

After the concert she and Aunt Delma were going to the Blue Bird Tea Room. And then she was invited to a quilting bee. Such a flurry of activity, she told herself. She was never idle, and she was never alone. Yet she was usually bored and quite often lonely.

She was never bored or lonely when Aaron was with her. But he was off on another of his hateful trips. This was the third trip in a month. And it had started the very first morning of their marriage. He was always vague about these trips. He would say, "Oh, it's just a silly case, Joleen. The details would only bore you. A fight about a land title down in Wilkinson County. Boring as sin. . . ." But it wouldn't bore her, not if he would tell her every little detail. Nothing that had to do with Aaron bored her, no matter what. She became bored and lonely and upset only when he evaded her questions and excluded her from his law practice and his travels.

She would gladly go with him, even to inspect obscure land boundaries in remote counties. She would go anywhere with him. She was so eager and so happy when he took her around Natchez and introduced her to people who spoke German and Italian. They shopped in tiny stores on crowded streets with the goods spilling out all over the sidewalks. These stores sold strange spices and teas and cheeses and sweets. Her family would never shop in such places. Aaron told her it reminded him of market streets in Europe. They would shop and take coffee in a dim, smoky little café. Or they would browse through cluttered bookstores. Or Aaron would take her dancing in a hall filled with Germans and Italians who spoke little English.

She found it sad that Aaron had no family. This drew her nearer to him, and though she was always in awe of him, it made her want to protect him. She was intrigued that he had lived in Germany, in a town called Munich. He had traveled all over Europe, and he could speak several languages. And he knew so much! He read books constantly and could talk about anything, not just planting and cotton prices and parties and weddings.

Their best times were after supper when they were home alone. They sat in the parlor, and Aaron drank brandy and read to her from one of the books that filled the shelves in the room. She felt she was so ignorant and uneducated. She had started reading herself, shyly asking him to recommend books. She found it difficult to finish a book. She admitted honestly she'd rather be out on her horse. But she always finished a book he recommended. They were usually history books, and she learned of slavery in other times and also something of the ways that Jews had been persecuted.

On the evening before his last trip, Aaron read her some poetry by a Scotsman named Robert Burns. She liked the poetry. One poem was about freedom, and one line, "A man's a man, for all that," kept coming back to her. Most of the poems were about love.

She memorized a poem that ended:

> And fare thee well, my only love.
> And fare thee well, awhile.
> And I will come again, my love,
> Though it were ten thousand miles.

It was beautiful. She felt it was meant just for her, that Aaron would go away but that he would always come back to her.

Often they went to bed quite early. They made love a long time and fell asleep in each other's arms. The lovemaking sessions were intense and adventuresome. He taught her many variations, and each new one excited her more than the last one. She felt they were not only husband and wife but lovers in some fairy tale, that they were two parts of an identical being and were total only when their bodies were joined together in bed and they exchanged vows of love.

And then Aaron would wake up and get on his horse and ride away!

Joleen twisted on the seat. She glanced about the room. Would the man never finish playing his violin? She swore that if there was one more piece she would leave, and manners be damned!

Finally she sat in the Blue Bird Tea Room with Aunt Delma.

"Did you enjoy the music, dear?" Aunt Delma asked. They sat at her favorite table by the window.

"Yes," Joleen said. "Though I must admit I became restless."

"Some musicians do seem to get carried away," Aunt Delma said. "We're quite fortunate here in Natchez, you know, Joleen. They say there's not a better violinist between here and Philadelphia than Signore Carlini."

Their tea came. Joleen sipped the hot tea carefully and stared out into the street. A heavy rain fell, and the street was muddy. People scurried along seeking shelter and trying to avoid the mud flung up by horses.

"When does Aaron get back, dear?"

"What? Oh, tomorrow, for sure," Joleen said. "He promised to be back tomorrow without fail. I keep hoping he'll come back tonight. Aunt Delma, I hate it when Aaron travels so much."

"He has his profession, dear," Aunt Delma said. "And I suppose if he is to defend landowners with disputed boundaries in court, he must see the land for himself. Though it does seem he travels more than any three lawyers combined."

"I wish I could talk him into plantin' the land Daddy gave us," Joleen said. "Oh, I'd love to live in the country again, Aunt Delma. And Filch could run the place. But Aaron hasn't the slightest interest in growin' cotton. Or in livin' on a plantation. Why, he doesn't even seem interested in buildin' a house on our land. Sometimes I don't understand him at all."

"What do you mean, dear?"

"He has the oddest attitudes about things. Take the niggers. He won't hardly let them do a thing for him. He doesn't mind a bit if I do somethin' for him, but just let Norvina try, and he jumps up and does it for himself."

"Yes, I've noticed that when I visited," Aunt Delma said. "He didn't have any people of his own before the marriage, did he?"

"No," Joleen said. "He hired two free niggers to cook and clean. I didn't know there were any, Aunt Delma."

"Any what, dear?"

"Well, any free niggers," Joleen said. "Until I moved to Natchez, I thought they were all owned by white people. I thought . . . It never occurred to me a nigger would want to be free. I mean, I don't understand how they can take care of themselves and all. Oh, well, what am I sayin'? Surely somebody like Cellus or

Filch could, but they certainly wouldn't want to go away and be free. Would they, Aunt Delma? How does a nigger get to be free? Aaron told me that in the North all the niggers are free and that they live just like white people. I guess I knew that about them, in the North. But I never really thought about it. When I talk to Aaron, I do a lot more thinkin' than ever. I know so little, Aunt Delma. I know at times Aaron must think me the most ignorant of girls."

"Now, that's nonsense," Aunt Delma said. "You're very bright, and Aaron loves you and he's proud of you. It's obvious every time he looks at you. And even a man like Aaron, with such a good mind and so much learnin', well, dear, the last thing he wants is a wife who thinks too much for her own good. That's not why he married you, Joleen. As for the free niggers, yes, there are some in Natchez. Not many, but a few. They hire themselves out, do about the same kind of work as if they'd been hired out by their owners. From time to time someone will free a faithful slave. I've made such a provision for two of my people in my will. With ample money for their well-being. I do believe a few exceptional niggers can be free. But they must be provided for. As for the general lot of them, why, it's unthinkable. They'd be miserable. Most of the free ones take to drink, dear. Maybe in some other life. Maybe in a millennium, when they change and all. . . . But enough of this talk."

They drank tea again and engaged in light gossip about friends. Joleen talked without enthusiasm. She stared at the rain and thought of the boring evening ahead and of another whole night without Aaron.

The door opened. Joleen glanced around. It was the redheaded woman who had smiled at her during the concert. Other people were looking at the woman and leaning together and whispering.

"Aunt Delma, who is that?" Joleen asked.

"That, my dear, is Lavon's unlikely wife. They're quite reluctant to serve her in here. Some of the ladies have protested. But she persists in comin' back, as though she herself were anything but trash. At least, I see she's learnin' to dress properly."

"She smiled at me durin' the concert," Joleen said. "As though she'd like to get acquainted."

"I'm sure she would love to become acquainted," Aunt Delma said. "Of course, it's out of the question. Lavon has become a despicable man! Tradin' in flesh, associatin' with people common as bug dust! As far as the Deavorses are concerned, Lavon is dead. I hear he's makin' a fortune with his tradin'. But none of it will matter. He can have all the money in Adams County and it won't buy back his honor or his social status. And if that pitiful woman ever approaches you, Joleen, simply cut her dead. Why, did you know her father treats sick niggers, though he has no medical degree? Most of those he touches die horrible deaths, but the man makes a fortune, and I hear Lavon shares his profit. Despicable work, Joleen. The dregs of the earth. Men like Lavon and his father-in-law are sorrier than the sorriest nigger that ever walked a cotton row."

"I know every time Daddy hears about Uncle Lavon it upsets him," Joleen said. "When I was out at the Columns last week, Daddy heard somethin' that upset him so much he went into the study and stayed there the rest of the day. Everybody hates those traders and men with nigger dogs and all, don't they? And yet people buy from them and use their services. Just last week the Delsanos bought two mechanics from a trader. It all seems so odd to me, Aunt Delma. Hatin' those men and yet dealin' with them. I know the men disturb Aaron, too. We'll be out in town and come across a trader, and suddenly Aaron gets real angry and says something bitter. But then he goes right back to bein' his usual cynical self."

"You haven't told me all the news of your visit to the Columns," Aunt Delma said. "How is everybody? How are Lawton and Lucinda gettin' along?"

"I guess everybody's fine," Joleen said. "Mama and Daddy are all right. And Lawton and Lucinda seem fine, too. I think she likes livin' on the plantation. She's really come out of her shell a lot. They seem to have a good marriage, Aunt Delma. They really seem happy. But I don't think Lawton's gotten over the barn burnin' down with all that cotton in it."

"Did they ever find out what caused the fire?"

"No, they never did," Joleen said. "Daddy even had the sheriff out. Lord, Lawton takes the blame, since he talked Daddy into holdin' the cotton off the market. You know, Aunt Delma, I think Lawton'd feel guilty about anything. Sometimes I think he feels guilty because the sun comes up."

"And what about Tillman, dear?"

"He's about the same," Joleen said. "Stays by himself a lot and hardly ever says a word."

"Lord, that boy's growin' up to be the strangest Deavors that ever lived," Aunt Delma said. "He spends too much time alone. He should start comin' into Natchez more and meet children his own age. The boy's goin' on fourteen, but you'd never know it except for his size."

"That's probably a good idea," Joleen said. "He could stay with me. I could use the company."

She sipped her tea. It was cold. She looked out at the rain. She didn't believe she could spend another whole night without Aaron.

Chapter 38

Joleen picked at the fried chicken. Norvina hovered behind her chair.

"Can I fix you somethin' else, Miss Joleen?" Norvina asked.

"I'm just not hungry," Joleen said.

"Maybe some pork chops," Norvina said. "You always did like a good pork chop."

Joleen shoved her plate away. "No, I'm not hungry. Please, Norvina, leave me alone. I don't want anything to eat."

She went into the parlor. The room was dark. She

did not light a lamp. She walked to the window and looked out at the rain that churned the drive into mud. Puddles stood on the lawn. A hot breeze rippled the curtains. She stood with her hands held in front of her and stared out at the rain for several minutes. The sound of carriages and horses beyond the shrubbery made her loneliness more acute.

She dared herself to cry. But she wanted to cry. Or scream. Or throw something across the room. She was miserable. This had been the longest day of her life. And the loneliest. Despite the concert and Aunt Delma and the tea room and the quilting bee.

When she was with Aaron she was so happy that she gave him the benefit of all her doubts. She felt his love for her, and he seemed to enjoy being with her as much as she enjoyed being with him. Each pleasant thing they did in the course of a day had a thread of sensuality that ultimately led them to bed and to love-making.

But on an evening such as this, all her doubts poured out.

She had doubts about these frequent business trips he would never discuss. She had doubts about his explanation for the night she had saved him from the slave patrol. She even had doubts about why he seemed so cynical and foppish in public and yet with her was often serious and always assertive and strong. She had tried to believe that it was just his way of dealing with a world he found largely not to his liking, a way of avoiding any involvement with people he did not consider worth his while.

On this hot night in May she felt she did not know Aaron at all. He was certainly posing, but for reasons she did not begin to understand. And he was lying to her. She was sure of that. Joleen stepped to the table and poured a glass of sherry. She told herself she could take no more of this. She had tried to love Aaron and make him happy. And she just knew that he was content and that he loved her when they were together.

Then why did he run off all the time? Why did he continually lie to her? She knew there might be another woman. Yet she felt it was something more than a rival. But what? She had no idea, and he wouldn't tell her. Then, when they were together, she was so happy that she did not let herself think about the kind of misery she suffered on a night like this.

She sipped the sherry. A cawing sound caused her to look around. It was only LeRoy, the parrot Aunt Delma had given them. "Caw, caw yourself," she said as she walked to his cage.

LeRoy tilted his head and looked up at her with one eye. He was an orange-and-green bird who had never learned to speak a word, despite all Joleen's efforts to teach him.

Joleen returned to the window. She remembered when her uncle had first returned to the Columns. He told them about dining in a garden filled with date palms. orange trees, and cages of bright, jabbering parrots. Her father had been so happy when Lavon returned. Now her uncle had become the worst sort of man, and her father was deeply hurt.

Joleen drank more sherry. A horse was galloping up the street. It might be Aaron, she told herself. But the horse galloped past the house. She thought of her uncle again. And of seeing him this evening as she returned from the quilting bee.

The rain had let up as she sat in the back of the open carriage. She was eager to hurry home, hoping against hope that Aaron had returned. But Filch drove the horse slowly along the muddy road. At an intersection just outside the city limits they came on a new brick building. Joleen saw eight slaves, haltered by chains at their necks and wrists, standing outside.

"Filch, stop the carriage a minute," she called.

He reined up the horse. The slaves were being examined by a very fat white man. An even fatter black man held an umbrella over the man's head. Joleen stared at the scene. There was a Negro locked in a set of stocks by the door.

"Filch, what is that?" she asked. "What's happenin'?"

"That there's a nigger pen, Miss Joleen," he said. "Them niggers, they been brought down here from

Carolina or Virginny. They goin' to be put up for sale. Places like this—they more and more of 'em springin' up in Natchez."

"And that man in the stocks?"

"Well, like as not he's bein' punished for somethin'," Filch said. "We better be gettin' on home now. Norvina, she be upset if her supper's cold when you get back."

"No, wait a minute," Joleen said. "I've never seen anything like this, Filch. People chained like this. And in stocks. Why are they chained up? It must be painful. Have they come all the way down here chained like that? Oh, look!"

The fat man slapped a Negro in the face. Joleen had never seen anyone hit a slave before. Though she remembered that her Uncle Lavon had slapped Cellus. Her thought seemed to give birth, for at that moment Lavon walked from the building and said something to the fat man.

Then he turned to the slaves. He spoke and nodded to the door. They did not move. He cracked his whip in the air. They stumbled forward and went through the door. Lavon and the two fat men followed.

"That's terrible," Joleen said. "I've seen traders from a distance a couple of times in Natchez. But never anything like this, Filch. That's my uncle. He's a Deavors."

"Yes'm, I know," Filch said. "I knowed from the moment I saw him come up the house road in that old buggy, drinkin' his whiskey, I knowed he was sorry news, was goin' to bring grief to the family. Well, we better be gettin' on."

"No, wait, Filch," she said. "What goes on in that buildin'? They're goin' to sell those slaves? Men go in there and examine them and bid on them? Is that all that happens? What if the slaves don't like their masters? Where all did you say they came from? They must be scared, so far from home. And don't they have families? Why are there only men?"

"Miss Joleen, better you ask Mist' Aaron or your daddy 'bout these things," Filch said.

"Don't drive off," she said. "I want to go inside. I want to see what's happenin'."

Filch turned around. "Miss Joleen, you can't do that. Ladies don't never go into slave pens. Now, we better get on home."

"Damnit, I want to see what my uncle's goin' to do with those niggers, Filch. I can go inside if I want to."

"Miss Joleen. I couldn't let you do that."

"You couldn't let me? Filch, how dare you talk to me this way!"

"Miss Joleen, you be a married lady now, and mostly growed up, but you still young," he said. "Your husband, he not here, and your daddy, he done charged me to look after you. I couldn't let you go inside that place."

"I dare you to try and stop me! I can do what I want! And I won't be bound by any orders from any nigger! Oh, Lord, I'm sorry, Filch. I didn't mean to say that. I don't know what's happenin' to me. Seems like nothin' is the same since I moved into Natchez."

"Yes'm, you right," Filch said. "We was all better off back to the Columns. We all done seen too much, got ourselves to thinkin' too much and askin' too many questions. Let's go home now, Miss Joleen. Norvina, she done fixed chicken for your supper."

"Yes, let's go home, Filch," she said.

Joleen set her empty glass on the table. It was early, but she decided to go up to the bedroom. She would read awhile. She knew she wouldn't be able to sleep. And tomorrow she would insist on a long talk with Aaron.

LeRoy cawed his disapproval as she walked from the parlor. She was halfway up the stairs when she heard someone at the front door. She pivoted and ran down two steps. She stopped. If that was Aaron, she was not going to run to him. Filch opened the door. He was talking to someone. She could not hear what was said, but obviously it wasn't Aaron.

The door closed. Joleen walked down the stairs.

"Who was that?" she asked.

"Just some nigger who wanted to speak to Mist' Aaron. Said it was important business. I told him to come back tomorrow."

Joleen opened the door and ran down the flagstone walk. It was raining harder.

"Wait a minute," she called.

The Negro turned. He wore a hat. He did not remove it when she approached him, as a Negro was expected to do.

"What do you want with my husband?'" she asked.

"Just some law business, Mrs. Clauson," he said. "It can wait till he comes back."

"But you told Filch it was important. Maybe I can help you."

"No, I'd have to speak to your husband, ma'am. Good night, now, Mrs. Clauson."

"What's your name?" she asked. "Who's your master? Why are you out alone this time of night?"

"My name is Clarence Lee. I have no master. I'm a free man."

"Tell me why you want to see my husband. I insist. Tell me why you want to see him."

"No, ma'am, I really couldn't. It has to do with him bein' a lawyer. Well, now, good night."

"Damnit, don't walk away from me! How dare you walk away from me! Free or not, you're still a . . ." She bit off the sentence. The rain fell harder. She was soaking wet. Water dripped from her face. "I'm sorry," she said. "May I be honest with you? I've never met a free black man in my life. My husband will be back tomorrow. I'll tell him you called."

"Yes'm, thank you, good night." He walked away.

Joleen returned to the house. She found the staircase endless. Each step brought a new thought, a new worry. Why would this freed slave be calling on Aaron? Freed slave . . . She smiled at the thought. She had apologized to two black men in a few hours. One was a slave and one was free.

She wanted no more of Natchez. She wanted to go back to the Columns, where she could be young and naïve and not worry and everything was familiar and in its proper place. And where everybody loved her and where she was never, never lonely or alone.

Joleen reached the top of the stairs and looked down the hall toward the dark bedroom. She swore to herself that if Aaron did not talk honestly when he returned that she would pack her things and go right out to the Columns.

Chapter 39

"What a lovely baby you have," Joleen said. "What's his name?"

"Thomas," the woman holding the baby answered. She made cooing sounds, and Thomas smiled and clutched her gloved finger with his little hand.

The Deavorses gathered around the woman. Lucinda and Estelle and Joleen played with Thomas, who had blue eyes and reddish hair. The woman who held Thomas was dressed in a black silk dress. She wore a black bonnet and a veil that covered the top part of her face and shadowed her mouth and chin.

Aaron stood back and watched the scene with amusement and some apprehension. They were in the lounge of the paddle-wheeler *Kentucky*. The family had come to see him and Joleen off. He was taking her on what he called a business trip to Ohio.

The veiled woman was the first part of that business. She was introduced to the Deavorses as Mrs. Campbell, the widow of a Wilkinson County farmer. Actually her name was Lucy. She was an octoroon and a slave.

The baby she held belonged to a fat blond woman who sat across the lounge sipping a glass of port. The woman, whom Aaron knew from Ohio, was named Mrs. Steuben. She and her husband had come down to run a store and gotten involved in the Underground

Railroad's activities. Her husband had died of smallpox a month ago, and now she was returning to Ohio.

When Aaron decided to dress Lucy as a wealthy white woman, Mrs. Steuben had suggested Lucy carry the baby, to make her disguise complete. Such caution and cleverness were necessary. Lucy's master, Harry Thornton, had been in Natchez the past few days. He and his agents haunted the docks. He offered a two-hundred-dollar reward for Lucy's return. And he made it clear that he would kill anyone who assisted her.

Lucy had escaped twice and been recaptured. If Thornton caught her again, her punishment would be severe. He was willing to whip and perhaps maim a valuable slave and then sell her downriver to a sugar-cane plantation at a financial loss, as an example to his other slaves.

Thornton stood by the gangway as the *Kentucky* boarded its passengers. He was a hulking man with two pistols in his coat. Aaron walked a few feet behind Lucy. There was a moment of anxiety as Lucy passed her master. But he paid no attention to her, and now she was safely on board.

Lucy wanted to escape because six months earlier she and her husband had been separated in a sale in Lavon's slave pen. Her husband had escaped to Canada. He got word downriver for her to join him. Clarence smuggled the message to Lucy. Now, on her third attempt, it seemed she would be successful.

This was Joleen's first trip out of the South, and she bubbled with excitement. Aaron was glad to see her so happy. He knew how much misery he had caused her, a misery he had underestimated to a nearly fatal degree. Joleen had been on the verge of leaving him a month ago, in May.

He thought of the scene when he returned from his trip almost a full day late. At first Joleen was quiet and sullen. Then her anger flared, and she smashed a cup against the wall. She accused him of having another woman, of not loving her, of lying to her about everything, including his true destination the night she saved him.

Neither his declarations of love nor his denials of having lied could calm her. In desperation he promised that she could accompany him on any future trips. After several tense hours they went to bed. Their lovemaking was urgent yet tender. Aaron lay curled against her damp body while she slept, and realized just how much he loved and needed Joleen and how unfair he was being to her.

Yet what could he do? He was committed to the Underground Railroad, and many people depended on him. And he could not take a chance on being honest with Joleen. She was beginning to change, now that she lived in Natchez, in what he called the "real world." Her mind was opening to new ideas. She was beginning to think and to question things she had always taken for granted. Slave auctions and the mistreatment of slaves shocked and angered her. But so did any mention of abolitionists or freeing slaves or any criticism of the institution itself. He knew precisely the path her thoughts were taking. She realized that many aspects of slavery were wrong. She would work tirelessly to improve these aspects, to end the abuses of slaves, to end slave trading.

But to free slaves, to do away with the institution itself—why, it was unthinkable. Yes, "unthinkable" was exactly the word for Joleen's beliefs. She could not even let herself think of such a thing as ending slavery or freeing slaves.

Aaron didn't travel for a month. He courted Joleen with love and flattery and gifts and sex. And he thoroughly enjoyed every minute of it. Then he was summoned north by Levi Coffin. He had to go to Ohio. And now he had to take Joleen along with him.

Aaron stood there in the lounge and watched Joleen's cheeks crease into dimples as she smiled. He told himself he had to tell her the truth very soon. But what if she rejected him, stopped loving him, revealed his secret to her family?

Aaron finished his whiskey and put the glass on the bar. The paddle-wheeler's whistle sounded three times. The black waiter announced that all visitors must go ashore.

Athel gathered his family together. Everyone hugged and kissed Joleen. Athel and Lawton shook Aaron's hand. The Deavorses left the lounge. The whistle sounded three more times. Aaron walked over to Joleen. She smiled. Her face radiant. At such times he felt that all the beauty and intensity in her face was meant as love for him.

Joleen kissed his cheek. "I know kissin' you in public will shock everybody," she whispered. "But if they only knew what we do when we're alone! Oh, Aaron, thank you for takin' me with you today. I don't ever want to be away from you again."

Her happiness was infectious. Aaron told himself he had never been more content. Then he looked past Joleen's face, and a chill shot up his back.

Harry Thornton was walking into the lounge. Lucy had seen Thornton too. Her hands were trembling. The baby started to cry. Thornton walked directly toward Lucy.

Thornton sat beside Lucy and played with the baby as the *Kentucky* pulled from the dock. Aaron sat across the lounge and tried to remain calm.

"What's wrong, Aaron?" Joleen asked. "You seemed so full of spirit a few minutes ago. Now you're glum and you're not talkin' at all."

"Just thinking about a case, Joleen," he said. He forced a smile. "It was thoughtless of me."

"Where you headed to, ma'am?" Thornton was asking. Behind him, Mrs. Steuben twisted on her seat.

"To . . . to Cleveland," Lucy said. "To visit my family."

"I'm sure they'll be glad to see you and that fine boy," Thornton said. His face was red. He was gulping whiskey. "I take it they haven't seen their grandson yet."

"No, this will be the first time," Lucy said. She sat so that Thornton could not look directly into her face.

"You travelin' alone?"

"No, I've got my . . . nigger girl waitin' in my cabin."

"You think it's safe to take your nigger to a

Yankee state like Ohio, ma'am? Can't never tell what a nigger might try, once she gets to Yankee land. Mighty near to Canada. You don't think she might try to run away?"

"I'm sure she won't," Lucy said.

"Well, if she does, or if them Yankee abolitionists give you any trouble, you just call on old Harry Thornton here," he said. "Lucy, one of my nigger gals, done run away, third time. But I'm goin' to track her down. I know she's headed for Ohio. Got a runaway nigger husband 'round . . . well, from what I could find out, 'round Cleveland."

Thornton drank more whiskey. Mrs. Steuben got to her feet, but sat down again.

"Seein' as how you're a widow lady, perhaps you'll do me the honor of takin' supper with me some evenin' in Cleveland," Thornton said.

"Take supper with you?" Lucy asked. "Why . . . why . . . I would be delighted."

"You mighty young to be a widow," Thornton said. "And goin' off alone to Ohio. Good thing you got family there. Why, I hear Cleveland is a hotbed of abolitionists. Course, when I find my nigger up there, and I will, ma'am, oh, yes, I will, when I find her, the courts'll have to give her back to me. That there's the law. And God help anybody who's hidin' her. See, I know this farmer up there, he knows some of the places the abolitionists hide runaway niggers. We goin' to barge right in and flush out my nigger. And I'll make sure she don't get on no boat to Canada."

"I'm sure you will, sir," Lucy said.

"See, I got me a nose for niggers, ma'am," Thornton said. "Can smell one a mile off. Can't no nigger hide from Harry Thornton. Yessir, I could tell my Lucy half a mile off."

"You're very clever, Mr. Thornton," Lucy said. She stood up. "Now, if you'll excuse me, I better see 'bout puttin' Thomas to bed for his nap."

"Pleasure talkin' to you, ma'am," Thornton said. He got to his feet and bowed to Lucy.

Lucy left the lounge. A moment later Mrs. Steuben bolted up and followed her.

"Now, that there was a lady of quality," Thornton said to Aaron and Joleen.

Thornton went out on deck. Aaron talked idly to Joleen, but his pulse was racing.

"Why don't we go to our cabin, Aaron?" she asked.

"Yes, I'd like that," he said. They looked at each other. There was a faint smile at the corners of her lips as they walked out.

Chapter 40

Joleen had discovered the pleasure of making love in the afternoon.

Dinner, the heaviest meal of the day, was at noon, when the weather was hot and humid. Joleen always ate heartily, and since her marriage she drank wine with dinner. She left the table full, sometimes slightly intoxicated, and often sleepy. Aaron taught her that many Europeans take what he called a siesta after all the food and wine. So an hour of rest was now natural on a hot afternoon. And the lovemaking that followed was better than love in the morning or at night.

It was the same this stifling afternoon on the boat. They ate dinner in their cabin. They drank a bottle of Chablis. Joleen had more than her usual share. She slept for half an hour. When she awoke, Aaron was staring at her. She kissed his cheek. He brushed a strand of wet hair from her forehead.

Their love play was leisurely at the beginning, soft kisses and gentle touches of tongue and fingers. Joleen's excitement built quickly when Aaron kissed along the scar on her thigh and tantalized her vagina with his tongue.

"Come to me now, please," she whispered. "I want you inside me. Go inside me, Aaron."

They made love the first time with Aaron lying between her thighs. Aaron's slow pace maddened and delighted Joleen. She and Aaron climaxed at the same time.

A quarter-hour of petting aroused them again. Joleen lay on top of Aaron. She savored the feel of his penis in her vagina as she moved up and down. She brought herself to a quick climax, then watched his face as his own release built inside her body. She squeezed the muscles of her vagina. Aaron groaned, and his hands slid around on her firm buttocks. Their eyes met at the instant of his climax.

Then they slept again, wrapped against each other, until supper.

At Cairo, Illinois, they changed to the paddle-wheeler *Brutus*, which took them up the Ohio River. Then they took an overland coach to Cleveland. Mrs. Campbell and her son, Thomas, and Mrs. Steuben shared the coach.

Aaron and Joleen checked into a hotel. After dinner Aaron suggested a walk along the Lake Erie docks. A ferry was loading passengers for Canada. Joleen was surprised to see Mrs. Campbell boarding the ferry. Thornton and two rough-looking men stood at the gangway.

"My family's over in Canada," she told Thornton. "My poor Aunt Ellen is sick with the fever in Port Stanley. You could come callin' when I get back, Mr. Thornton. We live at the corner of Elm and Harwood."

"I'll look forward to it, ma'am," he said. "I'll come callin' on you. And I hope you find your aunt's recoverin'."

The gangway was lifted up. The ferry moved from the dock. Mrs. Campbell stood on deck. When the boat was a hundred feet from the dock, she suddenly tore off her bonnet and veil.

Thornton gasped. The color drained from his face.

"That's Lucy!" Thornton shouted. "That's my nigger! Stop the boat! I want my goddamn nigger!"

The ferry did not stop. Lucy smiled and waved. A black man appeared at her side. He put his arm around her waist.

Thornton's face was bright red now. He sagged against the railing. The last Joleen saw of Thornton, he was being held up by one of his men while the other gave him a cup of water.

Joleen had come to like "Mrs. Campbell" and to dislike Thornton. Lucy's escape did not upset her. She did not even think in terms of abolitionists or slavery. As she and Aaron walked away, she was merely amused and impressed by Lucy's audacious escape.

They stayed in Cleveland two days, and though Aaron took Joleen on three Lake Erie cruises, she was unhappy most of the time because he left her alone while he went off on one business appointment after another. She did not meet a single person Aaron knew in Cleveland. The same was true when they visited Mechanicsburg. Aaron left her alone a whole afternoon. Joleen did not meet anyone.

But in Cincinnati everything changed. Joleen loved the city. It lay right at the Kentucky border and was very Southern, yet it was full of Germans. She met many people Aaron knew from his childhood and from his years of practicing law.

Often Aaron spoke in German, but he was always careful to translate everything for Joleen. She was delighted when she began to understand a few phrases. They dined in German restaurants. Joleen ate German food that didn't exist in Natchez. She drank thick, dark German beer. She had never tasted beer before, and she didn't much like it.

One day Aaron took her to the Jewish section. He showed her a small building he called a synagogue—a Jewish church, he explained. The people seemed very German, yet they were different. They spoke a kind of German called Yiddish.

By this time Joleen knew a great deal about what Jewish people believed. She had been disturbed when Aaron told her they did not believe in the divine birth of Christ. She told him she could never accept this. He merely smiled and told her no one was asking her to accept it. She seldom thought about the fact. Her mind was not tuned to theological matters. She was a Presbyterian who accepted the church's teachings but paid little attention to them. The church was accepted as an important institution, but it played a very small part in her life or that of her family.

Very few of Aaron's friends were Jewish. And those who were seemed as little interested in the religion as he was.

Joleen and Aaron stayed in Cincinnati a week. There was a continual round of parties. Joleen was always the center of attention. Aaron was unusually indrawn at these parties. He would stand back and drink his whiskey very slowly and let Joleen talk.

And at every party the talk soon turned to the South and slavery. Many of the people sympathized with the South. They wanted slavery to be legalized in Ohio. But other people were openly critical of the institution, which surprised and disturbed Joleen. She had always accepted the fact that many Yankees hated slavery, but to find herself drinking punch at a party in her honor and defending the institution was quite another matter.

It had never occurred to her that one might actually have to defend slavery. It just was. Like, well, like the government and the churches and the family. What other system could one have in the South, with all the niggers? How could the cotton be planted and harvested without slaves? It was the natural condition of black people.

Yes, she would admit, on occasion, a particular slave could be freed, though from what she knew in Natchez, free blacks usually took to drink and came to no good end. Yes, she did know some slaves who might actually do well as free men. There was a slave on her plantation in Mississippi, named Cellus, who helped run the place and could certainly get along as a free man. But he was the exception. And she was certain Cellus never thought of being free. He was quite content. So were her family's other slaves. Why, they would be terrified if they had to leave the Columns and take care of themselves.

Perhaps in some other life, perhaps in hundreds of years, black people would change. But not very long ago, why, they were living in the jungles of Africa! Oh, it was well enough in the North, she supposed. Let the niggers be free up here if that was what white people wanted. All the people in Mississippi asked was that the Yankees leave them alone to handle their niggers as they saw fit.

What? Well, of course, niggers were human beings. And she hated slave traders, and she thought it was terrible when slaves were mistreated. But that didn't happen often. Why, her father would never hurt one of his people. And he never bought or sold slaves.

The arguments would go on until she was exhausted and irritated. And she would look to Aaron for help. But he never entered these arguments except to make some caustic comment or to indicate that the whole topic bored him.

The discussions always came to an impasse. Joleen realized that these people would never understand slavery in Mississippi, and she certainly wasn't willing to accept their arguments. They weren't speaking from experience. They would have to go down South and live with black people to understand them and to see what slavery was really like and how well it worked.

By the time she got to the fifth party, she refused to discuss slavery at all.

But a Kentucky planter named Conway Pearson would talk to her of nothing else. He was overjoyed to find someone from Mississippi, who he assumed shared his beliefs. Pearson advocated slave trading and the breaking up of slave families if expedience and profit demanded it.

"The niggers were put on earth by God to serve white people as their slaves, Mrs. Clauson," he said. "And we whites can do with the nigger as we please. We can work him till he breaks. Whip his black back when he disobeys. Nigger's not a human bein'. He's without a soul, like some beast. Treat him like a human and he gets lazy and rebellious and starts usin' that little mind of his to think up mischief. Me, I work my niggers till they drop in the fields, and whip 'em at random just to keep 'em scared all the time."

Within five minutes Joleen despised this fat, red-faced planter. She told him his beliefs were abominable. And when he smiled in a condescending manner and dismissed her as a child, she startled him—and herself—by discussing slavery in Greek and Roman times. She had never before used the knowledge that Aaron's books and her other readings in history had given her. She made comparisons between slavery in the South and other forms of slavery at other times. She used historical facts to refute Pearson's arguments, and ended up by stating that in some ways Southern slavery was crueler than that of the Romans.

Joleen stopped in the middle of a sentence. She asked herself what in the world had gotten into her, to talk this way about slavery. She'd had too much punch, that was for sure.

She turned abruptly from Pearson and walked over to Aaron, who had been standing a few feet away listening to the argument.

"What a terrible man," she said. "Let's dance, Aaron. I'm sick of talkin' and all."

They danced again and again. Joleen had even more punch. Soon she was able to rid her mind of all those awful contradictory feelings about slavery and to smile and flirt and make the kind of party talk with which she was comfortable.

Joleen enjoyed the trip, but she was relieved when the boat docked at Natchez. She didn't think she ever wanted to leave Mississippi again. She had heard and seen too many disturbing things in Ohio. She wanted to stay down here where everything was in its proper place.

Several porters and carriage drivers offered their services as Joleen and Aaron disembarked. Aaron declined their offers. One black man was insistent.

"No, I always give my business to a man named Clarence Lee," Aaron said. "Isn't he here to meet the boat? Do you know him?"

"Clarence . . . the free nigger?" the man asked.

"Yes," Aaron said. "What about him?"

"Well, no massuh, he ain't here. He ain't free no more. He's been sold to a sugarcane plantation."

"What in hell happened?" Aaron asked.

The Negro backed away. "I don't know, massuh," he said.

A white man had been listening to the conversation. He walked over to Aaron. "Why, bunch of farmers caught that free nigger and a white Yankee preacher name of Lewis, caught 'em red-handed helpin' four niggers to escape. White man, they branded his forehead and give him thirty lashes 'fore turnin' him over to the sheriff, and word is he'll get at least ten years. The nigger, they done branded him in the palms of his hands and whipped him good. He's been sold to a fellow owns a sugarcane plantation 'cross the river in Louisiana. And that's too good for him. Why, they ought to have killed him."

Joleen was repulsed by what the man said. And Aaron was actually trembling. His lips were pinched together. He was deathly white. His hands closed into fists.

"Hey, what's wrong, mister?" the man asked.

"Aaron, are you all right?" Joleen asked. She touched his arm. He jerked his arm away. She had never seen such a look on his face.

"Let's go home," he muttered. He hired a carriage and told the driver to load their luggage.

"Aaron, please tell me what's wrong," she pleaded. "You knew him, didn't you? The nigger. He came to the house one night while you were away."

"Damnit, Joleen, I don't . . ." He swallowed hard. "Yes, I knew him. I can't . . . Please, please, let's not talk now."

They climbed into the carriage. Joleen wanted to touch Aaron, to comfort him, but she feared he would reject her comfort.

They started up the hill. Joleen huddled miserably in her corner of the carriage. She knew something was wrong, something even worse than what had happened to those poor men.

BOOK V

The Brothers

Chapter 41

Lavon stood up in the stirrups and looked past the last of his land and onto land that belonged to the Columns. He could see Athel's slaves working on the horizon. He settled down in the saddle and brushed at the tiny August flies that buzzed around his head.

A week earlier, Lavon had decided to reveal that he owned these three hundred acres adjacent to the Columns. He could not resist the satisfaction he would get from Athel's reaction to the news that Lavon was now his neighbor. And according to Essie, Athel's reaction was disbelief and anger.

Lavon savored the idea of also letting Athel know that, through Jason Colfax and other agents, he now owned five additional units of the twelve land parcels that surrounded the Columns. But that pleasure would have to wait. Athel was no fool, and if he were aware of Lavon's plan, he might well be able to buy some of the remaining land himself. No, Lavon told himself, Athel wouldn't know, not until he discovered that the Columns was surrounded by Lavon's land.

By then Lavon would own even the road from Benton and Natchez, the only road onto the plantation. The Deavorses never even thought about that road or considered the fact that they did not own the land that contained it. The owner, Lavon had discovered through records in the courthouse, was an elderly Frenchwoman named Antoinette LeBeau, who had moved to New Orleans thirty years ago. Colfax tried to buy the land, but she wasn't interested in selling. She had no need of money. However, her only heir, a spendthrift nephew named Alain, told Colfax that his aunt was dying of a wasting disease and that the day he inherited her property he would gladly sell the land.

Then what will the Deavorses do? Lavon asked himself.

He would strangle their goddamn plantation as surely as if he had his fingers around its throat. He would charge Athel an exorbitant amount merely to cross over the land to get in and out of the Columns. Athel would have to pay Lavon's price. And one day Lavon would tell Athel: You can no longer cross my land, and if you trespass, I'll have the sheriff on you.

And while he physically strangled the plantation, he would also strangle it financially. Athel was so locked into his tight little world of being a planter and nothing else that his only cash income was the cotton his slaves took out of the ground. Of course, the slaves themselves were worth a fortune, but Athel would starve before he would sell a single slave.

Lavon's enormous cash flow from slave trading gave him increasing power in both Natchez banks. One fine March day Athel would ride confidently into Natchez to finance the year's planting and discover that Lavon's men controlled both banks. Already Lavon could count on the support of two members on each bank's board of directors.

A rider appeared on the far horizon. Lavon wondered if it was Athel. Or Lawton. He could not tell at this distance.

Lavon reined his horse around and trotted along the rows of ripening cotton plants. He brushed sweat from his face. Prospects for a good harvest were improving, and he was pleased at the profit it would bring him, yet he would gladly have seen every damn pod in the county wither so that Athel wouldn't make a dime.

Even in good year Athel would soon be in trouble. Lavon now secretly owned forty-five percent of the Benton gin. By the end of the year, he had been assured, he would own more than half. The gin would process no more Deavors cotton after that. Athel would have to haul his cotton halfway across the county to be ginned. And some critical year, when the plantation was about to go under financially, Athel might as well not gin the cotton at all. Because Lavon would see that the barges carrying the Deavorses' cotton sank mysteriously before reaching New Orleans.

When Essie had burned down the barn full of cotton, Lavon realized how truly vulnerable Athel was. Lavon was angry that Essie acted on his own. He warned Essie there would be hell to pay if he did something like that again. But Essie wasn't caught. And Athel suffered a severe financial blow.

Yes, Athel was quite vulnerable. Other cotton could burn up or be destroyed. At a crucial planting or harvesting time, there could be many kinds of sabotage. The plantation would be physically strangled or financially ruined. Lavon didn't care which tactic succeeded first, though he rather liked the idea of turning the plantation into an island.

One day in the future, Lavon Deavors would be master of the Columns, he told himself, and if his family showed enough humility and contrition, he would be lenient with them. Yes, the Columns would be his. Every goddamn acre and every goddamn slave. And that fine house that was his home, his birthright! He would no longer sell slaves. He would be the wealthiest planter in the county. He would have his honor, and people would respect him.

Frannie was eight months pregnant. He was confident that his child, all his children, would grow up on the plantation. It would be his heirs, and not Athel's, who inherited the Columns.

Lavon's optimism began to fade as he rode toward his overseer's cabin. He recalled his talk two days earlier with Jason Colfax. Lavon had come to assume that the new state constitution now being prepared would contain no provision that outlawed slave trading. But Colfax said he had met with several members of the state legislature and learned that such a prohibition would almost certainly be included.

Lavon knew there would still be a demand for slaves, and he knew he could eventually get around the prohibition one way or another. But for months his profits might be greatly reduced. Just when everything was going well and he could nearly feel his hands squeezing the life out of the Columns, his cash flow would be severely cut.

The constitution wouldn't become law until May 1833. That was nearly a year. He could make a small fortune in that time . . . if only Purvis Swan didn't get half of every dollar he earned. Swan was growing fatter and lazier. The bastard seldom worked. He just wallowed in his obesity and waited for Lavon to turn over half the money. Lavon had tried to buy Swan out. He would pay anything Swan wanted. Swan refused.

Lavon had come to loathe the man. Swan lumbered around town squandering Lavon's money and acting pompous and arrogant. He drank excessively and kept a dozen valuable slaves to wait on him hand and foot.

Lavon wondered if Swan's sanity wasn't going, as though the fat was squeezing his brain. In May, Nester and Blue, two of Swan's dogs, were run over by a wagon. Swan not only hired the preacher from the Blood of the Lamb Baptist Church to conduct the dogs' funeral, but he built a small marble mausoleum in his front yard and buried the dogs there.

When Lavon objected, Swan said, "If it wasn't for Nester and Blue, sir, you'd still be stuck down there on them mud flats, without a pot to pee in."

Lavon was seething with anger as he rode past his slaves, who were hoeing out weeds, and Rayford Blackledge, the overseer. Blackledge was from Tennesee. He had cost more than Lavon wanted to pay, but he came highly recommended, and Lavon needed a dependable man, since he himself knew nothing about cotton. Also, Blackledge was young, ambitious, and greedy. Lavon didn't doubt the man would do anything Lavon asked him to do, as long as he profited from the scheme.

Lavon dismounted at Blackledge's cabin and waited while a boy hitched up his carriage. Chickens scattered as he paced the dry dirt. He thought about Frannie. During the past two weeks she had complained of severe pains, and Lavon was finally convinced that the pain was real and that something might be wrong with the unborn baby.

Lavon took out his watch. What was keeping Dr. Gatlin? He had agreed to meet Lavon at the Red Lion Tavern so they could discuss Frannie's condition. Dr. Gatlin had examined her earlier in the day.

Lavon was finishing his second brandy when the doctor arrived, all haste, importance, and apology. "I swear, I've never seen as much sickness as the past week," the doctor said. "Fevers, the flux, broken limbs. It seems everybody in Natchez wants my services, Mr. Deavors."

"Yes, well, what about Frannie?" Lavon asked.

"Frankly, I'm rather worried," Dr. Gatlin said. "My examination didn't reveal anything new. But those cramps and pain are real, and they're serious. And she's not gainin' weight as she should, Mr. Deavors. In all honesty, I don't know what to do next. I'm most concerned about the delivery."

"Then you think I should take her to New Orleans?" Lavon asked. He looked into the doctor's nervous black eyes and felt an intense dislike for the man, as though he were responsible for Frannie's condition.

"Yes, Mr. Deavors. I'm afraid her condition is that serious," Dr. Gatlin said.

Lavon nodded. Gatlin was considered the best doctor in the state. If he admitted he could not help Frannie, then her condition must indeed be serious. Lavon decided they would go to New Orleans the next day.

On a misty October morning Lavon stood at the rail of the paddle-wheeler *Kentucky* and watched six slaves tie the boat to a Natchez dock. Frannie and her mother sat behind Lavon. Frannie held their two-month-old son, Lige. Only the skill of two of New Orleans' best doctors had saved Lige at his birth. Lige had weighed only three pounds. He was still in frail health, but the doctors said they could do no more for him. He needed nourishment and close care, and they could be provided at home.

Lavon had gone back and forth on paddle-wheelers so often in the past few weeks that he was sick of the trip. As a result, he had had to turn over most of the trading to his agents, and on the last coffle—some 260 slaves—they had bought too dear in Virginia and sold too cheaply in Natchez. In all those weeks that goddamn Swan waddled into the slave pen only one time. He hadn't lifted a fat finger to ensure the best profit when the slaves were sold.

Lavon thought back to his arrival in Natchez on a paddle-wheeler when he had returned from Europe. He had been destitute then, and now he was a wealthy man. And if it wasn't for that fat fool, his wealth would begin to double!

Lavon thought of crawling through the mud flats under the hill. He thought of Lige. He did not want Lige to grow up in the world of Purvis Swan and the Runnels. Damnit, he was already a plantation owner and a wealthy man, and yet he had no sense at all of having regained his honor or pride or self-respect. Still no respectable planter's door in the county would open to him and Frannie. Aunt Delma snubbed Frannie in public. Athel and Lawton passed Lavon on the Natchez streets and did not acknowledge his existence.

But damnit, they would pay! He would have their precious plantation and their precious niggers. He would make them come crawling to him. He would make them acknowledge that he was a Deavors. He would take over the family home and the family land, and he would be the one to continue the Deavors line.

Lige would grow up a proper Deavors, with his rightful heritage. But all this could take years, and Lavon was impatient.

If only he could break that goddamn contract with Swan. . . .

The gangway was put down. Passengers began to disembark. Lavon helped Frannie down the gangway and decided to go right out to Swan's house and settle something with him, no matter what it cost.

Chapter 42

Lavon walked up the steps to Swan's porch. He had no idea of how to deal with the bastard. This frustration increased his anger.

"He's not here, Mist' Lavon," Swan's cook said. "Ain't been here much since the death. Just ain't been hisself. Took to drinkin' more. . . ."

"The death? What death?"

"Why, just last week, Jackson, he done died of the colic," she said. "Mist' Purvis, he set up all night tryin' to save that dog. When he ain't drinkin' now, he been goin' to church a lot."

Sure enough, when Lavon turned to leave, he saw another grotesque little mausoleum in the front yard.

Lavon located Swan at the Blood of the Lamb Baptist Church on the bluffs at the Natchez city limits. Swan was fatter than ever. His face bulged with flesh. His eyes were red from whiskey or crying, or both. He was sitting on the church steps. He looked like a Buddha statue sculptured by an artist who hated Buddha.

Swan managed to get to his feet. "You heard the terrible news?" he asked.

"You mean about the dog?"

"Jackson's been taken from us," Swan said. "I just come out here to talk to the preacher 'bout movin' the graves of all three dogs to the church cemetery. But he ain't here."

"Swan, you can't bury dogs in a church cemetery," Lavon said. "Get hold of yourself. They were only dogs."

"Only dogs! Yes, but they was the finest dogs in the state. Each one of 'em smart as a whip. Smart'n some people I know. I never had me no family. Never had no wife, no children. I was mighty close to them dogs."

"All right, all right, Swan, they were fine dogs," Lavon said. "I just returned from New Orleans, and I want to discuss business."

"Oh, pardon me," Swan said. "How's Frannie and young Lige?"

"They're doing fine, Swan," Lavon said. "Let's go somewhere and talk. It's starting to rain."

"Let's walk back here behind the church," Swan said. "Here, just a minute. Got me a jug in the carriage."

"Hell, let's go to a tavern."

But Swan took the jug and stumbled off around the church. Lavon followed. He cursed beneath his breath. Swan paused to drink. Whiskey dribbled down his three chins. He led Lavon through tombstones to a bare spot at the back of the cemetery beneath a chinaberry tree and ten feet from a bluff overlooking the Mississippi.

"All of them dogs, they done loved a chinaberry," Swan said. He drank again. "Here, you want some whiskey?"

"No, I don't want any whiskey," Lavon said. "And I'm sick of hearing you talk about your goddamn dogs, Swan."

"I was thinkin' of buryin' 'em here 'neath the chinaberry tree," Swan said. "Now, that preacher, he might be hesitant, but I'm willin' to make a big contribution to the church if he's willin'." Swan looked up at Lavon suddenly. It seemed to have taken a minute for Lavon's words to sink in. "What you mean, you sick of talkin' 'bout my goddamn dogs? They was half yours. You become half-owner when we signed that there contract. I never loved nothin' more'n I loved Jackson and Nester and Blue, and I done give you half of 'em. Give you half of what they earned when you didn't have a pot to pee in. And you stand here 'neath this chinaberry tree and mock their memory."

Swan's face was red. He drank again and shook his head. He stepped back to the trunk of the tree.

Lavon advanced on him. "Listen, Swan, I've had

a hard day, and I've come to talk serious business. Now, you haven't lifted a finger to do any work in months, goddamn months. And I'm goddamn sick and tired of bringing down the niggers and selling them and doing every goddamn thing else while you drink and babble about three dead dogs."

"You mighty uppity 'bout me and the dogs now, ain't you?" Swan said. "Why, if it wasn't for me and them, why, you'd still be down there on them mud flats. That's why you talk this way 'bout the dogs. You never did love them dogs, never did 'preciate their hard work, just took it for granted they'd go on workin' for you. I know what you goin' to say. You been schemin' some way to make me break that contract, ain't you? You don't want to give me no more money."

"Swan, I'll buy you out. I'll make you wealthy. Name your price."

"Nossiree, we done signed that there thing all legal," Swan said, "when I had me the dogs and the carriage and the horses and two niggers and the house and a little money in the bank, and you didn't have shit. And I ain't breakin' that contract. You'll never get me to break it. And what you worried 'bout, anyhow? Lord God, you a rich man. Ain't you satisfied with what you got? I sure as shit am, and I ain't givin' it up."

Swan drank again. The motion of drinking made him sway, and he had to take three backward steps to regain his balance. He was only a few feet from the bluff, but he didn't seem to realize it.

Lavon advanced on Swan again. He did not know what to say. Half a dozen lawyers had examined the contract and found it iron-tight. Swan might live for years. Lavon's anger and frustration caused the blood to pump at his temples.

Swan swayed and took another backward step. "See, I done found the Lamb, in the face of the dyin' of them I loved," Swan said. "I done joined this here church. I'm goin' to start tithin', give 'em part of what I earn. I'm rich in this world, and now I got to start thinkin' of the next one. Goin' to get everythin' off my conscience. Goin' to offer that there preacher half my money if he buries the dogs here."

"Damnit, Swan, be reasonable. Do you know how much money that is?"

"It's my money, sir. First thing tomorrow, goin' to have the papers drawed up."

"Christ, Swan, I won't let you do that."

"Not a thing on earth you can do 'bout it," Swan said. "And you might ought to start thinkin' of yourself, as concerns religion. And start thinkin' of young Lige, what nearly died. Start thinkin' 'bout his soul, so you can bury him in consecrated ground here 'side of Nester and Blue and Jackson."

"Bury Lige beside your goddamn dogs? Swan, listen to me one final time. You're not giving all that money to these bench-jumping Baptist fools. That's my money, now. I need that money. You haven't worked in an eternity. I want that money. I'll buy you out."

"Nossiree," Swan said. "I'm keepin' my half-interest, and when I die, it's all goin' to the Blood of the Lamb Baptist Church so they'll have money to do the Lord's work for many a year. And tomorrow, when I draw up the papers, that preacher, he goin' to say, 'Yessir, Brother Swan, Jesus be proud to bury your dogs in our cemetery'."

Lavon stared at Swan. The fool was going to do it. He was going to sign over half of all Lavon gave him. Lavon's hands closed into fists. Swan lifted the jug, but it seemed too heavy. He dropped it to the ground. Whiskey spilled out and flooded a bed of black ants. Swan swayed back and forth. He was looking at Lavon, but his eyes didn't seem to be focusing. He shook his head.

"Swan, goddamnit, Swan, you're crazy," Lavon said. "You're not just drunk. You're crazy. Crazy! I'll have you declared insane. I'll . . ."

Swan smiled. His massive lips opened. A gurgling laugh came up from his throat.

"No, not a thing you can do," Swan said. "I never intend to do 'nother day's work. I got me a hard-workin' Deavors to keep me rich the rest of my days so's I can enjoy everythin' and dedicate myself to the

Lamb. You always looked down on me, always thought I was trash. Thought I was a fool all this time. Well, who's the fool now, Mr. Deavors?"

Lavon stared at the mocking, red-veined eyes. His rage made him tremble. Only once in his life, when he had had malaria in Italy, had he felt such fever.

"You're contemptible, Swan," Lavon said. "A pitiful mound of flesh. You're hardly human. No wonder you're obsessed with those dogs. You probably all came from the same litter. Or maybe you came from some dung heap."

"And what litter did you come from?" Swan asked. "All highfalutin 'bout bein' a Deavors, ain't you? Tell me my own mother was a bitch! Well, she wasn't no whore, sir, and that's more'n you can say. You and your precious Deavors blood! They was lots of talk when you was born that you wasn't no pure Deavors. Fella stayin' out to the Columns, paintin' portraits, word was he was your daddy! Well, what you got to say now? How proud and proper you goin' to be when I start remindin' folks 'bout that?"

Swan laughed again. He swayed. He balanced himself. He half-turned and seemed to see the bluff for the first time. It was only a foot away. He leaned forward and squinted, then drew back sharply. He placed a plump hand on Lavon's arm. Lavon flung it away. Then, in a sudden fury, Lavon shoved Swan toward the cliff. Swan's bulk resisted a moment. Then the clay gave way, and Swan suddenly plunged over the cliff. His fingers clawed the air.

Swan screamed once, then hit a boulder twenty feet down. He rolled the two hundred feet down the rest of the bank into the river.

Lavon watched Swan sink. He did not come up. Lavon smoothed down his hair and wiped sweat from his face. His heartbeat was erratic as he staggered through the tombstones to the front of the church.

There was no one in sight. Lavon bolted into his carriage and whipped the horse to a gallop.

Chapter 43

Lavon could not sleep that night. It was not conscience that kept him awake, but fear of becoming involved in Swan's death, even though there were no witnesses. To his vast relief, there were no repercussions at all. Swan's whiskey-glutted body washed ashore several hundred yards down the river. The jug was found on the bluff. Swan's behavior was considered erratic, and his drinking was a Natchez legend. It was assumed he fell off the bluff while drunk. There was not even an inquest into his death.

Swan had no family. He left no will. Lavon was his partner. Swan's property went to Lavon. DuPre, Swan's obese driver, became Frannie's driver.

Lavon's income doubled. He felt no remorse about Swan's death. He easily rationalized everything. The man was pawing him. He merely wanted to push him away. Anyway, by this time, Swan had become less than human and clearly insane, Lavon told himself. The way Swan swilled whiskey, he would probably have killed himself soon in some drunken accident. But not before Swan would have had ample time to spread malicious gossip about Lavon's birth.

Each time Lavon thought of Swan's charge that he was illegitimate, he felt a new intensity of hatred for the dead man. Of course, it was only a vicious, drunken lie. But Lavon could not endure the idea that people might whisper behind his back that he wasn't a real Deavors. Despite Lavon's wealth and influence, he was still too near the low world of Swan and the slave pen to tolerate such gossip.

As Lavon rode toward Natchez one rainy November day, he did not think of Swan at all. He chanted a ritual to himself, a ritual of his wealth, of his influence, of the success of all his plans. He ran figures through his mind, dollars, slaves, profits. But the ritual did nothing to pull him from his depression.

He was soaking wet, hot, and tensed with anger and frustration. Despite his wealth and the success of his plans, he was weary of every aspect of his life. He loathed every person he dealt with, black or white. He knew it could be years before he became master of the Columns.

And he was worried sick about Lige. The baby cried constantly and seldom slept. Hardly a day passed that Dr. Gatlin wasn't summoned to treat Lige. Now the doctor was afraid his left leg wasn't forming properly. Frannie was frantic with worry and fatigue. She cried and complained and was nigh impossible to live with. Several times recently she had left the baby with slaves and disappeared for hours.

As Lavon rode into Natchez, he decided he needed a drink. He headed for the Red Lion Tavern. The rain stopped, and the sun came out suddenly. This only made him hotter and did nothing to improve his spirits as he thought of taking Lige back to the doctors in New Orleans.

Then he saw the Deavorses on the corner. Athel and Estelle and Joleen and Lawton and Lucinda and Tillman, all standing there talking calmly in the sunshine, all tall and smiling and straight and healthy. They probably thought the sun came out just for them, Lavon told himself. Except for Tillman's occasional fevers, the Deavorses had always been healthy. No Deavors had ever been deformed.

This was the first time Lavon admitted to himself that Lige might be crippled for life. Why should he and his son be cursed this way? He was a Deavors, too! He thought of Swan's words and felt a chill through the damp heat.

Lavon rode past his family without looking at them. They did not acknowledge him with so much as a glance.

To hell with sitting in that dull tavern and drinking, he decided. He headed for the river. Frannie had not let him touch her for four days, and he was gnawed by the kind of tension that only sex or violence could cure. He left his horse at a stable near the docks and walked quickly over the wet wooden sidewalks.

Lavon sensed more than the usual hovering of violence under the hill. He was not surprised to meet Sheriff Crandall.

"Afternoon, Mr. Deavors," the sheriff said.

"Afternoon," Lavon said. "There must be big trouble down here to bring you under the hill, sheriff."

"There was a murder, down to Annie Easter's barge," the sheriff said.

"A murder at Annie's? That's never happened before. Was it someone prominent?"

"This wasn't no garden-variety murder, Mr. Deavors," the sheriff said. "It was Annie herself. Got her face blowed away with a pistol shot."

"Christ! Who did it?"

" 'Fraid it was her son who killed her."

"Her son!"

The sheriff nodded. He said her eighteen-year-old son, Paul, had been away in a fancy Eastern school for years. Annie visited him from time to time. But he never came to Natchez. He thought she was a wealthy and respectable lady who lived on a plantation. By chance some school friends who lived across the river in Louisiana invited Paul to visit them. He accepted their invitation because it would also give him the chance to pay a surprise visit to his mother.

They arrived in Natchez late last night, the sheriff said. His friends told Paul they would take him to the best whorehouse on the river. They were drinking and joking about the whores in Annie's lounge when she walked in. Paul's friends had met Annie on her last visit. They made cruel remarks to Paul and left.

"The boy went plumb crazy," Sheriff Crandall said. "He cursed Annie. He hit her. Then he pulled a pistol and shot her in the face. He wrestled another pistol from a customer and shot himself in the head. Both of 'em died instantly. Lord, we're goin' to miss Annie, rest her soul. Well, got to get on my way. Afternoon, Mr. Deavors."

Lavon nodded. The sheriff walked away. Annie had told Lavon she had no family except Paul. She had talked of selling her barge and its whores. Lavon had been interested because of the important men who frequented the barge. But he realized the place must earn a fortune. If the new state constitution outlawed slave trading, the barge could become an excellent source of income.

Lavon hurried back to his horse. He was anxious to find his lawyer so he could take the necessary measures to secure the barge and its girls. But the horse was so exhausted when they reached the top of the hill that Lavon had to dismount and let him rest.

Lavon had the feeling he was being watched. He looked around. Tillman stood beside a crabapple bush.

Lavon remembered the day of his first slave sale, when he had leaned against the rum bar, filthy and sick and nearly sobbing, while Tillman stood down the street and stared at him. Tillman was taller now, but he was very thin. His clothing hung from his body as though it did not fit. His face was pale.

Tillman had been a quiet, strange boy when Lavon was at the Columns. Perhaps he had grown stranger as he grew older. He must be at least fourteen, Lavon told himself.

"Hello, Tillman," Lavon said. "How are you today?"

Tillman nodded.

"That's good. Are you . . . ? How is your schooling. Still have the same tutor?"

Again Tillman nodded.

This was getting on Lavon's nerves. Was the boy incapable of speaking?

Tillman glanced around frantically. He ran behind the crabapple bush. Lavon sighed and mounted his horse. To hell with the little bastard. He picked up the reins and rode off.

Chapter 44

Athel sat at the corner table in the Red Lion Tavern. He hoped no one he knew came in. Athel rarely drank in a tavern, but he wanted to be alone for a few minutes, to relax and think about his problems. The women were shopping for shoes. Tillman had returned to Aunt Delma's. And Lawton was buying eight new plows.

This was the first time Lawton had taken the responsibility for buying supplies without Athel's or Cellus' assistance, and his reluctance had been quite obvious as he walked away from his father. Athel was worried about Lawton. In every way possible he encouraged his son to take more responsibility and to show more self-confidence in his work. Lawton was intelligent. He was hard-working. He loved the Columns. The people respected him. His marriage with Lucinda was solid. But still Lawton held back from the potential that Athel knew he had.

Lawton simply would not make independent judgments. And he seemed to doubt the quality of any work he supervised. Unfortunately, the one time he had suggested a drastic change at the Columns, the result was a disaster. The idea of holding back part of the harvest until prices rose was a sound idea. Lawton wasn't responsible because the barn burned down. But he took the loss so badly, one would think he had set the fire himself.

Sheriff Crandall was convinced someone had set the fire. The sheriff was unable to discover who was responsible, but he told Athel it was no act of nature. Yet Athel found it difficult to believe someone had sneaked onto the plantation and burned the barn. And he knew none of his people would do such a thing. Not even Essie.

Athel took a sip of whiskey. He was exhausted and knew it was less from physical work than from worry. Loss of the cotton was a severe economic blow. And the loss came just after he had paid for Joleen's wedding and her land.

All Athel's life the Columns had prospered without any difficulty. There was a bad year here and there, when rain damaged a crop or the price of cotton dropped. But everyone knew the following year there would be prosperity again. And there always was. The land was rich, plentiful, and cheap. The Columns had unlimited credit at the Natchez banks. Athel told himself it would have been almost impossible not to make good money growing cotton in Adams County.

But the barn-burning forced Athel to accept some harsh realities. He was in the worst financial situation of his life. There had been constant rain this fall, and unless the rain let up soon, the harvest would be a poor one. Thousands of people were pouring into Mississippi. The price of land had nearly doubled in less than a year.

Athel drained his glass and ordered more whiskey. He sank back against his chair. As if all these problems weren't enough, he had just this week learned something of Lavon's schemes. The old waiter shuffled over with more whiskey. Athel took a sip. He tried to remember how long it had been since he had sat alone in a tavern in the afternoon and drunk whiskey. He could not remember.

Athel thought of Lavon and how naïve he had been to think his brother merely wanted to raise a great deal of cash quickly and return to the Continent, without being dependent on his family. Even when Lavon had remained in Natchez, Athel thought it was only greed that kept him at his wretched trade a few months longer. Athel was not even suspicious when he learned that Lavon had purchased four hundred acres in the northern part of the county or that he had bought a home in Natchez. And when he was told that Lavon had purchased three hundred acres adjacent to the

Columns and put them into cotton, Athel's reaction had been anger that his brother's land should touch the Columns. He was repelled by the idea, as if any land Lavon owned might contaminate the plantation.

Three days earlier, though, Riley Ferguson, who was on the board of directors of the First Agricultural Bank, had told Athel that Lavon had also purchased four other land parcels bordering the Columns, all through his lawyer, Jason Colfax, and other agents. And that Lavon, with his huge cash income, was becoming a power in both the Agricultural Bank and the Mercantile Bank. Ferguson said he was afraid Lavon's allies would control First Agricultural's board by the first of the year.

There was no mistaking the clear evidence. Lavon intended to squeeze the family out of the Columns!

What convinced Athel of Lavon's intention was that, of the five land parcels which Ferguson described, two were only swamp. It was absolutely useless land. A man would be crazy to buy it for any purpose other than strangling the Columns, cutting off the plantation from the outside world.

Of course, Athel now understood why Lavon wanted to control the banks. The Lord only knew what other schemes he had under way. Why, it was probably not beneath Lavon to burn down that barn full of cotton! Athel thought of confronting Lavon. But he had sworn he would never speak to his brother again. The confrontation would do no good, anyway. Lavon was beneath contempt. Surely, despite his wealth, he must be the most miserable of men, driven only by hatred and the desire to ruin the Deavorses. And married to that girl who was little more than a whore, if the stories were true, running around with one man after another.

Well, Athel told himself, Lavon might be both clever and ruthless, and he might grow to be the wealthiest man in Adams County, but he would never own the Columns. Athel would do whatever was necessary to keep the plantation in the family's hands, and as far as he was concerned, Lavon was no longer a Deavors.

The thought did not go down well. Athel drank

his whiskey as though he could swallow away the connection this thought made with something that lay deep in his mind. Another swallow did not help. Athel sighed and closed his eyes. Even in the past months, as he grew angrier and more disgusted with Lavon's activities, he had not let himself remember the possibility that indeed Lavon was not pure Deavors.

Athel had been only ten when Lavon was born, but he had heard fragments of the whispered talk and he recalled the quick departure of that man who had been painting portraits around the county. Athel's mother died in a steamboat accident and he overheard one old slave mutter: "Missus seems to want to die and pay for her sin." But Athel's father accepted Lavon as his own son and ended all the talk. Over the years, as they grew up, and particularly after the death of their father, Athel took great care to provide for his younger brother and to make certain he was accepted as a Deavors. He knew that was what his father wanted. And over the years Athel simply willed any thoughts of his mother and the painter out of his mind.

Athel stood up. He did not know for certain what he would do. He wanted to talk to more people and find out what else he could about Lavon's scheme. However, he would take steps immediately to see that Lavon did not surround the Columns. There was that old lady who lived in New Orleans who owned the land that held the road, he remembered. He would go to New Orleans and purchase the land. And while he was there, he would seek financing with a New Orleans bank, even if the financing was more expensive.

He walked from the tavern. A mist was falling. The street was a foot deep in mud. He hired a carriage and told the driver to take him to Aunt Delma's. As he settled back in the carriage, he tried to relax, but it was impossible. He thought of discussing the situation with Lawton and Cellus. No, he decided, he would wait until he knew more about the scheme and had decided on a definite course of action. And Lawton had enough to worry about as it was.

Chapter 45

Tillman ran through the trellis of scuppernong grapes. He glanced over his shoulder as he reached the cluster of oleander bushes that screened the Negro quarters from the big house. There was no one around. He listened to the noise from the party. Aunt Delma wouldn't miss him, because she was busy with her guests.

Tillman ran past the Negro houses and along the shrubbery-lined alley to the street at the end of the block. He stopped and caught his breath. Then he walked slowly down the sidewalk. His head was swimming. He had difficulty breathing. There was a shout and the sound of horses.

Tillman looked up in terror. He jumped back to the curb. He hadn't realized he was in the middle of the street.

He hoped Aunt Delma would stay busy with her party. If she missed him, she would send her slaves out to find him. She didn't like for him to go off alone at night. But he wanted to go off alone. He didn't want to stay at Aunt Delma's. He didn't want to stay in Natchez. He wanted to go back to the plantation and sit under the house and play with his soldiers.

But his parents insisted he visit in Natchez and meet children his age. He didn't like the children. They made fun of him, and Millie Clark laughed at him when he told her about playing with his soldiers. No, he did not like Natchez. He was repelled by all the things he saw when he sneaked around the streets and alleys at night. Yet all these strange things also attracted and excited him, and he fitted them into his fantasies.

Tillman kept to the shadows as he started down the long street that led to the river. The lights of a paddle-wheeler were brilliant on the dark water. Tillman's heart pounded. Of all the things he had seen in Natchez, the one that most excited and repulsed him was this place under the hill. Just thinking of the people and the barges and the sights and smells made him go warm. He glanced around guiltily. His father said that only terrible people went down under the hill.

Tillman realized he was walking too fast. He did not want to fall down again like he had last night. He forced himself to walk more slowly, but it was difficult on the steep hill.

Last night, as he had crept along the wooden sidewalks, his shoes damp from the water and his body dripping perspiration, he had seen a white man and a black woman in a shanty. The man tore off the woman's dress. He took down his pants. He climbed on top of the woman. Their groans drew Tillman closer to the window, and he stared into the filthy room, lit with a low, flickering lamp, until the woman saw him and screamed. The man cursed and pulled out a knife. Tillman lurched down the sidewalk and nearly fell into the water.

Tillman knew what they were doing was wrong and that it was wrong for him to watch them. It made him feel strange and hot, and he wanted to play with himself, the way he did under the house or in his bed at night.

It must be terribly wrong. His father had said so. Tillman had been at the edge of the house and overheard his father say that Lawton had done that to Nettie. And she had a baby. And they sent Nettie away, and she never came back. And Lawton had to go live in New Orleans alone. It was bad when a man did that to a woman. But the worst thing was when a white man did that to a slave.

Lawton had done that again, too. He did it to Lucinda. They did it at night when they thought no one would know. Tillman climbed an oak tree one night and looked into their room and saw them. Lucinda was so pretty, but when Lawton did that, her face looked all twisted, as though Lawton was hurting her. Tillman masturbated while he watched them. Then he felt sick.

The next night he climbed another tree and saw his father do that to his mother. Tillman nearly cried out. His stomach churned. He climbed down and started running, and he ran until he collapsed out in the fields. He didn't masturbate then.

Why did his mother and father do that, if it was so wrong? His mother fussed at him and punished him when he did something wrong. Would she be punished for what she did?

When Tillman reached the bottom of the hill, he had to sit down and rest for several minutes. His head felt as though it would explode. He stood up and looked into the bright lights of the paddle-wheeler. The lights hurt his eyes. He looked away and hurried onto the wooden sidewalks, where it was dark.

Tillman crept along the sidewalk. He stayed in the shadows, though occasionally he peeked into a tavern or gambling den. Blood was drying and turning rust-colored on his shirt. He had watched a black rooster and a brown rooster fight in a pit. When the brown rooster's talons ripped the black rooster's head, blood spurted over the crowd, and several drops wet Tillman's shirt.

Negro women called to him from a barge. He stopped and stared at their naked breasts. A tall woman smiled and stroked her large brown nipples. He was very warm. His penis began to swell. He backed into the shadows again.

He walked away from the barge. He felt bad, all hot and damp and guilty because it excited him when the girl stroked her nipples. It was wrong to be excited. But he could not help himself.

The shadows ended a few yards ahead. He saw a long red barge blazing with lanterns and torches. There were no women displaying themselves on this barge. Its windows were shuttered. A man with a rifle stood by the gangway. The door was closed. Tillman moved out of the shadows. He heard people talking and laughing behind the shutters. Someone was playing a spinet. He stopped in front of the gangway. The man with the rifle looked at him but didn't say anything.

The door opened. Two well-dressed men walked out. Tillman thought he recognized one of the men. The man worked for a bank. Tillman decided to run away.

Then his Uncle Lavon walked out. He was dressed in a blue jacket and pants, and there were ruffles at his wrists. He smoked a cigar and laughed and talked to the men. Again Tillman turned to leave.

"Tillman!" The sound of his name stopped him. "Tillman," his uncle called again. "What in hell are you doing down here under the hill this time of night?"

Lavon said something to the two men. They laughed and walked away. Tillman backed up as Lavon stepped toward him.

"What's wrong?" Lavon asked. "Don't be afraid, Tillman. I'm not going to hurt you. What are you doing down here? Christ, you've grown since I knew you. How old are you. You must be nearly fifteen."

Tillman swallowed hard. His throat was raw. "Fifteen next January," he mumbled.

He had wanted to run away, but he had stayed, and he told himself he had to talk now. He remembered Lavon's stories about Morocco and Spain and France and England. Maybe if he stayed and talked, his uncle would tell him more stories. But everybody said his uncle was bad because he sold slaves. Tillman remembered the day he had seen Lavon on Seville Street, when his father came and took him away. Tillman glanced around. Would his father come and take him away now? He did not want to go away. He did not want to go back to Aunt Delma's.

"Hell, you're almost grown," Lavon said. "I've seen you in town before. Alone. You must get bored out on the plantation." Lavon smiled. "Fifteen is old enough, Tillman. Come on inside. This is grand-opening night. Everything's on the house. It's time you found out how much fun you can have if you get away from your family. Come on, boy. Let's be friends. Wouldn't you like something cold to drink?"

"I don't know," Tillman said.

Lavon put his arm around Tillman's shoulder. Tillman let himself be led up the gangway. He had seen his father put his arm around Lawton's shoulder and around other men's shoulders. No one had ever put his arm around Tillman's shoulder. It made him feel grown-up. No one else treated him like he was grown-up.

"This is my nephew Tillman," Lavon said to the man with the rifle. "He's always welcome here. He's going to become a man tonight. And then he'll be back often. Won't you, Tillman?"

"I reckon so," Tillman mumbled.

Lavon led Tillman along a dimly lit corridor. He opened a door, and Tillman walked into a long room that dazzled him and made his head swim.

Chapter 46

Chandeliers burned like suns, and wall lanterns blazed with high white flames. The walls, curtains, and rugs were bright red. The bar was covered with red plush. The furniture was ebony. The black waiters, who carried silver trays, wore red jackets, shirts, cummerbunds, and pants.

And all the women were dressed in red, though no two dresses were alike. The women were young and beautiful. The light glistened on their bare shoulders and breasts. A girl near Tillman was jet black. Beside her stood a girl whose skin was chestnut. Tillman glanced around. Other girls were chocolate and bronze, rust and yellow. Tillman sucked in his breath, and his nostrils were tantalized by the women's perfume and by incense that burned in silver braziers.

Tillman had never seen a party like this. He had never seen Negroes dressed up this way. The girls all acted just like white people as they drank from long-stemmed glasses and talked with the white men.

"Are the girls all niggers?" Tillman asked. "I mean, are they all slaves?"

"Oh, they're slaves," Lavon said. "But they're not like any niggers you've ever seen. They're all from New Orleans. They can sing and play the spinet and talk intelligently. They've got good manners. And they're very . . . sophisticated. There's not another place on the Mississippi with women like this, Tillman. Come on, let's get you something to drink."

"I'm not allowed to drink whiskey or wine," Tillman said.

"Christ, that was before tonight," Lavon said.

"I better not," Tillman said.

Lavon sighed. "All right. How about some champagne?"

"Champagne? I don't know if I'm allowed to drink champagne."

Lavon motioned to a waiter. He handed Tillman a glass. Tillman took a sip. The bubbles tickled his nose. He liked the champagne. It was bubbly and sweet, and it tasted good. It wasn't whiskey or wine. They were the only things he wasn't allowed to drink.

Tillman was introduced to several men. They were drinking and smiling, and one man had his hand on a black girl's breast. Tillman knew Mr. Thigpen from the bank. And he knew Sheriff Crandall. He was afraid they would tell his father he was here. But if they were here themselves, it must be all right.

Tillman was drinking his second glass of champagne when Lavon took him back to a spinet in the corner. A girl with copper skin stopped playing and stood up. She smiled at Tillman. She was very young. Her breasts were enormous, the largest breasts Tillman had ever seen. His warmth grew into fever as he stared at them.

"Ginny, this is my nephew Tillman," Lavon said. "I want you to be very nice to Tillman. He hasn't . . . had any experience. Tillman, this is Ginny. She just came upriver two days ago. Come to think of it, you two are damn near the same age."

"How do you do, Mist' Tillman?" Ginny asked.

"Fine, I guess," Tillman said. His throat was dry. He drank more champagne. A waiter filled his glass. He looked around. Lavon was gone. He couldn't see him in the crowd.

Tillman gulped champagne. His legs were weak. He was nearly shaking with fever and excitement. A waiter refilled his glass.

"Where's my uncle?" Tillman asked Ginny. The bright lights hurt his eyes.

Ginny smiled again. "He's busy for a few minutes," she said. Her voice was soft.

Tillman drained his glass. "I better go home. . . ."

"Not yet, Mist' Tillman," Ginny said. "Come on, let's go back here."

"Where?" Tillman gasped. His glass was full again.

"I'll show you," she said. "Come on." She took his free hand. He stiffened. She held his hand firmly and led him to a door. He was soaked with perspiration. The perfume and incense and heat were smothering him. He stumbled along and spilled champagne.

In the corridor behind the door it was cool, and there were shadows. Ginny took him into a room and closed the door. Everything in the room was royal blue. A small chandelier was turned low. Wind chimes crinkled in a breeze from an open porthole.

Tillman's hand shook as he gulped champagne. He told himself he had to run away. It was wrong to be here with Ginny. She was a slave girl. It was wrong to be excited like this because of a slave girl.

"Come on, let's sit down on the bed," Ginny said. "See, there's more champagne there in that silver bucket."

"I can't . . ." The words barely came out.

"Sure you can," Ginny said. "We just goin' to drink some more champagne and talk like friends."

Tillman sat down on the edge of the bed beside Ginny. He gladly accepted more champagne. He was already intoxicated, and so sexually aroused that his penis ached against his tight pants.

Ginny asked him questions, and he was shy, but

she coaxed him with smiles and champagne and the touch of her fingers. His eyes darted from her breasts to her dark, innocent eyes. When he spoke, Ginny was interested in everything he talked about, particularly his soldiers. No one had ever talked to him this way. He drank more champagne. When Ginny kissed his ear and stroked his leg, he forgot what he was supposed to be talking about.

Tillman thought he was sitting up, but he realized he was lying on his back. Ginny was undressing him. He whimpered. He tried to get up. She put her hands on his shoulders and shoved him down. He closed his eyes. When he opened them, Ginny was naked.

She hovered over him, her young girl's face and her exquisite breasts. The black nipples brushed his lips. He groaned. His body was rigid, but he trembled when Ginny rubbed against his penis and licked his ears and the inside of his mouth.

"No . . ." he gasped as she squeezed his penis with her hand. He dug his nails into his palms. Slowly his penis was sucked into a vise of hot flesh that terrified him and excited him to near-madness.

"No . . . Don't . . ." He made gurgling sounds.

"Shhhh," Ginny purred. She licked his lips and tongue. "No! Don't move. Just lie still."

Tillman felt the craziness rise in him as Ginny squeezed her vagina and slid up and down, up and down, so slowly, and then slower still.

He screamed and bit his lips. He was overcome with pain and ecstasy. His penis exploded.

Then it was over. His loins ached. His stomach churned. He gagged and tasted regurgitated champagne.

Ginny crawled from his body. She kissed his cheek.

"I'll be right back, Mist' Tillman," she whispered. She left the room.

Tillman lay still a moment, fighting for breath. Then he scrambled out of the bed. He could hardly stand up. His head was throbbing. He was nauseated. His fingers trembled as he put on his clothes.

He had had sex with a slave! He had done the worst thing a white man could do!

Ginny would have his baby! She would be sent away, and she would never come back. And he would be sent to New Orleans alone, like Lawton.

He stumbled against the champagne bucket. It fell to the floor. He lurched down the dim corridor and smashed into the wall. His shoulder ached, but he kept running. He tore open a door. A black girl was sucking a man's penis while he licked a yellow girl's thighs. Tillman fled the room.

He found the door to the lounge. He ran into a waiter with a tray of drinks. The glasses crashed to the floor.

Tillman ran blindly across the room. He could not see clearly. Tears blurred his vision. He bumped into a man, then a woman. Someone screamed. There were shouts.

"Tillman!" Lavon called.

Tillman ignored him and ran from the barge. His toe caught between two wooden slats in the sidewalk. He fell forward and hurt his knees, but he got up running.

Finally he was out from under the hill. He doubled over with pain and nausea.

"Mist' Tillman . . ." Tillman looked up. It was Dilson, one of Aunt Delma's slaves. "Mist' Tillman, where you been? You got to come on home now."

He couldn't go home. He had done a terrible thing. They would punish him and send him away. What would his mother think of him? He saw her face and heard her voice.

The paddle-wheeler was pulling from the dock. Tillman staggered toward the retreating lights. Dilson ran out onto the dock after him.

Tillman stopped at the end of the dock and stared into the black water. He could no longer be a Deavors. He had done such a terrible thing that his father would make him live alone in New Orleans. He saw his mother's frowning face in the water.

"Mist' Tillman . . ." Dilson touched his arm.

Tillman swayed on the edge of the pier. Dilson touched his arm again. Tillman dropped into the water.

Chapter 47

Athel sat down wearily at his desk. He was staring out at the heavy rain when Cellus came in.

"What did the doctor say 'bout Mist' Tillman?" Cellus asked.

"He's over the fever," Athel said. "And the delirium has passed. The doctor says he's out of danger. Here, sit down." Cellus sat down beside the desk. "Now, I know what happened, Cellus. Why Tillman tried to kill himself. Once his delirium passed, he couldn't wait to confess, to tell me what happened. Yet he was terrified that when I knew what happened I'd send him away. Damnit, what can I do, Cellus? Tillman's not quite . . . right. I guess we've all known that. Now something like this happens to the boy."

"What happened, Mist' Athel?"

"My goddamn brother, Cellus." Athel nearly choked on his anger. "Lavon opened up that whore barge, had a grand opening. Tillman sneaked down under the hill and ran into Lavon. Lavon took him into the barge and got him drunk on champagne and gave him a whore. Afterward Tillman went berserk. He was overcome with guilt, with fear. He tried to punish himself."

"Least he's all right now," Cellus said.

"I can't conceive how a man could sink to such depths," Athel said. "My own brother! Tillman's not quite fifteen years old. Lavon knows he's had his problems. What can I do about Tillman, Cellus? I just don't know what to do with the boy."

"Time passes, he'll get better," Cellus said. "He needs rest. You know, Mist' Athel, sometimes children, they grow out of these . . . moods. But that Lavon. I don't know what to say 'bout him. He's bad, through and through. Always has been."

Athel started to ask Cellus about Lavon's birth. But he decided against it. "You've been over the books?" he asked.

"Yessir. And I talked to the drivers. Doesn't look too promisin', Mist' Athel. 'Less this rain lets up mighty quick, we could be in trouble."

"That's just what Lavon is waitin' for, Cellus," Athel said. "Last week I found out that he has a definite plan to squeeze me out of the Columns. And he's gone a long way toward puttin' his scheme into effect. It's time we talked this over and made some decisions. Is Lawton back from the Sumralls'?"

"No, sir, not far as I know," Cellus said.

"Well, we'll talk when he gets back, then," Athel said. "I want Lawton to understand everything and be a part of whatever we decide, Cellus. I've already decided to go down to New Orleans, and I'm goin' to have to turn over more responsibility to Lawton while I'm gone. I only hope he can handle it better than he usually does."

"I know you worry 'bout Mist' Lawton, but I think he'll come along just fine when it counts," Cellus said. He looked out the window. "Rain seems to be lettin' up. The sky's gettin' brighter. That's a good sign."

"I hope so, Cellus," Athel said. "We could use a few good signs."

It had rained for three straight days. The slaves had not been to the fields during that time, and some of the cotton was beginning to rot in the pods.

Cellus left the parlor. Athel studied the books, but he couldn't concentrate on Cellus' figures about the plantation's finances or the amount of cotton that had been harvested and ginned. Finally Athel walked out to the porch and looked past the columns. A mist was falling. The sky was bright on the horizon. The sun was about to come out.

Estelle joined him. "I know how upset you are," she said. "But try to stop broodin', Athel. Tillman's out of danger."

"It's not just Tillman," Athel said.

"Athel, we both know what kind of man Lavon is," she said. "But there's nothin' we can do about him."

"No, I don't think I quite knew what kind of man he is, Estelle. Oh, I thought him weak and without character. Even despicable. But now I see that he's vicious, vindictive. . . . And I know now . . ." No, he told himself. No need to worry Estelle with Lavon's schemes.

"Athel, look at me," she said. "I know how upset you are. I've never seen you angrier. But there's just nothin' we can do. If you get back to work, it will be better than worryin' all the time. See, the rain's stopped. The niggers'll be back in the fields soon."

"Yes, I guess I should get my mind off all this," Athel said. "I was waitin' for Lawton. We were goin' to look at that rocky land and see if it's worth clearin' and puttin' into acreage in the spring. Think now I'll go out there by myself. Lawton'll pass by there on his way back from the Sumralls'."

Estelle took his hand, and they walked down the gallery.

"Somethin' sure smells good," Athel said as they stood on the back steps.

"Beatrice is fixin' chicken and dumplin's for dinner," Estelle said. "Please don't be late. You know how it upsets her when people are late for dinner."

"I wouldn't be late for chicken and dumplin's," Athel said. He kissed Estelle's cheek and walked down the steps.

Lucinda was coming from the storeroom. "Looks like we're finally goin' to get some sunshine," she said.

"Sure looks like it," Athel said. "By the way, Lucinda, I was meanin' to ask you. There's an elderly lady livin' in New Orleans, moved there from Adams County, oh, must have been thirty years ago. Her name's Antoinette LeBeau. I never met her, but I understand she's well known there, and I was wonderin' if you might know her."

"Antoinette LeBeau?" Lucinda said. "Why, no, I don't really know her. But I've met her. She is pretty well known, but she's a strange old lady. She mostly keeps to herself, from what I remember. I really knew her nephew, Alain. He came courting when I was in school."

"I'm goin' down to New Orleans," Athel said. "I've got to speak to Mrs. LeBeau on a business matter, and it would help if I had some kind of introduction to her, Lucinda."

"Oh, then I'll write to Alain," she said. "Nothing came of his courting, of course. He was too wild and all for me. But we're good friends, still. Oh, I'm sure he'll be glad to introduce you to his aunt."

"That's fine," Athel said. "Why don't you go on and write that letter, if you don't mind. But, Lucinda . . . please don't tell anybody I'm goin', just yet. I don't want Lawton or Estelle to fret over nothin'."

"I won't tell a soul," Lucinda said, and smiled.

Athel's boots creaked in the mud as he walked toward the barn. He thought about Lucinda. She had gained some weight, and she looked prettier every day. Beatrice said Lucinda was the best natural cook she had ever seen. The girl had really come into her own in the past few months. And she was an ideal wife for Lawton.

"How's Mist' Tillman?" Ed asked when Athel entered the barn.

"He's all right now, Ed," Athel said. "The danger's past." He turned to Ambrose. "Saddle my horse, will you?"

While Ambrose saddled the horse, Athel and Ed discussed the rain and the crops and the need to buy fodder for the horses and mules. When Athel rode out of the barn, the sun was shining. He smelled the wet earth as he rode through the fields and headed for the acres he wanted to plant in the spring. He felt a flush of excitement, brought on by the earth smell and the thought of growing cotton in land that was now only a rocky field.

Lavon's head pounded. His stomach churned. The taste of whiskey tormented his dry mouth. The earth smelled fetid, and he cursed the rain and the mud and whatever impulse had brought him out here with such a hangover.

The grand opening of the barge had lasted for two days and nights. Bankers and lawyers and judges and planters had come in droves. They accepted free champagne and whiskey and enjoyed themselves with the beautiful mulatto women. And damn them, Lavon thought, many of those same men would still slam the door in his face if he visited their homes.

But there was nowhere else in Natchez to find the quality of women he had. When the men returned to the red barge, they would pay dearly for the whores' company. They would help make Lavon a wealthy man. They would reveal their sexual whims and secrets. Some of the men would become obsessed with certain girls. Others would not be able to afford the girls and would have to accept credit or charity. Yes, one way or another, Lavon told himself, he would use sex to manipulate these proud and influential men or make them suffer for snubbing him.

But these thoughts gave Lavon no pleasure on this wet, earth-stinking morning. The alcohol had taken too much of a toll. And Lavon was worried sick about Lige, and angry with Frannie. The New Orleans doctors said that Lige would be crippled for life. Crippled! His own son! Lige screamed constantly. The slaves couldn't do a thing with him.

And Frannie had not been home in two days, and her family had no idea where she was.

Lavon hated the thought that his son was deformed. He even hated Lige, despite the love he felt for him. He hated the doctors who could not make him normal. And he hated Frannie for bearing a son in this condition.

Before his impulsive ride out here to wander along the rows of rotting cotton pods, Lavon had visited the slave pen. The new coffle was sullen and rebellious. Two men had to be put in the stocks. Another had to be lashed. The man's screams tormented Lavon. After eight lashes he could stand no more, and he grabbed the whip from his agent and ordered the slave to be spared further lashes and be put in the stocks instead. Lavon had never seen such hatred as that which burned in the man's eyes as he was released from the whipping post.

Six slaves had died of cholera on the march down. And two more lay dying in the courtyard. The slaves stank. The agent was drunk and reeked of whiskey. Four children still cried for their mothers.

Lavon had stood there in the rain and smelled the agent's putrid breath and smelled the sweat and grime of the sullen Negroes and smelled the disease that was killing the two on the ground. He had stalked out and mounted his horse and started riding blindly in the rain. He hated the goddamn slaves and he hated the goddamn agent. He hated owning the slaves, he hated trading them. He hated himself and his goddamn life and his crippled son and his wife.

On the horizon in front of him, Lavon saw another rider. The man was on land belonging to the Columns. Lavon reined up his horse. He watched the rider disappear, and wondered who he was. The horizon was the end of cultivated land on the Columns. What lay between the horizon and his own land was filled with stones.

Lavon dismounted. He was exhausted. And he faced the long ride back to Natchez. He asked himself why in hell he hadn't had the good sense to take a carriage out. He was soaking wet, but at least the rain had stopped.

He pulled off a cotton pod. Unless the rain ended, the crop would be devastated. He hated to lose money on his own cotton, but he hoped it rained for a month. He hoped Athel didn't make a penny this year.

Damnit, he had to accelerate his plans somehow. He couldn't continue with this life much longer. He wanted the goddamn plantation, and he wanted it soon. Nothing would change in his life until he was master of the Columns.

Lavon had reached the edge of his land. He inhaled, and smelled rotting cotton and pungent earth. The smells did nothing for his unhappy stomach. The slaves had not been in the fields for three days, and already weeds were strangling the cotton plants. Left alone a short time, this whole field would be overgrown with weeds and vines. The fecundity of the land was awesome, almost frightening.

Lavon crossed over into land that belonged to the Columns. He picked up a stone, then threw it back down and turned to leave.

The horse was almost on him before he heard it in the soft earth. He looked up into Athel's face.

Chapter 48

They stared at each other for a full minute. There was something odd about Athel's face. The blue eyes were narrowed, and the lips were taut.

Athel dismounted. Lavon sensed his brother's anger before he spoke. Since he had never seen Athel this angry, it was an unknown and ominous quality.

"I thought I'd never speak to you again," Athel said. His voice was unusually high. "Your despicable life and trade put you beneath contempt and beyond pity."

"My goddamn life and my goddamn trade are my own affair," Lavon said. "Don't preach to me, Athel."

"Yes, they're your own," Athel said. "They are very peculiarly your own. You have an instinct for gettin' involved with whatever is most wretched in our society. As for your trade, I've supported the new constitutional prohibition with all my influence."

"That constitution will make no difference to me," Lavon said. "As you'll find out in good time. If you only knew . . ."

"Oh, but I do know, Lavon," Athel said. His voice had changed. He was calmer. "I know all about your schemes to take the Columns away from me."

Lavon was stunned. He cursed his hangover. He couldn't think clearly. Surely Athel was bluffing or making a wild guess. How could he know?

"You're buyin' up land, all the land around the Columns," Athel said. "You think you can strangle me out. And you're tryin' to take over the Natchez banks to squeeze my credit. Don't deny it. Riley Ferguson told me everything. For all I know, you burned a barn full of my cotton. But none of it will work. You'll never own the Columns, Lavon. No matter how wealthy you become, you'll never be anything but trash, and your lot will always be with people like Purvis Swan and the Runnels. Soon as I get back to the house, I'm sittin' down with Cellus and Lawton, and we'll put an end to your threat."

"No, you're wrong," Lavon said. "You may know about these plans. But there's nothing you can do, Athel. One way or another, I'll be master of the Columns!"

"Save your threats," Athel said. "Don't you understand? You will never own the Columns. It's just that simple. But I didn't ride over here to discuss your schemes or your wretched life. I came over because of what you did to Tillman."

"Tillman?" Lavon asked. "What I did to him? Christ, he's fifteen. He was probably the last fifteen-year-old virgin in the county. I didn't lead him under the hill. He went of his own free will. And he went because he wanted something, something he doesn't get from the plantation or his family. He fucked that girl readily enough. Nobody forced him, Athel. I can't be responsible if he felt bad afterward. Hell, I should be angry at the way he ran out, breaking things and knocking people down."

"He tried to kill himself," Athel said. "Tillman tried to kill himself, damnit. He jumped off the dock."

"I didn't know that, Athel," Lavon said. "I swear I didn't know the boy tried to kill himself. You can't blame me. Tillman's always been a little strange."

"No, Lavon, you can't be blamed for anything," Athel said. "You justify everything you do, no matter how vicious or how foul. I want to give you this warnin', and I want you to know I mean it. I'm takin' steps to see that you never own the Columns. And if you ever cause harm or grief to a member of my family again, I'll see that you pay dearly, brother or no brother."

Lavon's lips quivered at the corners. He felt a hatred of such intensity that he trembled. And his hatred was made all the stronger because it was tinged with desperation and a sense of futility. Now that Athel knew of his plan, he might never own the Columns!

And he feared what else Athel might know. He had discovered so much. What if he had learned of the cholera-ridden slaves dumped in the bayou? Or about Swan's death?

Lavon swallowed. He tasted stale whiskey.

"The Columns is as much mine as yours," he said. He realized he was nearly whining, and he hated himself for the way his voice sounded. A mist was falling, and he cursed the rain. "Damnit, I will own the Columns. I swear I will, Athel. My son will grow up there. He'll inherit the Columns."

"I have nothin' more to say to you," Athel said. "But take fair warnin' about my family."

Athel turned to mount his horse. Lavon grabbed his arm and spun him around.

"Your family!" Lavon shouted. "Your precious goddamn family! Your whore of a daughter! Everybody knows that lawyer was fucking her before the marriage. And as for your son-in-law—this new member of the sacred and pure Deavors family—well, how does it feel to welcome the first Jew into the family, to know your grandchildren will have Jewish blood?"

Athel shook his head. "You poor bastard. What do you think? That you can hurt me with your impotent hatred?"

"It's true!" Lavon shouted. "Joleen is a whore! Clauson is a Jew, and your grandchildren will have Jewish blood."

"I have no more time for you," Athel said. "I

don't share your aversion to Jews, Lavon. And as for your pitiful taunts about Joleen, I assume you're merely reflectin' your own experience with your wife, so that you think every woman is a whore and roams the Natchez streets."

Lavon trembled with rage. Suddenly he knew that what Athel said about Frannie was true. That was why she was never at home! Lavon tried to speak, but he merely made a gurgling sound. Words choked in his throat.

Athel was staring at Lavon. He nodded, as though he had decided something. "Since you wish to speak of pure Deavors blood, Lavon, there's something you ought to know. I haven't ever spoken of this, but perhaps it explains your behavior. You see, my father was not your father. You carry bad blood from another man."

"No!" Lavon screeched. "No! It's not true! Damn you to hell, Athel! Damn you for telling me this!" Tears fell down his cheeks. His lips opened, but they only quivered.

"No, it's true, Lavon," Athel said.

"You're the bastard! I'll own the Columns! I'll see Estelle and Joleen so hungry they'll beg to whore for me under the hill! I'm a Deavors, goddamnit! Me, Athel, I'll be the one to continue the Deavors line at the Columns."

Athel shook his head. He reached for the reins. Lavon stumbled forward and drove a fist into Athel's side. Athel fell back with the blow, but when Lavon swung for his face, Athel ducked and shoved Lavon to the ground.

"You're gettin' soft and slow for a man your age," Athel said. "You been livin' too long with your whores and your whiskey."

Athel ran a few feet and caught his horse's reins. The horse reared up, but Athel steadied him.

Lavon climbed to his knees. He nearly vomited. His head fell forward. Through hazed eyes he saw his brother steadying the horse. Lavon crawled forward. His hand touched a large rock.

Frantically he clawed the rock from the mud. He

staggered up just as Athel moved to mount the horse. Lavon held the rock in both hands. Athel heard him coming. He glanced over his shoulder.

Lavon smashed the rock against Athel's head.

Athel swayed a moment, then fell to the ground. Lavon dropped to his knees alongside Athel, raised the rock in both hands, and brought it down on Athel's head.

Athel lay on the ground. He was groaning and holding his head. Blood trickled through his fingers.

Lavon staggered up with the rock still gripped in his hands. Athel rolled over and raised himself to one knee.

Lavon again raised the rock in both hands. He held it overhead and hesitated. Then he smashed it down on Athel's head.

BOOK VI

The Whip

Chapter 49

A mist began to fall as Lawton rode slowly across the field. He had decided to ride straight out to the fields from the Sumralls', since he was an hour late in returning. The rain had let up, and Lawton thought his father might have gone out to inspect the acreage without him.

He saw a horseman racing across his Uncle Lavon's fields, away from the Columns' land. He turned in the saddle and watched the man, who rode as though the Furies were pursuing him. The man looked like Lavon, though the mist obscured Lawton's vision somewhat. Yes, he told himself as the rider disappeared on the horizon, the man was definitely his uncle.

The mist fell heavier. Lawton had been hopeful when the sun came out. Now the sky was gray in a winter way, a total and full gray that threatened rain for days.

Lawton's horse had difficulty with the mud, so Lawton had to slow his pace. He was riding through rows of dripping cotton plants. The stone-covered field lay a hundred yards ahead, beyond a small grove of mulberry bushes that had suddenly sprung up in the field two years earlier.

He rode from the bushes and saw his father's horse standing two hundred yards away. Lawton reined up. The land was flat and barren, except for weeds, but he saw no sign of his father. The horse whinnied and pawed the ground. It began to circle what looked like a mound of mud and rocks. Lawton stared at the mound a moment.

A chill started at the base of his neck and shot through his body to his shins. He rode very slowly for several yards, straining forward to see better in the heavy mist. That was no mound of dirt and rocks, he knew, and for those few yards he feared what he would discover. Then he tried to gallop the horse, but the mud made a gallop impossible. Lawton cursed. He rose up desperately in the saddle, as if his urgency could move the horse faster.

"Oh, Lord, no!" The words choked in his throat. His father was lying face-down in the mud, covered with rocks. Lawton dismounted and stumbled through the mud. He fell to his knees. He tore rocks from his father's back and head. Blood trickled from the head and back, and the hair was matted with oozing blood.

Lawton's hands trembled as he turned his father over. He flinched at the sight of the face, lacerated and swollen and soaked with blood. The eyes were closed.

Lawton touched the face and jerked his hand away. He doubled over and gagged. Chills and fever wracked his body. He willed himself to act, and each physical thing he did was a sheer act of will. Though his legs nearly gave way, he managed to lift his father and put him across the horse's back, in front of the saddle. His father was still breathing, he realized. Lawton mounted clumsily, his foot slipping twice on the wet stirrup. He jerked his head around as though his uncle might be still in sight. He trembled with anger, but the emotion was an indulgence, and he cursed himself for the precious seconds it cost him.

Slowly, awkwardly, he moved his father upright and held him around the waist as he headed for the house. The ride seemed endless through the wet, empty fields. The mud resisted all efforts to trot the horse. And Lawton was hesitant to trot, afraid he would hurt his father. Blood dripped from the face and head, staining the horse's mane and flanks. Lawton saw the blood, and tears stung in his eyes.

Finally he rode along the house road. He glanced about wildly for someone, a slave in the fields, anyone. But no one was out in the rain. There was less mud on this road, and the horse trotted now.

As Lawton rounded the wall and trotted toward the house, he began to shout. He shouted until he was hoarse. But no one appeared. He rode up to the house and sat in the saddle, holding his father. He was shaking, and he didn't think his legs could support his weight.

Cellus ran across the porch. "My Lord, Mist' Lawton, what's . . . ? Lord God, that's Mist' Athel!"

"He's hurt bad," Lawton mumbled. "I'm afraid he's already dead, Cellus. I don't know what to do."

Cellus lifted Athel from the saddle and cradled him in his arms. He walked up the steps. Lawton dismounted and stumbled after them. Lucinda came running out the door, followed by Bonita and Flora. Lucinda gasped and shrank back.

"Don't look, Lucinda," Lawton said. He went to her, and she put her arms around him.

"You, Bonita, go get Miss Estelle," Cellus said. "She's in the storeroom. Then tell Ed to ride for the doctor. Tell him it's Mist' Athel, and he's hurt bad. You, Flora, run get Aunt Froney. Move, both of you!"

The girls ran down the gallery. Cellus carried Athel up the stairs. Lawton stood and watched his father's disappearing body. He put his hand against the door.

Lucinda touched his face. "I . . . Don't cry, Lawton," she said. "He'll be all right. I know he will. Lawton . . ."

He turned to her, his eyes red and filled with tears. She put her hands on his shoulders and looked into his eyes. She was crying, too.

"Better get upstairs," Lawton muttered.

They held hands and started up the stairs. By the time they reached the top, he was leaning against Lucinda. He dragged himself down the hall, and they stood in the door of the room where Cellus was bathing Athel's face.

"What can I do?" Lawton asked, but he wasn't speaking to anyone.

"We just have to wait . . . for Aunt Froney and the doctor," Lucinda said. "You can't do anything, Lawton. Here, Lawton, don't look at him that way. Look at me. Lawton. Please . . ."

Lawton put his arms around Lucinda, and she

hugged against his body. He cried then, the sobs shaking his body.

"It was my uncle," he gasped. "It was Uncle Lavon. He did this. I saw a man ridin' away—it must have been him. He did this, Lucinda. With stones. He . . . he stoned my father. I don't . . . I can't . . ."

"Hush, hush, Lawton," she said.

"With stones, Lucinda," he said. "He was lyin' there, covered with stones and dirt and blood."

He looked past Lucinda's shoulder. Tillman stood in the door of his room. He was naked. He looked very pale. His eyes were wide.

Slowly and awkwardly, as though walking in his sleep, Tillman came across the hall. Lawton pulled from Lucinda's arms.

"Tillman . . ." he started. He went to his brother. Tillman walked by him as though he did not exist.

Tillman went into Athel's bedroom. Lawton stared at his brother's back, then looked past him to Athel's gashed and bleeding face.

Cellus turned from the bed. "Mist' Tillman," he said. "You better not . . ."

Tillman screamed. The sound cut Lawton like a razor. He ran to Tillman, who turned at his approach. His face was white as paste, distorted, twisted. He continued to scream. He pushed past Lawton and fled into his room.

"Tillman," Lawton called. He took a step toward Tillman's bedroom, then turned.

His mother was hurrying along the hall.

"Mother, wait," he said. "Wait, before you go in . . ."

"What happened? she asked. "Where's Athel? Bonita said he's hurt bad. "

"Mother . . ." He did not know what to say.

She ran into the bedroom. She stopped. She took a step. Another. With the next step her right leg gave way. Cellus had to help her to a chair.

Tillman screamed from his room. Lawton glanced across the hall, then at Lucinda.

"My mother . . . I must help my mother," he said. "Lucinda, can you see about Tillman?"

"Yes, Lawton," she said. She brushed her hand against his arm, then ran across the hall.

Lawton walked into his father's room as Aunt Froney came up the steps.

Chapter 50

Athel died at two minutes past one in the afternoon.

The slaves gathered on the front lawn. Most of them cried with grief. A few whispered and worried. Though it was the Deavorses' policy never to sell their people, rumors spread among the slaves, and they feared this change in their lives and feared they might be sold, feared Lawton might not be the kind of master his father had been.

Estelle tossed in a fretful sleep. The doctor had given her a strong sedative. Tillman passed abruptly from his screaming fit into a catatonic state, and Lucinda stayed in his room.

Lawton and Cellus sat in the study. There was a glass of whiskey on the desk in front of Lawton, but he had not touched it.

"They things we better talk about," Cellus said. "The sheriff, he got to be notified. And Miss Joleen. Better somebody from the Columns give her the news, so she doesn't hear it secondhand. And Miss Delma, I believe she's in New Orleans, so word got to be sent down to her."

"Joleen's supposed to come out here tonight for a visit," Lawton said. He stared into the whiskey as though it might reveal something that would comfort him.

"But word will get back to Natchez 'fore then," Cellus said. "I'll ride into town now. It's better if I tell Miss Joleen. And I can notify the sheriff."

"No!" Lawton said. He turned to Cellus. "I'll ride in myself."

"Mist' Lawton, you needed here," Cellus said. "Your mother, Mist' Tillman . . ."

"No, damnit, I'm goin' into town," Lawton said. "I'll make damn sure my uncle pays for what he did."

"Mist' Lawton . . ."

Lawton stood up. "I've got to go, Cellus. Don't you see that? It's my responsibility, damnit. My duty. I'm the one to deal with my uncle and to tell Joleen."

Cellus protested, but Lawton was adamant. He sent word to Ed to saddle his horse. He drank a glass of whiskey he did not want, then took a pistol from his father's desk, and went out to the barn.

Lawton pushed his horse so unmercifully that he had to stop an hour from Natchez and rent another horse from a farmer. And he pushed himself with a desperate nervous energy that overcame his grief, but not the rage he felt toward his uncle, nor his own sense of guilt. He galloped through the rain and thought of that summer with Joleen, of Nettie, of fleeing to New Orleans, of the barn of cotton that burned, of being late this morning. If only he had not been late . . .

And now he was master of the Columns. The thought frightened him so much he could not dwell on it. How could he take his father's place? How?

At the Natchez city limits he paused beneath a sycamore tree, caught in a frenzy of indecision. Should he go to Joleen's first, or should he contact the sheriff?

He trotted off. No, he would find his accursed uncle himself. He would deal with him. It was his duty as his father's son.

He tried the slave pen first. Lavon wasn't there, nor had anyone seen him since the early morning. Lavon wasn't at home, either, and there was a sense of fear and uncertainty among the slaves.

Yes, Lavon had been home for a few minutes, but he had left in a hurry. He took Miss Frannie and young Lige with him. Two slaves had accompanied them. Those who remained did not know exactly where

Lavon had gone. One man said he thought Lavon had gone up the Natchez Trace. A woman said, no, they had gone to take a paddle-wheeler to New Orleans.

Lawton raced down to the docks. There were no New Orleans boats there. But, yes, a man said, a paddle-wheeler had left for New Orleans less than ten minutes earlier. No, there were many passengers, and the man did not know if Lavon Deavors was aboard.

Lawton forced his reluctant horse back up the hill. He felt he had failed in this, as in everything else. His uncle had slipped away because he was slow in getting to Natchez.

On his way to Joleen's he stopped at the sheriff's office.

"Athel Deavors?" Sheriff Crandall asked. "Murdered? By his own brother? I can't believe it."

A few seconds of Lawton's fury, and the sheriff began to believe. He said he would hunt Lavon down, no matter where he had gone. And he himself would get right out to the Columns, to the field where Athel had been killed. The sheriff was clearly shocked. He spoke of Athel with respect and offered his condolences.

Lawton used his last reserves of strength to comfort Joleen. She was nearly hysterical for a few minutes, but Lawton and Aaron finally calmed her down.

They set out for the Columns in a pouring rain. Filch drove the carriage. Joleen sat huddled against Aaron. Lawton sat opposite them. No one spoke. Lawton stared into the wet undergrowth, but he saw nothing clearly.

The pistol pressed against his thigh. He had forgotten it. He asked himself what he would have done if he had found his uncle. His rage had subsided now. He would be damn sure his uncle was brought to trial and convicted. That was the right way to handle the matter. The rage tried to surge up again, but Lawton lacked the enthusiasm for it. He was so exhausted, he nearly trembled.

His father's battered face appeared in his thoughts. Lawton would have cried, but he had no tears. He merely whimpered once and hoped Joleen and Aaron didn't hear him.

His father was dead. If only he had not stayed late at the Sumralls'. If only he . . . What was the use? It was his responsibility and his guilt.

He was head of the family. He was responsible for the Deavorses, for the Columns, for the crop, for the people. He watched the rain pour off gray moss and broad oak leaves. Would the rain never stop? The crop would be ruined. What could he do? What would his father have done?

He saw the face again. He whimpered, and then he cried, though there were no tears.

Chapter 51

Some four hundred people attended Athel's funeral in the Benton Presbyterian Church. The rain stopped at dawn the day of the funeral. After burial in the church cemetery, Lawton led the family and slaves back to the Columns. The carriages and wagons moved slowly through the drying mud.

The kitchen and dining room were filled with pots and dishes of food brought by neighbors. But no one was hungry. The slaves returned to the quarters and sat around their doorsteps. The Deavorses separated in the house as though each person wanted to be alone with his grief.

Lawton chose the parlor. He felt odd sitting behind his father's desk. He tried to pull himself from his sadness and lethargy and examine Cellus' figures about the cotton harvest, the bales to be picked and transported and ginned and shipped downriver, as well as the latest word on the New Orleans and European cotton markets. But he could not concentrate. He was staring at a fat spider whose web reflected the sunlight when Cellus came in.

"You want to wait to tomorrow to talk business?" Cellus asked.

"No, I guess we better talk now, Cellus," Lawton said. "The people need to be in the fields at first light in the mornin'. I'd rather do somethin', get to work today."

"Yessir, that's how I feel," Cellus said. He sat down. "First of all, I better tell you that last time I talked to Mist' Athel he said he knew for sure that Lavon had a scheme all worked out to take the Columns away from the family. He didn't tell me nothin' definite . . . wanted to wait till we three could talk it over together."

"And you don't have any idea what the scheme was?" Lawton asked.

"No, I don't," Cellus said. "Course, with Lavon run off this way and the murder hangin' over his head, we don't have to worry about any of his schemes now. And that's fortunate. 'Cause we got worries 'nough as it is."

"Do you think that's why Lavon killed my father?" Lawton asked. "Do you think he confronted Lavon about the scheme?"

"Could be," Cellus said. "Likely, we'll never know. And to my way of thinkin', it more probably had to do with what happened to Mist' Tillman. In any case, we shouldn't dwell on it now."

"No, I guess not," Lawton said. He looked at the spider for a moment. His guilt crept out again. If only he had not been late returning from the Sumralls'. . . . "We better go over the situation with the harvest and all."

"Yessir, reckon we better," Cellus said. "And it's goin' to be pretty bleak, Mist' Lawton."

An hour later Lawton knew that at best, with no rain and if the current market prices held steady, the cotton would bring only about seventy percent of the plantation's usual profit. It would be the worst year the plantation had suffered in Cellus' memory. And with the loss of the barn full of cotton and the expenses for

Joleen's wedding and her land, the family was in serious financial difficulty.

Cellus closed the ledger and stood up.

"I was thinkin'," he said, "if we should consider hirin' an overseer."

"An overseer?" Lawton glanced up at Cellus, then looked away quickly. "I don't . . . Why do we need an overseer?" he asked quietly. He looked around the room, anywhere but into Cellus' face. "We can hardly afford that kind of expense, Cellus. And we never had any luck with such men before. Don't you think . . . we're capable of runnin' the place ourselves?"

"I'm sure we are," Cellus said. "I was just thinkin' 'bout it."

"Maybe for the spring plantin'," Lawton mumbled. "Maybe I'll see who's available for the spring."

"Don't you brood on it, Mist' Lawton," Cellus said. "I wasn't hintin' you couldn't bring in the harvest just fine yourself."

"No, it's somethin' to consider," Lawton said.

Cellus left the parlor, and Lawton sat without moving for several minutes. He stared down at the ledger and thought of the overseer and of the fact that Cellus didn't think him capable of running the Columns without help.

There was no more rain during the harvest, and cotton prices held steady. Because of the rain, the last cotton was not picked until the first week in December.

The urgency of the harvest occupied Lawton for weeks, and he found little time for his guilt or grief. He was in the fields before the slaves each morning. He stayed out all day, even taking his dinner with the people in the field. Each night he sat in the parlor with Cellus and reviewed the day's work, the wagons sent to the Benton gin, the bales headed for Natchez and New Orleans.

Estelle had not fully recovered from her shock and grief, and Lucinda had taken over more and more duties of running the house. Lucinda obviously enjoyed the responsibility. The slaves liked and respected her. They had come to accept her as their new mistress.

No matter how hard Lucinda worked, she was always dressed up for supper. She kept the conversation going around the table. She was particularly good at getting Tillman to eat and occasionally to say a word or two. Lawton remembered his worry when he brought Lucinda home to the Columns, a shy, pale, and easily exhausted city girl. Now she moved about the plantation as though born here.

Lawton was always exhausted when they went to bed, and many times he did not think himself capable of making love. But Lucinda could always arouse him with her slim fingers and her lips. There were very few nights during the harvest when they did not make love.

The sight of the last wagon of cotton leaving for the gin had a profound effect on Lawton. He stood on the porch and watched the wagon disappear and felt the last strength dissipate from his body. He felt so weak he could hardly walk.

The harvest was over, and there was nothing he could do now. There was no physical work to hold back his misery and lack of self-confidence. Nor his anger. For Lavon had not been indicted for Athel's murder, despite Lawton's visits to the sheriff and the outrage and pressure of the Deavorses' friends.

"Looks like we can't bring that indictment, as things stand now," Sheriff Crandall told Lawton. "See, both Lavon's overseer, Rayford Blackledge, and his lawyer, Jason Colfax, they done swore under oath that Lavon was in Natchez the mornin' of the murder, that he didn't go out to his land at all. And you done admitted it was rainin' hard and that you had some doubts at first that the man ridin' away was your uncle."

"Damnit, the man was Lavon!" Lawton protested. "I'm sure it was. There was only a mist, not a hard rain."

"Well, be that as it may, there still them two witnesses," the sheriff said. "They both honest men. You was wrought up that mornin', 'bout bein' late, you done told me that. And even a mist makes seein' clear difficult. What I'm workin' on now is that your daddy was murdered by one of them abolitionist agents. The ones what stirs up niggers. Blackledge said he seen a strange white man sneakin' 'round out there. Now don't you worry. It's a terrible crime, and I won't rest till I catch the man what did it."

"Damnit, Lavon Deavors is the murderer!" Lawton shouted. He went into such a rage that the sheriff backed down and said that when the grand jury convened again he would try for an indictment.

But the jury met, and Lavon was not indicted.

"Long as Crandall's sheriff, I doubt he will be," Haskell Sumrall told Lawton. "I've done everything I can do. It's a goddamn outrage. But I suspect your uncle owns Crandall, lock, stock, and barrel."

Lawton took to sitting in the parlor alone, sipping whiskey he did not want, and brooding about the harvest and the spring planting and the murder. He was also worried about an immediate decision—the annual harvest ball.

Cellus and Estelle advised against having the ball, both because of the tragedy and because of the family's financial situation. But the ball had been held for generations, and Lawton was determined that he would not be the first master of the Columns to stop the practice. However, he did make some compromises. The entertainment and the refreshments would be less lavish. And the ball would be combined with the Christmas party.

The ball began with an air of forced gaiety, but slowly everyone gave in to the music and the alcohol. For the first time in weeks Lawton enjoyed drinking whiskey, and he laughed and danced and forgot his problems.

Aunt Delma had returned to New Orleans after Athel's funeral. She was talking now of selling her plantation and moving to New Orleans. Joleen came out for the ball and stayed a week. Aaron came, too, but he returned to Natchez after three days.

Lawton found that Joleen was beginning to change since her marriage. She was less confident and enthusiastic and often lapsed into long silences. And she read a lot of books. When she was living at home she couldn't have been bribed to read a book that wasn't assigned by her tutor.

She even had opinions on politics and slavery. Lawton wondered if that visit to Ohio had had some effect on her, or if her husband was changing her views. Aaron never talked about slavery himself, and his idea of politics was to tell some amusing or cynical story. But Joleen spoke bitterly about the treatment of slaves in Natchez and about slave traders, and at times she actually speculated about what Mississippi would be like if there were no slavery. Yet, the next instant she would launch into a defense of the institution, citing history and the Bible, and to an audience that hardly needed to be convinced.

Lawton wondered about the marriage. He had come to like Aaron a bit more, though he doubted they would ever be real friends. Joleen was obviously happy with Aaron. Lawton could tell from the way she spoke to Aaron and the secret ways she looked at him. When Aaron left, she became moody and bad-tempered. Twice on an impulse she sent a slave galloping into Natchez—"to make sure he's all right and doesn't need anything," she said. Each time, she waited anxiously for the slave's return. Lawton had the feeling that her moodiness and anxiety came not only because she missed her husband but also because she feared what he might be doing in her absence.

But Lawton spent little time worrying about Joleen or anyone else. The day after Christmas he had the slaves back to work again. He drove the people far harder than his father ever had. Work was the only way to expiate his guilt and keep his worries from driving him crazy. He stalked the plantation and ignored the grumbling as he supervised the clearing of the fields, draining of ditches, repair of fences, and myriad other winter tasks.

Lawton kept up an appearance of confident hard work and revealed only a fraction of his misery and uncertainty. Lucinda begged him to talk to her, to be honest about his feelings. Some nights as they lay snuggled together in bed he wanted to cry, to pour out his fears, to ask her to hold him and comfort him.

But he kept his feelings in check, and the weeks crept forward toward March and planting and the trip to a Natchez bank.

Chapter 52

Joleen led Norvina down the crowded street. Merchants spilled their displays of vegetables, fruits, and meat out into the sidewalk, and the smell of spices was pungent on the humid March morning. Norvina had been reluctant to come. She lectured Joleen that "proper ladies" definitely did not shop on such a jumbled street filled with German and Italian and Spanish people who could barely speak English.

"I need some spices, and there's nowhere else in Natchez to get them," Joleen said. "Now, come along."

Joleen bought basil for the tomatoes, something Aaron loved and said he seldom ate. She bought thyme and sage and oregano. She had been cooking more and more the past few months, despite Norvina's annoyance at having her kitchen constantly invaded to cook what she called "all that foreign food."

Joleen loved to please Aaron with a German or Italian dish, and she found she not only enjoyed cooking but was quite good at it. She also knew quite clearly that she spent an increasing number of hours in the kitchen each day so that she would not give in to her grief and fear. It was not only the lingering grief from her father's murder. It was a sorrow for her whole family. Her mother had not yet fully recovered. She spent hours simply sitting in her room, wrapped in a shawl, staring out the window. Tillman would lie in bed for two days at a time, then suddenly go into a kind of fit, raving about a baby and a whore and his uncle. And poor Lawton, all guilt-ridden and uncertain, with the family and the people and everything depending on him.

Joleen had only to think of Lavon for her grief to become anger. That anger still festered after all these months, because the sheriff believed Lavon's overseer and his lawyer and refused to have the grand jury indict Lavon. The sheriff discounted Lawton's testimony that he saw his uncle fleeing the murder.

Twice Joleen had gone to sheriff herself and insisted he take some action. She listened impatiently while he explained about Lavon's two witnesses and dismissed Lawton's evidence. "The rain, Miss Joleen, in that rain he couldn't see no fast-movin' rider clear 'nough to identify him for sure."

And, Sheriff Crandall added, Lavon was so far away, nothing the law did would have any practical effect.

"Sheriff, his runnin' away the very mornin' of the murder shows his guilt," Joleen snapped. "He ran out of Natchez so fast if anybody got behind him he would have choked him with heel dust."

"Now, now, slow down," the sheriff said with a nasty little smile that angered Joleen further. "It all makes sense, you see. He took his boy to the doctors in New Orleans and then took passage to Virginia to carry on his tradin' business."

Joleen did extract a promise from the sheriff that if Lavon came back to Natchez he would be arrested promptly and brought before the grand jury. She told herself constantly that she must stop grieving, must stop being angry, told herself in the most logical manner that there was nothing she could do. It was a useless dialogue, and at times when she was alone, she still cried.

And for the past month, when she most needed Aaron to be with her constantly, he had started making his hateful little trips again. She had come to fear these trips, and even more she feared to discover the truth behind them.

This sense of fear had become part of her feeling for Aaron since that day the previous summer when they had returned from Ohio. He had calmed down soon enough and dismissed the incident with his usual cynicism. And nothing really happened for a long time. He was affectionate, he was charming, he courted her as though they were yet to be married and he desperately wanted to win her hand. They made love frequently, and it was better than ever.

Yet there was something about Aaron that was different after that incident on the docks. There was a hardening, a bitterness in his nature that he couldn't hide from her. He took only one trip all summer. He went over to Louisiana on what he called urgent business. He returned the next day exhausted and depressed. Again he courted her, almost desperately, she realized.

She could not get him to discuss things with her, and she soon quit trying. She knew he lied to her. She knew it with all her being. Yet she dared not confront him or threaten to leave him. She loved him and desperately wanted to be with him under any circumstances. And she felt he loved her, no matter what his lies meant. He seemed to need her as much as she needed him.

So the summer passed, and autumn came, and they played at their love and dependence, and she let things be unsaid. Then came her father's murder and the aftermath. Aaron was with her constantly except for a few days when she stayed at the Columns without him. The first week in February, Aaron made an overnight trip to inspect some plantation boundaries across the river near Valdalia, Louisiana. He made a second trip, then a third. He promised each trip would be the last. But he made five trips in a month, all without Joleen. And yesterday he had crossed the river again.

Joleen had sworn to herself a dozen times in the past two weeks that she would confront him and force him to tell her the truth. But she could not bring herself to do it. The pieces of a puzzle floated at the back of her consciousness, and she dared not put them together.

Joleen handed Norvina a package of cumin. "Let's go home," she said. She felt no more pleasure at the thought of cooking for Aaron. Joleen shoved through the crowd and hurried to the corner. The carriage wasn't there yet.

"Damn Filch," she mumbled. "Let's walk home, Norvina."

"Filch, he be here in a minute," Norvina said. "He had to have the horse shoed, most likely he got delayed with the shoein'."

"No, I feel like walkin'."

"Miss Joleen, it's not proper for a lady to—"

"Don't you lecture me on manners, Norvina. I just dare you to try."

As she turned to cross the street, a coffle of twelve slaves blocked her way. They were linked by chains around their necks and left wrists. They moved very slowly, as though to a man they might collapse the next moment. Joleen saw the exhaustion in their faces and the fear in their eyes. One man had an ear missing. Another man's chest was crossed with deep lash marks. They were all men, and Joleen thought of their wives and children and their loneliness.

A white man in the street cracked his whip and drove them faster. His whip stung the last slave's back, and he screamed.

Joleen watched the white man come around the end of the coffle. She gasped.

The man was Lavon Deavors.

Joleen and Lavon stared at each other. He was as startled as she. She could not believe he actually stood here in front of her. He had murdered her father, his own brother, and gone free. Now he was abusing slaves and selling them. Joleen had never felt such hatred for any living thing.

She advanced on him. "You murdered my father!" she shrieked at him. "You stoned your own brother to death. And you have the gall to walk the public streets in daylight! You'll be sorry you ever came back. I swear to God you'll regret the day you ever returned to Natchez."

"Just a goddamn minute," Lavon said. "Don't slander me with Athel's death. I have no guilt. Just ask the sheriff—"

"You murdered my father!" she screamed. "Lawton saw you ridin' away! Do you think you can kill my father and go free, to get rich with your filthy trade? Do you think you'll own the Columns? You'll wind up at the end of a rope!"

"Get out of my way, Joleen," he said. "I have business. I don't have time for hysterical little girls."

"Your business!" she said. "Whippin' and sellin' slaves! If I was a man I'd take that whip from you and show you how it feels!"

"Well, now, you're not a man, are you?" he asked. He smiled. "And I doubt if you're married to one. Are you? What kind of man is your Jew?" He stepped closer and lowered his voice. "And, Joleen, I *will* own the Columns, and in a short time."

"If my husband were here he'd show you what kind of man he is," Joleen said. "And you'll never own the plantation. Never! Lawton won't let you."

Lavon laughed. "Lawton? You really think your brother can stop me? Or you? Do you think you can stop me? No, nothing will stop me, Joleen. I'll be master of the Columns. And my son will become its master when I die."

"Your son?" she asked. Now she laughed. "You mean that pitiful little thing that came from . . . Was it your wife or one of your whores on the river? You're trash, pure and simple. You're one of those white men who's fortunate in being born white. If you were black you wouldn't be a mechanic or a house nigger. You'd be a lazy, worthless field nigger, and a drunken one, at that."

A crowd had gathered. A man snickered. Lavon glanced around furiously.

"Go on and sell your niggers quick," Joleen said. "Because I'm on my way to the sheriff."

"The sheriff knows I'm back," Lavon said. Again he lowered his voice. "He won't touch me. And neither will anyone else. And, Joleen, the Columns *will* be mine, damnit! As for you, when I'm finished with the Deavorses, you just might find yourself begging me to work as a whore on my barge."

"No, if your wife gets tired of all the men there,

you'll just have to find someone else to take her place," Joleen said.

The crowd snickered again. Lavon's face reddened.

"Miss Joleen . . ."

Joleen looked over her shoulder. Filch was running toward her.

"Sorry I'm late," he said. "You got trouble with . . . this man?"

"This man?" Lavon said. He turned his fury on Filch. "A nigger doesn't talk about a white man like that, boy. Now, you apologize, damnit!"

"Let's go, Filch," Joleen said. "I want to go to the sheriff."

They walked away. Lavon ran after them. He grabbed Filch's shoulder and spun him around.

"Apologize to me, damnit!" Lavon shouted.

"No, sir, I won't," Filch said. "Not to a man like you."

"Goddamn you, nigger!" Lavon slapped Filch. Blood spurted from his nose. Filch's hands clenched into fists at his sides. He trembled.

"Don't you dare hit him again!" Joleen screamed. "You hit a black man because of what I say to you! You coward! You murderin' coward! You're the one who should apologize. You should apologize for the day you were born!"

"I'll see him whipped!" Lavon shouted. His face was scarlet. He brought up the whip. Joleen grabbed the whip with both hands and surprised herself by pulling it from Lavon's grasp. He turned his hate-filled face to her.

Joleen lashed at Lavon with all the force of her anger. The whip sliced into his face. He screeched as the flesh split open along his left cheek. Blood poured out. He grabbed his face with both hands and stumbled back. He screamed and sank to the street.

Joleen dropped the whip. A convulsion shook her body. Blood rushed to her head. She turned from the writhing, screaming figure on the ground and hurried away.

Chapter 53

Joleen stood at the parlor window. It was nearly midnight. LeRoy was asleep in the hooded cage behind her. The slaves had gone to bed.

Joleen could not stand still more than half a minute. She began to pace the room again. The lamps were low and cast shadows among the furniture and shelves of books. The room depressed Joleen. So did the whole house. For months she had begged Aaron to buy them a new house, as he had promised. And to start building on their land. All she got were promises.

"Promises and lies," she said aloud.

She returned to the window. The street was quiet. She listened to the crickets and locusts. Her mind was as restless as her body. She walked from the window, thinking of Aaron, and then, four steps later she was recalling her encounter with Lavon.

They had shouted insults at each other in the public streets. And she had actually taken his own whip and lashed his face! The night was humid, but she shivered at the memory of his screams, of the flesh that fell open on his cheek, of the gushing blood. The memory made her sick, yet she did not regret what she had done.

The audacity of the man! Returning to Natchez this way, after murdering his own brother. And he drove those poor slaves right down the street in broad daylight as though he had nothing to hide. She became angry again when she thought of her uncle, and furious when she recalled her visit to Sheriff Crandall.

"Yessum, I know he's back," the sheriff said. "I know I promised I'd take some action if he returned. First thing tomorrow I'll have him here in my office, I'll have that lawyer and that overseer . . . Now, wait a minute, ma'am. This is a serious matter, and I can't call those men liars and fly off half-cocked and do somethin' rash. . . ."

Joleen stormed from the sheriff's office. It was obvious her uncle owned the wretched man and that he would never be arrested. He would go free, to sell his slaves and get rich and scheme to steal the Columns.

Joleen found herself at the window again. She was miserable. She hated all this. Her life had been so simple when she was young and lived at the Columns. Oh, she was still young, she knew, but she felt like an old woman.

She wanted to erase the past few months. Erase her father's murder and the suffering of her family and her marriage to Aaron. No, no, there had been so many good days and nights with Aaron, she told herself. No matter what she felt now, she did love him, and she wanted to be with him. Even through her misery and anger she lapsed into a brief fantasy of lying in bed with him once more, of kissing him and staring into his eyes and making love.

The parlor finally depressed her so badly that she went back to the kitchen. She poured a glass of milk. But she slammed the glass to the table without taking a sip. She had made up her mind. When Aaron returned from Louisiana, she would insist he tell her the truth. And if he refused, she swore that she would pack up her things and go back to the Columns.

She had reached the hall door when she heard a scraping sound along the outside wall. She paused. She heard whispering. The back door creaked open. A Negro man inched inside. Joleen sprang back into the hall shadows. The door opened wider.

There was a white man's arm around the Negro's waist. It was Aaron! He was helping the Negro into the kitchen. The Negro's leg was bleeding. And Aaron's shirt was ripped, and he was bleeding, too.

Joleen ran several steps into the kitchen. "Aaron?" she called. "Aaron, what . . . what's wrong? What happened?"

She recognized the Negro. It was Clarence Lee,

the man who had been sold to the Louisiana sugarcane plantation.

"Oh, Lord, no," she whispered.

She knew then. She had known for many weeks, but she had never let herself solve the puzzle. She stared at Aaron. She felt she was looking at a stranger. She saw his dark eyes, his lips, the strand of hair across his forehead, his ears, his Adam's apple. Each part of him seemed alien.

Aaron eased Clarence into a chair and walked toward Joleen. He was clutching his side. She backed away.

"Joleen . . ."

She shook her head. "Don't . . . Stay away from me, Aaron. I know. I've known a long time. You . . . you've been lyin' to me. . . . Everything you've said is a lie. I loved you, and I . . . You lied to me, Aaron. . . . You've been usin' me and my family, and all you care about is helpin' niggers escape. . . . You're a criminal, Aaron. . . . And I loved you."

"Listen, Joleen," he said. "Listen to me. I don't have time to talk now. I had to come here, to bring Clarence here. He's badly hurt. I must get help for him. There's no other place I could go. The sheriff has dogs after us. He may be here any minute. I want you to leave. Go out to the Columns. Get out of here. But . . . yes, I've lied about everything . . . except that I loved you. I do love you very much."

"No, you don't love me!" she cried. "No! I hate you!"

She flew at Aaron, hitting him with her fists. He staggered back. His face was twisted with pain.

"I'm . . . I'm sorry," she said. "Here, let me . . . I don't know what to do." She glanced wildly at Clarence. "I'll help you, Aaron. But not him. I won't help him! I want that nigger out of my house!"

Blood seeped between Aaron's fingers. Joleen was terrified at the sight of the blood.

"I've got to go up and find some dressings for Clarence," Aaron said. "And some of that salve Aunt Froney gave us. Joleen . . . please . . . I do love you. . . . Get out of here. Get Filch to drive you to the Columns. Damnit, go on!"

He brushed past her, and she watched him scrape his hand along the wall. He paused at the stairs, then gasped as he took the first step.

"Oh, Aaron, wait!" She ran to his side. "Wait down here. I'll get whatever you need. You'll hurt yourself."

"No, I've got to go up," he said. "There are some things hidden . . . maps I must destroy in case the sheriff comes. Help me. Help me up the stairs, Joleen."

He put his arm around her, and she helped him up, step by step, and each step made him gasp. At the top he nearly doubled over, and had to lean against the wall for a full minute.

"The bedroom," he said. "I must go to our bedroom."

Again she helped him walk, but by the time they reached the end of the hall he had found some reserve of strength and he pulled away and moved without her help. But the grimace on his face told Joleen of his pain, and she stood there trembling with fear and anger.

"I can't leave you like this," she said. "I can't just run away. You're hurt so bad. I don't know what to do. . . . Why did you do this to me, Aaron? Why did you lie? Didn't my love mean anything to you? You just married me because I'm a Deavors. That's all. You just wanted to be a Deavors so no one would suspect what you've been doin'."

"I married you because I love you, damnit!"

"And that night. Those men. You did kill those three men, Aaron. Oh, my Lord! How many more have you killed on your trips? You hate us all, don't you? You'd free every nigger in the county! And set them against us!" She backed away suddenly as though he had something contagious.

"Yes, I killed them, Joleen," he said. "And I've bitterly regretted the killings. I've cursed myself many times for ever pulling my pistols that night. But that was the past, Joleen. There'll be no more killings. And no more lies. . . ."

"How many men have you murdered altogether, Aaron?" she asked. "I've never known a . . . a murderer before. That's what you are, a murderer . . . and a liar!"

"I can't talk!" he said. "Will you get out of here, Joleen? I . . . Believe me. I've suffered for those killings. And for the lies. But I never lied when I said I loved you. I never lied about that. And aren't you lying to yourself now? About slavery. You know it's wrong, damnit! You know it's evil. I've watched you change over the months. I've listened to you, Joleen. You just won't admit what you've come to believe."

"No, Aaron," she said. "You're wrong. Oh, I see the abuses of slavery. But I don't . . . What about the Columns? And the people there? What about my family, Aaron? Do you think they're evil? You do, don't you? My father and Lawton and all of us. . . . Damn you, Aaron! Yes, I'll leave. And I don't care what happens to you. I hope they do catch you and that nigger."

Horses were stopping in front of the house. A dog barked.

"Get out the back," Aaron said. "Get the hell out of here!" Aaron took a pistol from his chest of drawers.

Joleen ran to the door. "I will," she called. "And to hell with your lies and your niggers, and I don't care if you bleed to death."

She ran down the stairs. Tears smarted her eyes. Her face was feverish. She hated Aaron. All she wanted was to get away from here, get out to the Columns.

Someone was pounding on the front door. Joleen stopped in the hall. She looked at the door. No, she told herself, I'm not going to help him. And she took two more steps down the hall toward the back door. She stopped again. The last Yankee abolitionist they caught had been whipped and branded and put in prison. She glanced at the stairs. Oh, Lord, she told herself, that's what they'll do to Aaron!

Joleen swallowed hard. She wiped at her eyes. Then she turned, walked to the front door, and opened it.

Chapter 54

Sheriff Crandall and several men with rifles stood there.

"Good evenin', Sheriff Crandall," Joleen said. "The hour's a little late for callin', isn't it?"

"Yes, ma'am, it is," the sheriff said. "But this an urgent matter. You see, ma'am—"

"Oh, I understand," Joleen said. "You've finally done somethin' about my father's murder, after all these months. You've come to tell me that Lavon Deavors has been arrested. Of course, sheriff. I don't mind bein' disturbed for that kind of news."

"No, ma'am, wait up," the sheriff said. "That . . . that ain't why I've come. Oh, I'm workin' right along on that murder, and pretty soon I'm sure I'll have somethin' to report. But what we come about tonight is somethin' different. See, they was this trouble 'cross the river near Vadalia. This vicious nigger escaped from a sugarcane plantation, and this white man helped him. They was tracked to Natchez. And, well, I don't know how to say this, ma'am . . ."

"You don't know how to say what, sheriff?"

"Well, ma'am, this here white man was seen, and a fellow said he kind of resembled your husband. And then, the dogs, they done led us here."

"Sheriff Crandall," Joleen said, "do you mean to stand there and tell me . . . insult me, sir, with the accusation that my husband has helped some nigger to run away?"

"Ma'am, the dogs led us right here," a red-faced man said. "And they got true noses. They don't lie."

"Are you suggestin' that I'm lyin'?" Joleen asked. "You'd take those hounds' noses against my word, sir?"

"Now, now," the sheriff said. "Rancy didn't mean

nothin' like that, Miss Joleen. But if you'd let us have a look around . . ."

"You mean search my home?" Joleen asked. "That's preposterous, sheriff! Do you for a minute think I'd harbor a fugitive nigger? Why, my family has owned slaves in Adams County since the last century."

"Miss Joleen, nobody would question a Deavors' word," the sheriff said. "But . . . well, frankly, your husband's a different matter. He not bein' a Deavors, and all. See, that there white man, he was hurt pretty bad. Lost some blood. So if we could just talk to your husband for a minute, then we'd know he wasn't the man."

"You're still accusin' me of lyin'."

"No, ma'am, Miss Joleen. I'd take your own word for anything. But your husband, he could do things you don't know nothin' 'bout. He could have sneaked out tonight . . ."

"He's been here all night," Joleen said. She avoided the sheriff's eyes and sought the right lie. She was desperate. If the sheriff and his men got past the door, everything was lost. "It's just that . . . well, my husband was feelin' po'ly. He went to bed early with a fever, and I can't disturb him."

"Now, really, ma'am," the sheriff said. "Po'ly or not, we goin' to have to talk to him. And there's no two ways 'bout it. He couldn't be that sick. So you either goin' to have to fetch him down, or I'm goin' to have to insist that I—"

"You wish to speak with me, sir?"

Joleen glanced around. Aaron stood behind her in the door. He had changed into a powder-blue suit and wore fresh lace at his wrists. He smiled as though amused, but she saw the pain in his eyes. And he held his body rigid, with his arms pressed against his sides. One hand moved to his waist. She didn't know whether he meant to hold his wound or reach for a pistol. Then she nearly gasped aloud.

There was a tiny spot of fresh blood on his coat!

"Why, yessir, Mr. Clauson," the sheriff said. He told Aaron about the incident in Vadalia. "Don't mean to insult you with the accusation you helped. But the dogs led us here. And they was this fellow thought it was you. Course, you haven't been hurt bad tonight. That's for sure."

"Insult me?" Aaron said. "Why, sir, you both flatter and amuse me. I find it rather droll to be accused of helping some nigger escape from a sugarcane plantation. There are only two problems with the matter, sheriff. One is that I really can't tell one nigger from another. If I had to help a certain nigger escape, the poor fellow would have to wear a number or uniform so I could tell him from all the others. And then there's the problem of my lace, gentlemen. Wouldn't the task of helping a nigger escape be very damaging to one's lace?"

Two of the men wanted to search the house and grounds. But the sheriff wouldn't hear of it. He apologized for the intrusion and led the men away.

Aaron closed the door and collapsed against the wall. His arm fell from his side. His shirt and coat were damp with blood.

No white doctor could be trusted, so a free black man who knew some medicine treated Aaron and Clarence. Once the bleeding was stopped, Aaron's wound didn't seem too serious, though he was quite weak from loss of blood. Clarence's leg was badly hurt, however, and he tossed feverishly on a mattress in the cellar. The free Negro promised to return the next night. Norvina and Filch knew what had happened, but the other slaves were not told.

At four o'clock Joleen and Aaron lay awake in bed. They had not said a word to each other since coming upstairs. Aaron had slept for an hour, but Joleen's eyes did not close. She stared at the ceiling and waited out each minute that brought morning closer. She was drained of feeling. Earlier her mind had boiled with anger and hatred. But it had boiled too long and now seemed blanched of any intensity.

"Joleen," Aaron said when he awakened. His voice was hoarse, and saying the one word seemed to tire him.

She didn't look at him, "No, don't talk, Aaron," she said wearily. "Try to sleep some more. We have nothin' to talk about. I've made up my mind. I'm not goin' to stay with you. I won't betray you. But I won't continue to be your wife. In the mornin' I'm movin' back to the Columns."

"Joleen . . . I've been cruel to you," Aaron said. His words came with heavy breathing, as though he had just run a race. "I can't defend what I've done. But damnit, I love you! I love you in a way I've never loved anyone. And . . . need you. . . . Don't you understand my dilemma all this time, how it's torn me up inside?"

" 'I love you . . . I love you,' " she mocked. "You use words so easily. Just as easily as you've used me. And my family. Married to a Deavors, you've been beyond suspicion for your criminal activities. That's what you've needed, Aaron. I want you to get out of Natchez. I don't even think I hate you anymore. I just don't care. I want to go back home and try to forget this nightmare."

"Did you really whip your uncle in the street?"

"What? What if I did? It has nothin' to do with you and your activities. How did you know?"

"Filch told me," Aaron said. "If you despise slavery enough to whip your uncle on a Natchez street . . ."

"Slavery had nothin' to do with it," Joleen said. "It was because of my father's murder. And because my uncle was goin' to hurt Filch."

"Yes, and Filch is a slave," Aaron said. "Don't you see? Look at yourself, Joleen."

"I didn't do it because . . . I don't want to talk about this anymore, Aaron. I can't talk to you. You're too clever. You're too deceitful. You've manipulated me with your cleverness and your lies and your books."

He forced himself up on one elbow. "Damnit, listen to me, Joleen."

"I don't want to talk," she said. "And you should rest."

"Not until I finish what I want to say. I came to Natchez only because of my work with the abolitionists, Joleen. I abhor slavery, and I'd do anything to end the practice and see every black man set free. I make no apologies for that or for anything I've done. I do apologize for my cruelty to you. I love you, I really do love you, Joleen. I love you desperately, and I hate myself for my deceit. But what in hell could I have done, torn between something I dedicated my life to ... and my love for you? What could I have done, Joleen? It's been agony, all these months of lying and keeping my true self from you. But how could I have been honest with you? No, wait a damn minute. I've hoped beyond reason that you'd change. I knew you'd change and come to see the evil of slavery. And you have. I know it now. It's not easy for you to admit, I know, but ... Oh, hell. I can't live one day without you, Joleen. I simply can't. You make me feel whole."

Joleen put her finger to his lips. "No, Aaron, save your pretty speech. You're just sayin' words. I can't trust you. And I can't be a part of what you are. I can't help niggers escape. I love the Columns. I love my family. And our people. They don't hate us, they don't hate me. They don't, Aaron. I have a loyalty, don't you see? No, don't kiss me. Oh, look, you've hurt yourself."

"I'm all right," he said. "We must talk. We must work this out. Don't you see how much—?"

"No, no, no!" she said. "I've made up my mind. I can't ever believe anything you tell me again. And I can't be a part of your Yankee schemes. I can't! Now, you've got to get out of Natchez, Aaron. You've got to. But first thing tomorrow, I swear to heaven, I'm goin' back out to my family. I'm so tired. I wish I felt something. I wish I was even angry or full of hate. But I'm just tired. Let's sleep now. If you say another word, I swear I'll scream."

She turned away from Aaron. He didn't say anything else. She did not look at him again all night. She lay awake and watched the sun come up.

Chapter 55

Lavon touched his scar as he watched the new slaves being washed down and given clothes. There were 238 of them. Nearly one hundred were mechanics and field hands, but the majority were young women who would be good breeders. The new constitution that prohibited slave trading would become law in May, just two months away, and many men who supported the prohibition were rushing to buy slaves before the ban took effect.

Over the din in the courtyard Lavon heard the sound of bricks being slapped against mortar. He glanced to his right, where four black masons were adding a new wing to the pen. Lavon smiled as he thought of the plan that he and Jason Colfax had devised to stay within the letter of the law, yet effectively circumvent its intention.

The constitution prohibited professional slave traders from importing slaves into the state and selling them. But it did not prohibit a legitimate, established farmer from selling slaves to his neighbor in a private transaction. Lavon and his agents would continue to bring in slaves, and Lavon would set them to work on his own land. They would plant or pick or do whatever legitimate work was needed. Then, after a few weeks, the slaves would be sold, in a "gentlemanly" manner, to some desperate farmer.

Lavon even planned to plant cotton on the ten acres that surrounded the slave pen. He owned parcels of cotton land, with slave quarters, all over the county. Once he planted these ten acres, he could claim that the former slave pen was now nothing more than particularly elaborate quarters for his slaves.

"Get those new niggers dressed and looking good," Lavon shouted to Luke Simmons, his chief agent. "There's an auction this morning. And cut out that high-yellow, second from the end. With some training and polish she might make a fancy lady for the barge."

Lavon walked out of his carriage and told Silas, his driver, to take him to the Mercantile Bank.

The road was filled with horses and carriages. In the months Lavon had been away, Natchez had received a glut of new people. New homes were springing up on every available piece of land around town. Thousands of acres were being cleared for planting. There were even more slave pens, despite the coming prohibition. But none of the pens was as large or as successful as Lavon's. During his absence he had traveled from New Orleans to Virginia, and with skillful buying and the use of Luke Simmons and other good agents he had flooded Natchez with slaves, just as farmers began to panic because of the new constitution.

There was no fat, lazy partner to siphon off half the profits now. And Columbine LeClerc, whom Lavon had hired in New Orleans to run the whore barge, was a clever and efficient woman. The last month alone, Colfax estimated, the barge had earned more money than some of the county's smaller plantations earned in a year. Part of this was due to Columbine's suggestion that she add high-stakes gambling to the barge's attractions.

Lavon touched his scar again. It itched with a dull pain. Two days earlier Dr. Gatlin had told Lavon that the scar would not go away. He would be scarred for life. For life, damnit, he mumbled. His son was a cripple, and he would wear this scar to remind him and everyone else of his public humiliation at Joleen's hands! His anger seemed to increase the itch along his cheek. And Silas had taken the carriage over half a dozen deep holes.

"Damnit, stay out of those holes, nigger!" Lavon shouted.

"Yessuh, Mist' Lavon," Silas said.

Joleen will pay for this, Lavon swore to himself for the hundredth time since he lay writhing in the mud. Damnit, she would pay! And in a very short time.

The moment Lavon heard that Sheriff Crandall had traced a fugitive Negro to Joleen's house he set his agents to investigating and following her husband. Lavon felt it was too much of a coincidence that Clauson could be innocent of both this and the incident during the Nat Turner insurrection.

Lavon did not doubt that his agents would trap the man in the near future. And if he could prove nothing against Clauson, then he would fabricate whatever evidence was needed to convict the man. It wouldn't be difficult. Clauson was already under suspicion. Only his marriage to a Deavors had saved him so far.

Lavon didn't think his niece was involved in any abolitionist work, though she might lie to save her husband. But if Clauson was caught, Joleen would surely be charged with the same crimes. Lavon scratched the scar. What might his proud, arrogant niece do if she were confronted with overwhelming evidence and given the opportunity to save herself and her husband? She would probably subjugate herself to anything! Lavon permitted his fantasies to roam. First of all Lavon would take his own sexual pleasure with her, in ways he had learned in Morocco and that even his most jaded whores disliked. Then he would put Joleen to work on the barge and see that she serviced only the most demanding and perverse men. She would end up with many scars, and the physical ones would be the least damaging.

Then, of course, Lavon would turn the evidence over to the sheriff and see Joleen and her husband whipped and branded and imprisoned.

The carriage hit another hole.

"Damn you, Silas, I'll have you in the fields if you don't drive better," Lavon shouted.

Silas mumbled something and leaned forward with his head bowed. Lavon tried to relax and forget the maddening scar and the hatred it kindled. But the itching tormented him even more, and he found himself thinking of his fight with Athel.

Though his mind now called the incident a fight, it had taken many weeks for the horror of what really happened to fade into his usual rationalization.

Lavon had maimed two horses fleeing into Natchez that morning. Two hours later, he and his family were headed for New Orleans. Once safely on the boat, he had beaten Frannie severely for her infidelity.

For weeks he drank heavily, all the while moving about constantly and throwing himself into his work. He had nightmares about stoning Athel, and many nights the vision of Athel's battered face woke him, and he staggered across the room and gulped whiskey from a bottle.

Rationalization came very slowly, but it came finally, faithful as always. Hell, Lavon told himself, Athel's death was the last thing he wanted. Having Athel penniless and at his mercy when he took over the Columns was his principal motivation. He would have gone out of his way to see that no harm came to his brother.

But Athel had insulted him, provoked him beyond reason. And Athel had tried to take away his birthright, his right to be called a Deavors! Athel had slandered him as the bastard son of some portrait painter. That was a despicable insult, and any man worthy of his honor would have demanded satisfaction in a duel. Instead, he and Athel had fought with their hands. And he, Lavon, had won the fight.

Lavon wished he had not killed Athel. But he felt no guilt for the act. And he would never be tried. Sheriff Crandall had assured him of that by messenger, before he returned. The sheriff was a poor man who visited the barge several times a week and enjoyed the whores for nothing. Lavon was quite pleased with himself for having the foresight, even in the panic of fleeing, to set up his alibis with Colfax and Blackledge.

Thinking of the murder was a daily ritual for Lavon, as ritual as stroking the scar. And thoughts of Athel always led him to thoughts of the Columns.

Lavon had been stunned that rainy day to learn that Athel knew his plans. Fortunately Athel mentioned that he had yet to reveal those plans to Cellus or Lawton. Now everything would be much easier. Lawton was young and inexperienced, and his lack of confidence was obvious to everyone.

While away, Lavon had feared that Lawton might learn something of his plans. Fortunately, Athel had been rash enough to tell Lavon that it was Riley Ferguson of the First Agricultural Bank who had warned him about his brother. Jason Colfax discovered that Ferguson was an incurable gambler and owed several large notes to Natchez gamblers, notes he could not possibly pay. Colfax bought up the notes and demanded that Ferguson stay quiet. If not, he would demand payment and ruin the man.

Also during Lavon's absence, Colfax had bought two more land parcels adjacent to the Columns. And old Mrs. LeBeau, who owned the land with the road, was nearly dead. Her nephew, Alain, was anxious to sell the land when he inherited it.

Lavon now controlled a majority of the First Agricultural Bank's board members, as well as three members of the Mercantile Bank's board. Though three was not a majority, Lavon was able to manipulate Hal Thigpen, Mercantile's president.

Another year, maybe sooner, Lavon told himself, and he would be master of the Columns.

Half a dozen men were waiting to see Thigpen, but Lavon was ushered past them.

"Lawton came in earlier this morning," Thigpen said. "He had already been to the Agricultural Bank, and apparently they were reluctant to give him the cash he needs. It's far more cash than usual in a planting loan."

Lavon had arranged for Lawton to be cordially but firmly refused at the Agricultural Bank.

"And what did you tell my nephew?" Lavon asked.

"I told him . . . what you suggested I tell him," Thigpen said. He talked rapidly and avoided Lavon's eyes. Thigpen was a wealthy and proud man whose grandfather had founded the Mercantile Bank. He was obsessed with a seventeen-year-old mulatto whore named Renée. He had offered Lavon a small fortune, but Lavon wouldn't sell her, though he hinted that when he owned the Columns he would give the girl to Thigpen.

"Well, did he sign the note?" Lavon asked.

"No, he's not that young and stupid," Thigpen said. "He insisted on taking time to consider the rather . . . stringent terms. I'm surprised he came in at all without a lawyer or someone to advise him. I played up his youth and the fact that this was the first time he'd signed, and emphasized the sizable amount of cash he wants. And I told him the board is meeting this afternoon and that they won't meet again for two weeks. All right, Lavon, I'm sure he'll come back this afternoon and sign. I did as you wanted. But in all honesty, I—"

"But what?" Lavon asked sharply. He softened his voice. "We've talked this over before, Hal. I understand your feelings. And you have my word that when I own the plantation it will be only a formality. Lawton and my family will continue to live there and plant there, as they've always done. I'm in a hurry now. Drop down to the barge tonight, and we can talk then. And, oh, yes. Renée is over the grippe. She asked about you. I've been thinking of that little trip downriver with her that you mentioned. We can discuss it tonight."

Lavon was smiling as he walked from the bank.

Chapter 56

Lawton's horse pawed the hard earth. When the horse stopped pawing, its hooves were hidden in a ground fog. Lawton shivered and huddled tighter inside his coat. It was unusually cold for the last week in February. If the nightly frost continued, it would kill off the azaleas and japonicas that budded at the beginning of March.

Lawton looked back at the quarters. Why didn't the drivers have the people up by now? Damnit, he expected them to be in the fields by sunrise.

There was always so much winter work, and it seemed to Lawton that the work was going much slower than in previous years. There were still buildings to be repaired and fences to be mended with new rails. Ditches had to be dug, and others had to be drained. Tools and implements had to be repaired. And all the old cotton stalks had to be cut down for the March planting.

Lawton glanced at the quarters again. Damn the drivers! Then he heard the horn and watched lights come on in the cabins.

He trotted toward the quarters to hurry the people along. But he reined up abruptly and rode back out into the fields. The deeply shadowed swamp brought a memory of a summer day when he had followed Joleen and masturbated as she swam naked.

He had submerged his guilt about the summer with Joleen for a long time, and he felt betrayed that his mind could delve it up now. But each morning as he waited impatiently for dawn, some guilt or worry always troubled him. Usually they concerned the Columns and his family.

He did not know if he could get the Columns through this year, given the plantation's financial situation. He did not know how much financing he could get from the bank, and he was uncertain how to go about it or whose advice to take. He did not know if he could work the people and supervise the cotton from planting to harvesting to market. He decided one day to hire an overseer, and the next day he rejected the idea.

He worried about his mother, who still spent long periods alone in her room. And he particularly worried about Tillman, who grew stranger with each week. Tillman was making a nervous wreck out of his mother.

At times she became exasperated and shouted at Tillman. He would run away and hide out in the swamps and not come back for hours. Usually Tillman never spoke a word. When he broke his silence, he screamed about a whore and about a baby and about his uncle.

Two weeks earlier Tillman had attacked a pregnant slave. He had to be dragged from her stomach, which he was clawing at as though he was actually trying to rip the baby out. Dr. Stacey had a long talk with Tillman. But he told Lawton there was nothing he could do for his brother.

"Sometimes, people have something . . . wrong with their minds or their nervous systems," Dr. Stacey said. "Medicine can't help them. It's something we doctors know nothin' about, really, and I'd be less than honest if I pretended I could help the boy, Lawton. There are places down in New Orleans where you can . . . have him committed, but I don't think you'd want to send your brother to such a place."

Lawton shuddered and stared blankly at the red sun just appearing on the horizon. No, he would not even consider sending Tillman to some madhouse. And, as Dr. Stacey said, Tillman was under the double strain of his experience with the whore and his father's murder, and he seemed to feel that he was responsible for the murder in some way.

"He's still young, Lawton," the doctor said. "It could just be a phase he's passin' through. He might well grow out of it."

The first slaves were heading into the fields, carrying their snacks for the noon meal. Lawton heard the breakfast bell and realized how hungry he was. He nodded and spoke to the slaves as he galloped toward the house.

The day he learned of Lavon's return Lawton rode into Natchez. But Sheriff Crandall was adamant. He promised to question Lavon and talk to Blackledge and Colfax again about their sworn testimony, but he made it obvious that no indictment would be brought against Lavon.

Lawton left Natchez without learning of Joleen's scene with Lavon. News of the whipping reached the Columns the next day. Lawton was stunned and pleased and angry at himself because his sister had done exactly what he should have done—taken a whip to his uncle.

Later that same day Joleen arrived at the Columns, with several trunks. She announced that she and Aaron had separated and that she would under no circumstances return to him. She refused to discuss their troubles. She was unusually quiet and took a long ride alone at dusk.

The next morning she was up at dawn and ordered the trunks put into the carriage. With no explanation and hardly a good-bye, she headed back for Natchez.

Lawton brooded about Joleen for the rest of the day. But his sister and her marriage were far back in his thoughts when he woke up the next morning. The fields had been cleared. Manure had been spread. Plowing was under way. And he had to go into Natchez for the loan that would see the Columns through the year.

He sought advice from Haskell Sumrall and Juan Delsano. On a Natchez visit he sought out Riley Ferguson, who often advised his father on business and banking matters. Ferguson was surprisingly formal and, in fact, rather cold for a man who had known Lawton since his birth. And he was no help at all.

The first week in March had passed, and Lawton watched the second week creep along, day by day, without making a decision about what kind of loan he wanted and the terms he was willing to accept. He told himself he had so much work to do on a given day that he could not spent the time in Natchez. He knew quite clearly what he was doing and why he was hesitating. But he could not force himself to confront the Natchez bankers.

On Wednesday evening Lawton sat in the parlor and talked to Cellus.

"I been sayin' to think things out and don't rush into nothin'," Cellus said. "But time is here for you to make up your mind on our needs and on what kind of note you goin' to sign. I'd say you ought to get into town first thing in the mornin'. Cash money is in short supply this year, from what I hear tell. You wait too late, banks might have put out all the money they can afford for one year."

"I know, Cellus," Lawton said. "I've got to go in tomorrow mornin', for sure. And I'm goin' to have to get more cash than usual, even if the terms are not the best."

"Yessir, we need the cash," Cellus said. "Payin' off last year's loan has 'bout wiped us out. Come the summer, we goin' to have less cash money than we've had in, well, I reckon in my memory. But we can squeeze by in lots of ways. I'd be mighty careful 'bout the terms I get, if I was you. Talk to both banks first, then we can talk again. We got to read all the fine print, have a lawyer look things over. And you know, well, even then, what with your uncle back and all, and him rich and influential in Natchez, you can't ever tell where that influence might be. You know, Mist' Lawton, you might ought to consider goin' downriver to New Orleans and talkin' to a bank down there 'bout financin'."

But Lawton wouldn't consider going to New Orleans. Hadn't his family always financed through a Natchez bank? The people at the First Agricultural Bank and the Mercantile Bank respected the Deavorses, and they had always dealt honorably with the family. Lavon might be ruthless and have his schemes and his influence, but certainly not with the kind of men who ran the banks.

If they wouldn't give the Columns the financing it needed this year, it would be a personal reflection on Lawton. No, he would be careful, and he would be shrewd. But after all, he was dealing with men of honor.

The next day, as he waited for his carriage to be hitched up, Cellus came out to the barn.

"Mist' Lawton, maybe I ought to ride into town with you," Cellus said.

"Damnit, that's not necessary," Lawton said. "I

appreciate your concern, Cellus. I'm not going to do anything rash. I'll come back out here tomorrow, and we'll have all weekend to decide what's best before I sign anything."

His mother came out as he mounted the driving box. She also advised that he be cautious and talk things over before he made a decision.

"I know you'll do just fine with the bank, son," she said. "I have every confidence in you."

She kissed his cheek. Lucinda ran out from the kitchen and kissed his lips. Lawton cracked the whip, and the horse trotted off. He sat erect and did not look back at his family. He was afraid his face would betray the anxiety that nearly made him tremble.

Chapter 57

Lawton was totally discouraged as he walked from the First Agricultural Bank. The people there were cordial, but they were quite reluctant to advance the Columns the amount of cash that was needed. They said there was an outside chance the board might approve the loan but that Lawton shouldn't depend on it.

Lawton talked to three men at the Agricultural Bank, and he had the same feeling as when he had sought advice from Mr. Ferguson. The men talked about how much they respected the Deavors family, but Lawton sensed that they were uncomfortable in dealing with him. Did everyone in Natchez think he was incapable of running the plantation? He walked slowly toward the Mercantile Bank and asked himself what his father would have done in a similar situation.

Of course, he told himself, his father would not be in such a situation. He would simply go to the bank and get the cash and the terms he wanted, as he always had.

After talking to Mr. Thigpen over a glass of sherry at the Mercantile Bank, however, Lawton's spirits picked up. The banker was warm and expansive and said he had no doubts that Lawton could run the Columns as well as any man in the county.

"The master of the Columns has no need to worry about financin' a year's cotton," Thigpen said. "Why, my family has dealt with your family for decades. Last year was a bad one for all the planters. Oh, there are some people we'd be hesitant to back, but certainly not you, not under any circumstances."

Lawton accepted another sherry. He was elated when Thigpen said that the bank could almost certainly give Lawton the money he needed. Though of course, Thigpen added, the full board of directors would have to give its approval. The only problem was that Lawton had waited so late to ask for the money.

Lawton's elation faded as Thigpen mentioned some of the conditions of the loan. The interest rate was high. The note had to be paid by the first of the coming year, which was three months earlier than usual. And the bank retained the right to sell the note.

"But these are formalities," Thigpen said. "Just bankers' terms, the sort of thing we must put down on paper. Why, everybody feels there'll be a bumper crop this year. And needless to say, if you do experience some little difficulty with the terms, why, we'll simply talk things over again and make whatever adjustments are necessary to extend the terms of the note. Here, your glass is nearly empty, Lawton."

Lawton tried to bargain on some of the harsher terms but found himself confused by the detailed bankers' language. At times Thigpen might as well have been speaking Greek.

"I'm sure what you say is true," Lawton said. "About renegotiatin' the terms and all. But I'll have to . . . seek some advice, Mr. Thigpen. Some legal advice. And I must have time to think things over."

"Of course, of course, son," Thigpen said. "I'd expect you to think things over and seek advice from older people. Particularly since this is the first time you've been old enough to even sign a note." Thigpen leaned forward. "I'll tell you frankly, son. It's only because of the high esteem the bank has always felt for your family that we'd advance so much money to a . . . to a man of your youth and inexperience. How many hours do you think you need to think things over?"

"Well, actually Mr. Thigpen, I was thinkin' in terms of a few days. . . ."

"I don't want to rush you into anything, Lawton," Thigpen said. "I know that you find all this difficult and that you're hesitant to commit yourself . . . though to be a successful planter, son, you have to be able to make up your mind and be resolute. You have to be your own man. You see, my only concern is this. For my own part, I'd say take a day or two to consider the note and seek advice. It's just that the board of directors is meeting this afternoon. And if you could make up your mind during dinner and come back here this afternoon to sign, then I'm sure the board will accept the terms of the note and vote to give you the cash. They don't meet again for two weeks, and by then, well, it's late as it is. But don't let me rush you into anything, son."

Lawton declined another glass of sherry. He promised Thigpen that he would make a decision and return to the bank in the afternoon.

Joleen kissed Lawton on the cheek. They were standing in the front door of her house.

"You and Aaron come on out to the place soon," Lawton said. "He hasn't been out in a coon's age. And you—you hardly stay long enough to unpack. You know, Joleen, you and Daddy once joked about me gettin' too citified in Natchez. Now you're the one who's gettin' citified."

She laughed. "Don't you worry about that," she said. "I wish you could stay till Aaron gets back from the courthouse. Or why don't you go over there and talk to him? I think you ought to, Lawton. I don't know a thing about notes and loans and all, but you ought to talk to somebody like Aaron before you sign anything."

"Maybe I'll go over there," Lawton said. He knew he had to talk to someone about the note. But he didn't really want to see Aaron. He could tell there was something very much wrong about Joleen's marriage. Joleen wouldn't talk about her problems, but she was more indrawn than Lawton had ever seen her. A sense of anxiety permeated the house. Filch and Norvina hovered about the kitchen and wouldn't look Lawton in the eyes.

Joleen touched his arm. "Lawton?" she said. "Lawton, do talk to Aaron or some other lawyer. Or go back out and talk to Cellus or Mr. Sumrall or somebody. I can tell how uncertain you are. Anybody would be, the first time they deal with a bank this way. I know you're worried about what's goin' to happen to the Columns."

"Damnit, I can run the plantation just fine," he said. "I appreciate your concern, Joleen, but I get sick and tired of people thinkin' I can't run the place the way . . . it's always been run. I'm not goin' to rush into anything at the bank. And, Joleen, don't worry about the plantation or anything. Everything will be all right. We're goin' to have a damn good crop this year, just you wait and see."

"I know everything will be all right, Lawton," she said. "I really believe you'll do . . . what's best. It's just, with Lavon back and all, well, he's so ruthless, Lawton. You know, Aaron and I have some money. We could help you out. Really, we could. Why don't you wait, and we'll talk to Aaron. And you know what else? I could . . . we could sell that land Daddy gave us. Lord, I hear land value has doubled. And with that money, you wouldn't have to get so much cash from the bank."

"Joleen, I couldn't consider such a thing," Lawton said. "That's your dowry! I want you to keep that land and build on it and maybe plant someday. Don't you see? I'm . . . I'm head of the family now. I've got to do things like . . . like a man. I can't go takin' your land and your money right here at the beginnin'. I'd be admittin' I'm not capable of dealin' with the bank. You know Daddy would never have taken charity from anyone, family or not."

She sighed. "All right, Lawton," she said. "I understand how you feel. And I know you'll do the best thing for the Columns."

She smiled as he walked away, but he knew it was a forced smile. She didn't really believe he was capable of doing the right thing. He climbed into the carriage and scolded himself for being so ambivalent. He would talk to Aaron and talk to Mr. Ferguson again. And he would visit Wayne Nester, a lawyer and old family friend. He would take their advice, and if necessary he would refuse to sign the note until the terms were changed. In any case, he decided, he would insist that he go back out to the Columns and return tomorrow after discussing the loan with Cellus.

But Aaron wasn't at the courthouse. Lawton waited half an hour, then left. Mr. Ferguson was in, and his clerk said he would be glad to see Lawton but that Lawton would have to wait a few minutes, as he was with a client. Forty-five minutes later Lawton left the office without seeing Ferguson.

Lawton had two quick glasses of whiskey that seemed to resent the presence of the earlier sherry and took out the resentment on his stomach. The bank closed in twenty minutes. He hurried around to Wayne Nester's office, but the lawyer had not returned from dinner.

Lawton stood in the street, overcome by urgency and indecision. A minute passed. Another. A clock chimed the quarter-hour.

The bank's board wouldn't meet again for two weeks, he told himself. If he failed to return this afternoon, they would think him weak and indecisive.

He ran the two blocks to the Mercantile Bank. Mr. Thigpen was leaving for the board meeting and seemed in a great hurry. Thigpen said he assumed Lawton had taken his business to the First Agricultural Bank and that, on further thought, perhaps that was best, as he had talked to two board members and they were reluctant to give out any more large planting loans this year.

Lawton asked for a glass of sherry. He gulped the sherry and tried to hurry through all the complicated terms of the note as he avoided Thigpen's impatient eyes.

Ten minutes later, Lawton signed the note. Collateral, as usual, was the Columns and its slaves. Thigpen signed for the bank and assured Lawton the board would approve the loan.

Lawton was relieved and celebrated the loan with another sherry in a tavern. He had no money worries, he told himself. Now he could truly be master of the Columns and concentrate on bringing in the best cotton crop the plantation had ever seen.

Chapter 58

Lawton rode slowly through the rain. The horse's hooves sank into mud where cotton should have been planted a week earlier. But the rain had been relentless for days. It was early dusk, and the swamp was a dark hulk all along the horizon. Lawton told himself that, left untended, and given excessive rain, the swamp would creep right back out and devour the fields that his great-grandfather had cleared.

His great-grandfather had left a tobacco plantation in North Carolina and marched his family and slaves overland a century ago. He had settled here in Mississippi and tamed the wild growth and carved out a plantation. He had fought Indians and bandits and French and Spanish, cholera and smallpox and weevils, droughts and floods. He had lived in a cabin, then built the house, bringing the original columns for the house downriver on flatboats and stonemasons up from New

Orleans to set them in place. His son had enlarged the Columns, and the place had prospered. Lawton's father had inherited the plantation, and the prosperity continued. And then the Columns had come into his hands. And he, Lawton Deavors, the fourth master of the Columns, had been master for less than five months and he was on the verge of losing the place.

He heard the supper bell. Its sound was very faint. He could barely see the house through the mist, and he had the sudden illusion that it was moving away from him in the rain. He shook his head. What was happening to him, thinking about things this way?

He rode toward the house, though he was not at all hungry. He smelled smoke from the quarters and heard a baby crying. The new wood of the cabins glistened in the rain. His father had given the people new, comfortable homes, and he, Lawton, was about to deliver the people to Lavon.

He knew now that Lavon would almost certainly own his bank note at the end of the year. Just as he now controlled both Natchez banks and all those men of honor Lawton had trusted.

A week after signing the note, Lawton had returned to the Mercantile Bank and first asked and then begged Thigpen to rewrite the note. Thigpen refused even to discuss the matter. As Lawton left the bank, he encountered his uncle for the first time since his father's death.

"You murderin' bastard!" he shouted as he advanced on Lavon, his hands opening and closing at his sides. He cursed his uncle in the foulest language he knew.

"Learn to hold your whiskey, boy," Lavon said. "I assume you've been drinking or you wouldn't rave like this. You'll come to regret using such language with me. After all, I'm head of the Deavors family now."

"You're the head of nothin' but your own wretched family and your barge whores," Lawton said. "You're no Deavors, not any longer."

"I *am* a Deavors!" Lavon shouted. His face grew white, and he turned slightly, as though thrusting his scar into Lawton's face. There was a crazed look in Lavon's eyes. "I'm a Deavors, boy," Lavon said in a whisper. "I'm a Deavors. You poor, weak bastard. I'm a Deavors. I'll be the only Deavors. This time next year I'll be master of the Columns."

"No! You'll never set foot on the plantation again, and if you do . . ."

Lavon shook his head. "You'll never meet that note, boy. And even if you do, well, it's useless. Whatever you do, I'll still be the Deavors who owns the plantation, and you . . . If you're good and learn to keep your place, I might hire you on as my overseer. If you prove competent enough, which I doubt."

"I swear on my father's grave you'll never own the Columns. Never! And you'll pay for his murder. I saw you ridin' away that mornin'."

Lavon stroked his scar. "No, the law will never touch me for . . . for what happened. And I've already paid. Thanks to your goddamn sister. That's a debt I'll collect tenfold. Though I have to admire her spirit and her courage. It's fortunate you're the man and Joleen the woman. I might have difficulty if she were master of the Columns. But with you, no, I'll have no trouble, boy."

Lawton lunged for his uncle. Lavon stepped back and pulled a pistol.

"None of you is ever going to lay a hand on me again," he said. "You move, and I'll shoot you, so help me God. But only in the leg. Actually, you might like that, Lawton. You could tell yourself you lost the Columns only because you were crippled."

"God damn you!" Lawton said. His nails dug into his palms.

Lavon backed up. He and Lawton stared at each other a full minute. Then Lavon's face twisted into a grotesque smile, and he walked away.

Lawton had never seen Cellus so angry.

After supper Lawton had retreated to the parlor and was drinking his second whiskey when Cellus came in. Lawton ordered him out, but Cellus moved to the desk and looked down with an expression that made Lawton turn away and stare into the cup.

"Drinkin' whiskey like this!" Cellus said. He sat down. "What you think you goin' to find at the bottom of that glass, Mist' Lawton?"

"Damnit, leave me alone," Lawton muttered. "I need to think. I got to work things out."

"Think? Work things out? You not thinkin', Mist' Lawton. You just broodin' and worryin' and enjoyin' ever' minute of it."

"Enjoyin' it?" Lawton asked. "What the hell do you mean, enjoyin' it? I told you about seein' Lavon and what all he said."

"And you reactin' the way you been reactin' to ever'thing lately," Cellus said. "You come here and take out the whiskey and tell yourself how weak and helpless you are."

"Get out of here, damnit!"

"You're right," Cellus said. "You keep this up, your uncle goin' to take the Columns away from you, boy."

"Don't call me boy, goddamnit! I'm your master, and I'm a grown man."

"You my master," Cellus said. "But you actin' like a boy, not a man."

"What in hell can I do?" Lawton asked. He drank whiskey. "If this rain keeps up, we're goin' to be ruined. There's no place I can turn. Lavon seems to own Natchez lock, stock, and barrel. And don't say it again. All right, I was stupid to sign that note. It was stupid, Cellus! There, I admitted it. Are you satisfied?"

He reached for the whiskey. Cellus shoved the glass away.

"Satisfied?" Cellus asked. "Lord God, what's eatin' you? You wallowin' in your guilt and fear like they was some kind of drug, kind of thing them people down to New Orleans smoke and can't give up. This worryin' and all, it become a luxury for you, Mist' Lawton. Lord God, far back as I can remember, you been feelin' guilty 'bout one thing or another. Now you got the bank note and your uncle's threat to latch on to. But if it wasn't them, it'd be somethin' else. You goin' to lose this place for sure, you don't straighten out."

"Cellus, please . . ."

"No, now, you hear me out, Mist' Lawton. You a smart man, you hard-workin', you love the Columns, the people respect you. But you shilly-shally 'round, change your mind all the time. One day you reject good advice, and then, when it's too late, you decide to accept it. You got no good opinion of yourself at all. Here you is, twenty-one years old, and runnin' a big plantation already. Course, you make mistakes. Men twice your age, they make mistakes too, Mist' Lawton. But most men, they learn somethin' from their mistakes. Not you. You enjoy all your worryin' and sufferin' and self-blame. Well, 'less you straighten up quick and start actin' like a Deavors, you might as well just hand the Columns over to your uncle right now."

"Give me that whiskey!" Lawton shouted. "And get out of here, damnit. I don't need sermons from niggers."

"Boy, you need everythin' you can get," Cellus said. He shoved the whiskey across the desk and stood up.

"Damnit, don't leave," Lawton said. "Please, Cellus, sit down. Sit down and let's talk . . . let's talk like two grown men."

Cellus sat down again.

"I'm sorry I shouted at you that way," Lawton said. "What you said, everything you said, it's all true. I just don't understand it, Cellus. You're right, though. My worryin' and all, it's just a habit . . . but I can't seem to stop it. What am I goin' to do? I'm worried sick. I'm afraid. I'm honestly afraid. I need help. I don't know what to do." He felt tears in his eyes. "Oh, God, I don't want to cry. A man shouldn't cry."

"Mist' Lawton, it sometimes takes a real man to admit he wants to cry," Cellus said. "Your Daddy, I seen him cry, and he wasn't ashamed."

Lawton wiped at his eyes. "My father? I never saw him cry, Cellus."

"The night his brother come back, he cried, and you saw it."

"Yes, I'd forgotten."

Cellus poured two drinks. They sipped the whiskey and did not talk for a minute. Lawton brushed at the tears. Whiskey rode in his tight throat, and he had difficulty swallowing. He sniffled. He hesitated and was conscious of each inch his head turned, but he forced himself to look into Cellus' face. Cellus smiled and made a gesture with his cup. Lawton touched Cellus' cup with his own.

"That Lavon, he not goin' to take the Columns from us," Cellus said.

"No, damnit, he's not," Lawton said. "This is only March. That note doesn't come due until next January. We've got ten months to come up with the money. By God, we'll make this the best cotton crop the Columns has ever seen, rain or no rain!"

"Yessir, we'll do that for sure," Cellus said. "The people, they'll work extra hard. Word gets 'round the quarters, and they know now 'bout your uncle's threat. You know what they think of the man. They'd work till they dropped to keep Lavon from bein' their master."

"We'll cut our expenses to the bone," Lawton said. "There'll be no harvest ball or big Christmas party. . . ."

"And we won't buy nothin' in town this year," Cellus said. "We usually spend a lot of money in Natchez over a year's time. But the people, they'll have to make everything we need, from plows and harnesses to clothes and shoes."

"By God, we can do it, Cellus."

"Yessir, we can," Cellus said. "But let's be practical. Even with all that savin', even with good weather and a good crop, we likely to fall short of the cash we need to pay back that note. So we goin' to have to do a couple of things we never done before. First off, we goin' to have to make certain that Lavon, he don't work no mischief here on the place."

"You think he had that barn full of cotton burned down?" Lawton asked.

Cellus nodded. "Your daddy and the sheriff thought it was set by somebody. So we got to watch the people good, see if Lavon's bribed any of 'em. And we got to make certain don't no strangers get on the place and do no damage." Cellus drained his glass. "And we got to allow for rain or a bad market in the fall, Mist' Lawton. We got to take steps now, in case somethin' happens then. And I was thinkin'. That land of Miss Joleen's. It's just settin' there, goin' to weed. Why don't we think 'bout puttin' it into cotton? And then both she and your Aunt Delma, they got some money they could lend us. . . ."

"No, that land belongs to Joleen, damnit, and I don't want charity," Lawton said. "We Deavorses have never asked for charity, and I won't be the first one to ask. I'm not askin' anybody for a penny."

"You're on kind of a high horse, Mist' Lawton," Cellus said. "Miss Joleen, she's family. And puttin' her land into cotton ain't charity. It's a sin to let rich land like that go to waste. A thousand acres more to plant, that could be a lot of money when the harvest's in."

"But who'd work the land? . . . All right, all right. . . . I don't know why I'm arguin' with you. It makes good sense. I'm not askin' Joleen or anyone else for money, but her land should be planted. Labor would be a problem, though, and competent drivers. . . ."

"Some of the young people, and old ones, too, will have to work more," Cellus said. "And you could get some of your Aunt Delma's niggers, Mist' Lawton. She's only plantin' half her acreage, and she's frettin' 'bout what to do with her idle hands. You can spend some time over to Joleen's place. If need be, I'll take up some of the slack in the fields here."

"You? In the fields, Cellus? You've never . . ."

"We all goin' to have to do things we never done before," Cellus said. "Don't fret 'bout me."

Lawton poured them each a short drink. Again they touched glasses.

"Only thing now, Mist' Lawton," Cellus said as he stood up. "You got to . . . forget all your feelin' sorry for yourself and your broodin'. If you be like a Deavors, like your daddy's son, then we goin' to come out of this thing just fine."

Cellus left the parlor. Lawton finished his whiskey. He stood up and turned toward the door, but he paused.

He formed a resolution to be strong, to give up the luxury of his guilt and brooding.

He smiled at himself and walked out. He knew that resolutions meant nothing. All that mattered was his behavior when he woke up in the morning, and the next morning and the next.

Chapter 59

The day Joleen returned to Aaron, they sat in the parlor and argued for hours. In the late afternoon, despite Aaron's wound, they made love.

Afterward they lay on opposite sides of the bed and touched with their fingertips.

Joleen was angry and confused, hurt and anxious. She was also full of love for Aaron. After ten minutes of silence she asked the same question she had asked before they made love.

"So you won't . . . give up this abolitionist work, Aaron?"

"I can't give it up, Joleen," he said. "It's . . . it's too important to me. If only you could understand that fully, if only you could join me . . ."

"No!" she said. "No, Aaron. I've said no a thousand times already today. How can I join you? I know the abuses of slavery. I've seen them, and I hate them, too. I guess I do believe a great deal of . . . of everything havin' to do with slavery is wrong . . . but there should be some drastic reforms and . . . and not just do away with it. What about the Columns? And all the niggers there, Aaron? They're content. They don't want to be free."

"That's only because they've been kept down, kept in ignorance."

"No, don't talk like that," she said. "You're talkin' about my family, about my mother and . . . and my daddy, and about Lawton. If slavery's such an evil, then what can I think about my family or even about myself? No, Aaron, I won't be any part of your abolitionist schemes and killin' and all."

"There won't be anymore killing," he said. "I've already promised you that, Joleen. Don't you see that in time, damnit, you're going to come around to opposing slavery? I think you do already, if you'd be honest with yourself. I'm not saying your family is evil. But the entire damn premise of their wealth and their life is . . . damnit, it's so wrong. I can't give up this work. Yet I love you, and I . . . can't live without you, Joleen. I'd have lost my sanity if you hadn't come back from the Columns."

"Oh, this is hopeless, Aaron," she said. "I should have just stayed out there, no matter how I feel about you. I can't endure this kind of life. I love you, and I want to be with you. I can't imagine anything else. But you're a criminal, Aaron, no matter how cleverly you explain it. And what if you get caught? What then? They'll catch you sooner or later. After this, they'll be suspicious of every move you make. And what happens to me when they catch you, Aaron?"

He touched her cheek, then brushed a strand of hair from her eyes. She rejected his hand with a toss of her head.

"I'll be very cautious in the future," he said. "I know how precarious my position is now. And I'd do anything to protect you. I even . . . well, I've been thinking that we should move to Ohio. I can continue my work there. And you'll be in no danger. But I can't give everything up because of you, Joleen. If I gave it up because of you . . . Don't you see?"

"Yes, I understand what you mean," she said. "I guess I do. If you gave up your crusade with the niggers, you'd hold me responsible and—"

"Not responsible. That's not what I mean, Joleen."

"Yes, that's exactly what you mean, Aaron. We've just come to an absolutely hopeless point. I don't want to live in Ohio. And in any case, I can't run away now. Lawton and them are in trouble, Aaron. I've got to do whatever I can to help. I've been meanin' to ask. Could we . . . if necessary later on, could we lend Lawton some money? He's goin' to need it with that note he signed."

"Of course we can," he said. "But we can do that from Ohio. Joleen, we don't have to make a decision right now. Think it over for awhile. And don't worry. I'm not going to do anything the least bit dangerous. Let's just compromise for awhile and not argue and just . . . just be together."

"Nothin' dangerous?" she asked. "What about that nigger in the cellar? What if somebody finds him there? I want Clarence out of this house, Aaron. The first day his wounds heal, I want you to send him away. We'll give him whatever money he needs, but I want him to leave. Poor Filch and Norvina are frightened and confused, and it's just a matter of time until the other niggers find out he's down there, and Lord knows, they might start gossipin' . . ."

"As soon as he's healed, I'll take him away," Aaron said.

"Oh, no," she said. "Please don't go away with him. They'll catch you for sure this time, Aaron. We'll give him lots of money, but you can't go with him."

"Joleen, I promise that I won't do anything . . . anything at all involving the abolitionists . . . not for weeks, at least. But I must help Clarence escape."

Joleen tossed away from Aaron's hand. She curled her body up and refused to talk anymore.

The compromise pleased neither of them, but they clung to it with some desperation. Aaron suspended all activity with the Underground Railroad. He and Joleen did not speak so much as a word about their dilemma. They were together more hours of each day than at any other time since their marriage. They made love more and more frequently.

It was during a thunderstorm four days later that

Joleen and Aaron began to suspect that their house was being watched and that they were being followed. A man stood in a shallow doorway across the street from their house. He was soaked by the heavy rain but made no effort to find better shelter. The next day, when Joleen and Aaron went to the market, the same man followed them. Later that day they attended a concert, and another man walked a block behind them and waited up the street until they left the concert. By the following day they realized that only Aaron was being watched. When Joleen went out alone, no one followed her.

At first Aaron thought the men were working for the sheriff. But Joleen convinced him that they were her uncle's men. She almost welcomed the ominous men, for she hoped their presence would convince Aaron not only that he couldn't return to his abolitionist work but also that he couldn't even consider helping Clarence to escape.

Aaron admitted the danger, but he was adamant about seeing Clarence safely up to Rodney and aboard a paddle-wheeler.

"It will take only a short time," Aaron said. "A few hours at most, Joleen. And then I won't . . . then I'll tend to my law practice for awhile, and we'll have time together, like now. And your uncle will finally call off his agents. I have a plan. A very simple one. They're always the best kind."

Aaron's plan was to disguise Clarence in one of Norvina's outfits, complete with bonnet and veil. They would drive away from the house in broad daylight and drive innocently around Natchez until they lost Lavon's agent. Then they would go up to Rodney, and he would put Clarence on the boat.

Joleen argued that the plan was too dangerous. But she could suggest nothing better.

"All right, then," she said one evening as they sat in the parlor. "But I'm comin' along. You need me."

"No, Joleen, I can't let you do that," he said. "No, absolutely not."

"You've been trying to talk me into joining your abolitionist work, Aaron. Now, when I want to help, you tell me I can't. And don't forget, your wound's still healing."

"I didn't mean taking a risk like this," he said. "If we're stopped, I'll have to . . . I don't want anymore killing, but if we're stopped, I'll have to use my weapons. As for my wound, it's all but healed."

"You won't be stopped with me along," she said. "Don't you see? It's perfectly normal for me to go out in the carriage. And right up out of the city that way when I go to one of those silly quiltin' bees. Why, last time, Norvina went with me. And I am a Deavors, Aaron, and I've had pretty good luck at protectin' you in the past."

"I won't even consider it, Joleen," he said. "I refuse to take the chance. I'll see Clarence safely away, and then we can have a little time together, without worry. I hope you've been thinking seriously about our moving to Ohio. I see no other solution to our dilemma."

"I can't leave my family now, Aaron," she said. "And I see a very simple solution to our dilemma, once that nigger is safely out of the house. And it'll be lots safer for you both if—"

"No, damnit, you're not coming with me," he said. "Now, let's not argue about it any longer, Joleen."

The argument ended there. They had sherry, then went upstairs and made love. Later, as Aaron slept, Joleen stared at the ceiling and began to formulate a plan that would get Clarence to safety and yet protect Aaron.

Chapter 60

"Mist' Aaron, he's goin' to have our hide for this," Norvina protested as she helped Clarence into one of her dresses. "Lord, child, you can't take this kind of chance."

"She's right, ma'am," Clarence said. "It's too big a risk."

"Now, listen here, damnit," Joleen said. "My mind is made up. Aaron's bein' followed, and I'm not. Nobody's goin' to stop me or question me."

Filch joined the protests. He even refused to drive them. Joleen had come to realize in the past few days just how sympathetic Filch was to the abolitionists and to Clarence. And she, herself, had come to like Clarence, had stopped thinking of him as "that nigger in the cellar." As he was being dressed, she saw the lash marks across his back and chest and the deep branding scars in his hands. She was angered and horrified.

"Well, Filch, will you get the carriage or not?" Joleen asked. "I'm perfectly capable of drivin' myself, and by God, nothin' is goin' to stop me!"

Filch brought the carriage to the front. Joleen and Clarence walked out and climbed into the carriage. At the street Joleen nodded at two passing ladies and the maid from the house next door.

Traffic was heavy. The carriage crept along the street, and Joleen caught herself glancing frantically at men on horseback, at pedestrians, at carriages, to see if they were being followed. Finally she forced herself to look straight ahead.

She wondered if their horse was lame. It seemed incapable of moving with any speed at all. A man on the sidewalk tilted his hat and nodded. Joleen nodded and forced a smile.

"Please, go a little faster," she called up to Filch.

"Can't do it in this traffic," he said. "And it might look suspicious."

"Yes, that's right," Joleen said, more to herself.

"We be out of town shortly," Clarence said.

His deep voice from behind the veil startled, then amused Joleen. The amusement was a relief. Filch drove around a corner, and the relief turned to near-panic.

Lavon and Sheriff Crandall were standing on the

opposite corner. The sun glistened on Lavon's scar. Another carriage blocked their way. A horse shied. In another second, traffic was hopelessly snarled.

Joleen realized that Lavon was staring at her. His face was as white as paste. All the color had drained to the scar. He looked bizarre in the bright sunshine. His eyes were glazed, and his lips curled tightly at the corners.

Joleen straightened up and spoke to Clarence. She laughed lightly, as though her maid had said something amusing.

"Mornin', Miss Joleen," Sheriff Crandall called.

"Mornin'," Joleen said. Her eyes met Lavon's. Other people were staring at them. Everyone in Natchez knew she had taken a whip to her uncle.

Lavon looked past Joleen. He was looking right at Clarence! He took a step toward the carriage.

But he stopped abruptly. He turned and said something to the sheriff. Joleen knew that if she were not holding herself so rigidly she would be trembling. If the sheriff or her uncle came over now, she was lost. Would they . . . would they lash her, too, and brand the palms of her hands and . . . imprison her for ten years.

Filch cracked the whip. The carriage inched forward, then moved faster. Joleen stiffened her back. They rode fifty yards. A man shouted. She tensed. A hundred yards. Half a block. The man was shouting at a runaway horse, she realized. At the next corner she glanced over her shoulder. Lavon and the sheriff were walking away.

"Oh, Lord," she sighed, and sank back against the seat. Only then did she realize that Clarence had a pistol in his hand, hidden by the folds of the skirt.

"Another few minutes, we'll be out of the city," he said. "You all right now?"

"Oh, I'm fine," she said.

I'm fine, she repeated to herself. The delusion lasted less than a minute. She heard a fast-moving horse and jerked her head around. The man passed them and rode on. A minute later, for no reason at all, she glanced back again. Hadn't she seen that tall man trotting along on the chestnut mare? Was he one of the men who had been following Aaron?

Twice in a half-minute she glanced around frantically at the man on the chestnut horse. She turned back and smiled weakly to assure Clarence she was all right.

She held her hands in her lap to keep her fingers from trembling. The other times, when she had acted bravely to save Aaron, had been on an impulse that gave no time for thought or fear. But now she was so afraid of being caught that she felt nauseated.

She tried to talk to Clarence, but the high pitch of her voice frightened her. She fidgeted with her hands another minute and stared up at the road, the endless road she would have to endure for another two hours. Then, in Rodney, would come the real danger.

Joleen glanced around at the horseman again.

Aaron dismounted, gave the reins to the stable boy, and walked toward the house. He knew something was wrong the minute Norvina opened the door. She looked from his eyes and turned away.

"What's wrong?" he asked. "What's happened?"

"It's Miss Joleen," Norvina said. "She done took Clarence in the carriage with Filch."

"Damnit, why didn't you stop her?" he shouted. "When did they leave? Where did they go, up to Rodney? Were they followed? Damnit, why did you and Filch let her do it, Norvina?"

"We tried to stop her, Mist' Aaron," she said. "I begged her not to go. So did Clarence. Filch, he said he wouldn't drive, and she said she'd go without him. You know Miss Joleen, once she sets her mind to somethin'." Norvina started crying.

"All right, all right," Aaron said. "Tell me where they went. When they left. Tell me everything."

Norvina told him, between sobs. Aaron cursed and ran into the parlor. He stuck two pistols in his pockets. As he ran down the hall, Norvina called to him. He stopped.

"Mist' Aaron . . ." She came to him, her head bowed. "Mist' Aaron, I don't know how to say somethin' like this. And I know how much you love Miss

Joleen and how she feels 'bout you. But you . . . you done put her and all of us in lots of trouble with your abolitionist doin's." She looked up into his face. "I don't say I'm not glad to . . . see some niggers go free. And Filch, he been changin' lots since he lived in Natchez. I worry 'bout him, 'less he gets hisself in a heap of trouble. But Mist' Aaron, that Lavon, he mean and smart, and he goin' to catch us all, see we whipped and branded and throwed in jail."

"Norvina, I can't . . . Yes, yes, I know the danger. After this, after today is over, things will be different. I promise you. I can't talk now. I've got to go find Joleen."

Aaron caught the stable boy as he was preparing to unsaddle his horse. He grabbed the reins from the startled boy and mounted. He galloped up the driveway, but slowed down and trotted into the street.

What got into Joleen, he asked himself as he cursed the slow-moving carriages and horses. He was angry at her, angry at Clarence and Filch, angry at himself. She was so damn young, so damn naïve, and so damn certain the name Deavors would protect her forever. And she was too damn brave for her own good.

He dug his heels into the horse's flanks and rode around a lumbering coach drawn by four old horses.

Damnit, she would get them all caught! What if she was followed? Even now she might be in Lavon's hands somewhere up on the trace.

Aaron glanced back. Yes, that goddamn man had a horse, had mounted it, and was following *him!* In his anger and haste, he had forgotten the blasted man. He was leading the man directly to Joleen and Clarence.

"Damn it! Damn it!" he muttered.

This was what happened when his anger got the better of his judgment. He relaxed the horse's pace and turned down a narrow street, then turned again, so that he was heading south. He did not look around.

After two more blocks he rode into an alley lined with vine-covered shrubbery. He reined in behind a tall bush and pulled a pistol.

The horseman came abreast of the bush. Aaron rode out and thrust his pistol at the man's chest.

"Hold up, sir, and keep your hands on the reins," Aaron said.

"What in hell . . . ?"

"Keep your horse and your hands steady or I'll shoot. That's right. You've been following me. For days. Who hired you to spy on me?"

"Listen, you ain't got—"

Aaron shoved his pistol under the man's chin and tilted the man's head back sharply. "I'll give you five seconds to answer," he said.

"I can't . . . You ain't . . . It was Mr. Deavors . . . Mr. Lavon Deavors . . . and he goin' to be on you tooth and toenail when he hears what you doin' to me."

"Dismount," Aaron said. "Damnit, get off your horse!"

The man cursed as he dismounted.

"Throw me your pistol," Aaron said. "And you'd better throw it very carefully." Aaron caught the pistol and grabbed the reins of the man's horse in the same motion.

"You can't rob me this way!"

"You'll find your horse and pistol down the street a couple of blocks," Aaron said. "And I don't want to see you outside my home again or find that you're following me. The next time I encounter you, sir, I'll call you out. I promise you that. And you tell Lavon Deavors he'll rue the next time he sets an agent on me or any member of my household."

Aaron led the man's horse out of the alley and trotted for three blocks before releasing the reins and throwing the pistol to the ground. He hurried down a long street, then headed north again.

Aaron cursed Lavon as he galloped along the trace. If Lavon or any of his agents had so much as spoken to Joleen, he would kill the man.

But his abolitionist work had become impossible, even without Lavon's vendetta against his family, Aaron told himself. From the day he married Joleen, his effectiveness had been compromised. He asked himself how he could have thought it would work out. How could he have jeopardized not only Joleen's love, but her very life? Why in hell hadn't he taken her to live in Ohio months ago?

He gave up his miserable thoughts and strained in the saddle as he saw a carriage ahead. But it wasn't Joleen.

Another carriage came in sight, then another. Aaron rode faster. Something had happened to her! She had had ample time to put Clarence on the boat and be at least this far back along the trace. She's over an hour late, he realized.

Aaron cursed God and all creation. But mostly he cursed himself. She's been caught, he repeated again and again. There was no telling what they might have done to her already! Why hadn't he taken her to Ohio and continued his work there? Why, damnit? Why had he endangered her by staying here, staying here and actually owning slaves himself, slaves who had grown interested in freedom but to whom he had paid no heed? Why in hell hadn't he helped Norvina and Filch escape?

He realized that his horse was giving out. There might not be a stand for miles. The horse nearly stumbled. Aaron swore that if the horse went lame he would take a mount at the point of a pistol.

The horse nearly stumbled again. Aaron reined up. He closed his eyes a moment and thought of Joleen, and for the first time in many years he felt like crying.

When he opened his eyes, Joleen's carriage was fifty yards up the road, coming toward him. Filch drove up and stopped. Aaron dismounted and stumbled into the carriage.

"Thank God you're safe," he mumbled.

She hugged him and kissed his cheek. He put his hands on her shoulders and held her away.

"But damn you, Joleen," he said. "What possessed you to do such a thing? I've been worried sick. What if you'd been caught? Do you have any idea what they might have done to you? Don't you ever do anything this foolish again."

"You're hurtin' me, Aaron," she said. He released her shoulders. "And I did get away with it." She smiled. "I told the drunk old captain I needed some furniture brought downriver. I offered him a lot of money and flirted with him, rather shamelessly I'm afraid, and all this time, while we sat in the cabin, the mate helped Clarence sneak on board and hide in the hold."

"Damnit, you make it sound like a game, Joleen!"

"No, Aaron, it was no game," she said. "I've never been more afraid in my life, believe me. At one point I was sure we were bein' followed. But I was determined to do it. And I did. And we're safe now. You're safe. And I'm hungry and tired and thirsty and . . . Oh, I was terrified. Please don't fuss at me, Aaron. Please."

Aaron took her in his arms and buried his face in her hair and whispered that he loved her.

Chapter 61

For the first time in memory the Deavorses' slaves worked on July 4. Lawton promised them two extra holidays after the harvest in compensation. The promise pleased the slaves, but they would have been willing to work July 4 in any case. They were motivated by an obsessive fear that Lavon would become master of the Columns. Consequently, work this summer was progressing far better than usual, despite the fact that Joleen's land had been put into cotton and twenty of the Columns' people were now working those thousand acres, along with twenty-two of Aunt Delma's slaves. Her overseer had quit, and much of her land was nearly farmed out, she told Lawton. She planted only half her usual acreage and talked of moving to New Orleans in the fall.

To make up for the slaves who worked Joleen's

land, Lawton sent all the older and younger people—all the quarter-hands and half-hands, who usually worked only at harvest time—into the fields each day. He was both pleased and proud that not one of them complained.

Even Flora and Bonita volunteered to hoe weeds a few hours each day, though this meant they had to get up an hour early and go to bed quite late. Since the Columns was making every item of clothing and every household necessity this year instead of buying them in town, the house slaves had to work many extra hours. Ed and the wheelwrights and the carpenters also put in extra time to keep everything in good repair and to build or forge many items that usually came from a Natchez harness or hardware store.

Estelle had not recovered from Athel's murder, so the full burden of supervising all the extra work fell on Lucinda. She was up with Lawton an hour before sunrise each morning, and many nights she was still mending or sewing when he went to bed.

Lawton and Cellus alternated overseeing Joleen's land and the Columns, and the sight of Cellus' tall, rigid figure riding the fields spurred the people to work even harder.

July 4 was cloudless, and the temperature hovered near a hundred. Lawton rode back and forth along the cotton rows, shouting encouragement and advice to the drivers and slaves. But he worried that he pushed them too hard in the murderous heat and decided to give them an extra half-hour off at noon.

The weather had been good for the past three months, and Lawton was confident he would bring in a record harvest. From time to time he caught himself lapsing back into his guilt and brooding, but he was able to smile at himself and pull out of the mood. And the satisfaction of anticipating Lavon's possible schemes and taking steps to thwart them made Lawton so euphoric that Cellus had to caution him against overconfidence.

Lawton felt that this new confidence was well justified, however, and that it would be quite difficult for his uncle to sabotage this year's cotton crop. Beginning with the planting, he and Cellus had examined every possible point at which they might be vulnerable, then made sure they were not. They started with the seed and discovered that several sacks contained ragweed seed instead of cotton seed. Next they set up day and night patrols to ride the perimeter of the Columns and of Joleen's land. Twice so far the patrols had driven off men who had tried to sneak in and damage the growing cotton.

Then Lawton discovered that outsiders now owned sixty percent of the Benton gin. This discovery angered the Sumralls and Delsanos and other nearby planters. They were still embittered about Athel's murder and sympathetic to Lawton's plight. Six planters met at the Columns and agreed to boycott the local gin and go to the trouble of transporting their cotton twenty miles to the next nearest gin. This gin served small farmers, and as an inducement to secure the tonnage of cotton the planters promised, the gin's owner lowered his charges to each of them. Therefore, not using the Benton gin would be to Lawton's financial advantage.

Lawton arranged for someone from the Columns to watch each wagonload of cotton through the entire ginning and baling process. And instead of the Natchez teamsters who were usually hired to take the bales from the gin to the river barges, Lawton had decided to use the Deavorses' slaves and wagons. Already Ed and the wheelwrights and carpenters were building the extra wagons that would be needed.

Finally, Lawton and Cellus had realized how easily Lavon might sink a barge full of cotton on its way to a New Orleans broker. So Lawton, Cellus, and several slaves would ride on each barge. The men who tried to sneak onto the place at night had escaped the patrols, so Lawton had no proof so far that his uncle had done anything criminal. He hoped desperately that Lavon would make just one slip in the future, so he could be prosecuted.

Lawton stared past a hoe gang and into the swamp, where the sunlight ended abruptly. Back in

February and March, the swamp had frightened Lawton as he thought how easily the growth could devour the land and the house. During the worst of those miserable hours, Lawton even let himself imagine that some evil had seeped out of the bayous to curse and contaminate the Deavorses. Now he looked at the moss-hung cypress trees on the horizon and thought of draining and clearing some of the marginal swamp acres for spring planting.

When he turned back to the field, he saw Lucinda walking toward him. He trotted over to meet her.

"What brings you out here in the heat?" he asked as he dismounted.

"Well, I hate to bother you when you're workin', Lawton, but I think it's important," she said.

"Let's walk over here and talk in the shade," he said. He led her to the open-sided shed where the mule teams ate and rested at noon. "I thought Pearl Sumrall was visitin' you this mornin'. Is . . . is somethin' wrong with Tillman again, Lucinda?"

"No, he's quiet this morning," she said. "He's playing with his soldiers under the house. Mrs. Sumrall did visit for a spell. And she said something about New Orleans that made me remember a talk I had with your father on . . . that day, Lawton. I should have remembered it before, but I've blotted out everything about that day. Anyhow, he asked me if I knew a Mrs. Antoinette LeBeau in New Orleans and said he had to go down and see her on some urgent business and needed an introduction."

"Mrs. LeBeau?" Lawton asked. "I think she used to live here in the county. I never met her, but I've heard people talk about her. As far as I know, she's lived in New Orleans for a long, long time. Do you know her, Lucinda? Do you have any idea why my father felt it urgent to go down and see her?"

"I don't have any idea what he wanted with her," Lucinda said. "He just mentioned business. And, yes, I've met the woman, but I don't really know her. But I was . . . I was real good friends with her nephew, Alain. He used to come courtin' some when I was in school. I told your father I'd write Alain and that I was sure he'd introduce him to Mrs. LeBeau."

"Come to think of it, Lucinda, Mrs. LeBeau owns some land around here. I think it's that land that the road's on. The one out from Benton and Natchez."

Lawton looked at the swamp. His eyes swept the horizon. Hadn't he heard some talk that a fool Natchez lawyer had bought up several thousand acres of deep swampland on the other side of the Columns? Some of the swampland could be drained and planted, but this swamp was hopeless, and Haskell Sumrall had joked that the lawyer must want to start an alligator farm, because the land was useless for anything else.

Lawton moved his gaze along the horizon in the direction of his uncle's land that bordered the Columns. What if his uncle had used some lawyer to act as his agent in buying that swampland? Then he'd have half the plantation surrounded. And what if . . . ?

"Oh, God," Lawton mumbled.

"What's wrong?" Lucinda asked.

"My uncle," Lawton said. "My damned uncle. Lucinda, somebody bought up lots of worthless swampland borderin' the Columns. What if Lavon's the real owner? What if he . . . ? Goddamnit, what if he bought the land from Mrs. LeBeau? Except for her land, there's no reason on earth why my father would think of goin' to New Orleans durin' harvest. Don't you see? Lavon can buy up all the land and completely surround us. He can strangle us out of here. It might already be too late. I've got to talk to Cellus. I'll have to ride over to Joleen's."

"Cellus came back from there a few minutes ago," she said.

"Come on, I'll give you a ride," he said. He helped her into the saddle and climbed up behind her. The slaves turned to stare as he galloped toward the house.

Cellus agreed that Lavon was probably buying up all the land around the plantation. There was no other explanation for Athel's sense of urgency in contacting

Mrs. LeBeau. And worthless swampland being bought was too much of a coincidence.

"We been caught for fools, Mist' Lawton," Cellus said. "Here we proud as peacocks thinkin' we stopped all his schemin', and all the time he's laughin' at us. When your daddy mentioned New Orleans to me, I thought it had to do with seein' a bank down there. Lord, we got to find out the truth, and find it out quick. There's nothin' for it, you goin' to have to go into Natchez tomorrow, and you goin' to have to go down to New Orleans and speak to that lady."

"I can't afford to go down to New Orleans until after the harvest," Lawton said. "And what if she's already sold the land to Lavon? Anyway, where can we find the money to buy any land?"

"We'll have to get the money somehow, that's all," Cellus said. "Important thing, you got to go down right away, or send somebody you trust. 'Cause I'm sure as anything what you goin' to find out once you start checkin' land titles in Natchez and start askin' questions."

"Why can't I go?" Lucinda asked. "After all, I do know the family. Alain LeBeau is an old friend, and I'm sure he'd do me a favor. And it's time I paid my aunt a visit anyhow."

"But you don't know anything about business, about buyin' land," Lawton said.

"But my aunt knows lawyers who do," Lucinda said. "All I have to know, really, is exactly which land parcel the road's on, so I can be certain I'm discussin' the right one. Buying it's not too important right now, is it? I mean, if I get a promise that they won't sell to Lavon, that if they sell in the future they'll sell to us—wouldn't that be enough for now?"

"Maybe," Lawton said. "But after my experience with Natchez bankers, I'm a little wary of people's word and their honor."

"But the LeBeaus aren't like that," Lucinda said. "I can take care of it, Lawton. Please trust me. Like you said, you can't possibly leave now. I can go into town with you tomorrow and catch a paddle-wheeler."

"Yes, all right, Lucinda," Lawton said. "You'll

have to go down and deal with them. I only hope it's not too late. My God, I feel so stupid for not realizin' what Lavon was up to."

"Don't go to broodin' now," Cellus said. "We don't know for sure that Lavon's tryin' to buy up all that land. And even if he is, now that we know, we got a chance to stop him."

They left Cellus in the study and walked out onto the front porch.

"You know, Mrs. Sumrall mentioned something else," Lucinda said. "And it set me to thinking. You know, when we heard about the sheriff's posse trackin' that nigger to Joleen's house, we thought it was just some of Lavon's doings. But Mrs. Sumrall said there's lots of talk in Natchez that Aaron really has been involved with the abolitionists. She said she herself thinks Lavon's just spreading those stories because he hates Joleen after what she did to him. I'm sure that's it, Lawton. But talk like that worries me."

"Well, I'd heard a little of that talk myself," Lawton said. "And it worried me some, but I just refused to give it any heed. How could Joleen be caught up in something like that? She'd leave Aaron in a minute if those stories were true, Lucinda. No, I'm sure it's just more of Lavon's schemin' to hurt the family, and of course he must hate Joleen. Aaron's an ideal target for that kind of slander—bein' a Yankee and havin' been caught up in that slave-patrol shootin'. But they're supposed to come out tomorrow, and I'll talk to them then. They've got to be careful, no matter how innocent they are. Lavon's perfectly capable of tryin' to do somethin' terrible."

"I guess I better go start packin'," Lucinda said.

"And I better get back out to the fields," Lawton said.

They separated in the gallery. Lucinda kissed his cheek, and he watched her walk up the stairs.

Lawton's mother was coming from the storeroom as he walked down the back steps. He told her Lucinda was going to New Orleans but didn't trouble her with the reason.

"Why don't you go down with her?" he asked. "The trip might do you good."

"No, I don't think so," she said. "I'm just not up to it. And I'd worry too much about Tillman while I'm away. I swear, I just don't know what to do with him anymore, Lawton."

"We've got to do somethin', that's for sure," Lawton said. "And he's gettin' to be too much for you to have to put up with. Why don't you let one of the slaves look after him for awhile so you can get some rest and all?"

"No, Lawton, I couldn't let somebody else do what I ought to do as his mother," she said. "It's just that lately he's started blamin' me for what happened with that nigger on the barge. He says such awful things to me. And sometimes he says things I don't understand. He seems to have the idea somehow that his baby is inside my stomach. But he's been quiet today, and that's a good sign. Well, I better get out of this sun."

Lawton kissed his mother's cheek. As he mounted his horse, he told himself that something definitely had to be done about Tillman.

Chapter 62

The journey back from Natchez the next day was slow and quiet. Lawton leaned forward in the driving box. He stared at a long stretch of loblolly pines and thought of being without Lucinda for nearly a week.

Joleen and Aaron sat in the back of the carriage. They had had only one conversation since leaving Natchez. Lawton couldn't help but overhear their talk, and he was surprised to hear them argue about moving to Ohio.

"No, now, I've told you a hundred times, I'm not movin' away while there's all this trouble," Joleen had said. "Not with the Columns in danger. I just won't consider such a thing, Aaron. Not right now, anyway."

Not right now, Lawton said to himself. That meant Joleen might well move up north in the near future. And though he was glad that she wouldn't go immediately, he was upset that she seemed to be staying only because of the threat to the plantation. Perhaps she would have left months ago, Lawton told himself, but she didn't think he was capable of saving the plantation without her help.

Lawton asked himself why on earth anyone would want to move up to a place like Ohio. Of course, it could be because of Lavon's harassment and the vicious rumors he was spreading. Lawton had heard that the rumors were hurting Aaron's practice.

Lawton told himself that his brother-in-law was probably the kind of man to run away from such gossip and slander. He would hardly stand and fight for his reputation. Lawton hoped Joleen wouldn't be hurt by all this. Lavon must hate her for taking the whip to him. Lawton didn't think Aaron was capable of protecting Joleen or himself. So, as head of the Deavors family, it was up to him, Lawton, to protect them both.

The rhythm of the horse's hooves and the steady humming of insects in the dusk shadows were the only sounds. Lawton thought of Lucinda again. He didn't think he could endure the time she would be away. And of course, until she returned, he would not know about the LeBeau land. For all he knew, when he drove down that road in a few minutes, it might be the last time he or anyone else from the Columns was allowed to use that road.

He scolded himself for his morose thoughts, but it was difficult to fight back the brooding and worry that had begun to reassert themselves in the past two days.

In Natchez he had confirmed that someone was definitely buying up the land surrounding the Columns. At least eight of the twelve land parcels had been bought in the past year, and though the title to only one was in Lavon's name, Lawton had no doubt that his uncle owned all eight parcels. Lawton had hired Wayne Nester, a lawyer and family friend, to investigate further and try to buy the remaining land for the Columns. Lawton didn't know where the money would come from, but by now he was resigned to borrowing it from Aaron or Aunt Delma, if he had to. And Nester had warned that since the remaining parcels were owned by absentee owners, Lavon might already have purchased the land and not yet recorded the transfer of titles.

Lawton was giving into his worries when the sound of a galloping horse pulled him back to reality. Ambrose reined up beside the carriage.

"It's Mist' Tillman!" Ambrose shouted. "He gone crazy wild, Mist' Lawton, and I was ridin' over to fetch Cellus. Done locked him and your mama in her room and took to screechin' 'bout whores and babies and 'bout your uncle, 'bout your mama bein' sinful with your daddy. Door's locked, and the windows shuttered tight."

"Give me your horse!" Lawton said.

He mounted the horse from the carriage and galloped for the house.

Lawton ran into the house and sprinted up the stairs. Half a dozen slaves stood outside the door to his mother's room. Ed and two field hands were throwing their weight against the door.

"We can't budge that door!" Beatrice cried. "It's oak and strong as iron, Mist' Lawton. Lord, lord, they done fell quiet inside."

"An ax!" Lawton shouted. "Somebody get an ax." He pounded on the door. "Mother! It's me, Lawton! Are you all right? Tillman? Mother? Tillman, please open the door. Say somethin'."

Lawton and Ed threw their weight against the door, but it was useless. Lawton pounded the door with his fists and shouted for his mother and Tillman to answer. There was only silence beyond the door.

"Shutters locked tight as a vault," Beatrice said.

"Two boys, they up to a window now with a ladder, but not makin' no headway tryin' to break in."

"What set him off this time?" Lawton asked.

"Well, best as I can reckon, Mist' Lawton, he seen one of the pregnant girls walkin' 'cross the yard," Beatrice said. "He got all crazy and started yellin', and run into the kitchen, knockin' over everything. Your mama, she brought him upstairs, and she was yellin' at him to be quiet. And then they both got quiet all quick-like. I come runnin' up here and found the door locked."

"Where's that nigger with the ax, damnit!" Lawton shouted.

The man came running down the hall. Joleen and Aaron were behind him.

"Where's Mother?" Joleen called. "Lawton, what's happenin'?"

"Stay back, Joleen," Lawton said. "No, please, stay back there."

Lawton swung the ax. The blade ate into the wood. He swung again and again. On the eighth stroke the door gave way and fell from one hinge.

Lawton and Ed forced the door open. The room was dark, with the shutters closed. Lawton stumbled into the dark and turned up the lamp.

He looked onto a scene that brought bile up into his throat and over his lips.

His mother had been disemboweled. She lay amid her intestines and her blood, and Tillman lay curled beside her stomach, a butcher knife in his hand, and his thumb in his mouth.

Tillman smiled up at his brother and sucked his thumb.

BOOK VII

Columns of Fire

Chapter 63

Lawton walked to the slave jail and looked through a crack. Tillman was playing soldiers with Randall, the slave who had become his guardian and constant companion. Lawton stepped back and took a deep breath. It had been two weeks since the murder, and still he could not look Tillman in the face or stay in the same room with him for more than a few seconds. And the thought of dragging his grinning brother from his mother's body nauseated him.

He mounted his horse and rode toward the fields. Essie was returning from Joleen's with a wagonload of implements to be repaired. Lawton waved to Essie and thought of Cellus' suspicion that Essie's good behavior was in some way unreal. But Lawton was pleased with Essie's change in attitude and told himself Cellus was being too harsh on Essie because of past mistakes.

Lawton smiled at Aunt Froney, who stood on the nursery steps. He had to keep up an appearance before the people. At night with Lucinda he could give in to his grief. But his mother's gruesome murder, so soon after his father's death, had shaken many of the slaves and affected their work.

Lawton had nearly strangled Tillman when he pulled him from their mother's body. Ed had to restrain him until his rage subsided. But the rage passed quickly, and as Lawton surrendered to a desperate anguish, he decided to protect Tillman from the consequences of the murder. He would not have his brother tried for murder, nor would he allow him to be locked away in some madhouse dungeon in New Orleans.

Lawton instructed the slaves present, under threat of punishment, to say that a runaway slave had murdered his mother and escaped. He didn't ask Joleen and Aaron to play the lie. He told them.

Sheriff Crandall accepted Lawton's story that the runaway had escaped. The sheriff didn't talk to anyone else, and he left within five minutes to fetch slave dogs and form a posse.

Word of the murder spread quickly. All that day and into the evening people arrived at the Columns to offer sympathy and to talk bitterly of the way the abolitionists were stirring up the slaves again. The sheriff caught several runaways and brought them out to the plantation, but in each case Lawton said the sheriff had the wrong man.

Tillman was locked in the slave jail, with comfortable furniture and his soldiers, and Randall moved in as his guardian. Randall was a huge man. He was nearly sixty but was still incredibly strong. He had never married and was considered "simple" by the slaves. He was a deeply religious man. He seemed happy to be spared field work, and he preached his primitive Baptist beliefs and played soldiers with Tillman.

Eventually Lawton wanted to bring Tillman back into the house, into a bedroom that would be shuttered and always locked, a room that Randall would also share. Lawton weighed the chance he was taking. If Tillman ever went crazy again, if he ever got his hands on another butcher knife . . .

But the alternatives were a murder trial or the madhouse.

At dusk Lawton trotted his horse back toward the house. He had worked hard enough all afternoon to spare himself the recurring grief and horror of his mother's death. And soon he would be alone with Lucinda and she would comfort and heal him with her love.

He had come to depend on Lucinda, on the strength he had not suspected when he had brought her up from New Orleans. Her confidence in him bolstered his own growing confidence in his ability to run the plantation. And Lucinda had provided the final element to make his confidence complete. She had returned from New Orleans with a written promise of intent from Alain LeBeau. When he inherited the land from his aunt—and the doctors said she could die at any moment—he would sell the land to Lawton.

Lawton gave way to his confidence for a moment. His uncle could no longer strangle the plantation. It was all but impossible for Lavon to sabotage the cotton crop, and the crop promised to be a record one, with market prices high. And since Lawton had finally agreed with Cellus that to borrow money would be no terrible mark on his manhood, he didn't see any possible way Lavon could take the Columns away from him.

No, he scolded himself, he wouldn't get overconfident again. But he enjoyed that moment when he felt he was truly a man, truly his father's son, truly the master of the Columns. The thoughts of Lavon and his desperate schemes to hurt the family and own the plantation reminded Lawton of what Cellus had said about Lavon.

"There was lots of talk, and I believe in my heart it was true, that Lavon's father was this here artist that was visitin' the place," Cellus said. "But your granddaddy and your daddy both wanted Lavon accepted as though he had pure Deavors blood, and I've held my tongue all these years and made sure all the other slaves did, too. But I think you ought to know, Mist' Lawton. Maybe it explains somethin' 'bout why Lavon's turned out so bad."

Lawton heard a shout. He saw Joleen and Aaron riding toward the barn. Joleen rose up in the saddle and waved.

Lawton reminded himself that he never had talked with Aaron about the abolitionist rumor. There had been a slave insurrection in east Texas, and anti-abolitionist feeling was running high. Lawton knew that Joleen would never stay married to a man involved in Yankee schemes. But it wouldn't hurt to have that talk and make damn sure.

Lawton smiled as Joleen reined up beside him. But it was not a true smile, because last night Joleen had announced that she was moving to Ohio in the near future.

"Who, me, Lawton, caught up with those unlikely abolitionists?" Aaron had said in their after-supper talk. "It's your uncle. He's spreading those lies, and without a shred of proof. I suppose that since I'm a member of the family he's included me in his vendetta."

The talk seemed to satisfy Lawton, though he told Aaron he was worried that Lavon would try to hurt Joleen and that he doubted Aaron was capable of protecting her.

"I assure you I am," Aaron had said. "And in any case, we'll be moving up to Ohio soon."

Aaron walked slowly through the rose garden, digesting the talk and thinking of Joleen, who had gone back to visit Tillman. In her own impulsive way, Joleen had suddenly told Aaron two nights earlier that she had decided slavery was wrong and that she could no longer live in Mississippi. But she said she couldn't possibly leave her brothers yet.

When Aaron warned Joleen that Lavon would surely seek some revenge against her, when he said he suspected that the abolitionist rumors were some part of a plan by Lavon to affect that revenge, when he begged her to leave with him immediately, she readily agreed that they were both in danger but insisted that he go upriver alone and said she would join him later.

"Joleen, your uncle has limitless money and resources," Aaron argued. "And I'm vulnerable, damnit. And through me, so are you. I'm half-surprised Lavon hasn't taken steps to have me arrested already."

"Yes, I've worried about that, too, Aaron," she said. "And I know if he has some evidence and he has you arrested, then I'll be in trouble. That's why you've got to leave without me. Don't you see? I don't care what he plans or how much he has on you, if you're gone, then nothin' will happen to me. If you get away now, we'll both be safe. You're the Yankee, the outsider. I'm still a Deavors, and I'll be safe at the Columns."

"Damnit, I'm not leaving without you," Aaron said.

"Then let's both stay out here at the Columns, where we'll be safe," she said. "Just a little longer, and then we can go."

So they stayed out at the Columns. Aaron had abandoned his law practice. He reasoned with himself that, after all, Lavon had called off the men who were following him. Perhaps Lavon had given up altogether, or perhaps he, himself, was imagining more danger than existed.

Aaron picked a yellow rosebud for Joleen and put it in his pocket. When she set her mind to something, there was no getting around her, danger or no danger. And Aaron knew that forcing her to leave, to confess to Lawton her true feelings about slavery, to almost literally renounce her family, was too much of a burden so soon after her mother's death.

That murder, he thought. In all his life he had never seen anything as grotesque as that boy lying in his mother's body, holding a knife, sucking his thumb, and smiling. He was only glad he had been able to turn back in time to shield Joleen from the sight.

How could so much horror come to one family? he asked himself. It was as though they were cursed in some way. When he sat with Joleen and dried her tears and rocked her in his arms to calm her hysteria, he had the almost desperate impulse to force her to flee the Columns, as though she would be the next Deavors to suffer some unspeakable death.

Aaron heard horses up on the road. They were coming fast. He watched them appear in the moonlight, though he couldn't make out their faces. He supposed it was a slave patrol. With the new talk of slave insurrections, the patrols were active once more.

He watched them disappear, and picked another rosebud. A horse whinnied. There was a shout. A woman cried out.

"Joleen!" Aaron started running. Could Lavon have had the audacity to send his men onto the Columns?

He rounded the wall. Some of the men had dismounted. And someone was lying on the ground.

"Joleen!" he cried.

A man was helping Joleen to her feet as Aaron reached her. The man was Haskell Sumrall. Juan Delsano was also there.

"My God, are you all right?" Sumrall asked. "I didn't see you until you were right in front of me."

"Joleen . . ." Aaron started.

"I'm . . . I'm fine, I guess," she said. "I was just goin' out to surprise Aaron, and I heard the horses, but my mind must have been a thousand miles away. I'm all right now."

Aaron put his arm around Joleen and took her into the house. It wasn't like her to let her mind wander in this way.

Sumrall and the other planters had come over to discuss news of a new slave insurrection in Louisiana, and the news convinced Aaron that he and Joleen had to leave immediately.

Chapter 64

Lavon scratched his scar as he stared at Lige's right leg.

The left leg was fat and healthy, but the right one was thin and twisted. Lavon reached out, but he pulled his hand back. He wanted to stroke the leg, just as he constantly stroked his scar. Yet he was repulsed by his son's deformity.

He left the nursery. Frannie was coming down the hall.

"Is he asleep?" she asked.

Lavon nodded. "Yes, he's finally asleep. Where's

that nigger? I sent her down for some water, and she didn't come back."

"She'll be right up," Frannie said. "She had to go out to the well."

"Stay with Lige till she gets here," Lavon said. "I don't want him left alone."

"Couldn't you come in and sit with me awhile?" Frannie said. "Just a little while, Lavon. We never spend time together anymore."

"No, I've got work to do."

"Please, Lavon . . ."

"Damnit, don't start whining again," he said. "You cry more than Lige does, Frannie."

"I'm sorry, Lavon," she said.

He stiffened as she kissed his cheek. He walked down the stairs and out the front door. He had not touched Frannie since their return to Natchez. He could barely stand to be in the same room with her. He cursed himself for being saddled with a woman who was either whoring around town or always underfoot whining and loving and being dependent. He told himself he would divorce her before the year was out. When he and Lige took over the Columns, there would be no place for a woman like Frannie.

"Silas, where in hell are you?" Lavon called.

Silas ran out from under a magnolia tree. "I'm right here, Mist' Lavon."

"Drive me to the slave pen," Lavon said as he climbed into the carriage.

Silas made a clicking sound in his cheeks as he drove off. He popped the whip over the horses' backs. Lavon was proud of the two chestnut stallions that pulled the carriage. He had bought the matched pair at an auction. They were the talk of Natchez horse people.

The scar was itching worse than usual, and Lavon felt the chill that sometimes accompanied the really bad itching. He reached under the seat and pulled out a whiskey jug. He took a deep swallow and wiped his chin. Dr. Gatlin said there was no connection between the scar and the chills, but Lavon was convinced there was, and he had decided to visit a New Orleans doctor in the near future.

His hand sought his coat pocket, and he was startled to see that his fingers were trembling. This was the second time in two days. Damnit, he would definitely have to go downriver for treatment. If it wasn't the scar, then he must have picked up some fever that was causing him to shiver and tremble.

He pulled some salt from his pocket. He poured the salt into his palm and studied the grains as they sparkled in the sunlight. Then he licked up the salt and washed it down with whiskey. His cook had told him that salt was good for stopping a chill.

He cradled the jug in his lap and told himself that salt could also be good for something else. Salt could be sowed into the Columns' cotton land. The ripening cotton plants would wither and die, and for generations nothing would grow on those acres. The goddamn plantation would be like Carthage after the Romans salted the fields and streets. Barren for generations. Barren, like his life now, goddamnit.

"No, no," he mumbled.

He had to stop such thinking now that he had a certain plan to ruin his family and become master of the Columns. In a few days his barren life would end, the life of a despised slave trader, the owner of a whore barge, the life of a man ostracized from Natchez society and whispered about and mocked and humiliated on the public street by a girl.

By God, he swore, he would have salted those acres, if necessary! But now he didn't have to. Soon his life would become honorable. He would be master of the Columns and the wealthiest planter in the state. He and Lige would travel in Europe. He would return to all the grandeur and high society to which he had been accustomed. His wealth would buy Lige the best doctors on the Continent.

And he would renovate the Columns and make it the grandest house in Mississippi. He would bring marble from Carrara and cedar from the Levant. There would be glassware from Dresden and fine furniture from France. He would give lavish balls. Men with titles would visit from London and Paris.

By God, he would be respected and feared, and

the planter families would realize he was a real Deavors and accept him as one of them. They would, damnit! Or he would destroy them one by one, as surely as he was about to destroy the Deavorses!

"Damn them all," Lavon mumbled. From his whining whore of a wife to that weak-kneed sheriff who was backing away from him, from that suddenly self-righteous banker Thigpen to Riley Ferguson, that gutless bastard who had slandered him with a suicide note.

Nothing had been the same since Ferguson had shot himself and his note was found. Ferguson blamed Lavon for his suicide. He wrote that "If Lavon Deavors isn't stopped, he'll sap the honor of decent men with his venom, just as he ruined me because of my weakness for gambling."

After Ferguson's death, three bankers had told Lavon outright that they wanted no more of his schemes, despite the promises of wealth or any threats he could muster. Planters and judges stopped visiting the barge. Men crossed the street to avoid him.

And yesterday Hal Thigpen had told Lavon he wouldn't see Renée again. "I've been weak, I'll admit," Thigpen said. "I let myself believe you meant no harm to your family but only wanted the Columns in your name. I was a self-deluded fool, Lavon, deluded by my obsession for that nigger. Well, that's finished. I want no more truck with you at the bank. And I'm going to ask the board to renegotiate that planting loan with Lawton."

They were all deserting him suddenly, all those proud, wealthy, influential men he had so carefully manipulated with money and women and blackmail. They were drawing in together, returning to their class. They would be wet-eyed and guilt-ridden and repentant. They would move to help Lawton. But it would do them no good, goddamnit!

The carriage hit a bump, and Lavon felt the hint of a chill.

"Damnit, watch the goddamn road!" he screamed at Silas. He scratched his scar until it hurt.

He settled back in the seat and thought of his plan, his beautiful, final plan to revenge himself and ruin his family. Lawton had surprised him with his tenacity and cleverness, but one night very soon Lawton would learn what it meant to stand in the way of Lavon Deavors.

The plan would have worked in any case, but the recent slave insurrections in Texas and Louisiana provided just the right climate of fear and hatred in Adams County to make the plan perfect. The slave patrols were out every night, and the runaways, who were always numerous and who usually received lenient treatment when caught, were being hunted down with a vengeance and whipped or branded by men who feared a local uprising. Lavon told himself that it was ironic that Estelle's murder by a runaway had helped to increase that fear.

Feeling against the Yankee abolitionists was running high. Rumors were rampant all over the county that Yankee agents were pouring into Natchez to incite and arm the slaves. Just the day before, an innocent Yankee trader had been beaten in a tavern.

And Lavon smiled as he thought of the handbills his agents had circulated. The handbills called for the slaves to rise up and murder their masters and destroy the cotton. It promised that Yankee agents were in the vicinity with arms for the slaves. The appearance of the handbills intensified the already explosive situation. And Lavon had his agents create enough mischief at night to make people think that indeed an uprising was imminent.

Lavon had taken Aaron's threat seriously and called off his men. But he made sure Aaron was constantly libeled as an abolitionist.

And one night this week Lavon would lead a slave patrol to the Columns. Lavon would first trick Lawton into leaving the place. Then he would have to deal with only Joleen and Aaron. Lavon had arranged whiskey for the patrol, and he would work the men into a frenzy of hatred and fear. And to increase that frenzy, he would have a member of the patrol shot in Benton and claim that he saw the slaves who did it and that they belonged to the Columns.

Lavon drank whiskey. Yes, damnit, he would turn

the patrol loose on the plantation and goad them to use their right to administer mild whippings. He knew that the whippings would get out of hand and that branding irons would be used. Let Lawton see how incompetent he was at protecting his slaves!

And he, himself, would see that Cellus was both lashed and branded. As for Joleen, he would be the last man to enjoy her body before it was branded. Afterward, he would blame all the excesses on the drunken men.

These same men—and Lavon would be careful to lead only men who had no connection with him, men no one could say were in his pay—would stumble onto overwhelming "evidence" that Lawton and Joleen and Aaron were all abolitionist agents. They would find a printing press and abolitionist pamphlets and handbills, they would find forged letters signed by Lawton and the others, and they would find a cache of arms and ammunition. Essie had smuggled the evidence onto the place over the past few weeks, stopping to pick up a few items each time he drove his wagon from Joleen's land to the Columns.

And to make certain that the evidence was found, Lavon would see that Sheriff Crandall got a search warrant and followed him out to the Columns. Crandall had been backing away from Lavon recently, and Lavon knew the sheriff would be appalled by the violence at the Columns. But Lavon and the patrol would have a good half-hour before the sheriff reached the plantation.

Even the Deavorses could not escape certain and severe punishment with all that evidence against them. Everyone, including their planter friends, would turn against them. The entire cotton crop would be lost. And the bank would be glad to have Lavon buy up the note Lawton had signed.

As for Joleen's husband, Lavon hoped the man tried to interfere. Because Lavon would be protected by a poleman named Creech Flanders. He was considered the best shot under the hill and was said to have killed more than thirty men.

Lavon smiled and drank whiskey and scratched his scar.

"Master of the Columns," he mumbled.

Chapter 65

Joleen sipped her tea and looked from the window of the Blue Bird Tea Room. She was waiting for Aaron to return from the courthouse, but he was late, and she wished she had gone with him. She had never seen such ugliness on the Natchez streets. She found it difficult to believe that the groups of angry, red-faced men who clustered on every corner were the same men she used to pass on leisurely Saturday mornings when she came into town with her family.

And the talk she had heard! Why, people seemed to believe that every slave in Adams County was about to take up arms and murder all the white people. And that an army of black and white abolitionists was on its way downriver to aid the slaves. She knew that the first reports of a bloody uprising in Louisiana had been greatly exaggerated and that the uprising had consisted of half a dozen slaves who killed a white man and were hunted down in the swamps and hanged. But those men out on the streets either didn't know the truth or didn't want to believe it.

She thought about the handbill she had seen a few minutes earlier. It did call on the slaves to rise up and kill their masters. She didn't understand that at all. Aaron had told her that his abolitionist friends were gentle men who did not believe in violence. He said they would never incite slaves to insurrection and murder. Then who had printed the handbill?

She sipped the tea. It was cold. She shoved the cup away. There was a rising din of talk around her.

She wasn't sure, but she suspected that some of the ladies were staring at her and making comments behind her back. Once she had clearly heard a woman mention something about Aaron's being a Yankee.

For the first time in her life she felt somewhat alien. She didn't care about the gossip—as gossip. Why should she care what these silly women or those men out on the street thought about her? But she worried that all the talk meant even more danger for Aaron than she had imagined. And now he was several minutes late, and she was worried.

Joleen stared into the teacup and realized she would probably never come back to the Blue Bird Tea Room. Each thing she did now in Natchez had a finality to it. In a few days she and Aaron would take a boat upriver. She had no idea when she might return.

Her change of feeling about slavery had crystallized quite rapidly in the past few weeks. She had come to detest the institution. It was that simple. She wanted to see all the black people free, just as she and Aaron were freeing Filch, Norvina, and their other slaves.

As always with Joleen, this change involved no long, drawn-out intellectual process. She had resisted the final, drastic step in her feelings largely because of her family and the people at the Columns. Then one day as she rode through the fields at dusk she saw the people trudging back to their cabins after fourteen hours of work, and she told herself that they were slaves only because they were black, and their children would all be slaves, and their children's children.

Even before she turned against slavery she began to feel a sense of alienation from the people she had known all her life. She felt little kinship with the women in the tearoom or the men on the street. She felt no rapport with or affection for the Sumralls and the Delsanos.

She was Aaron's wife. She loved him. He loved her. She wanted to be part of his work. She wanted to know his real friends in Ohio, the ones involved in what he called the Underground Railroad.

She felt no sadness about the alienation with either the town or with lifetime friends. But her sadness about the Columns and Lawton and Tillman brought her to the point of tears. She would visit the Columns one time—perhaps a final time. She would say good-bye to her poor, insane brother. And she would tell Lawton of her new beliefs and her new feelings. The telling would be almost unbearable.

She loved Lawton, and always would, beyond any concern with his owning slaves. She would miss him terribly. And she knew that no matter how much she disliked slavery, she would always feel ambivalent about the Columns and the slaves her family owned and cared for so much.

Several horsemen raced past the window. Someone shouted down the street. Where was Aaron? Joleen told herself that she had been naïve not to realize how truly serious Aaron's warnings of danger had been. Any Yankee in town was in danger today, and Aaron was a Yankee who had been labeled an abolitionist for weeks.

She decided that if Aaron did not come back in five minutes she would go out and look for him.

Aaron returned as she was getting up. He ordered coffee.

"My friends have nothing to do with those handbills," he said. "Believe me, they don't put out such rot. And until I'm safely away, they'll be quite cautious about doing anything at all in Natchez."

"But who could have printed them, Aaron?" she asked. "You've said there are other groups in Pennsylvania and all, and maybe they're responsible."

"No, I just don't think it's a handbill the abolitionists would print," he said. "Realistically, it makes no sense if you think about it. It only makes our work much harder and does the slaves no good at all. I don't have a shred of proof, but it wouldn't surprise me if your uncle wasn't behind the handbills, though I can't imagine what he hopes to gain."

"Well, whoever printed them has certainly got people stirred up," Joleen said.

"Yes, I've had a bad time of it this afternoon," Aaron said. "I almost got into two fights."

"You shouldn't have come into town," Joleen

said. "You're not safe at all. Why, those drunken men could attack you at any moment. And I'm worried sick that Lavon has found some evidence. I should have come in and supervised the packing by myself."

"No, no, I couldn't let you come alone," Aaron said. "And I do want us to get home and finish the packing so we can get an early start back to the Columns. I don't want to be on the road after dark."

"You think it's goin' to be dangerous on the roads tonight?" she asked.

"Yes, I do," he said. "Those patrols could get drunk and go beserk, just as they did during the Nat Turner insurrection. Thank God we're leaving at the end of the week. I only wish it were tomorrow."

As they walked out, Joleen realized the tearoom was nearly empty.

They couldn't find a carriage, and decided to walk home. The streets were crowded. The taverns were full. Gangs of white men ran down the few Negroes who were out and demanded each slave's pass. On the Mercantile Bank corner a slave without a pass was beaten to the ground. The slave's owner came to his rescue. The mob nearly attacked the white man when he denounced their actions and they learned he was a Yankee.

Aaron took Joleen's arm, and they walked faster. There were no planters on the streets now, no lawyers or doctors. Few merchants were open. Most people had gone home and locked up their families and their slaves, if they owned any. Natchez was being left to the polemen and poor farmers, the mechanics and teamsters, the drifters and woodsmen, to all those who owned no slaves and let the misery and poverty of their lives pour out in their hatred of Negroes and their genuine fear that the slaves, who made the wealthy even wealthier, while they themselves had to break their backs for a living, were about to rise up and murder them.

Joleen had come to accept many contradictions about a slave society, and one of the oddest was that these same men who hated the planters and had little reason to defend slavery would actually defend the institution with their lives. In addition to the fear of a slave uprising, just the thought of Yankee interference in slave matters enraged them. And any talk of freeing slaves had one very bitter translation for these men: it meant that suddenly there would be thousands of black men competing for the jobs they now held.

Aaron turned Joleen from the street they usually took. The street passed the jail, and Aaron had seen the glow of a white-hot fire. He knew what that meant. Runaway slaves who had committed some petty offense and were usually given mild punishment, if any at all, were being branded on the forehead or in the palms of their hands. A scream frightened Joleen. Aaron put his arm around her and hurried her along.

"Aaron, I'm really scared now," she said as they reached their house. "You know, you're right, of course. We should have gone on and left earlier. I should have already told Lawton. I'm so afraid Lavon's up to something."

"Then you're willing to cut short your visit to the Columns?"

"All right, yes," she said. "Really, all I have to do is talk to Lawton and tell him everything. Putting it off a few days won't make it any easier. Why don't we plan on going upriver the day after tomorrow?"

They walked slowly over the flagstones. A shot startled them; they heard horses racing down the street. They were both relieved that the horses passed the house without stopping.

Chapter 66

Lawton and Joleen walked down the gallery toward the parlor for the talk Joleen dreaded. At that moment, Ed came running in and said there were riders on the house road. Lawton walked to the front porch to meet them.

Joleen watched from the window as Lawton talked to a dozen roughly dressed men. Their faces were angry in the light of the torches they carried. She couldn't make out what they were saying.

"What's wrong, Lawton?" Joleen asked as he returned to the parlor.

"They wanted to search the place," Lawton said. "Claimed a white man had been wounded by some niggers outside Benton. Claimed the slaves who shot the man were from the Columns, though they didn't know their names. Of course, it's not any of our people. That's ridiculous. But it worries me."

Ed had been waiting in the gallery. Lawton sent him out to make sure that all the slaves were in their cabins except for the ones who were guarding the plantation against Lavon's agents.

"And find Cellus and send him in here," Lawton added. "I don't know where he disappeared to, but I'm goin' to ride around and check things in a few minutes, and I want him in the house."

Lawton and Joleen sat down. Lawton offered her sherry, which she gladly accepted. She surprised him by gulping it down and asking for another glass. She forced herself to sip at the sherry as she made hesitant small talk and avoided Lawton's eyes.

"It must be somethin' bad," he said. "The way you're hemmin' and hawin' and gettin' nervous. Now, come on. It can't be all that bad, Joleen." He smiled.

"Oh, Lawton, dear Lawton," she said. "Yes, I'm afraid it's that bad."

She took a deep breath. She sipped the sherry. Then she looked into his eyes and told him the truth about Aaron and herself. He did not interrupt, but his cheeks grew red as she talked. When she finished, he poured half a glass of whiskey and drank it in one swallow.

"I just don't understand," he said. "Joleen, you can't mean . . . It's Aaron, damnit. He's done somethin', he's taken advantage of you because you're young and naïve."

"No, Lawton, it's me, not Aaron," she said. "I'm a grown woman now. I've seen lots of the real world since I left the Columns. All my beliefs have changed, Lawton. I've come to . . . dislike slavery, and I want to see it end."

"Many a time when he lay here in the house after that patrol shootin', I wished him dead," Lawton said. "And he was guilty, after all! My God, then, he murdered three men, Joleen. I wish his wounds had killed him. I wish I'd killed him myself!"

Joleen stood up. "Lawton, look at me," she said. "This isn't Aaron's fault. These are all my own decisions. I've come to believe all this myself. I know you find it difficult to understand . . . to even begin to understand. But I do believe slavery is wrong. And I intend to free Filch and Norvina and my other niggers. It just makes me so . . . Oh, I don't know how to say it, Lawton. I feel like cryin'. I love you. And Tillman. And the place and the people and all. And I know you're a good master and you'd do anything for the people. But don't you see? I have to . . . to believe what I believe. Please don't look at me that way."

"Joleen, to disapprove of slavery, well, that's one thing. But to be an abolitionist. To break the law. To be a criminal, a murderer . . ."

"It's not like that, Lawton. All those laws are wrong. If they passed a law up in Washington sayin' you couldn't have slaves, why, you'd disobey it, wouldn't you? Because you really felt it was terribly wrong? And I . . . we don't want to hurt anybody. Aaron's not ever goin' to . . . to shoot anybody again. I promise you. Oh, Lawton, it's just impossible for us to talk about this. We can argue till doomsday and we won't change each other's way of thinkin'. I know how hurt and disappointed you are, but let's not talk—"

"But damnit, we've got to talk," he said. "I can't let you do this to yourself, Joleen. Of course, now I see why you want to run off to Ohio. Damnit, damnit, what you and Aaron are doin' is criminal! You're goin' to become everything we were taught to despise. An abolitionist. A spy. A liar. A criminal. Turn against your family and your friends. Damnit, where is Aaron? Is he still upstairs takin' a nap? I won't let him—"

"No!" she said. "No, you listen to me, Lawton. There'll be no confrontation between you and Aaron. Whatever you have to say, say it to me. We might as well have this out right now."

"Joleen, oh, God, Joleen, I love you," he said. "Please don't do this to me. To yourself. What's happenin' to the Deavorses? Mother and Daddy murdered, Tillman crazy as a loon. You're all I've got left of the family, and you stand there and tell me . . . Oh, God, what can I do?" He drank another half-glass of whiskey and nearly choked.

"Lawton, let's talk later," she said. "Tomorrow morning. When you've had a chance to calm down, and when you don't have to worry about the slave patrols and all."

"No, we'll talk now, damnit!" he said. "You know I love you and I'd do anything in the world for you, Joleen. You know that. And nothin' you say would make a whit of difference in how I feel about you. But you might as well have come in here and told me that . . . that you'd just murdered a hundred people . . . or burned down all of Natchez. Don't you see? Mother and Daddy—our whole family—our friends, everything we are or ever have been is based on slavery. Why do you hate it so? Our people are content. And I'd walk fire to take care of them. I just don't . . ."

There was a sound. They turned. Lucinda stood in the door.

"I heard part of your talk," Lucinda said. "And I just can't believe it, Joleen."

Lucinda walked over and put her hand on Lawton's arm. She kissed his cheek.

"No, and you probably never will," Joleen said. "I can't begin to explain my beliefs in any way that you'd understand, and it's useless to argue. Just hopeless. Now, please, I wanted to be honest with you before I left. But there's really no more to be said."

"Hell, there's a lot more we have to talk about," Lawton said. "If you think I'm lettin' Aaron just take you off to Ohio after what you've told me, then you're mistaken, Joleen. I intend to—"

A shot interrupted Lawton.

"Damnit!" he shouted. "That shot was near enough to be on the place! I hope it's not another drunken patrol with its poppycock about the abolitionists stirrin' the niggers up and some of my slaves off shootin' white people."

Lawton looked at Joleen in a way that made her go cold.

"No, Lawton," she said. "No. Aaron and I have nothin' to do with any nigger uprisin', real or imagined."

"But you would, wouldn't you?" he asked. "If not here, then somewhere else. What else do you abolitionists do but stir up niggers and incite 'em to riot and run away and all? What else, damnit! And what if Aaron's involved in somethin' you don't know about? He sure was for a long time, and he lied his goddamn head off to you and everybody else. My God, for all I know, on one of his Louisiana trips he was stirrin' up those niggers that shot the white man."

"He wasn't!" Joleen said. "Listen to me, Lawton. Aaron's honest with me now. He hasn't had anything to do with the abolitionists for weeks and weeks. And no matter what, Lawton, they don't stir up the niggers, like you seem to think."

"How can I believe you?" Lawton asked. "How can I believe him, damnit! Damnit! Damnit! I'm harborin' a Yankee criminal in my own house. And, my God, Joleen! All those rumors about Aaron were true. I thought they were just Lavon's work. How did Lavon know? What else does Lavon know? What else is true about Aaron that I don't know, Joleen?"

"Lawton, please. There's nothin'—"

"Don't you even begin to understand? Lavon must know all about Aaron. God only knows why he didn't have him arrested, the way he must hate you. And you'd get caught up in it, too, if they arrested your husband. And so would all of us here at the Columns. Don't you see? Do you and Aaron have anythin' . . . incriminatin' with you? What if one of those drunken patrols found some abolitionist stuff on the Columns? With the mood they're in, and a man just shot up in Benton . . ."

Lucinda touched Lawton's arm again. "Lawton, please calm down," she said. "You know Joleen wouldn't lie to you, no matter what."

"Wouldn't lie?" he shouted. "She's been lyin' to me for months, Lucinda. Joleen, I want to know the truth, and I'm goin' to have it if I have to drag your Yankee husband out of bed by the heels. I won't have the Columns put in danger like this."

There was another shot. This one was closer.

"I've got to see what's happenin'," Lawton said. "I'll be back soon, and we'll get Aaron and we'll finish this talk to my satisfaction. And you can just forget goin' to Ohio with him."

Lucinda walked out with Lawton. Joleen picked up the decanter of sherry but decided she didn't want another drink. She went upstairs.

Joleen told Aaron about her talk with Lawton and how badly it had gone. She felt like crying, but he comforted her, and they made love. She was both physically and emotionally drained and wanted to sleep. But Aaron said he was restless, and he went out for a walk.

A few minutes later thunder and lightning woke her up, and she couldn't get back to sleep. She went downstairs and found Lucinda alone in the parlor. They agreed they both needed a glass of sherry. Lucinda was picking up the decanter when they heard horses on the road.

They ran out to the porch. Torches lit the sky. Even before the riders' faces became visible Joleen sensed that Lavon would be with the patrol. She started to run for help but didn't want to leave Lucinda alone.

Lavon rode at the head of some twenty men. The torch he held made his scar glow red, as though it, too, were burning.

"Lucinda, you better get inside," Joleen said. "And send somebody for help."

"No, Joleen, you go on yourself," Lucinda said.

"I'm mistress of the Columns. I'm not runnin' away. Lawton or somebody'll be here in a minute, I'm sure."

Lavon and a tall man with a rifle dismounted. Joleen saw that a Negro was slung over the back of Lavon's horse. She recognized Lonny, who had been on guard duty. Blood trickled from a hole in his neck.

Lavon grabbed Lonny's arm and jerked him to the ground. Lucinda gasped and shrank back.

"That's one nigger'll never shoot another white man," somebody shouted. Other men laughed and passed a jug.

"Get out of our way, Joleen," Lavon said. "The Deavorses' niggers have been on a tear tonight, murdering and raping and trying to get other slaves to join the insurrection. We're here to put a stop to it and to all your abolitionist schemes."

"Get off this place!" Lucinda shouted.

Lavon laughed and scratched his scar. "Where's Lawton? Did he run off and hide when he saw us riding up? And you, Joleen? Where's your husband? He hiding too? It won't do them any good. We'll find them and the printing press and all the other abolitionist stuff you use to stir up the niggers. Tell me, Joleen, where is your Jew-boy?"

Joleen moved to slap Lavon, but he caught her wrist, and she screamed in pain. She thought that her wrist would snap off, the pain was so great.

Suddenly Lavon let her go. A scream choked in his throat. Joleen saw him hurtle through the air. Lavon hit the ground, with Cellus, who had come out of nowhere, on top of him, the huge fingers around his throat.

The tall man swung his rifle at Cellus. Cellus ducked, but the butt caught him a glancing blow on the side of his head, and he fell to the ground. Two men raised their rifles, but Lavon held up his hand.

"No killings," he said. "There'll be no lynchings, damnit!" He climbed to his feet. "But I recognize this man. He's the one I told you about, the one I saw riding away from Benton with the nigger we shot. Now, we killed Lonny because he tried to escape when we found him out on the house road. But this nigger, Cellus, now he can't escape, can he? So he goes to the law."

"Aw, shit, Mist' Lavon," a bald man said.

"But first we have a legal right to use corporal punishment, like I told you earlier. We have the right to brand the man and lash him, and any other Deavors slaves we suspect of being criminals."

Joleen flew at Lavon again. And again he caught her wrist and hurt her. Another man held Lucinda, who looked as though she was about to faint.

Cellus was getting to his knees. Two savage kicks to the ribs knocked him back to the ground.

It took six men to hold Cellus down. The bald man heated a branding iron over two torches. Cellus' fingers were pried open. A man kept the fingers open with his boot.

Joleen screamed and fought Lavon, but she was helpless. Ed ran from the house. He was clubbed to the porch.

Lavon twisted Joleen's arm behind her back and pulled her a few feet away. "There'll be lots of branding and whipping before tonight's over,'" he whispered. "And not just niggers, Joleen. And these men will find enough evidence to put you all under the jail, and then the sheriff will come along. But before you go off to jail, I'll enjoy your body. And you'll learn what a branding iron feels like, and it won't be in the palm of your hand."

Joleen cursed and struggled, but Lavon twisted her arm, and she half-fainted with the pain. Lucinda had already passed out.

The iron was white-hot now. It was lowered to Cellus' palm. Joleen choked as she heard the sizzle of flesh. Cellus' face distorted, and he gasped, but he didn't scream.

The men were passing around two whiskey jugs. Some of them already seemed too drunk to stay on their feet.

"Go on, now!" the tall man shouted. "Hunt down all these vicious niggers and give 'em a taste of the iron and the lash. Show 'em what happens when they plot to murder white people!"

"And look around for that abolitionist press and all," Lavon said. "And be careful. Some of the niggers are armed, so you better shoot first."

Several men ran toward the quarters. Others went into the house.

The iron was pressed into Cellus' other palm. Joleen gagged as she smelled the burning flesh. A feeling of utter helplessness swept her body, and she sagged in Lavon's arms.

Chapter 67

Aaron stood in the backyard and thought of the plantation's vastness. A nebulous but growing sense of danger had brought him out to search the place, but he did not know where to begin.

He knew that there was not a shred of proof that Lavon had hidden incriminating "evidence" on the place, but in his work with the Underground Railroad Aaron had developed a sense of danger that had little to do with evidence, and this sense seldom misled him. Lawton's natural reaction to Joleen's confession was a fear that such evidence might be found by a patrol. And a patrol had already accused Deavors slaves of shooting a white man. And there were those mysterious handbills.

What better opportunity could Lavon find—or create—than this one? Aaron asked himself as he stared at the barn. A Yankee who was rumored to be an abolitionist was at the Columns, the county was fevered with fear and rage against such men, vicious handbills were being mysteriously printed. . . .

If one of the patrols did happen to find "evidence" of abolitionist activity at the Columns in a climate like this, even the Deavors name and reputation wouldn't be enough to save them. Yet Lawton had had the plantation guarded for weeks. How could such evidence have been brought onto the place? And by whom?

Aaron decided to stop worrying and start searching. If nothing else, it would keep him busy so he wouldn't brood about what seemed an inevitable confrontation with Lawton. He heard a sound from the storehouse, and his hand moved to the hilt of his pistol. It sounded like someone crying. Then he saw a light through the cracks of the slave jail and remembered Tillman.

He walked over and looked through a crack. Tillman and Randall were both crying. They were down on their knees with their hands clasped and their faces raised.

"Lord Jesus goin' to come 'gain," Randall said. "Not the water, but the fire this time. He goin' to purify everythin' with the fire. Flames goin' to wipe away all our sins."

Poor child, Aaron told himself. What must go on in Tillman's mind, to have committed so horrible a murder? If that fire-and-brimstone religion gave him any comfort, he certainly deserved it.

The moon came out from behind a cloud, and Aaron thought he saw a shadow moving across the yard toward the barn. It disappeared. Aaron walked toward the barn but stopped abruptly. There was a second shadow now. This one was larger and quite distinct. Aaron pulled his pistol and crouched down low.

The shadow materialized into a man at the barn door. It was Cellus.

"What . . . ?" Aaron started.

Cellus motioned for him to be quiet and led him away from the door and behind a wagon.

"That's Essie just went into the barn," Cellus whispered. "And all the people not on guard duty, they been told to stay in their cabins."

"What could Essie want in the barn?" Aaron asked.

"I don't rightly know," Cellus said. "But I had this hunch to keep my eye on him tonight, with all the trouble brewin' in the county. Somethin' 'bout Essie just don't set right. He give us lots of trouble for a long time, then he got all quiet and hard-workin'. It's just a hunch, but you can bet he's up to no good, sneakin' into the barn like this."

"He drives a wagon, doesn't he?" Aaron asked.

"Well, normally he's a mechanic," Cellus said. "But lately, like all the niggers, he's been doin' some extra work, and he volunteered to drive back and forth 'tween here and your place. And that sure ain't like Essie."

Aaron told Cellus of his suspicion that Lavon might try to trap the Deavorses with evidence someone had planted on the Columns.

"Lord A'mighty, that's it, then," Cellus said. "Every trip, Essie been takin' just a little too long to get back and forth. I thought he was just bein' lazy. But he could've been pickin' up stuff and hidin' it in the wagon."

"We better see what he's doing," Aaron said. "Is he alone?"

"Far as I know," Cellus said. "But he could be meetin' somebody in the barn."

As they moved from behind the wagon, a finger of lightning lit the sky, and they stopped and glanced around. Then it was dark again, and no more lightning came. But the thunderclap was loud as they entered the barn.

Two lanterns were lit, but they were turned low, and beyond the two faint circles of light there was a vast darkness filled with wagons, harnesses, plows, harvesting implements, and bales of hay.

Thunder boomed again as they crouched low and strained to hear some movement back in the darkness. Then they heard it, a scraping sound to their left. They inched toward the sound, and when they crept around a wagon, they saw a tiny light at the back of the barn.

The light came from a candle stuck into a beam. In its meager light Essie suddenly appeared, rising up from a hole in the floor with a bundle in his hand. He threw the bundle down and cut the rope that bound it. He began to throw sheets of paper around the floor.

Suddenly he stopped and turned slowly, as though afraid of what he might see.

The instant Essie saw Cellus, he jumped at him, knife in hand. Cellus stepped back and caught Essie's wrist and slammed him against the beam. Aaron knocked Essie unconscious with the butt of his pistol.

The papers Essie had been throwing around the floor were the same handbills that had infuriated Natchez.

"What's down those steps?" Aaron asked.

"That's an old fruit cellar," Cellus said. "Ain't been used for years."

Cellus lit a lamp, and they climbed down the creaking steps.

In one corner was a printing press, and dozens of bundles were stacked around the press. On the walls were maps of escape routes to Canada, detailed maps of Ohio towns, and lists of abolitionist agents along the river. And one entire wall was lined with rifles and crates of ammunition.

Aaron walked over to a large carton that was used as a desk. It contained letters to Ohio abolitionists, with forged signatures by Aaron, Joleen, and Lawton.

"This is enough to hang us all," Aaron said. "Even the Deavorses couldn't withstand this much evidence."

"That Essie, he must of brought in the press bit by bit," Cellus said. "Lord, he must hate the family. Guess he always did, but why he'd turn to a man like Lavon, I don't know. I'll go tell Mist' Lawton and—"

"He rode out to have a look around," Aaron said. "I don't know if he's back yet."

"Then I'll send somebody to fetch him," Cellus said. "But what we goin' to do 'bout all this, Mist' Aaron? The paper can be burned up easily 'nough in the yard. But what 'bout the guns and the press?"

"Send some of the slaves down here," Aaron said. "We'll have to dismantle the press and dump it and the guns in a deep bayou."

"I'll lock Essie up in the storehouse on my way out," Cellus said.

He disappeared up the steps. Aaron started dragging the handbills across the cellar.

Chapter 68

Aaron hurried up the steps and ran through the barn. He did not know how long Cellus had been gone, but the slaves should certainly have been here by now.

And then he heard the shots and the screams and saw the glow of fire through the door.

He ran out into a world gone berserk in the few minutes he had been in the cellar. The slave quarters were in flames, and smoke hung over the yard. Other flames leaped from the torches of men who rushed through the smoke in a frenzy, shouting and shooting their guns in the air. Above the drunken shouts, Negroes screamed for mercy.

Aaron stood choking in the dark smoke, immobilized and disbelieving. He heard the thud of the lash and inhaled a lighter smoke that came from burning flesh.

For an instant there were no screams or shots. That instant was punctuated by a woman's distant scream.

"Joleen!"

Saying her name brought motion and a sickening sense of belief. Aaron ran toward the house. He encountered a man who took a second to realize Aaron wasn't with the patrol. For that second he did not bring up the rifle he carried. Then he tried to fire from his hip. Aaron shot him through the chest and kept running.

He quietly slipped past four white men who were branding a Negro in the palms of his hands, forcing himself to keep to the smoke and shadows and ignoring the screams of a mulatto woman who was being raped.

He crashed through the corner of the vegetable garden and reached the front lawn, some twenty feet to the side of the house. One tall azalea bush blocked his view. He stepped around the bush, and was stopped by a scene that took only an instant to register—but that instant seemed an hour.

Cellus was tied to the furthest column of the porch. Aaron wondered if they had caught him before he locked up Essie. A torch stuck in the ground lit the deep lash marks that turned his back to pulp. His blood had stained the white column rust and red. Beside the column stood a tall man with a rifle.

And a few feet away, Lavon drank from a jug and stared into a charcoal fire where a branding iron was turning white.

Joleen's half-naked body lay at Lavon's feet.

Aaron started forward, but he had no feeling in his legs, no sense of walking. His throat began to contract. He breathed through his mouth.

"Hey, here comes the Yankee!" the man with the rifle yelled. "Want me to shoot him or save him for some branding?"

"Just wound him," Lavon said as he looked around. "Be careful. He's a good shot, I hear."

"Not with no pistol, not at this range," the man said as he raised his rifle.

Aaron's pistol came up so quickly that the man gasped. Before the gasp was finished, a shot had passed into his open mouth and blown out the back of his head.

Lavon grabbed his own rifle. He fired in panic. The shot went wide. Aaron took out his other pistol and deliberately shot Lavon in the leg. Lavon fell to the ground, writhing and groaning.

Aaron reached Joleen and sank to his knees. Her face and breasts were bruised, and she was unconscious. But she hadn't been branded, and she was breathing normally.

Aaron stood up. He advanced on Lavon, who clawed the ground and tried to crawl away. He collapsed after ten feet. Aaron aimed at Lavon's face, and his finger began to close on the trigger as Lavon babbled for mercy.

Aaron looked into the crazed eyes and felt a shudder of revulsion at the thought of killing Lavon. Aaron lowered his pistol and returned to Joleen. He covered her breasts and kissed her lips. He found Lucinda behind an oleander bush. She had no injuries and apparently had only fainted.

Aaron ran over and cut Cellus down. Cellus was still alive, but blood ran from his lips, and his breathing was erratic. Aaron laid him on the porch and returned to Lavon, who had crawled another twenty feet.

"Call your men off," Aaron said.

Lavon rolled over. He got to his knees and cursed Aaron as he held his bleeding leg.

Aaron raised his pistol. "Unless you get to your feet and stop your men, I'll kill you," he said.

Lavon climbed to his feet. Despite his bloody leg, he managed to stumble to the edge of the house. Lavon called a man who had just dragged a Negro woman behind a bush. He told him to go back to the quarters and call the men off.

Aaron sent the Negro woman to look after Joleen and Cellus.

"You still haven't beaten me," Lavon said through clenched teeth as the sullen, drunken men filtered from the quarters. "You'll all go to jail."

Aaron backed Lavon away from his men and made it clear that he wouldn't hesitate to shoot Lavon.

"No, we won't go to jail," Aaron said. "Because I found the press and the guns in the barn, and they'll all be destroyed before anyone knows they're there."

Lavon turned, and his lips twisted into a smile. He scratched his scar until it bled. Then Aaron heard the horsemen.

Lawton was riding at the head of the men. But right behind him was Sheriff Crandall. Lawton had encountered the sheriff and his men as he raced down the road and realized he had been lured away from the house. Now he dismounted on the run.

He was sickened by Cellus' bloody back, and his

nostrils were stung by the smoke that poured from the burning slave cabins. And when he saw both Lucinda and Joleen on the ground, he started trembling.

He ran to the women, lurched toward his uncle, then ran back to the women.

"They're all right," the Negro said. "Miss Joleen, she been hurt some, but nothin' too serious. Miss Lucinda, she seem to have just fainted."

Again Lawton started toward his uncle. The men stood in a semicircle among the flower bushes. They were silent and passed a jug around. Jerked abruptly from their drunken orgy of violence and hatred, they seemed to a man to feel guilty and embarrassed, and not one of them could look anyone else in the eye.

"I'll kill you for this!" Lawton shouted at Lavon. "So help me God!"

The sheriff stepped in front of Lawton. "Now the killin's over for the night, son," he said. "So get hold of yourself and let the law take over."

"The law!" Lawton said. "You might as well whore for my uncle on his barge, like his barge women, you bastard!"

"Now, listen here, son," Sheriff Crandall said. "I won't . . ." He bit off the sentence and turned toward Lavon. "But my God, Mist' Lavon, what got into you all? Burnin' and brandin' and killin'! And two white women lying on the ground. Lord God, there'll be hell to pay, and not no excuse of nigger trouble's goin' to justify all this."

"He told us to do it!" the bald man shouted. "He said we had the right and duty. And Christ, sheriff, it was him with them white women. We wouldn't lay a hand on no white woman."

"Shut up, you bastard!" Lavon said. "Sheriff, let me talk to you for a minute. About something far more serious than all this."

The sheriff walked over to Lavon, knelt down, and tied a tourniquet to his leg.

"You'll need a tourniquet for your goddamn neck!" Lawton said, and moved toward Lavon.

But Aaron intercepted Lawton. "Essie smuggled a printing press and guns and forged letters into the barn cellar," Aaron whispered. "If the sheriff finds it, we're all lost."

Lawton saw that Lavon was pointing back toward the barn. He knew he could back down a slave patrol, but there was no way he could stop the sheriff from searching the place if the sheriff insisted. Lawton glanced around and felt sick and defeated.

A torch on the ground caught Lawton's eye. He backed up slowly. Neither the sheriff nor Lavon saw him. He reached the cover of some bushes and ran around the house.

Lawton was gasping for breath as he stumbled into the barn. He hoped desperately that the paraffin jugs were still there. Only the fire from a paraffin explosion would be hot enough to melt and distort a printing press and guns.

Lawton searched frantically. Someone had moved the jugs! Then he found them behind a wagon. He took half a dozen jugs into the cellar, then picked up a lantern and threw it as he sprinted away. The explosion nearly knocked him down, but he kept his balance and fled the barn as flames began to devour the dry hay and old wood.

He heard shouts. Men were running around the house. He backed away from the inferno, toward the shadows of the storehouse.

Lawton heard the crying the same moment he tripped over Randall's body. He looked from the mutilated body and up into Tillman's pitiful eyes.

Chapter 69

The doctor warned Lavon to stay off his leg for at least two weeks, but Tillman's note brought him out of bed after only three days, and now he staggered through a grove of vine-choked plum trees. He cursed the darkness and the unseen vines that slapped at his face and irritated his scar.

Another few steps and he came out of the grove and stopped. He smiled and shivered. The Columns lay two hundred yards ahead. He scratched the scar and bit down to stop his lip from trembling. His leg was hurting again, but he ignored the pain.

He told himself that they all thought they had defeated and humiliated Lavon Deavors. But they were wrong, and they would pay!

The goddamn Deavorses would pay first. Then that turntail of a sheriff, who had charged him with half a dozen crimes. And that stupid Essie, whose blunder had given away the plan. He hoped Essie rotted in jail, but he also wanted his own revenge on the man. And those men in the patrol. He would ruin every one of those bastards, who had turned on him and blamed him for everything that happened on that night when he should have been triumphant.

Lavon started forward, but the pain was so bad he had to drag his leg. The pain goaded his frantic mind. Yes, goddamnit, he would still be triumphant! By God, he would sow the Columns' fields with salt. Nothing would ever grow again, and the family would have to abandon the place. Then he would take over! He would build a new house for the Columns, the grandest house in all of Mississippi. It would have to be a new house, because the house that lay silhouetted ahead would be ashes in a few hours.

"Ashes and salt," Lavon mumbled, and picked at his scar.

He thought of Tillman's note. It had said:

> Uncle Lavon, Please help me. They've locked me up in the slave jail, and I want out. I hate them all. I hate what they did to me, and I hate what they did to you. I want you to tell me those stories like you used to. And I want to see the woman on the barge again. The family is all going over to the Sumralls', all except Lucinda, who's in bed

with the shock. They'll be gone there over Sunday night. Come to the Columns then, Uncle Lavon. Come the back way and sneak down to the slave jail, where they keep me locked up. I've got jugs of paraffin to burn down the house, but I need help. Please help me, Uncle Lavon."

Your Nephew,
Tillman Deavors

Lavon glanced around as he neared the storeroom. There was no one in sight.

The door to the slave jail creaked open a few inches.

"Uncle Lavon?" Tillman whispered.

"Be quiet, I'm coming," Lavon said.

He stumbled to the jail and opened the door. Tillman's glazed eyes and the saliva dribbling from his lips startled Lavon, and he hesitated. But he entered the room, and Tillman rushed behind him and closed the door. Tillman turned the key in the lock and moved around in an odd, shuffling way, without taking either his heels or toes from the floor.

"There's the paraffin over there," Tillman said. He pointed with the key.

Lavon saw the jugs beyond a narrow bed and a table covered with Bibles. There was another bed in the room. The covers were turned down as though someone was expected to sleep there.

"The fire'll purify our sin and guilt tonight, Uncle Lavon," Tillman said.

"Yes, yes, that's right, Tillman," Lavon said. "Let's get started. By the way, why is that other bed made up?"

"That was Randall's bed," Tillman said. "And I keep it made up, because his soul comes back from God and sleeps there."

"Randall? Who's Randall? Isn't he one of the niggers?"

"They set Randall to watch over me and live with me after what I did to punish my mother."

"You killed Estelle? You mutilated your own mother!"

"And then Randall taught me about God," Tillman said. "And he taught me about the devil, Uncle Lavon. And because Randall loved God, the devil came and did bad things to him, and he died."

"Listen, Tillman, give me the key."

"And Randall died and went to heaven," Tillman said. "And I know it's a sin to lie, but God will understand why I lied to you in my note. God will understand that I had to trick the devil into coming back again."

Lavon stumbled toward the door. Tillman backed up and wiped saliva from his lips. A smile spread across his deathly white face, a smile so insane that it chilled Lavon.

Lavon lunged for the key. Tillman shoved it through a crack in the wall.

"Christ, you're crazy as a loon!" Lavon muttered. He grabbed the door handle and shook it. He shoved his weight against the door, but it would not give.

He looked around. Tillman was holding a lantern.

"Get away from the goddamn paraffin!" Lavon shouted. "Give me that lamp!"

Tillman smiled again and threw the lantern toward the jugs. The explosion slammed Lavon against the wall. A wave of fire lashed across the room, and the heat made Lavon scream. He crawled to the door and clawed at the lock.

"Help!" he screeched. "Please help me! I'm burning up! Help! Help!"

Lavon beat at the door. His coat caught fire, and he tore it off. Flames licked at his body, and he would have screeched in agony, but the smoke choked him.

Lawton was worried about Lucinda, and he was glad the Sumralls' party ended early. His worry caused him to drive the horse at a trot, despite the fact that Joleen and Aaron were being bounced around in the back seat. This would be Joleen's last visit to the Columns. In the morning she and Aaron were moving to Ohio.

Lawton was sorry he had left Lucinda alone, though he knew she would be in a deep sleep from the doctor's sedation. Dr. Stacey said she would be all right but that it might take her a full week to recover from the shock of witnessing such horror.

Lawton was so emotionally depleted that he had decided to let Joleen leave without any further arguments. And Joleen had suffered enough herself. He wanted to spare her even the slightest ordeal. He felt he should say something to her now as they rode along. She would be gone in a few hours. But he could think of nothing to say.

He and Joleen could never reconcile their differences about slavery. Yet there was a bond of love between them that would always remain. He would definitely visit her in Ohio. Perhaps in the future he could convince her how wrong she was. Perhaps after living in Ohio she would change her radical new beliefs. But for now he didn't have the heart for any controversy. He hadn't even protested when she and Aaron freed their slaves.

Lawton thought of Lucinda again, and of that night. Four slaves and two white men dead. A dozen other slaves mutilated, branded, lashed, raped. The quarters burned down. And poor Cellus. The doctor said any man of normal strength would have died from the abuse he suffered. Cellus would be scarred for life and bedridden for weeks. But all indications were that he would recover.

"Are you all right, Lawton?" Joleen asked.

"Sure," he said. "I'm just anxious to get back to Lucinda."

"You were thinkin' about that night, weren't you?"

Lawton nodded. "I know thinkin' about it won't change anything, but, well . . . there's been so much sufferin' and death and all. And all because of Lavon."

"He won't be a threat any longer," Aaron said. "He'll certainly go to jail."

"I guess I should be thankful for that," Lawton said.

"Lawton, you've . . . you've grown up so much

lately," Joleen said. "Daddy would have been so proud."

But Lawton was not listening. "Look, over there!" he shouted. "It's a fire. It's the Columns! Oh, my God, Lucinda's asleep in the house!"

Lawton whipped the horse's flanks. He strained forward in the seat. Smoke and flames billowed into the sky. They met a field hand riding to fetch them. Lawton didn't pause to hear what the man had to say. He drove his horse without mercy until they finally raced between the cedars and Lawton realized that the main house wasn't on fire. The horse was staggering with fatigue. When it refused to take another step, Lawton jumped from the carriage and started running.

He had realized that the storehouse was burning. Tillman might be trapped in the jail. Lawton ran around the house. Ed was supervising a dozen slaves, who were throwing buckets of water on the flames.

"Where's Tillman?" Lawton shouted.

"I'm 'fraid he's in there," Ed said. "Too hot for us to chop the door down, but we heard yellin'. Seems like there's two people in there. And it's not Atlee."

Lawton saw Atlee, the slave who had taken Randall's place.

"What happened?" Lawton shouted. "Did you leave Tillman alone?"

"No, sir, he tricked me. Sent me on an errand," Atlee said.

"Who else could be in there? Oh, no . . . Lucinda!"

"No, she's safe in her bed," Ed said.

There was nothing for Lawton to do but wait for the slaves to fight the fire down. Finally Lawton was able to approach the smoldering ashes. He was already prepared for the shock of finding Tillman, but still he had to choke back tears as he looked down at his brother's corpse.

Lawton didn't recognize the other body at first. Then he saw that, though the face was badly charred, the left cheek had been spared by the flames. And on that cheek, like the mark of Cain, was the frightful scar that the whip in Joleen's hand had inflicted.

Lawton put a protective arm around Joleen's shoulder. Aaron moved close and stood at her other side. Then, without a word, the three of them turned and walked slowly toward the tall white columns, beckoning to them reassuringly in the moonlight like old familiar friends.

ABOUT THE AUTHOR

GEORGE MCNEILL, born in Mississippi and graduated from the University of Mississippi, has worked as a journalist on various newspapers in the south and southwest, including the *Atlanta Journal.* Mr. McNeill has written numerous magazine articles and has also worked as an advertising copywriter. He has also written a number of paperback originals (using a pseudonym) and is now working on a sequel to THE PLANTATION.